Cill Darae

COPPER PENNY
PUBLISHING

Titles by Donald D. Allan

The New Druids Series
Duilleog, Volume One
Craobh, Volume Two
Stoc, Volume Three
Freamhaigh, Volume Four
Cill Darae, Volume Five
Gaea, Volume Six (coming in 2020)

Leaf and Branch (The New Druids Vols One & Two)
Stalk and Root (The New Druids Vols Three & Four)
Priestess and Gaea (The New Druids Vols Five and Six – coming 2020)

The New Druids Compendium (Volumes One to Six - coming 2020)

DONALD D. ALLAN

Cill Darae

A New Druids Novel
Volume Five

CILL DARAE: A New Druids Novel, Volume Five
Donald D. Allan

Copyright © 2019   Published by Copper Penny Publishing.

First Edition 2019 v1.1

Printed by Kindle Direct Publishing, An Amazon.com Company

This is a work of fiction. Names, characters, places, and incidents are the product of the author's imagination or are used fictitiously, and any resemblance to actual persons, living or dead, business establishments, events, or locales is entirely coincidental.

All rights reserved worldwide. No part of this publication may be reproduced, stored in a retrieval system, or transmitted, in any form or in any means—by electronic, mechanical, photocopying, recording or otherwise—without prior written permission. Please do not participate in or encourage piracy of copyrighted materials in violation of the author's rights. Purchase only authorised editions.

All inquiries should be addressed to:

Copper Penny Publishing
E-Mail: donalddallan@gmail.com
Web page: donalddallan.com

National Library of Canada Cataloguing in Publication Data

ISBN-13: 978-0-9958490-9-9

Cover Design—	Donald D. Allan
Cover Credits—	Images and art: Copyrights: https://www.123rf.com/profile_designwest, https://www.123rf.com/profile_1enchik, and http://www.123rf.com/profile_epantha. Use of the triskelion within this novel from http://en.wikipedia.org/wiki/File:Triskel_type_Amfreville.svg. The image is licensed under the Creative Commons Attribution 3.0 Unported license and is attributed to the author Cétautomatix (artéfact), Ec.Domnowall.
Interior Credits—	Images and art: Copyrights: http://www.123rf.com/profile_martm, http://www.123rf.com/ profile_olivier26, and https://www.123rf.com/profile_varunalight
Maps Credit—	Stephen Chase

To my father: Hector McLean Allan.
September 9, 1932 - December 7, 2018

Scottish to a fault, but always a father, grandfather, naval architect, and a professional engineer.

I miss you, dad.

Cill Darae

A New Druids Novel

Volume Five

Map of North Belkin: Munsten and Cala Counties

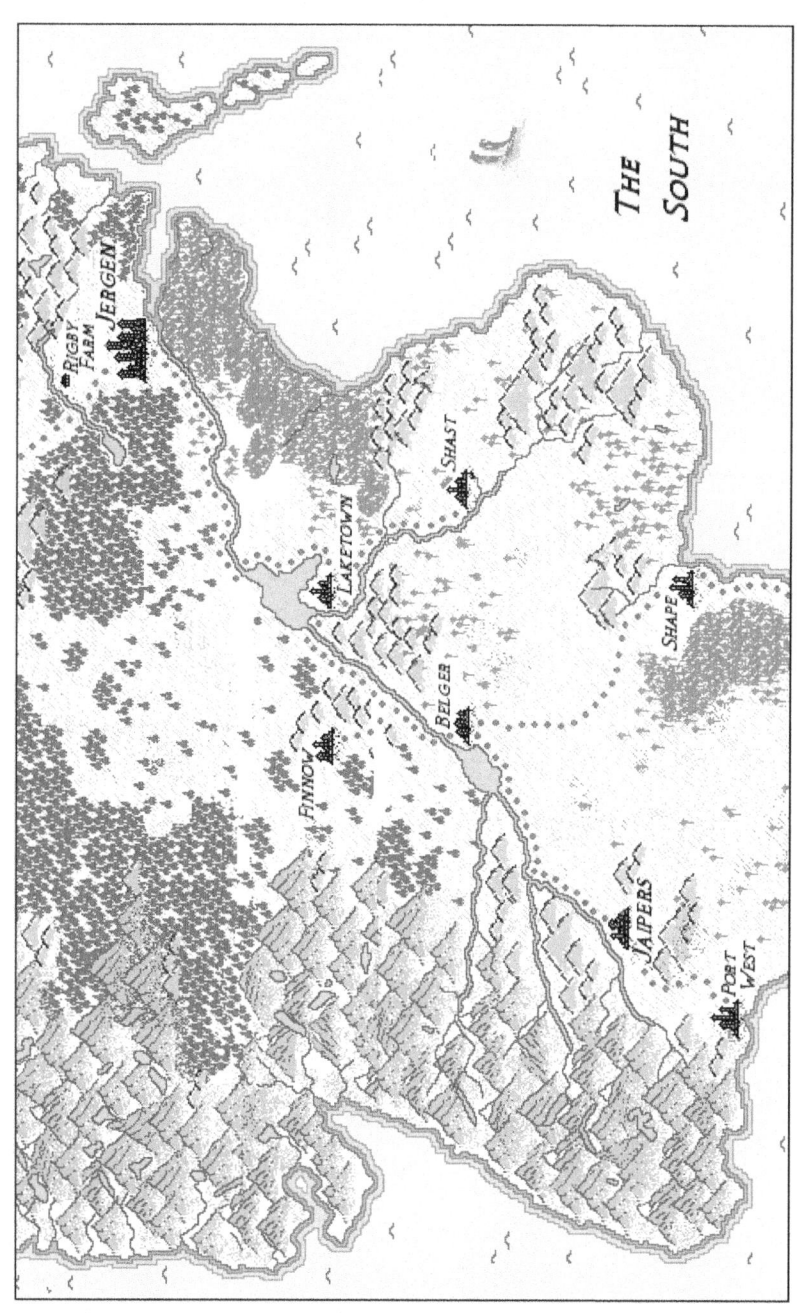

Map of South Belkin: Turgany County

What Came Before

THE FIRST FOUR novels of the New Druids series follow Will Arbor through his eyes. The next two novels, including this one, no longer follow Will Arbor. Readers may find the events leading up to this point confusing, especially after coming back to the story after an absence. I present a quick summary to better situate the reader in what came before:

The Realm of Belkin is a large island nation that has been under the rule of a monarchy for many, many generations. Beloved, or at least respected, by its subjects, the Monarchy is supported by an Army, Navy and a Constabulary to keep the peace in all the towns and villages. Within Belkin, there are three competing schools of thought: The Word, The Church, and the Druids (or draoi). The Word is a community of wordsmiths within Belkin that examine the world around them through reason, analysis, and logic; the scientist of the modern world. The Church of the New Order is a faith-based religion that subscribes to Seven Tenants of Morality. The Church strives to serve the spiritual needs of the people of Belkin, through faith in, and worship of, one true God. Over time, the Church has gained significant prominence in the world under the Kings and Queens of Belkin. Many people in the land prefer the comfort of their faith, and the tenets of morality that the Church preaches, over that of The Word and the teachings of the wordsmiths. Lastly, there are the draoi. Though few in number, these gifted and secretive people follow the teachings of Gaea, who reveals her intentions and desire for harmony through the male and female leaders of the draoi, the Freamhaigh and the Cill Darae.

The last legitimate king of Belkin, King Hietower, began a slow and gradual descent into insanity, and the Kingdom of Belkin began to suffer for it. Brother betrayed brother, and soon the lust for wealth and power prevailed throughout the land. King Hietower orders a "Great Debate" between The Word and the Church to settle the main source of discord within the Realm. When Gaea forces the Word as the winner of the "Great Debate," it ignited a Revolution, which further fed the chaos and suffering of the people of Belkin.

The leaders of the Revolution imprisoned King Hietower, and John Healy, a corrupt and power-hungry individual, came forward from the Belkin Council to create the position of Lord Protector, a pretext for ruling the land. As his desire for wealth and power grew ever larger, Brent Bairstow, the General of the Lord

Protector's Guard, began an investigation into Healy's nefarious dealings. Over the years, Brent exposed a complex web of corruption from the highest levels that spread across the northern counties of Cala and Munsten.

The Church was not exempt from the temptations of worldly power and mammon. Unbeknownst to everyone, the Church exposed the druids during an attempted Church coup against Healy. These peaceful people had been quietly and secretly working in the Realm against an unknown threat aimed at destroying Belkin and the rest of the world around them. The Church worked fanatically to destroy what they believed to be demons using a secret Church sect with ancient arcane powers. They purged the druids; all save one small child of the Cill Darae. The boy, Will Arbor, raised himself alone in the wild, protected and hidden by Gaea. Unknowingly, the Church sets into motion events that waken the druid powers in Will Arbor. Over time, Will's powers grow, and the truth and purpose of the druids becomes clear: they fight an ancient enemy named Erebus who seeks to destroy Gaea and change the world to a time long ago destroyed and forgotten.

In his search for truth, Will meets Nadine Opal, an aging druid, with no powers. For reasons of her own, Gaea returns Nadine to her youth, gives her powers matching those of Will, and declares her the new Cill Darae, the high priestess of the draoi. Will finds love with Nadine and together, at Gaea's urging, travel to Rigby Farm, outside Jergen, where they meet up with Steve Comlin and his now disbanded highwaymen, who have adopted a quiet farm life. But Rigby Farm, and its inhabitants, are destined to be the eye of many a storm as men and deities battle for supremacy in Belkin.

Erebus, using the Sect (the secret Army of the Church) as his puppets, attacks the farm, the highwaymen and the draoi. Many are slaughtered on each side. Using arcane powers, the dead are reanimated to fight for Erebus. Young Katherine Rigby watches her parents die in the attack, only to become reanimated living dead. From this experience, she is shattered; it is only her bond to Dog that keeps her sane. Erebus comes close to victory before General Brent Bairstow, using the powers of God, strikes the evil creature and turns the tide.

In the days and weeks after the attack, Will and Nadine decide to form a school for draoi at the farm and await the arrival of new draoi. Men, women, boys and girls, people from all walks of life, are summoned by Gaea to the Farm. Will is made the Freamhaigh, or leader, of the draoi. The school soon fills, and Will and Nadine begin the laborious and lengthy process to teach a new generation of draoi the craft and love of the land.

In a desperate bid to gain control of Belkin, Lord Protector Healy invites a foreign enemy force, who are themselves other puppets of Erebus, to assist him to win the county of Turgany and destroy the draoi. Will is torn. Should he answer his calling as Freamhaigh, (a calling to restore harmony in the realm) and eradicate Erebus? Or, should he join the fight against Healy and the invading army? Healy sends his joint army south against the army of Turgany, trained in Jergen under the tutelage of General Bairstow. The armies of Healy and Turgany clash at the Crossroads. When all seems lost for Turgany, Will arrives with the draoi and creatures of the land. Together, with the Turgany Army, they come close to winning the day. However, Erebus, the ancient enemy, reappears and again reanimates the dead of both sides to fight for him. Horrified, the Turgany Army is forced to flee, but not before Will and Brent join their powers, the power of God and the power of the draoi, to once again banish Erebus. Both sides retreat to their strongholds to lick their wounds, rebuild and plan for another day.

During this pause, Katherine and Dog leave Rigby Farm on a pilgrimage. Outside the northern city of Cala, they are asked by Gaea to sever themselves from her power and the rest of the draoi. Gaea believes that this action is the path to finally destroying Erebus for good. Once severed, Katherine and Dog discover another source of draoi power and in absorbing this new power, gain something of one another. The new power overwhelms them, and they nearly destroy the city of Cala before sanity returns. Gaea directs them to Munsten to confront Erebus. Erebus recognises the threat, and the reformed church sect is tasked to destroy Katherine and Dog, but they are no match for their new draoi powers, and the Sect is eradicated.

In his bid for ultimate rule in Belkin, John Healy declares himself the President of the Republic of Belkin, with the secret backing of Erebus. General Bairstow and select group of warriors from the Turgany Army, infiltrate the castle of Munsten and do away with John Healy. At the same time, Will and Nadine arrive in Munsten and join forces with Katherine and Dog to ensure the final destruction of Erebus. As Gaea's plan draws to a close, she appears and begs to be removed from the world, now that her ancient purpose is fulfilled. The draoi are split on whether to allow this, but as Freamhaigh, Will decides and allows Gaea to be removed from the world. With Gaea gone, the draoi turn to the new power that Katherine and Dog discovered, a power living throughout the land through Life Salt.

There can be no crowning of the new monarch, Edward Hitchens, until his bloodline can be validated. General Bairstow declares himself the Regent of

Belkin, holding the throne until the new monarch can be confirmed as the rightful heir of King Hietower. He commissions a small, but able, team of draoi and a trusted senior Army officer embark on a search for the remains of King Hietower, against which the draoi can confirm with Edward's blood, that he is the true heir to the throne. Will and Nadine retreat to Rigby Farm and resume their teaching of the draoi; however, the draoi are now on their own, without the guidance and controls Gaea once enforced. The future looks bright, but a political power vacuum has formed in Munsten. In this political vacuum, a new and sinister hidden power reveals itself and risks destroying everything the draoi have fought so tenaciously to overcome.

Prologue

Munsten Court Room, June 902 A.C.

REGENT BRENT BAIRSTOW winced and shifted his backside on the hard seat of the chair. After hours of sitting in the unforgiving seat, his bottom ached and his legs were cramped. Sitting where he was, to the right of the empty throne of Belkin, he was more than aware that all the Council members, plaintiffs and legal representatives could see him plain as day. Every movement he made was being scrutinised. He knew that his position as Regent was gossiped. Whispers occurred in backrooms discussing his suitability to hold his position. Every decision he made was questioned and debated. He was sick of it.

He had changed his title from Lord Protector to Regent once he had learned it was a more appropriate title. *I am holding the throne for Edward after all, not ruling the country. It also distances me from Healy.* The change of title had rippled across the city and caused more concern than good. Many complained about the loss of Revolutionary values and they were certain the realm would revert to the times of terror during the reign of the mad King Hietower.

With only months of being the Regent behind him, Brent was tired of politics. He had thought taking the mantle and asserting authority would be enough. *I was wrong*, he admitted to himself. *Wrong to think a man with a military background could run a country.* The Privy Council and Judicial Council fought him over every decision. He scraped and clawed for every advancement he felt he needed to make. Everything he touched was tainted by the years of corruption by President Healy. Brent's own investigation into Healy years ago had shown him just how bad the corruption was. As soon as he had taken power as Regent, he removed many of the people who had worked for Healy. The Council Chamber had been reduced by half and now looked empty. Thankfully, many of Healy's cronies had fled when Brent had assassinated him; making Brent's job easier, but Brent was certain there were more rats hidden in the ranks of government he didn't know about. He trusted no one. And no one trusted him.

With his military background he found the state matters regarding the army, navy, and guard much easier to deal with. Healy had removed, or had killed, all the senior leadership and replaced them with people loyal to him. All were suspect and Brent had asked Admiral Kingsmill to be Belkin's Knight General and weed out the bad ones. Cleaning up decades of Healy's influence would take a generation. Stripping the upper ranks was not the answer either. It took time to train officers for more senior positions and there was a vacuum that needed filling if the military was to rise strong again. Surprisingly, the Church came forward with a solution and offered to create a Church Guard to help keep the peace. Brent had accepted the help immediately and declared their authority. The Judicial Council had been furious over that decision.

Brent regretted becoming Regent. It had seemed a smart idea at the time, but now, more than ever, he needed Edward Hitchens to take his throne. Brent's thoughts drifted to Katherine, Dog, James, and Heather, who would soon be off on a quest to find proof that Edward is the rightful heir to the throne, and he prayed for their quick and safe return. *The sooner Edward sits here instead of me, the better for everyone.*

Brent shifted in his seat again and favoured his left cheek. He looked out at the long queue of people waiting to plead their case before him at the Regent's Bench. The room used to be the King's Bench, then it became the Lord Protector's Bench, and now it was his. Here his word was law, and despite his knowledge of legalities, it seemed every legal representative wanted to twist or bend those laws to suit their clients. It was enough for Brent to want to hang the lot. *The legal representatives at least*, he chuckled to himself. He changed his grin to a grimace when he noted two councillors now discussing his sudden smile. *God give me strength.*

He felt sorry for those in the line. The line disappeared out into the hallway. They were about to find out they would need to return the next morning to line up again, plead their case, and be given a priority to see him. Brent had asked for the line to be shortened today, but as usual his orders never made it to where they needed to go. Many of those in line had lined pockets with money to gain access to the hall. They would be angry to find out that all the remaining cases were being set aside to deal with the remnants of the Eastern army. Brent was eager to deal with them. Without their leader Mushir Adham, the Cian-Oirthear army had become a threat to security. They caused fights for the sheer pleasure of fighting. They caused disturbances for the sheer pleasure of disturbing people. They refused to assimilate to the culture of Belkin. They refused to learn the language of the land. Brent had had enough and ordered his staff to have them presented to him this afternoon for sentencing.

He pushed those thoughts aside and tried to focus on the barrister before him. She was addressing the audience who gathered to watch and was trying to sway his decision based on peer acceptance. Brent smiled to himself. *The woman drones on and on and yet I have already decided.* He watched the reactions of the public. They enjoyed the arguments. Since Brent had taken the position of Regent, the people of Munsten seemed to enjoy coming to watch him preside over the court. They would cheer and clap when he handed out punishments to those he found guilty of having aided and abetted President John Healy. The people were always looking for blood and it sickened Brent.

Since seizing power, Brent often regretted it. The manner in which he had enabled it gave him nightmares. It had only been three months ago when he had assassinated John Healy in his sleep; without a judge or jury and in front of God. He knew it had been the right thing to do and the best option to save lives, but now Brent lived with the repercussions. The act had been dishonourable. Admiral Kingsmill, who he had promoted to Knight General Kingsmill, had been against the act and kept his distance from Brent.

Once Brent had forced the Council to accept him as Regent, it had still taken two months to just settle the dust of having removed a tyrant who had ruled for decades. The entire politics and economies of the Realm were very much in turmoil. The cities and villages were suffering from upheaval. Mayors and leaders once in league with Healy were being hunted down and sometimes lynched. It was chaos across Belkin with the exception being Turgany County. The county had led the rebellion and now celebrated its victory. But the North was another matter. The Munsten and Cala counties were rapidly falling apart despite Brent's best efforts.

He needed men and women he could trust surrounding him. And he had no one, other than Martin. And tomorrow, James would leave with Katherine, Heather and Dog for Foula Island to follow a slim lead to find the remains of the late King Hietower. He had asked Will for a draoi advisor, but Will had declined the request except to identify a draoi stoc named Lana Turner who would always remain in Munsten, but not in the role of advisor. Brent was disappointed and more than a little angry at Will. He had wanted nothing more than to have someone next to him that could sort through the lies and find the truth. Will had said he understood but would not help in that manner. Nadine had seen the need and the two of them had argued for a time. As Freamhaigh, Will had decided and shut down the argument and they had departed back to Rigby Farm. Nadine had been furious, and Brent worried for the two.

The legal representative was now turned and facing him with a hopeful expression on her face. Her cheeks were splotched red, and she stole a glance at the woman she represented. "As you can see, Regent Bairstow, my client has been wrongly accused. As the sole owner of her estate, she has been accosted for years by those who represented President Healy. Her options were few: pay the amount demanded of her, or face gaol or worse. A single woman alone against the evil of the former government left her one course of action, to pay the demands and continue to exist." The woman glanced at her client once more and then locked eyes with Brent.

Brent admired her determination. She almost sounded sincere to his ears. The blotches of red on her cheeks spread further back and burned a deep red. Brent had seen her many times over the last couple of months. When she knew she was bending the truth, or hiding it, she would always burn bright red. *God watches her, and she knows it. Her shame exposes itself.*

Brent looked at her client. She was dressed in the highest fashion of Munsten. Her barrister had stripped her of her jewellery to hide her wealth, but Brent could see the untanned lines on her skin where the gems had recently lain. The woman couldn't possibly hide her wealth or stature. She sat with her back rigid, her hands crossed over her lap, and she wore a look of bored disinterest in the proceedings. Brent knew her type. For her, her wealth had always bought her passage through life and assured her continued survival.

"Trumpet, correct?" he asked her, and he watched as she jumped a little in her seat. Her barrister opened her mouth to respond, but Brent held up a finger and she closed it. He continued to stare at the woman until she nodded once. "What was that? I couldn't hear you."

A frown crossed the woman's face, and she looked at her barrister. The barrister leant over and whispered something. Brent heard the client whisper, "I won't!" and her barrister hushed her and spoke quickly. In a moment the barrister leaned away. Her client looked annoyed, but she finally looked at Brent. "Yes, Regent. My married name is Trumpet."

"I knew your son, Donal Trumpet. He paid for his commission. He started as a captain in the Army and then quickly moved over to the Guard."

The woman's lips thinned, but she said nothing.

"He made quite a name for himself. When I was the General of the Lord Protector's Guard I had to punish him several times for conduct unbecoming of an officer. Do you remember those times?"

Her barrister interrupted. "Regent, I must object. This is about Lady Trumpet, and not her deceased son! She still grieves him!"

"Noted. But this is about both of them. Don't interrupt. Where was I? Ah yes, your son. He was a disgrace. And one of the first to hunt down those Guard members who were loyal to the Realm. I have heard here how your estate was used by Healy's select as a base of operations. You opened your doors to them, Lady Trumpet. Fed them. Wined them. Supported them."

Lady Trumpet glared at Brent but said nothing.

Her barrister stepped forward. "Regent, Lady Trumpet feared for her life! No one could withstand the ire of Healy! She had no choice!"

"Silence! We all have choices! She made hers. She, like her idiot son, sided with a tyrant and slaughtered innocent men and women. Guards who swore allegiance to this Realm. I see you Lady Trumpet, glaring defiantly up at me. You disgust me. I have heard testimony that you even held the knife at times. There is blood on your hands and God sees that blood. You are hereby stripped of your land and belongings. You will be escorted to the gaol where you will serve a life sentence for your crimes against the Realm."

Lady Trumpet looked shocked and bewildered and looked about in confusion. Guards on either side of the plaintiff's table moved to her side. "Wh-what?" she stammered finally. She looked at her barrister. "Do something! Stop this!" When her barrister only looked away, Lady Trumpet screeched, the cry echoing loudly in the Council chamber. She looked up at Brent, despair now etched deeply into her face. "Please! I had no choice! My son, yes, he did those things, and he paid for it with his life! My only son! But I had no choice! What was I supposed to do?"

"The right thing," growled Brent, and he nodded at the guards. They stepped in and grabbed Lady Trumpet by the arms. She struggled and lost her footing. The guards dragged her toward the side door. She would be processed and thrown in a gaol cell in a matter of minutes.

She sobbed and cried out for help and the audience erupted in cheers, drowning her out. Brent closed his eyes and let the sound wash over him. The weight of leadership never seemed heavier than at these times. The sound of the door closing behind Lady Trumpet could barely be heard, and the audience chanted Brent's name. Brent snapped his eyes open. "Silence!" he roared. "Silence!"

Cill Darae

The noise from the audience faltered and then stopped. People looked at each other and Brent could see their confusion. The people of Belkin were spiralling into a place Brent hated. They needed the guidance of the church. They needed to hear the teachings of God and learn to avoid this lust. He glanced to his right and saw Vicar Martin Jordan and the draoi Lana Turner standing nearby looking out over the crowd. Martin looked pained.

"People of Munsten," said Brent to the audience. "I take no pleasure in the sentencing of that woman. She has been given a sentence that will see her in gaol for the rest of her life. Every day she will live with her sins. I have such pity for her. So should you. Have some respect, please."

The audience broke into a murmur, talking quietly to themselves. Brent looked at Martin once more, but Martin was gone from his spot. He looked about and saw him moving to the side door taking a female vicar with him. Brent watched Martin speak to the woman and then push her through the door.

Brent stood. The crier to his left snapped to attention and yelled out: "All stand!" Brent cursed inwardly as the entire chamber rose to their feet.

Brent smiled out at the people. "That will be all the court hearings for the day." He paused as the crowd started talking to one another. Those waiting in line cried out in anger. Brent raised a hand, and the noise quieted once again. "I have called for a special hearing. As many of you know, the remnants of the Cian-Oirthear army remain in our city. They cause great unrest and threaten the security of the Realm. For those in line, you will be each given a marker with a number. You will return in the morrow and resume your place in line. My apologies. Guards, clear the room of the unnecessary. We will resume in half-an-hour."

Brent stepped down from the dais and walked behind it and headed toward the back door. He heard the chamber erupt in cries behind him and the shouting of guards grew louder. Brent looked to his left and saw Martin walk over to stride beside him. They said nothing with the turmoil behind them and then passed through the doorway. It shut behind them and the noise all but disappeared behind the thick wood. Two guards flanking the doors came to attention and snapped a salute.

"At ease, folks," he said and then paused to look at the female guard on the right. Her eyes swivelled toward Brent for a moment and then snapped forward. "Lesley?" asked Brent.

Brent caught the quick look of sorrow that passed over Lesley's face before she nodded. "Sir, yes sir!"

"At ease I said," and Brent waited until they adopted the parade at rest position. Lesley looked at Brent. "I heard you survived, Lesley. It's good to see you."

"Yes, sir. It's been a while," Lesley swallowed before continuing. "I want you to know sir, we tried to protect Knight General Bairstow. It's a shame we bear. I'm sorry, sir."

Brent could see the guilt on her face, and he tutted. "Frederick was quite capable of taking care of himself. There was nothing you or anyone could have done to stop it. It's not your fault. Frederick thought in his stupidity he could rescue me. He died trying. I suspect he snuck away from those who were guarding him, correct?"

Lesley nodded. She opened her mouth to speak, but something caught her voice and she swallowed again. Brent looked at the other guard and saw the same guilt.

"You are guards, sworn to your duty. You did not falter, and you are not to blame for my brother's death. That lies at the feet of that bastard Healy. Do you hear me?"

The guards looked at one another.

"Do you hear me?" he demanded a little louder.

The guards nodded.

"Good, now Lesley, and Brett, isn't it?" The other guard nodded and looked surprised at hearing his name. "I want those guards who stayed by my brother's side to come to my quarters tonight. I'll order you all freed from your duties. Tell them to bring their thirst. Tonight we honour your duty and my brother. We will put this shame and guilt where it belongs. Tonight after the dinner watch."

Brent watched the eyes of the guards open a little wider. They looked at one another and then nodded vigorously. "Aye, sir. We'll let them know."

Martin chuckled and clapped Brent on the shoulder.

"Good." Brent resumed walking down the corridor and turned into a small room with refreshments laid out. He picked up a plate and handed it back to Martin. "Fill up, you will need the energy. This afternoon will be long."

Martin took the offered plate and started selecting cheeses and rolls. He filled a goblet with a summer white wine and sat at the small table. He started chewing on a thick chunk of cheddar cheese and looked thoughtful.

Brent chuckled. "That's refreshing. Normally people wait for me to eat first."

Martin looked horrified and stopped mid-chew.

"Relax, my friend. Relax. When have you and I ever put things like that between us? In the eyes of God we are all equal, are we not?" Brent took a seat across from Martin.

Martin relaxed and nodded and resumed chewing and swallowed. "True. Can I ask you something?"

Brent nodded and took a bite of a crusty roll.

"That last woman. Lady Trumpet. Are you sure of her guilt? I had heard that friends of her son had done horrible things to her. Did you not hear that?"

Brent nodded and took a sip of wine. "Aye, I did. We heard testimony she had been seen knifing one of the wives of the guards herself."

Martin looked thoughtful. "I hadn't heard that. Everything I heard was exactly as her barrister laid it out. I think perhaps you made a mistake with her, Brent."

Brent glowered. "Is that why you sent a vicar after her? To tell her you would have a word with me?"

Martin nodded.

"Wasting your time. It's decided. I can't be seen changing my mind on things."

"Even if she's innocent?"

Brent slapped the table startling Martin. "She's NOT innocent. Even if all she did was harbour those bastards she's guilty! She could have stood up to them. Helped families escape. Spread the word. Anything! Instead she did nothing! Nothing! She is guilty in the eyes of God, and my own. It is enough for me. You give her false hope. I will not change my sentencing. Have you anything else for me?"

Brent saw the look of hurt that crossed Martin's face and steeled himself. He was tired of disappointing so many. *I can only do what I think is right and if Martin is going to be another who judges me, so be it.*

Martin searched his face, but Brent remained steadfast. Martin rose and moved to the door before stopping and without looking back spoke. "In the eyes of God, who is creating the greater sin?" Martin slipped out and walked away.

Brent remained seated for a time. After a moment, he resumed eating. *God watches over me. Royal Law is clear on this matter. She is guilty as sure as the sun rises in the morning.*

* * *

Brent looked out over the two rows that made up the remnants of the Cian-Oirthear army. They were stripped of everything except pants and loose shirts. They were manacled together by their hands and feet. Each footstep they took as they traversed the chamber was loud and jarring and it set Brent's teeth on edge. They numbered twenty-three in total and stood in two rows. They stared defiantly back at Brent. Standing next to the army was a cowering man who was their translator. The man looked haggard and abused.

Brent looked out over the assembly. The eyes of the people were bright with anticipation. There was no love lost for these men. They were vile and repulsive.

They were the enemy, allowed to wander amongst them, seemingly without fear of retribution. Their crimes were numerous. Brent had had enough. He would deal with them once and for all. He rose to his feet and addressed the room.

"Gathered here are the remaining members of the Cian-Oirthear army. Brought to this land by the traitor John Healy. He opened this Realm up to the very enemy we protected ourselves against for decades. They come from a land with little respect for the values we hold dear in our country. They fear women. They fear our open ways. And their response is to kill that which they fear. They have been in our country for months and have made no effort to assimilate to our culture. They grab our women in the streets. They strike men who offer no offence other than to look the wrong way at them at the wrong time.

"I have read so many reports of the crimes these men commit in our city that it sickens me. I now find myself in the position of having to do something about that. Something permanent."

The assembly erupted in cheering that soon turned into a chant of 'Execute them!' Brent blinked at how quickly his words had turned into a desire for more bloodshed. He looked out at the lust-filled faces of his people. Men, women, and even children were chanting in unison, fists raised and pumping. He looked over at his court officials and they were smiling. The translator translated the words, and the shackled men glared at the people and some even bared their teeth. Then Brent caught sight of Martin at the back of the chamber. His face was lowered and when he raised it he looked right at Brent. From the distance Brent could still see the tears that tracked down his face.

Brent turned to the court crier and nodded. The crier stepped forward and banged the butt of the ceremonial mace on the stone floor. "Silence in the Chamber! Silence in the Chamber! If there isn't order, the Chamber will be forcibly cleared! Silence!"

The crier banged the mace harder and after a time silence once more settled over the Chamber. The audience was too afraid to be escorted out and miss the excitement. A dull murmur still rippled across the room and Brent waited until it finally stopped. He motioned to the crier to retreat, and he did.

"This realm has suffered such pain and anguish since the Revolution. Our streets are awash in our own spilt blood. We struck at a monarchy that had turned sour and evil. We forced people from the Church and slaughtered the draoi people who wanted nothing more than to help us all. We allowed one man to rise to such power that he very nearly drove us to a civil war that would have seen brother and sister pitted against brother and sister. At one point, Healy, desperate for control, invited Mushir Adham and his army into our Realm."

Brent paused when the army cheered at hearing the name Mushir Adham. The translator stopped speaking and looked apologetically up at Brent.

"Yes, Mushir Adham. Their finest warrior. Slain by a one-handed woman. This is the army that boasted they could best our Realm."

The audience cheered and cat-called to the Cian-Oirthear army. When the translator finished his words, the army rattled their chains. One at the end tried to move forward, but a guard drove the butt of his halberd hard into the man's midriff. The man bent over double and collapsed. The guard who had struck him grinned out at the audience and they cheered harder and Brent waited them out. In time, the man was lifted to his feet, but he remained bent over. The cries for execution was louder now. Brent noticed the face of one child screaming for the death of these men. The child was no more than ten and yet he leaned forward chanting with evident joy to execute these men.

These were men who did nothing more than follow the orders of their leaders. Men trained to do exactly what they had done. Brent could find no fault with them. He would expect nothing less of his own army. Those within the Belkin army who broke the law were always dealt with swiftly. The ones standing before him were far from home and lost in a culture they would never embrace or understand. They broke their laws and Brent would deal with them swiftly.

Brent motioned for silence and in time it was restored.

"I am foremost a military man. These men followed the orders of their leaders and fulfilled their duty according to whatever oaths they swore. I cannot fault them for that. I would expect nothing less of our own men and women in uniform. I have decided: these men are to be placed on Navy ships and escorted home. I charge Knight General Kingsmill to fulfil this task with the ships sailing in no more than forty-eight hours."

Brent pointed at the translator. "Except this one. If he so chooses, he may stay and work for the Realm. I have decided. So say we all."

Brent marched straight out of the hall and past Martin who smiled and nodded once to him. As Brent left the Chamber, it erupted behind him in cries. The newly renamed Regent's Guard moved to surround the Cian-Oirthear army. The guards at the door fell in step behind him and when the doors closed the cries shut off.

"Well done, sir," murmured Lesley, as he strode past her.

* * *

Two days later, Brent met the vicars of the church in their offices at the back of the Munsten Castle church. As he walked through the office area, he couldn't help but remember the horror that had occurred within the walls. It had taken quite a bit of effort to scrub the place clean and air out the death that had filled the rooms. Unbelievably, Healy had rounded up all the bishops and deans in Belkin, locked them in here, and then starved them to death. He had addicted them to *tears of the poppy* and then took it from them and locked them in. The horrors inside the church were beyond belief and Brent had ordered the information sealed. But of course, it leaked. Eylene used the information to garner more support for the Church. It reached sympathetic ears, and the Church was gaining favour once again.

As Brent strode toward the Receiving Chamber, he thought back to yesterday. James, Heather, Katherine and Dog had sailed away in the *Oriole* for Foula Island on an errand to prove Edward's lineage. Brent wished them Godspeed for he wished nothing more than to shed this mantle of power. It had pained him to watch his best friend James vanish over the horizon. He never felt more alone, and it surprised him. Martin was avoiding him more and more of late. Martin was certain something was amiss within the Church and he was often seen talking to all the vicars he could. Complaints about Martin were common. Many people had spoken to Brent and asked him to speak to him. That had resulted in Brent having to raise his voice to him, He had hated it, but sometimes the weight of being Regent meant he had to make the tough choice, even with friends.

Brent stopped before the double doors to the Receiving Chamber and shook his head to clear it. He reached forward and pulled open both doors at once and strode into the room. He nodded to the vicars who were gathered in the room sitting in the raised seating area against the walls. Central to the room stood a very large 'U' shaped table that filled the floor. At the centre of the table was where the Archbishop sat to preside over the deans and bishops. Today the seat was occupied by a woman Brent knew very little about, but he had come to value her counsel all the same. All he knew was that her name was Eylene Kissane, and she came from the city of Shape in southern Turgany. She wore the deep rich brown skin that marked the people of Shape, and the southern people of Turgany. The people of Shape kept to themselves and rarely ventured north of Belger. Their skin was a rare thing to see in the Realm and often they were stared at. Brent tried to avoid doing so now, but he knew he failed. It didn't help that she was stunningly beautiful with a rare exotic look. She looked timeless and much younger than her years. Her skin glowed, and she seemed to be the embodiment of female perfection. Brent swallowed against the sudden attraction he felt.

Eylene chuckled. "It's all right, Regent. You can stare. I'm used to it. God makes us in so many colours and shapes, He expects you to enjoy His handiwork, don't you think?"

Brent felt relief and warmed to her right away and walked around the table. He glanced at the vicars seated at the table. Most wore the same brown skin as Eylene, and they smiled and nodded up at him as he passed. Brent wondered what placed these vicars above the rest that they would be allowed to sit at the central table. Brent stopped and stood before Eylene. Her chair was central to the table and when he looked down at her, she beckoned to the seat beside her. "Please, sir. Have a seat."

Brent felt a moment of warning that came and went. He frowned and glanced about for Martin, searching for him amongst those seated around the room, and found him absent. "Where is Vicar Martin?"

Brent caught the flash of irritation that crossed Eylene's face before she hid it. "Indisposed at the moment, I'm afraid." Eylene motioned for Brent to sit beside her.

Brent scowled openly this time and remained standing.

Eylene looked up at him and arched an eyebrow. "Is there something the matter, Regent?" She looked around pretending to look for something amiss before her eyes alighted on the empty seat beside her. "Oh, I see! You feel you should be central and seated first, no doubt. I'm sorry, Regent. In this room, the Archbishop has the authority. Traditionally, the King sat next to the Archbishop and deferred to his leadership in this holiest of rooms. It is here that the souls of the people of Belkin are guided. I assure you, I am not challenging your authority, Regent. Whilst it is true that we are lacking an official Archbishop at the moment, I have been asked by my peers to preside over this meeting.

"Today we begin the process that will lead to a vote for the new Archbishop. We have therefore recalled all the vicars in the realm for this holy gathering. As it has always been, the bishops and deans will decide who will lead our church, and it shall be so today. We have strayed too far from our traditions. The Church will return to our most sacred doctrine and traditions. In the past, the deans and bishops decided who would be the Archbishop and the King would approve that decision. Without a King we have decided that we will vote and that will be it. The Realm must have an Archbishop watching over it. It is our sacred duty to see to that.

"Once we have a King again, he will have an Archbishop already in place ready to provide critical guidance to his rule. Surely you see the wisdom in that? And I might add, the Realm is tearing itself apart at the moment. An Archbishop providing critical and much needed spiritual guidance is needed most urgently, would you not agree?"

Without waiting for a reply, Eylene turned back to the gathering. The gathered vicars were all now seated and paying close attention to what was being said. Brent could feel the glares and felt uncomfortable and out of place. He knew little of church matters and he worried he might have offended the one organisation in Belkin that could truly help the land recover. She picked up a gavel and rapped it hard on the table.

"I call to order the sixty-third conclave to select the new Archbishop. I will remind the gathering that first and foremost we will raise within our ranks those vicars most deserving of being our new bishops and deans. We are all familiar with those who have been nominated. I expect the voting to occur quickly so we can focus on the question of who should be the next Archbishop. Time is of the essence. The Realm reels from a lack of governance...

As Eylene continued to speak to the assembly, Brent quietly sat down beside her and looked out over the vicars. He only knew a few of them and then only those who had been in Munsten when he was the General of the Lord Protector's Guard. He felt a disquiet settle within him. He hadn't been informed of the gathering until this morning, and it seemed almost an afterthought to him. He had searched for Martin and even demanded his presence. It seemed no one could find him. Brent looked over at Eylene and found her stealing a sideways look at him. He was surprised to see a small smile hidden there.

Cill Darae

Part One: Church and State

Cill Darae

One

Foula Island, June 902 A.C.

KATHERINE STOOD BEFORE the dark entrance to a cave on Foula Island. Moments before, she had transformed the tip of her black staff into a small sickle shape and placed it into the carved outline of a sickle central to what was a large door built into the side of an enormous boulder. A light had flared along the outline of the triskelion engraved in the door and then the door had crumbled to dust. Katherine took a moment to return the end of the staff back into a small dagger shape and then stepped up to the opening. James, Heather and Dog stood well back behind her.

Katherine could see stone stairs descending into the darkness of the opening.

Heather moved up beside her and whispered. "I've juist hud a thought. That's th' Cill Darae sickle, isn't it?"

Katherine nodded.

"That's pure Gaea, isn't it?"

Katherine nodded, but then turned and smiled at Heather. "It sure is. Should we head inside?"

Heather looked at the staff for a moment and nodded and pushed past Katherine and led the way down the stairs. Katherine took the first three steps and then stopped and looked back up toward the bright opening.

James' silhouette spoke down to them. "Sure, just walk right in. Go ahead. Not me! No, thank you very much. I'm staying out here."

Katherine smirked at Heather before responding. "Thanks, James. You've got our back. Stay vigilant."

Heather emitted a jolting laugh that Katherine rather liked. It reminded her of her mother's. It was odd: she had hated the sound at the family farm, but now she found the sound brought back fond memories of her mother.

I don't like it, grumbled Dog, standing beside James.

We'll be fine Dog, it's just a cave, replied Katherine, and they felt Heather agree across the bond.

No, Heather's barking sound. It scares away the rabbits, complained Dog and this time Heather roared in laughter and it echoed ahead of them.

"What are you laughing at, you daft girl? Keep your gob shut and listen!" yelled James from behind them.

They felt Dog sigh. *Now all the rabbits are gone.*

Sometimes Katherine wasn't sure if Dog was joking or not. She paused and then felt the mirth from Dog. *Dog! What's gotten into you?*

Dog didn't answer and padded down the stairs and past Heather into the darkness. Suddenly they felt him go rigid and he stopped. Katherine felt confusion from Dog and then excitement. Katherine sensed Heather pause on the steps below her.

Dog barked, the sound deafening in the stairwell. *I smell Gaea up ahead! And a dead person. But I smell Gaea!*

Heather glanced up at the staff Katherine wielded. *Gaea? Urr ye sure?*

Silence was the only answer.

Dog? Are you nodding?

They waited for a reply and heard nothing but silence.

Dog, are you still nodding? We talked about this. You have to use words; we can't see you. Dog, answer Heather with words.

Oh, sorry. Yes, I am sure and yes, I was nodding.

"Kin ye tell howfur lang ago?" asked Heather, out loud, and descended the stairs once more.

I am shaking my head now, replied Dog.

"You just have to say, no," snorted Katherine. "I swear you do this on purpose, Dog."

I am nodding my head now.

Heather barked a laugh before stopping on the steps. "We need a light. Ah cannae see anythin' gey weel. A'm feelin' a bawherr cut aff fae mah power. Dae yer feelin' that?"

Katherine's mind swirled trying to translate what Heather had just said. Her thick Cala accent was often annoying. Oddly enough, her accent also came across with her thoughts. Katherine was pretty sure Heather had just said she was feeling cut off from her power. Katherine stopped and peered ahead. Even using her power to improve her eyesight she could only make out a few more of the steps descending into the darkness. She *reached* with her powers but could only feel a little power coming from the opening behind them. It was barely a trickle. She had her reserves, but the motes in her body would drain her own energy if she pulled on that. "We need a light. Dog, go tell James we need a torch."

Dog rushed past them and scrambled up the stairs. They waited in silence for a moment before Heather spoke. "Ye ken Dug cannae speak tae James, right?"

Katherine groaned. "By the Word! Right."

"I'll be back. Bade 'ere."

Heather slipped past Katherine and ascended the stairs. Katherine found herself alone. She reached out with her powers to the staff and felt the power waiting there. She didn't know why, but she kept the secret of the staff from the other draoi. Heather had recognised the staff for what it was only moments ago. Katherine would need to have a long talk with her. She didn't know why she had kept this small part of Gaea present and safe from when they had erased her. Somewhere out in the world Gaea and the remains of Erebus were being eradicated, slowly but surely, and yet she held a small part of her safe in her own hands.

Once the solution to Erebus had been found, Gaea had demanded to be released from the world with him. She had tired of her role in the world. The decision on whether to eradicate Gaea had caused a split in the draoi. Many had not wanted Gaea to go. Others, like Will, had wanted to honour her wish and release her. It was the Freamhaigh who had decided, and Gaea had been destroyed. *Except this small part*, and Katherine rubbed the staff in the dark.

Killing Gaea had meant that Belkin had needed to be seeded with Life Salt, which they now knew was really the Simon motes: a man-made mote that now gave the draoi their powers. No longer did they fall under the control of Gaea, or the influence of Erebus. The draoi now decided their own fate.

While the Simon motes were almost everywhere in Belkin, they needed to be fully activated. To do so, the draoi spread the Life Salt they had found amassed in the Sect Chamber underneath Munsten Castle and used it to spark the activation. Using their *sight*, it was wonderous to watch when it happened. It was an eruption of magnificent colours and vibrant hues as the motes that made up the Life Salt dispersed across the land, pulsating and rippling in the wind. Everywhere the motes touched life it baptised and renewed the earth whilst spreading much needed draoi control. It was an awakening that brought such joy to the draoi. All across the land the draoi had travelled with Life Salt and spread their control. The motes now spread on their own, and in a matter of a few weeks they will have completed their task.

The bond between the draoi was alive and well. The transition to Simon motes from Gaea motes had been coordinated and controlled. None of the draoi had had to suffer what Katherine and Dog had endured when Gaia had severed her link to them. There had been a momentary loss of connectivity before it had reformed. Uninhibited from the rule Gaea had imposed, the draoi were free to use their powers as they saw fit. No longer were they constrained by doing no harm to others. It was empowering and frightening. Katherine remembered all too clearly what had happened to her. She had wiped out hundreds of people in Cala, all because the power had overwhelmed her. She could still clearly see the faces of those she had killed. They haunted her. *One day there will be a reckoning. Of that, I am certain.*

Katherine sniffed the air; she could smell exactly what Dog did, even though her sense of smell was not as developed. This was another secret she tried to keep from the other draoi. She and Dog had survived the impossible when they had been severed from Gaea and in the process they had joined minds for a moment. *We became one, and each left a part of the other behind.*

Katherine looked through Dog's eyes and saw Heather poking James' chest with a finger and with her face thrust in his. She kept pointing at Dog and yelling.

"Ah ken ye canna ken th' wee dug, bit he wis pul'in torches fae yer pack, wasn't he? Whit dae ye think that bloody means, ye dunderheided git? Now spark yin up 'n' haun it tae me."

"Would you calm down, woman? By the Word, you're a crabby thing. Your husband is probably falling asleep each night with a smile on his face with you gone. You need to calm yourself!"

"Lea mah husband oot o' this! Howfur dare ye remind me o' th' separation! Ye pure nasty thing!"

Katherine watched Heather turn and wink at Dog and Katherine laughed. *Oh, you are such a treat, Heather.*

Why, thank you!

Dog chimed in. *Did you know every time James gets upset, he farts a little?*

Heather paused in her tirade and then broke down laughing.

James stood with his arms on his hips. "What's the matter now? I swear, I'm leaving you lot here. I'm taking the *Oriole* home and leaving you here to rot!"

Dog took that moment to sniff at James' butt and then rubbed his snout with a paw. James swatted at Dog, but he bounded away. Heather was on the ground on her knees laughing and wiping at her eyes.

James stared at her in disbelief and then turned and untied a torch from his pack and removed the oilskin that covered the pitched end. He reached into his pack and pulled out a pouch and extracted a flint and a piece of steel. He sparked the steel over the end of the torch and then blew on a spark that landed on the pitch. The torch flared to life and James picked it up and swung it for a moment to catch the entire end. He handed it to Heather, and she stumbled away back to the cave mouth, still laughing. He looked down and caught Dog lifting a leg beside him and cursed and stepped quickly away.

"Dog! By the Word! Stop that, you dirty animal!"

Dog disappeared into the cave behind Heather and her laughter poured out of the hole.

Katherine laughed and then rubbed Dog's head when he came beside her.

I wasn't really going to pee on him, he said.

Katherine nodded.

Well, maybe just a little.

"No doubt," said Katherine chuckling and then blinked against the light from the torch carried in Heather's hand. She turned and looked down the steps. She could see they descended quite the distance into what looked like sparkling stone.

Heather examined it and then touched it. "Quartz, mabee. Solid. This cave looks tae be carved oot o' pure quartz."

"Which would explain our inability to reach the motes. There's no life here. Nothing to influence."

Katherine blew a strand of hair from her face. "No way to go but down. Ready?"

"Aye."

They descended the uneven stairs. The marks from chisels and hammers could be seen everywhere. It was clearly man-made and made through a lot of labour chiseling through solid rock. The stairs ended abruptly in a narrow hallway that bent around to the right. The floor, sides and ceiling were rough and natural.

The smell of Gaea and the dead person is much stronger, said Dog.

Katherine sniffed the air and Heather looked at her oddly. "Tis true then. Yer pairt dug."

Katherine frowned a little. "No, not part dog. Dog and I bonded in an unexpected way. My senses are a little stronger."

"Right 'n' Dug is juist a wee mair human. Speaking 'n' such."

"Uh-huh," replied Katherine. "I smell it too, Dog. The body I mean. Not Gaea."

Dog moved forward and then looked around the bend in the corridor. *There's a home down here.*

"A home?" asked Katherine and moved up beside Dog and gasped. Past the opening, the corridor opened into a large half-sphere. The ceiling arched to at least fifty feet above them. In this chamber, the walls were perfectly smooth, as if a bubble had formed and then burst leaving behind perfection. Heather stepped up beside Katherine and made a small sound. The light from the torch danced off the quartz and illuminated the object central to the chamber that shouldn't be here: a small house, complete with a thatched roof and small chimney.

"By the Word, what is this?" Katherine stepped into the space and then cried out when the walls and ceiling shimmered. Suddenly they were surrounded by a field in the middle of a vast forest. Above them the sky was blue with clouds drifting lazily past. Katherine staggered at the feeling of vertigo that swept over her. She squinted up at the bright sun and felt the warmth on her face.

I smell the grass and woods, said Dog and sniffed the grass at the edge of the chamber floor.

Katherine walked over to the grass and knelt and reached out to touch it. Her hand instead touched the cold of the quartz. Her eyes struggled to make sense of what she was seeing and what she was feeling. She stood and looked around. To her eyes, she was standing in front of a small home in the middle of a large field, surrounded by forest. She could smell the grass and trees. But then she noticed she couldn't feel any wind or breeze on her face despite the longer grass and leaves fluttering. *This is like living in a painting, it's not real.*

Heather, being more adventurous, put her torch on the floor, and stepped up to the door of the home and unbelievably knocked on the door. Heather looked back at Katherine and grinned.

You knocked?

Ye ne'er ken. Better tae be safe, aye?

Dog ran toward the forest and Katherine cried out to stop him. He ran maybe fifteen feet before he slammed into the side of the cavern. He yelped and fell back.

Are you hurt?

No. What is happening here? I'm confused.

So are we, Dog. We need to be careful here.

Okay.

Come over here with us. No running around.

Dog slunk over to stand beside Katherine, glancing over to the area where he had slammed into the wall. Together they joined Heather.

"No one seems to be home. You first?" offered Katherine.

"Ta."

Heather grasped the door handle and turned it. The door opened easily, and Heather pushed it open. She stuck her head in and called out. "Hullo?" Hearing no reply, she entered the home. Katherine and Dog followed in behind her.

Inside was a home that was clearly lived in. What caught their immediate attention was the body lying on the bed to their right under sheets as if sleeping. The room had a small table in the centre with two chairs. The remains of a small meal lay mouldy on a tin plate. A small journal lay open in the centre of the table. On the far wall, was a fireplace with a cooking pot hung over the remains of a long-extinguished fire. A small bookcase was near the bed and filled with books. A small wooden chest lay against the other wall, closed and latched. Otherwise the room was empty and very clean. The floor was made of the same stone as the chamber.

The three of them stood in the entrance staring about the room trying to decide what to do first. Dog decided for them and trotted up to the body and sniffed. He sneezed once and then twice.

Dead.

"We can see that."

Been dead for a long time. Very dry.

"Leave it be for now," said Katherine.

"Dae ye think it micht be Hietower?"

"Possibly. But why put him in a bed?"

"Och, right. That mak's nae sense."

Katherine went to the table and gently picked up the journal and marked the page it was open to with her thumb. She closed it and glanced at the cover and held it up for the others to see. "Look here, it has a tree and triskelion on the cover." Heather came closer and examined it. She reached out and traced it with a finger. Katherine watched Dog pad over to the cooking pot and sniff at it.

"It's oor symbol. Tis draoi."

Katherine nodded and opened the cover and read what she saw written on the first page. "Journal of Benjamin Erwin, 895 A.C."

"That's several years ago."

Katherine glanced at the body in the bed. "So this must be Benjamin Erwin. What's he doing here?"

"Nae weel, ah think."

"Ha, ha. Let's check him out."

Katherine placed the journal back on the table and opened it to the page she had kept marked. They went over to the bed and carefully peeled back the bedsheet. It was stuck to the body and resisted their efforts. They pulled a little more forcibly, and the blanket took a little of the body with it. Underneath lay a figure on his side with his face to the wall. He was dressed in what appeared to be simple brown robes. Other than a long white beard he could have been anyone.

"He could be anyone," stated Katherine.

"Ohh, aye. An old man by the looks o' him."

Dog was bolting around the small home sniffing frantically.

"Dog what are you looking for?"

I smell Gaea, she's here.

"How can you smell Gaea? Dog? What is it you smell?"

It's Gaea.

They watched as Dog ran around the entire home. Finally, he stopped and cocked his head to one side.

I think it's everything.

"Everything?"

Yes, the entire building. All this is Gaea.

Heather snorted. "Tis beyond our ken, that's fer sure. I mean look at this place. It's lik' bein' in th' forest, bit it's a' lik' a paintin. Juist sae real."

Katherine was silent and thinking. "This man died in here. Sealed in. This is a prison."

Heather shook her head. "That doesn't mak' sense. How come wid Gaea seal someone up? That's nae her nature. Is it? Benjamin was her Freamhaigh."

When Katherine turned to look at her, she had a look on her face that caused Heather to hesitate. "Yes, it is—was—rather."

Heather squinted her eyes. "Ye said *is*." Heather pointed at the staff. "That's Gaea thare oan that staff. Her essence. She bides in yer staff, doesn't she?"

Katherine glared at Heather and then sat in one of the chairs and placed the staff on the table. She thrust her chin at the other chair and Heather sat. Dog sniffed the body and sneezed again.

"Yes. It's her. I protected her from being completely wiped out. No one looked to it. No one cared."

"Th' Freamhaigh did. He ordered it. Said her wishes wur tae be follaed."

Katherine growled a little. "Perhaps."

"Mibbie? Katherine, ye gaed against him. Will will be chuffed."

"Will is not my Freamhaigh, Heather. Not exactly."

"Whit dae ye mean?"

"When I was severed, Dog and I, we left the draoi. We were on our own. We did...things. It was Dog and I against Erebus. A weapon forged by Gaea to get close enough to infect him. Then we won. And then Will was there with Nadine. Suddenly we were all this happy draoi family again. Except…

"Except ye don't cop lik' pairt o' that fowk, dae ye?"

Katherine looked hurt. She glanced at Dog and he padded over and laid his snout on her leg. "Not exactly. I do. And I don't. Dog and I are something different. I'm something different. Will worries only about harmony. Bringing nature into balance. For Belkin. You see that, don't you?"

"Aye, o' coorse. We a' cop that wey."

"I don't. I see a whole world out there. What has Erebus done to the rest of the world, Heather? Who is taking care of it? We have one Freamhaigh and one Cill Darae. That can't be enough. I doubt Gaea was only thinking only of Belkin. She said it was her last refuge, but I can't believe that. I needed to keep a part of her alive. Something to take with me out there."

"Oot thare? Ye mean ootside Belkin?"

Katherine looked at the table. For a moment, to Heather, she looked like a young girl, lost and confused, but when she lifted her face to stare at her, Heather saw eyes very different from those of a young girl. Heather gasped and lifted her hand to her mouth.

"Ye'v changed, Katherine. Ye hide this pairt o' ye, don't ye?"

Katherine looked away quickly. "Yes." Katherine stood up and went over to the fireplace. Dog trotted after her. "I'm not a nice person. Neither is Dog. We've done things." Katherine petted Dog's head and looked around the small home and gestured with her other hand. "This is a gaol. That body over there is probably Benjamin Erwin. He stole the bones of King Hietower and then came here and was trapped and died. But where is Analise Bracewell? Where is her body? Where are the bones of Hietower?"

Heather tore her gaze from Katherine's and looked around and then settled her eyes on the journal. "We need tae read this. Bit foremaist let me tell James whit's happening. He'll be whirlin` by noo."

Katherine nodded and moved over to the table. "Yes, go tell him."

Heather hesitated a moment, waiting for something more from Katherine as she pushed the mouldy tin plate away and glanced around. Heather kept an eye on Katherine until she realised Heather was still staring at her. Katherine turned and frowned at her, and then made a face. Heather shook her head and walked out of the small building and soon her footsteps faded away into the tunnel.

Katherine looked at Dog. "This is strange, Dog."

Dog sniffed the body on the bed again. *Yes, very strange. The body smells old. He was a man. Old.*

"Probably Benjamin. Either he was trapped here or opted to stay here. I'm tired of this chase after old bones. I feel the need to leave Belkin and head out into the world. Do you?"

Dog woofed gently in agreement.

"For now we'll stay and help sort this mess out. We can't leave yet. Belkin is in a right mess."

Dog remained silent and Katherine went out into the chamber to wait for Heather and James.

They both came back shortly after. James entered and gasped when he saw the chamber. Heather laughed and winked at Katherine.

"Ah didnae tell him anythin'. Ah wanted tae see his surprise."

James whistled and reached out to the grass and gave a yell when his hand hit the chamber wall. "What is this? More draoi magic?"

"Maist likely. Certainly, something beyond oor understanding."

"It's uncanny!" James looked around and up at the sky and then spotted the house. "A house? What is going on?"

Katherine laughed. "We aren't sure, but this is Gaea's work. Come inside. We found the remains of Benjamin Erwin, we think. And a journal."

James followed Katherine into the house and whistled again. "This is getting stranger by the minute." He noticed the body on the bed and went over and lifted the blanket to look at it. After a moment he covered it back up. "So this is the remains of the man who won the Great Debate and started a revolution? He died in this strange place all alone? Poor fellow."

Katherine lifted the journal off the table, still open to the last page Benjamin had opened it to. "This is his journal. It was lying open on the table. Hopefully it gives us the answers we seek."

Heather sat at the table and Dog sat next to her. James moved around the small single room and stopped at the chest. "Did you look in here?"

Heather shook her head. "Not yet."

"Maybe the bones of Hietower are in here?"

Dog chuffed.

"Dog doesn't think so. We would have smelled them."

James crouched and unlatched the chest and lifted the lid. The hinges protested loudly, but James had the lid up with little effort. Katherine peered over his shoulder and Heather leaned over to get a better look. James looked at Katherine for a moment. "Clothes. Maybe something at the bottom?"

Katherine looked disappointed and took the other seat at the table. "Keep searching. I'll read the last entry in the journal."

Katherine started to read and after a moment Heather gently kicked her under the table. "Out loud, if you don't mind."

"Ouch! Of course, I was just getting a feel for it. It's Erwin, for sure. He doesn't sound happy. Listen:

"I can feel the end is near. My heart struggles to beat. I welcome this, at long last. The pain of being separated from the draoi for so many years will soon be over, and I hope that I join the other draoi on my death. So much pain and suffering. It is over...

Katherine looked up at the others. "It ends there. We'll need to go back to the start and read it through."

James made a noise and lifted some objects out of the chest. He held them up for them to see. "A woman's skirt and a hair brush. There was a woman here at some point."

Heather nodded. "Analise Bracewell, I bet."

James put the items on the floor next to the chest and other contents. "Nothing but clothes. Well worn, too. Otherwise, it's empty."

Dog laid down on the floor next to Katherine. *I'm bored.*

Katherine poked him with a foot. "Get comfortable. We'll be here for a little bit."

Cill Darae

Two

Foula Island, June 902 A.C.

HEATHER SEETHED INSIDE. The last few hours provided little insight into what they needed to do next. James and Katherine could not agree, and Dog seemed determined to sleep wherever he could and as often as he could. Even the sound of James' breathing seemed to irritate her. *Everything is too topsy-turvy, but at least we buried that poor man.*

They had buried Benjamin and then they had each read the journal. Each of them had taken a different meaning from the content. One thing was clear: Benjamin Erwin had been a prisoner. And Heather was certain Analise had been the gaoler.

Heather stood in the door to the house looking up at the evening sky. It was hard to believe it wasn't real. The sky in the chamber followed the sky outside. She turned back inside to find Katherine still reading the journal and James sitting stretched out at the table with his ankles crossed. Heather spoke to the two of them. "It's plain as the day in his writing. Benjamin hated Gaea and figured out she was a spiteful thing. He threatened to expose her. He says so himself."

James stirred. "Aye, and Analise disagreed with him. It's Freamhaigh versus Cill Darae."

Heather blew a strand of hair from her face. "It's clear they disagreed. Analise, according to Benjamin, had turned from the draoi calling."

Katherine shook her head and placed the journal down on the table. "He didn't say that. He merely said they disagreed about the nature of Gaea."

"No, he didn't. He said '*Analise refuses to listen to me on what Gaea is. She went so far as to tell me the draoi are not what I believed them to be. She is so far from the Cill Darae I thought she was.*' That sounds like she turned from the draoi."

Katherine growled and even James looked up at the sound. It sounded far too dog-like to have come from her throat. "That just says they disagreed. Not that she turned from the draoi."

Heather strode forward and flipped through the journal searching for an entry. She found it and tossed the journal onto the table in front of Katherine. "Read that!"

Katherine glanced at the page and frowned.

"It says it right there."

"That was years after she had abandoned him here. I doubt his sanity."

"Abandoned him? She trapped him in here!" Katherine remained silent. Heather spun on James. "Say something!"

James looked startled. "Say what? That I agree with you? Well, I do. I've already said so. Nothing remains of Analise, but a skirt and a brush. Benjamin chronicled everything in that bloody journal." James counted on his fingers. "One, they left Munsten together after the King burned the bishop fellow. Two, they gathered the draoi and told them to spread out and calm the country. Three, suddenly the rebellion started. He says nothing about what happens next until, four, he and Analise steal the bones of King Hietower. He writes that Analise said Gaea wanted it done. Five, they come here of all places." James held up his other hand and stuck out a thumb. "Six, she abandons him here and runs off with the bones, places unknown."

Katherine sighed. "At least we know now that the bones are Hietower's. We aren't chasing our tails." Katherine looked at Dog, but he was asleep.

Heather tucked an errant strand of hair behind an ear. "True. The journal says nothing of why they took the bones out of Munsten. But we know they brought them here and then Analise took off with them."

Each grew silent in thought. Dog rolled onto his back and spread his legs wide exposing everything. James smiled at the sight and Heather scowled at him. *Men are all alike.*

Heather started when James looked at her and winked.

Such cheek!

James pushed himself back to a proper sitting posture and leaned on the table. The tin plate had been put away, and they had brought out their own fare and had a meagre repast. James poked the journal. "What about what Benjamin says about blocking Gaea? I thought that would give you two conniptions."

Katherine looked at Heather before speaking. Heather nodded and wondered why Katherine would defer to her on this. Katherine leaned back and answered. "It's interesting. Especially with what we know now about Gaea's nature. And Erebus. If there is a way to block the power of the motes I would like to know what that is. Heather, do you agree?"

"Aye, o' coorse. Ah wonder if it wid hae worked against Erebus?"

Katherine looked thoughtful. "I think so. They were the same. I would like to know more, but unfortunately it went with Analise. It was her belief. Perhaps if we can find her we can ask her."

"Ask her! You expect to find her alive?"

"Why not? They lived long after they should have passed from old age."

"She would be ancient! Well over a hundred years old!"

Katherine shrugged. "Probably not that many years if she could take power from Gaea. We should expect to live as long if not longer."

Heather gawked at Katherine. "Why? Why should we expect that?"

Katherine looked surprised by the question. "We control the Simon motes. We can repair most injuries to the human body. Our powers allow us unlimited years. You should plan for that. I'm surprised you haven't all figured that out."

Heather had her mouth open. She started to say something but stopped instead. *She's not wrong,* she thought. *This is miraculous. We need to speak about this as soon as I get out of this cave.* She shut her mouth when she realised James was smirking at her. "Shut your mouth, James Dixon!"

"It's not often I see you at a loss for words. It's pleasant."

Heather screeched and started toward James with her hands in claws. Dog rose from the floor and barked at Heather and she stopped and stared at him. They all stared at Dog until he sat on the floor.

Enough, where to next?

Katherine and Heather stared at Dog. James frowned when no one said anything. "Um, what did Dog say?"

Heather looked at James. "He said enough, where to next?"

James rose and ruffled the top of Dog's head. "I knew I liked you best, Dog." James sauntered out through the door.

Katherine hurried down the tunnel and back into the chamber. As always, the walls inside the chamber mimicked the time of day outside. The sun was just up and inside the chamber the sun was glinting through the gaps in the trees of the forest. Katherine had just spoken to Will and Nadine. She described what they had found and asked what they wanted them to do next. The lack of bones annoyed Will, and he said as much. Nadine had argued openly with Will and Katherine felt worry. For two people so very much in love they seemed to be more openly in disagreement with each other. It did not bode well.

The angst was making Katherine long harder to escape the shores of Belkin. Every day she worried about what was happening beyond the seas. *Was the virus I unleashed truly eradicating Erebus?* She needed proof. Otherwise all was for nothing. She knew Gaea was fallible. And she wondered if perhaps this business with the bones was another error on her part.

Belkin was not faring well, according to Nadine. Brent Bairstow was an excellent military leader, but a terrible political one. The people living in the villages and cities had not fully understood the sudden death of President Healy and the oath of fealty from the military toward Brent. Trouble brewed everywhere and everyone doubted what was truth and what was fantasy. And Brent was not responding to the threat well. What they were hearing from Munsten was the church was having a direct influence on Brent. He rarely listened to anyone but the church vicars; all of whom had descended on Munsten for some reason. He trusted few others, especially with Councils who had worked with Healy for years.

This is our world now. Gaea is gone, and we are left to our own devices and fears. Belkin needs a firm hand and Brent is too scared to flex his own muscle. And Will seems intent to distance the draoi from the politics of the land.

Katherine paused once she entered the chamber. She could see Heather and James sitting at the table. Heather thought she was fooling everyone, but Katherine could see the admiration she had for James. *I'm sure James knows it too and feels the same.* Thankfully, with James not part of the draoi bond, the bond wasn't sending that information for all to see and feel. That would be devastating for Heather and her family. Katherine felt sorry for them both. They could never be together. *It's easier to pretend to hate each other, I suppose.*

Dog bounded out of the building toward her and Heather and James looked hopefully out the door to Katherine. She entered, petting Dog, and stood just inside the doorway. "This place needs a third chair."

James frowned. "What did Will say?"

Heather frowned at James. "Whit did Nadine say?"

"Not much other than to continue our search. We have to find the bones, according to both Will and Nadine. We included Brent by using the draoi Lana Turner who's posted in the castle. Brent had some questions and then pointed us to Munsten."

"Munsten? How so? We just came from there!"

"He says Benjamin Erwin's belongings are stored in the lower levels of the Museum of the Revolution. He's says we're welcome to rummage through them."

Heather looked crestfallen. Katherine came forward and rested a hand on her shoulder for a moment. Heather looked up at Katherine and clasped the hand just as she pulled it away. "It's braw. Braw. At least it's in th' right direction."

Dog whined a little and placed his muzzle in Heather's lap. She stroked his head absently.

"I suppose," said James. "We are certain of this direction? Searching the belongings of Benjamin? What do we hope to gain?"

Katherine sighed. "There's nothing else here. No clue. Which is strange. Gaea meant for us to find the bones when the time is right. The clue led here and now nothing. We've come to a wall."

Heather shook her head but continued to rub Dog's head. "Ah hawp we trust Gaea in this. She led Analise 'n' Benjamin 'ere wi' th' bones. Then something happened atween th' twa o' thaim. Analise broke fae th' draoi, imprisoned Benjamin, 'n' teuk th' bones wi' her. Benjamin wouldn't ken whaur she wid hae taken thaim. Bit we ken she left him 'ere. Thare haes tae be a clue elsewhere. Something in thair bygane that micht point a wey. Gaea knew we wid fin' it. Otherwise, we ur done."

Katherine chewed her lip. "I don't like it. This isn't a direction I would willingly take. But Nadine and Will believe Benjamin's belongings will point the way, and so now we do that. I hope they're right." Katherine saw Dog now had his eyes closed enjoying Heather's attention. "Dog, stop that."

Dog stepped away from Heather and shook his body. *Bleah*, he thought. *Do we leave soon?*

Soon, yes. Were you not following along with the conversation?

Um, no. I was concentrating on not moving so Heather wouldn't stop.

James stirred from where he was flipping through the journal. "I don't get it. Why would Analise steal the bones away? Clearly Gaea wanted them found at some point. How could a Cill Darae abandon her draoi?"

Heather grimaced. "Thay lived thro' th' Purge. Thay gawked a' th' draoi perish aroond thaim 'n' yit cuid dae nothin'. It changed thaim. It hud tae."

Katherine shook her head. "Most likely they were inside here when it happened. They were isolated from the world. They wouldn't have felt the draoi bonds break. And Benjamin says nothing about it in his journal. They couldn't have been aware. They missed the deaths and torture."

"And then... started Heather and then raised a hand to her mouth in horror. "'n' then Analise cam oot 'n' wid hae found a world empty o' draoi!"

Katherine nodded. "Yes. That would have convinced her that she had been right."

They looked at each other in silence imagining the horror. Katherine understood better than anyone, other than Dog, of the horror of being severed from Gaea and the world.

James coughed and slid the journal around so the two women could see a page and he pointed out a passage. "This is interesting. Benjamin mentions a power source for Gaea. Do you know what that is?"

Katherine looked at the passage and shook her head. "I read that. He mentions Analise talking about it, but he says here he doesn't believe it. There's no other mention of it. I did sense it was a point of friction between them."

"I agree," said James. "What would a power source for Gaea be? I thought she was everywhere."

"She was everywhere. She was part of all life. Like Erebus. Her power came from each individual mote. I don't know how it worked, but I can't see there being one power source for all that. Do you Heather?"

Heather shook her head. "Na. Ah don't see howfur. How come dae ye mention it, James?"

"Because if I was Analise, and I wanted to upset Gaea I would head to where I thought her source of power lay."

"And you think she knew where that was?"

"Yes, and I think Benjamin might have, too. But kept it hidden from Analise."

Katherine slowly nodded. "So, Munsten is a done deal. We examine Benjamin's belongings in the museum. Maybe something there can point the way. Maybe to this power source."

Heather smiled. "Ah hae hope, Katherine. Ah hae hope." She glanced at James and found him looking at her.

Three

Munsten and Rigby Farm, July 902 A.C.

BRENT BAIRSTOW SAT at his breakfast table in his private chambers. The window next to Brent filled the entire wall and allowed an unobstructed view of the city of Munsten and its harbour. President John Healy had once enjoyed the view the table offered. He imagined Healy had probably gloated looking out over a city he once ruled with the trappings of a madman. As Brent watched smoke drift up lazily in the still air from the chimneys dotting the buildings, he could imagine that all the people below him were at peace and had no fear for their futures. He knew those thoughts were nothing but flights of fancy. The city and realm were in turmoil. Nothing he did seemed to make it better.

His breakfast lay untouched before him. Fine china and shining silverware lay unused before silver platters which offered everything he could want for breaking his fast. It annoyed him. Every day he told his castellan to provide him only with tea and some toast. And yet they continued to provide for him as they would for John Healy. Decades of pattern were hard to break.

He sighed and looked at his breakfast guests: Robert Ghent, the head of the Judicial Council, and Robert Hargrave, the head of the Privy Council. As normal, they refused to eat when they saw Brent was eating nothing. They sipped their tea and cast hungry glances at the platters of sausages, fried tomatoes and mushrooms, smoked fish, baked beans in molasses, and poached eggs. They met once a week in Brent's chambers to go over the more serious issues plaguing the land.

Brent set down his teacup. "Please, gentlemen. Eat! Don't let it go to waste."

The two Roberts looked at one another but made no move to take any of the food.

"I insist."

The two men looked back at Brent and then Hargrave, his large belly already pushing at the table, reached out and spooned baked beans onto his plate. Ghent hesitated a moment and then filled his own plate with poached eggs and smoked fish.

"Good," said Brent and sat back in his seat. He watched as the men filled their plates and he allowed them a moment to savour the food before speaking. "I understand the remains of the Cian-Oirthear army have sailed."

Hargrave nodded and chewed. Ghent glanced at Hargrave and spoke for him. "Yes, sir. They left yesterday morning with the tide. They were most upset about having to leave their horses behind. You would think we were taking their children from them. Such wails! Knight General Kingsmill had to have many subdued."

Brent nodded. He had heard the same tale. "And the people? I heard they had moved down to the docks in protest. Rocks and garbage were thrown? I heard two of our soldiers were hurt."

Hargrave nodded and swallowed before speaking. "Yes, sir. Except it was three soldiers, not two. One is in the hospital under the care of the chirurgeons. Nasty head wound. It is not certain if he will survive."

"Has the draoi Lana been summoned?"

A look of displeasure flitted across Hargrave's face. "I am told she was summoned. Edward insisted on it. He spends all his time with the chirurgeons and that draoi girl. He frequently skips out on his royal training. His tutors are most annoyed."

Brent scowled. "Find out if Lana has appeared. You should know that, not guesswork."

Hargrave looked surprised. "Sir, if I may. That is not my function. Matters of the military and the day-to-day activities of the chirurgeons are not my bailiwick."

Brent leaned forward. "It is your job to know everything that is going on in this city and the realm. Look into it and report back."

Hargrave's mouth drew thin. A splash of red crested up his jowls and high up his cheeks in angry splotches. Ghent looked confused. Hargrave opened his mouth and then closed it. Finally he opened it again. "Regent Bairstow, I am the head of your Privy Council. My role is to advise you on matters of the Realm. I am not your batman as I understand the role and position your army has. If you want to know more of minor military matters, I suggest you seek out the Knight General."

Anger rose fast and hot within Brent. His first impulse was to berate the man. He would never have suffered such insubordination from his juniors when he was a military man. The thought of the military suddenly kept Brent's mouth shut. *I'm not military anymore, and neither is Hargrave. He's quite right, by the Word. I hate this job. I'm not cut out to be a Regent.*

Hargrave must have sensed his small victory for he smiled and selected another poached egg to place on his plate. Ghent looked unhappy and uncomfortable. Brent looked out the window and sighed.

Below him the rising sun was brightening the morning and lighting up the streets, buildings, and parks. He looked back at the two men. "Fair enough, Robert. I am new to this role. I will make mistakes."

Hargrave had the face of someone who felt he was the better man. "Sir, you've been the Regent for many months. I would think you would have figured out much more than this. I am the head of your Privy Council. Robert here is the head of your Judicial Council. Our roles and responsibilities are quite clear and have been explained to you many, many times."

Brent stilled. Hargrave, oblivious to the change in Brent stuffed a large sausage into his mouth and bit down on the skin. The sausage burst and grease dripped down his double chin. Ghent moved back slightly in his seat putting a little distance between himself and Hargrave. When Hargrave finally looked up at Brent, he saw the open anger and froze.

When Brent spoke, he started at a whisper. "You go too far, Hargrave. That kind of insolence has no place here, or anywhere. I warn you for the last time. Be careful of what you say in my presence. I *am* the Regent, not some lackey in the Privy Council you can bully and jeer over.

"While you sit and stuff your face with sausages the realm reels with turmoil. I have asked the Privy Council countless times to provide me with options on how to best deal with the problem. You have offered me nothing but platitudes. Every day the number of crimes in the city rise. The army is having to quell violence and protests across the land. They are stretched thin—too thin—and every day I turn to you as the head of the Privy Council to advise me."

His voice had risen in volume and Brent slammed the table with a fist. The two Roberts jumped in their seats. "So *advise* me! Advise me on how to restore peace and prosperity to this realm before it all gets dumped down the latrine! Do your bloody job!"

Hargrave's face was flushed completely red. Brent could see his words had done little to change Hargrave's attitude. If anything, the man looked more stubborn than ever. Hargrave set down his fork and then lifted the napkin off his lap and dabbed at his mouth. He set the napkin down on his plate of food and then struggled to stand. He bowed once to Brent and then left without waiting to be dismissed.

Brent looked at Ghent. The man looked frightened and probably wanted to be elsewhere. "Relax, Robert. I have no issue with you. You have advised me in all the legalities of running the Realm and the court."

Ghent looked relieved and settled more comfortably in his seat. He reached for his fork, touched it, thought better of it, and pulled his hand back. He looked at a loss for what to do with his hand and settled it on his lap.

Brent smiled. "I need to know what powers I have over the Privy Council. Who decides who heads it?"

Ghent smiled a weak smile and coughed gently into his hand. "Ah, that would be you, Regent. We serve at your pleasure."

"Excellent. Is there a formal process?"

"Healy would simply have replaced the head. There is no formal process or paperwork to make it happen. It is a private council, sir."

Brent nodded. "Excellent. Now. Other matters. I want to increase the court sessions and provide a lower court system."

Ghent looked startled. "A lower court system? Whatever do you mean?"

"The court is hearing all manner of trivial cases. I want crimes divided into a higher and lower grouping. Much like we have in the military. Commanding officers have powers to try and sentence soldiers who have committed less serious crimes. The more serious crimes go to courts martial and more senior judges. We also have a jury system. I would like to see it applied to the lower court."

"Military law, I see," Ghent looked thoughtful.

"No, not military law, just the system of trying cases."

"I see. I will speak with the Knight General and ask for advice on the matter, is that acceptable?"

"Perfectly acceptable, just make it happen soon."

"Yes, sir. Now, if I may, I would like to brief you on the more serious crimes coming to your court this week. The Royal Laws in some cases can be quite confusing and often seeming to contradict one another, I assure you that the way forward is quite clear as far as the Realm is considered…"

Will Arbor added the henbane to the mortar and then looked about his table for the pestle. It seemed to have disappeared. He took a step back and looked under the table. He couldn't see it anywhere. He crouched down and moved the supplies stored on the shelf built under the table. He paused and thought and then stood up. *There it is, right next to the mortar. How had I missed it?* He snatched it up and returned to the mortar work.

Lately his thoughts did not seem his own. He felt disconnected. *I wish Gaea was still here. She would be able to sort through all this.* The pressures of being Freamhaigh were weighing on him and he was certain this was to blame. Nadine agreed with him. The truth was, the draoi were unhappy. They had spent weeks spreading Life Salt across the realm. Now activated, the motes the Life Salt was made of were duplicating and spreading and touching all life. Will could feel his powers reaching farther and farther. Gaea had normally worked with nature to ensure the harmony was maintained. Now that role fell to him and Nadine. The good news was it required little but their attention, although occasionally they had to interfere directly. The draoi wanted a larger role. Will disagreed. He had interfered with the politics of the realm too much already. The role of the draoi was limited to maintaining the harmony of nature. He would not let them become direct influencers of the politics in the realm. *That path leads to disaster*, thought Will. *Our powers are too great.*

The draoi openly argued amongst themselves and Will felt like a parent at times; he chastised and berated. Far too often he had to come between the draoi and making them see reason over some simple matter. Across their draoi bond, tempers flared. Gone were the days of contented bliss amongst the draoi. Gone were the feelings of strong family bonds. They were now an organisation, ruled by Will and Nadine.

As he ground the henbane leaves into the other herbs, he heard and felt the rest of the house waken and stir. In the other room, he heard Dempster shuffle into the kitchen and grunt when he found the stove already stoked and hot. It often was in the morning, Will rose earlier and earlier and always started up the stove. He drew strength from the land and found sleep nothing more than a distraction these days.

Upstairs he heard Anne slipping out from under the bedcovers. The large warm spot beside her was cooling now that Dempster was downstairs. Will smiled, happy for the two of them. Little Frankie was fussing, and Anne scooped her up and headed to the changing table to clean her up.

Also upstairs he could sense Nadine. Their bond burned bright white, and it led him to find her lying on their bed, on top of the covers, and wide awake. She was staring at the ceiling and Will knew she was watching him work in his laboratory—or his hideaway, as she sometimes called it.

I see you, Nadine, spying on me again. Being sneaky?

I'm not being sneaky.

What are you doing then?

Sneaking.

Will laughed out loud, and he felt Dempster turn to the sound before resuming his task of frying up bacon.

I love to watch you work, Will.

Come down here and help me then.

What? And get my hands all green? No, thank you. I'd rather just watch.

Dempster is getting breakfast started. You could help him.

No, thank you. I'm very busy at the moment.

Busy?

Yes, thinking up ways of bothering you later.

Oh, really?

Yes, just you wait, young man.

Will shook his head in laughter and resumed his work. He allowed his thoughts to roam the realm and he paused in a southern forest to count the rabbit population. The foxes were decimating the numbers and soon the foxes would be looking for food elsewhere. He still hadn't come up with a solution, but for now he merely watched. *I find it simpler to allow events to play out, eventually, as they often do, they sort themselves out...*

* * *

Later, after breakfast was over, Will and Nadine remained at the kitchen table drinking tea that was now not nearly hot enough. Will gave his cup a little surge of his power and the cup in his hands grew warm enough that steam rose from the contents. Will frowned at his cup.

"What's wrong, Will?" asked Nadine looking from the cup to Will's face.

"Our power is a little different," said Will. "Hard to describe. It just feels different."

"Hmm, yes. We've all noticed. It's a little too quick. Too strong, at times."

"It has a different flavour," mumbled Will, and he took a sip of his tea. It was blackcurrant, and he loved it. One of the draoi who had ventured up to Cala to spread Life Salt had brought it back. The draoi reported the city was still recovering from the horrors Katherine and Dog had unleashed. Will frowned at the thought. *What they had done was unforgiveable. Draoi should never take lives. Gaea saw to that.*

Nadine had pursed her lips. "Different flavour... yes, I suppose it does at that."

They grew quiet in thought and were startled when someone knocked on the front door.

Will looked at Nadine and then used his senses to probe for who was at the door. He was startled when no one was there. Nadine's eyes widened. Anne trotted down the stairs and opened the door. They could hear her from the kitchen.

"Oh, hullo Kennit. Will or Nadine expecting you?"

"No, they are not."

"Well come in, they're in the kitchen. Go on through."

"Thank you, Anne. How is Little Frankie?"

"Good thanks. She loves the rattle you gave her. Thanks again."

"My pleasure. I made them often in Shape for the babies. Back when I was a simple carpenter."

Will and Nadine heard Kennit Doirich approach the kitchen. With their senses they could sense nothing of him. Even the draoi bond was gone. There should be threads of power going from Kennit to every other draoi in the realm. But there were none to find. Nadine was struggling to her feet just as Kennit entered the kitchen.

Will stood up and moved beside Nadine and they stared at Kennit for a long moment. Kennit finally smiled and raised his arms up from his sides. "What do you think? Pretty neat, don't you think? Here, watch this..."

Will and Nadine were startled when the draoi bond to Kennit snapped back in place. Threads radiated out from him, one for each draoi. Immediately they could sense Kennit as they would any other draoi. They felt his heartbeat and his emotions, strong and familiar.

Will was the first to speak. "How?"

Nadine's question followed her husband's. "Why?"

Kennit chuckled. "I've been experimenting with our new powers. There is so much more to learn. I thought that perhaps I could shield myself from the other draoi. It's much simpler to do than you would think. It's more about applying your will to the problem."

Will shook his head. "But the bond? Where did it go? We never even felt it disappear. We should have felt that!"

Kennit smiled. "It's still there. I just hide it. I turn it back on itself."

Nadine frowned. "Show us how. Demonstrate it."

Kennit's smile faltered. "I will, just let me work on it a bit more first."

Will noticed his bond to Kennit flicker ever so slightly and he looked closer. Just then a powerful pulse of Nadine's power washed over her bond with Kennit and she grabbed it. Will felt the shock back along his own bond. All the draoi felt it. *I didn't know you could grab the bond*, thought Will.

Nadine moved up to stand in front of Kennit. "You just lied, Kennit. Why would you lie to me, the Cill Darae? Or the Freamhaigh?"

A flash of anger crossed Kennit's face and Will stared. The anger didn't surprise him that much, but not sensing it across the draoi bond did. Nadine looked back at Will and Will could see the concern there. She was worried.

Kennit stepped away from Nadine and held up his hands. "Another thing I've discovered. We can mask ourselves. Hide our emotions across the bond. It's wonderful, don't you think?"

Nadine growled and pulled on the bond she held. "No, I do not. The draoi bond is part of who we are, why would you want to hide yourself from other draoi?"

Will could see Kennit's discomfort with having his bond held to tightly by Nadine. Then Kennit scowled. "Have you forgotten the Purge? How the church used the bond to find other draoi? How about what Erebus and Katherine did across the bond? So many people in Belkin died from that pulse. We need to protect ourselves. I offer nothing more than that. I thought you would be pleased?"

Nadine growled again and stepped closer to Kennit. "You weren't even alive during the Purge. I was. How dare you accuse me of forgetting the loss of all my friends? The fight between Erebus and Katherine had nothing to do with the bond. You know that. This talent of yours, how many more know how to do this?"

Kennit flinched when Nadine tugged the bond. "Just me."

Nadine hissed. "Again, you lie." She looked back at Will. "Can you see it when he lies, Will?"

Will knew what she was hinting at. When he lied, his bond flickered ever so slightly. Will nodded.

Nadine turned back to Kennit. "Explain yourself."

Kennit frowned. "I don't think so."

Nadine hissed. "Excuse me?" Will stepped forward to speak but stopped when Nadine raised a hand to forestall him. Nadine's eyes bored into Kennit's. "You are speaking to your Cill Darae."

Kennit looked Nadine up and down for a moment. "I see a draoi who didn't listen to the other draoi. You let Gaea be destroyed. You murdered her! How could you do that?"

Will was confused. He struggled to make sense of what Kennit was saying. When they had confronted and beat Erebus, they had been able to destroy him. Gaea's purpose had been to remove the threat of Erebus from the land. Now that her purpose had been fulfilled, Gaea had asked to be removed from the world. Will had allowed the draoi to vote, against Nadine's wishes. Will had wanted to allow Gaea to go, others had not. It was an even split. There were many of the draoi who almost worshiped Gaea. She had so drastically changed their lives that their love for her had known no bounds. When Will, as Freamhaigh, had allowed Gaea to be destroyed, the draoi had split in reaction. They called it the *Gaea Decision*. Kennit was one of the draoi who had been the angriest when she had been destroyed. He openly blamed Will and Nadine, despite Nadine having voted to keep Gaea. It was lost on the group that Gaea had asked to be destroyed. They chose their version of the truth and clung to it despite the facts and evidence. It was this fracture in the draoi that kept Will awake at nights.

Nadine sighed and looked back at Will for a moment.

This seemed to make Kennit angrier. In a blink his bonds disappeared and Nadine's hold was gone. He stormed out of the kitchen. They heard the front door open and slam closed. Out on the farm, Will could hear draoi calling out to Kennit, but Will could no longer sense him or where he was.

Nadine reached out a shaking hand for the edge of the table and sank onto the bench seat. Will sat next to her. Across the draoi bond, they could sense the confusion from the draoi. Many had been focused on Kennit's bond and when it had disappeared questions poured in on Will and Nadine seeking answers.

Nadine clutched Will's hand. She felt her reach across their bond to him. *Look at who responds. Which of the draoi ask questions. Mark those who are silent. Can you sense them?*

Will reached out and after a moment he nodded his head at Nadine. Will could feel the despair enter Nadine's heart.

We are fractured, Will.

❦

Kennit cursed and entered the barn. He went to the back and climbed up to the hay loft and sat heavily into the chair he kept there. The smell of hay soothed him and reminded him of his days in Shape. He had been one of many close friends of Lana Turner and often she had taken him into a barn to educate him in on the finer things in life. He had known Eylene but only from a distance.

Memories of his times with her almost banished the dark thoughts he had at the moment. He cursed again and smacked his thigh in frustration. *I let them see what I could do! How stupid!*

Kennit had only meant to speak to Will and Nadine about the draoi. Plans were already well in place, but he had wanted to give them an opportunity to see reason. *Instead, I exposed my powers. It's too soon. Too soon. I have to warn them.*

Kennit had been slowly exerting his influence over Will. He constantly wove his power into Will's and influenced the decisions he was making. For some reason, Nadine was able to resist his effort and it frustrated him. It was decided to divide Will from Nadine. It was slow and careful work. If he pushed too hard, Will would notice. Lana had found the knowledge to new and unknown draoi powers in the Device in the Chamber in Munsten. Their new knowledge would allow them to gain control of the realm and support Eylene in her goals. Meanwhile, Lana was doing the same thing to Brent and others in the Councils. Slowly they were separating Will from the draoi bond and Brent from making the right decisions. The two of them had the potential to thwart the plans which had begun so long ago in Shape by Eylene.

He reached out across the draoi bond to Lana. He found her immediately, and she paused what she was doing to give him her full attention.

What's up, Kennit?

I made a mistake.

Mistake? What do you mean?

I exposed my power to Will and Nadine.

Lana said nothing. Kennit could feel her surprise and anger. After a moment, she responded. *What happened?*

I approached them to speak to them. I hoped they would see reason.

Reason? They have made their position clear. We spoke of this. You, me and Eylene. We know the better way. The old way of the draoi is over. We have a vision. A purpose.

Yes, yes. I know. I'm sorry.

What do they know?

Only that I can hide the draoi bond. Hide our presence.

Oh, Kennit. That is not good.

Kennit threw back his head and stared at the dust motes glinting in sunbeams high above him. *No matter. I will continue to work on Will. He has no idea. Neither does Nadine. My touch is so gentle. He suspects nothing. She is much harder and I've had little luck. The Device is giving us knowledge they will never possess. They have no idea.*

Kennit felt Lana's approval. *Good. Let me know if anything changes.*

I will. Give my regards to Eylene. I can't wait to meet her.

Kennit severed the link and lowered his head. Gently and carefully he found the bond to Will and eased his power along the thread. Kennit smiled and started his daily routine.

Katherine stood forward on the bowsprit and relished the cool sea spray as it washed over her. The *Oriole* was making terrific speed with a brisk following wind. The captain said they were doing fifteen knots. He measured the speed by having a sailor throw a rope with a series of equally spaced knots tied in it over the side and into the wake of the ship. The number of knots on the rope pulled into the sea over a set amount of time measured their speed. But it was no concern to Katherine what a knot was; she merely enjoyed the excitement of speed and the motion of the ship. It was so far removed from the farm life she had grown up with.

The *Oriole* skimmed effortlessly up over the swell top and then plunged down the other side. As the bow smacked the water at the bottom, a great deluge of water was forced up on either side. Some water sprayed over her and she grinned and spat out the cold, salty water. It was thrilling. She loved the sensation and the freedom it offered.

I can almost forget Cala at times like this, she thought, and her heart pounded with excitement as the ship rose up and started to climb the next high swell.

Please come away from the water, thought Dog from where he was in the cabin.

Katherine frowned. Dog had an irritating way of intruding at the worst times. *Shush, you.*

The water is not good for you. And it is salty. Makes you throw up.

Just because you don't like water doesn't make it bad for you. And you don't drink sea water, that's silly.

Silly human.

Katherine laughed out loud. Dog had discovered humour it seemed. He was often making cracks now. She loved it even though he was rarely funny.

Excuse me, Katherine? Heather asked across the bond. Her touch was tentative and a little unsure.

Katherine sighed. *Yes?*

Sorry tae intrude. Th' captain said tae tell ye that Munsten is ainlie aboot ten hours awa'. Th' foremaist island shuid be appearing soon. We shuid mak' Munsten harbour aroond midnight.

So you should stop what you are doing and get ready, added Dog.

You just want me to stop. I have nothing to get ready.

I could use a belly rub. Maybe James would like one, too?

Katherine felt the shock from Heather across the bond and laughed as the ship plunged down once again.

Dog, perhaps Heather could take care of both of you?

Katherine laughed as Cala curses erupted from Heather and then screamed into the wind with joy and abandon as more spray washed over her.

* * *

They reached Munsten after midnight, just as the captain had predicted. Katherine, James and Heather shook hands and thanked him and then crossed the gangplank with Dog to the shore. They walked a short distance away from the docks and stopped at a street corner, lit with a dim street lamp. They had yet to agree to what they should do next.

Dog immediately went to a lamp post and peed for a very long time. *That's so much better than trying to pee in that stupid bucket in the cabin. That was hard. Especially pooping. Why'd I have to do that?*

Heather and Katherine covered their mouths in laughter.

James looked around, and not being able to hear Dog, leaned in and whispered. "So now what?"

Heather chewed her lip. "Ah wid fancy a crakin' room in an inn. I'm tired o' sleeping in hammocks. Mah back's bent."

Dog sniffed around the area of the lamp post. Katherine watched him before looking up. "I say we head straight to the museum. The sooner this is over the better. I would like nothing better than to inform the others we found what we were looking for and be done with it."

Heather's gaze faded a moment, a sign of her using the draoi bond. "Huh, everyone's asleep. Lana, too. Right, so what's it to be then? Inn or museum?"

"The museum," answered James. "I'm with Katherine on this. Let's get it over with."

Katherine crouched down and Dog came over for a scratch. She looked up at James. "Dog agrees with you."

"Ach, weel. Thare ye hae it. Museum it is. Let's gang, ma wee bairns. James, leid oan, ye ken th' wey."

They followed James down many streets, all the while climbing higher and higher and closer to the castle. The *Museum of the Revolution* was an old mansion, owned by some noble who had been killed during the Revolution. When the new regime had seized the house they had forced the owners out into the streets. During the Revolution the building had lived on as the higher headquarters and coordinated all the actions of the Revolutionary active supporters. After the Revolution, they found the house filled with the maps and belongings of the more famous heroes of the Revolution and decided it was far easier to turn the place into a museum than to cart the belongings elsewhere.

At some point the curators had started going out and gathering items of interest; such as the items tied to the Great Debate. At some point, Benjamin Erwin's belongings had found their way into the building and stored to be added to the collection. According to Brent, everything the man had owned was down in the storage rooms.

They made their way up a steep set of stairs that opened onto a wide-open cobblestone street. The street lamps were brighter here and long shadows crisscrossed the road. A chill breeze blew steady here and Heather shivered and pulled her shawl tighter. Katherine tutted and drew power and warmed Heather.

"I'm so daft," murmured Heather in thanks. "I keep forgetting I've powers."

James looked up and down the street. "The museum is up past a guard station. We are almost there. Three blocks."

"Good, let's go."

They walked up the side of the street and turned a corner. Up ahead was a small square with a guard station on the far exit. Two guards were standing at the station looking around. They seemed alert, but relaxed, to James' eye. It was already well into summer, but the air was unseasonably cool due to the chill, northern wind off the ocean and so the men were wearing thick surcoats. They stirred on seeing James and the others and they said a few words to one another and watched them approach.

James stepped forward. "Good morning, I am Major James Dixon. How are you this evening?"

The guard on the right, a corporal by his rank insignia, was the one who spoke. "Morning, sir. How was your voyage?"

James froze for a heartbeat and then looked back quickly at Heather and Katherine before focusing in on the guard who spoke. "Do I know you, corporal?"

"No, sir," came the gruff reply. The guards looked at one another.

"Then how do you know about my recent voyage?"

The corporal looked blankly back at James and then looked sideways at his companion. James spotted a bead of sweat tracking down his temple. James looked around quickly, but all seemed quiet.

James frowned and then scowled. Then he noticed the guard look past him toward something above and behind him. *He looked up to the rooftops,* thought James. *That means...*

James turned to the others to give warning when the air filled with weighted bolts. James knew what they were at once and knew he was too late. The Guard sometimes used special heavy-weight crossbows to fire bolts tipped with lead-filled balls of cloth. They used the bolts to subdue people without killing them, but with enough force to incapacitate. The idea in their use was to target the head and knock people out. They were rarely used and only when the people were worth questioning. Provided they survived the blow. Often the bolts killed the person. James caught the look of confusion on Heather's face. He opened his mouth to cry out when he was struck in the head. He felt the ground reach up and pull him down into blackness.

* * *

The two guards rushed forward with saps after the crossbow volley and made sure the three people and the dog were indeed unconscious. The corporal rose and brought two fingers to his mouth and gave a shrill whistle. Shadows emerged from nearby dark alleys and walked into the streetlight. The first was Eylene Kissane dressed in the robes of the Church of the New Order. Slightly behind her was a female draoi, wearing the plain lightly weaved brown cloth they often wore. The others behind them were clearly military, but with their armour covered by a tabard bearing the symbol of the church. In moments, other church guards, carrying thick crossbows and quivers filled with more of the same bolts, descended from the rooftops and joined the others.

Eylene nodded to the two city guards and handed them each a small bag of coin. They bowed their heads and disappeared quickly up the street and out of sight. Eylene turned to the draoi standing beside her. "Good work, Lana. It appears you have control over what powers other draoi can wield, or sense. You hid my people well."

Lana Turner smiled a lop-sided smile. "My pleasure. Kennit has been a good teacher. We should hurry and place the collars on them. There's no guarantee they will work."

Eylene tutted. "Now, now. The device in the Chamber and the notes from Kevin Balfour were quite clear on how this would work. With the collars in place, I have full confidence they will not be able to reach their powers. We did test it on you, did we not?"

Lana grimaced. "Yes, you did. It was horrible. I will say it again; Katherine and Dog are unique draoi. Their powers are formidable. I cannot say for certain whether they can be contained. There is great risk here."

"Noted, dear Lana. Which is why the herb mixture you have provided will be mixed with all they eat. Both the collar and the herbs should do the trick."

"Pray that they do. The devastation Katherine and Dog levelled on Cala was frightening. Munsten would not survive. We really should examine Edward's journal. He knows more than anyone which herbs work best. Other than Will."

"I'll see if I can get my hands on Edward's journal. Remember, it is not Munsten I am worried about. It is the souls of the people of Belkin. The draoi must be dealt with. I can't have them running around loose in the country and doing who knows what."

Lana shot a glare at Eylene. "*Those* draoi, you mean."

Eylene moved closer to Lana and cupped her face in her hands and bent in to give her a soft kiss. "Of course, my love. *Those* draoi. Not Kennit's group."

"Good."

Eylene turned to the Church guards and barked an order. "Collars."

Eylene watched as the senior member of the gathered church guard pulled out three intricately made metal collars from a leather bag. The collars were featureless and shone with a dull sheen. He pulled at one collar and it parted effortlessly and swung open on a hidden hinge. He moved to Katherine first and lifted her head and worked the collar opening around her neck and then closed the collar. A soft click was heard, and the guard moved aside.

Eylene crouched beside Katherine and looked at Lana. "I just touch the collar?"

"Yes, you press a finger anywhere against the metal and hold it a moment. You will hear a chime and that will be it. Only you will be able to remove the collar after that."

"How does this work?"

"It is part of the power of the draoi. Will Arbor calls them the motes. We control them. The collars contain a small portion of the same motes. It doesn't need to be a collar, it could be anything really, but this way it cannot be removed. When you press your finger to the collar, it acknowledges you and the collar will be attuned only to you. No one can remove them, but you."

"Can they not be cut off with force?"

Lana smiled. "Yes. But the results would be devastating. You've heard of the black powder?"

Eylene nodded.

"The collars are filled with it. Tampering with them would be disastrous."

Eylene chuckled. "Good, good." Eylene pressed her right index finger against the metal of the collar. She felt a tingle on her finger and then a soft chime was heard. Eylene made a soft, pleased sound and looked up to Lana.

"That's it. It's locked and tuned to you."

Eylene smiled and looked at the Church guard. "Put the collars on the other woman and the dog. Tie up the man and then gag and bind them all. Make sure no one sees you bringing them into the dungeon."

Eylene and Lana watched as Heather and Dog were collared. James and Katherine were gagged and bound at their hands and feet with metal shackles. Eylene moved forward and touched each collar and the chime sounded from each one. A moment later, a horse and covered cart was wheeled into the square and the four prisoners were dumped into the back. The cart pulled away and the senior of the Church Guard bowed to Eylene before ordering his guard to follow on foot behind the wagon. In moments, the street was clear and quiet.

Lana lightly touched Eylene's shoulder. "I still say you should kill them, right now. They are a threat. Kennit worries about them."

Eylene shook her head. "Normally I would agree, but they were on a mission to discover the remains of King Hietower. I would know more of that first. Edward Hitchens can never be allowed to be King. He is a non-believer, and that is insufferable. My church will not be led by his ilk. Once I am Archbishop, I will deal with him. For now I thank God he cannot be confirmed as the rightful heir. I need to find the remains of the King and destroy them. I will replace the bones with the remains of gutter trash and remove him from any future thoughts of being crowned.

"No, we keep them alive. Besides, they may prove useful. Bairstow dotes on Dixon, and Will and Nadine have some kind of special relationship with Katherine. I would use that which will advance our goals no matter the cost. They are better left alive. So long as the collars keep their powers at bay they pose no threat."

Lana tucked an arm around Eylene's waist and then reached up and stroked the tip of her nose. "Yes, dear. You always were the smart one."

Eylene grinned and the street light gave her a feral look, with shadowed eyes and a contrasting bright smile. Eylene felt Lana shiver up against her and pulled her tighter against her. "Let's get out of the chill night air. You deserve a special treat after tonight."

Lana grinned. "Oh, goody."

Four

Munsten, July 902 A.C.

THE CHURCH GUARD escorted Brent Bairstow into the inner sanctum at the back of the Church of the New Order within Munsten Castle. He passed the icons of the Church and found peace. His faith had never been stronger. The past months had opened his eyes to the truth of the Church and God. The time in the dungeon when he had been held prisoner had strained his belief almost to the point of breaking. He had lain there a broken man certain his death was upon him. He had struggled with his faith. Martin didn't know to what extent.

Brent had cursed God many times. In the ways only a seasoned army officer could. But he had prayed constantly as well. He had pleaded for help; certain his prayers would be answered. Brent had wielded the power of God on the battlefield. He remembered Jergen and how God had allowed his power to free both him and Steve Comlin. As he lay there, broken in the cell, he had lost hope for a time. It deeply shamed him to admit it. Even now, Martin continued to look at him as some kind of saviour, or warrior of God. Every time he did so, Brent cringed a little inside. His shame was killing him. It made him doubt every decision he made as Regent. He wasn't worthy. And he knew it.

Brent had been coming to see Eylene every day for the past month. He had needed an outlet. Someone with whom he could confide his doubts. She listened to him and didn't judge him. Eylene had even forgiven him and he had cried in her arms like a child. She knew his most secret inner doubts. How he hated his brother for throwing his life away trying to save him. And how he blamed himself for his death.

We never found his body. We buried him in the mausoleum in an empty tomb. He deserved better.

Eylene had insisted on the ceremony. By doing so they had cleared Frederick's name and declared him a hero of the Realm. It had helped Brent accept his death a little more. *But damn, I miss the bastard.*

Eylene had been the one to suggest they meet regularly. She even went so far as to say that what Edward was saying about the health of the mind made sense to her. She said the Church was the best suited to helping people heal. Brent admitted pouring his concerns out to her was helping him. He felt his faith growing stronger. Eylene was quickly becoming a close friend and already a complete confidant. He looked forward to their sessions.

It didn't hurt she was so beautiful. He could gaze at her perfection all day. She had a way of making you feel wanted. Appreciated. The touch of her finger sent a thrill through him. She touched him often, and he was so very conscious of it.

Brent stopped before the double doors and waited for the Church Guard to announce him. He stepped inside and the doors were closed behind him. Eylene sat behind the ornate Archbishop's desk. He looked around and could see she had made herself more at home. He noticed a small bed had been placed in the corner and was puzzled.

Eylene rose from the desk beaming a smile at Brent that caused all his thoughts to flee. She held out her hands and Brent grasped them warmly and squeezed. "Regent, so good to see you this morning! You are looking well. Did you sleep better last night?"

Brent nodded and smiled. He couldn't help but smile at her bright eyes and perfect teeth. She shone. Her dark skin was so smooth, and unblemished. She looked radiant. She exuded femininity. *And sexuality*, he admitted to himself. *Something about her stirs a feeling of desire in me. She always does.* "Vicar Eylene, yes, I slept through the night. It was wonderful. I felt like a child asking for warm milk and honey, but it worked just as you suggested."

She laughed brightly and withdrew her hands, letting them linger just a moment longer than seemed appropriate. She waved a hand over to the couch area near her desk and Brent made his way over to the familiar area.

The Archbishop's office was a massive room compared to others in the castle. It was panelled from floor to halfway up the twelve-foot walls with rich oiled woods from all over Belkin. Above the wood, the walls were covered with priceless works of art. Carvings and Icons of the Church covered almost every inch of the walls and they were ancient and likely originals. Gold and silver gleamed everywhere Brent looked. A smell of something unfamiliar to Brent filled the air, but it was sweet and soothing, and he liked it. The office was more of a living space that shouted out for God to take notice.

The wealth in the room could feed half the starving people in Belkin for a year or more. This thought triggered a memory in Brent's mind. He had meant to ask Eylene how the distribution of the gold recovered from the Sect was faring. Martin had been so pleased to hand it over to the Church. Brent had heard nothing about it since. *I'll ask later.*

The couch area was something Eylene had added once she moved in. She had told Brent that talking across a desk was counter to her beliefs and not something people from Shape did. When dealing with people, she wanted them close and comfortable. She felt the need to better relate to people and the couch, for her, opened doors.

Brent settled on one end of the couch and watched as Eylene crossed over and lowered herself down at the other end. *She drifts across the room with such elegance, I wonder how she does that. The people from Shape have a way about them. And they keep to themselves for the most part. It's rare to see someone from Shape elsewhere in the Realm.* Brent had a stray thought. *I don't think there's a single person from Shape in the military. Strange that…*

Eylene interrupted Brent's thoughts by reaching out and touching his knee. "You're staring at me again, Brent."

He started and realised he had been staring. "I'm so sorry, Eylene, I'm lost in thought again. Did you say something?"

Eylene laughed a bright clear laugh. "No, dear. Not this time. Now tell me, what do you want to talk about, today?"

Brent felt his cheeks burning. He felt a familiar shame and guilt rise within him. It was always so hard to start talking. He looked away.

"Brent, we've been over this before. You are safe here. Tell me what worries you."

Brent took a moment to gather his thoughts. "I'm feeling stronger in my faith, Eylene. I no longer doubt myself. As much. You've helped me with that. God moves in mysterious ways, they say. I just thought… well, I thought perhaps there would be more. That God would speak to me again since that day in the dungeons. I know He is there, but He refuses to talk to me. I feel that I am failing Him. Like I am failing the people of Belkin and he doesn't approve."

Brent caught a glimmer of an expression cross Eylene's face. He would have called it anger, but he was sure he imagined it. She smiled at him and he relaxed.

"God does not work in that way. That he spoke to you at all is a miracle. He had a need for you to listen and He did wondrous things with you. You should bask in that attention. Those of us that work for the Church for our whole lives will never have that opportunity."

"Martin has been fortunate."

Brent was certain he saw annoyance cross Eylene's features, and he raised an eyebrow.

"Yes, our Vicar Martin. He has spoken often of his experiences. To anyone who would listen. Repeatedly."

"Martin is a man of great faith."

"Yes, he is. We are well aware of Martin's faith."

Brent waited for Eylene to say more but she remained silent. "He's a good friend. We've been through a lot together."

"Yes, you have."

Brent shifted in his seat. He had often watched Eylene change the subject when it came to discussing Martin. He didn't know why. Today he would ask for more. He had to understand her clear misgivings, but for now he would focus on the Realm. "I've received reports that the Church Guard is helping in the villages and cities. Thank you for your assistance. You are accomplishing what my people could not."

"That is the power of the Church, as you know, Brent. We reach the people through God and not through force. We stroke rather than strike. Reason is not a far-fetched idea! I've seen the reports and more. My own people report directly to me. What they see and hear. But I'm afraid not all is as well as they report."

"How so? I'm not hearing anything dire. Just the opposite in fact."

"Ah yes, well perhaps that is the price of being the Regent and head of the government. People may not be as forthcoming with news that is not good."

Brent scowled. "I have always been an approachable person. In the military the men and women often spoke frankly to me."

"You are no longer that military man, Brent. It is the weight of authority. It doesn't matter. You have the Church and you have me. I will always share our news. I would have brought this to you earlier, but I knew you had not been resting."

Brent felt unbalanced. Part of him felt that something was not quite right. He was surrounded by people he barely knew who all owed him their allegiance by his position. *But I feel like they are working behind my back. Doing things I would not approve of. Curse this position. Edward needs to take the throne as soon as possible*. Brent sighed. "Tell me."

Eylene rose and went to her desk. She opened a drawer and pulled out a thick file. She laid it on the low table in front of Brent and went over to the sideboard. Brent opened the file and began to read the contents. He heard the clink of crystal as Eylene poured them drinks.

What he read was no real surprise. Reading this report and mentally recalling the details of similar reports he could see where certain facts were being left out of what he was seeing. They were minor deviances, but altogether it spoke of great unrest still in the land. The people had no respect for him as Regent. His edicts were almost immediately being rejected. The army was being accused of using violence to subdue innocent protestors. It was a mess. The Church Guard was having much greater success it seemed. People trusted them when they refused to support an army that until just recently had worked for Healy. While the army trusted Brent and knew him, the people did not.

Brent finished the file and laid it down on the table and picked up the glass of Cala whiskey Eylene had poured for him. He took a large swallow and leaned back into the couch and eyed the report.

"What do you think?" asked Eylene. She took a small sip from her own glass.

"I think I need to make better use of your Church Guard. They seem to be doing more than the army can. I shouldn't be surprised. Healy made a right mess of it. He used the army to subdue the people. It's no wonder no one trusts them now."

Eylene laid back in the couch and smiled. "I was hoping you would say that. I have some ideas. The Church can do so much, Brent. You've seen the interest God has had in making sure you achieved what needed to be done. Work with me, Brent. We have the same desires here."

Brent took another swallow and then nodded once. "I don't see that I have much choice. I can trust no one else. What do you need?"

Eylene took a moment to herself and Brent glanced at her when she took a long time to respond. "Forgive me, Brent. This is difficult for me. It is hard to stay humble and say what I have to say."

"Please, you've listened to me go on and on about my problems. Say what you will. Go ahead."

Eylene looked relieved and took a swallow of whiskey before speaking. "Alright. There are many in the Church who would see me rise to the position of Archbishop. You know this."

Brent grunted.

"I know! I know! From Vicar to Archbishop. It's unheard of. But Healy decimated our ranks. The Church looks to promote those who can best serve the needs of the people. I argued against this, but as you can see..." Eylene waved around the office. "I've already taken up residence in the Archbishop chambers. I do the role in everything short of being formally recognised."

Brent patted the air. "You misunderstand. I just wondered what took so long. I had expected something some time ago and assumed the Church was happy with just continuing as it has. It pleases me that the Church wishes to make you Archbishop."

Eylene made a small sound which Brent assumed was one of delight. "That makes me happy! I was so worried you would disagree. The newly promoted cardinals and bishops would like to hold the ceremony next month."

"Ceremony? Next month?"

"Yes, silly. You don't just say 'you're the Archbishop, good luck'. There is a certain amount of pomp and ceremony that must be followed. Traditions. Just leave it with me."

Brent hesitated and then smiled and nodded once.

* * *

Shortly after Brent left Eylene's office, the door opened, and Lana slipped in and closed it behind her. She no longer wore her draoi clothes. Instead, she wore an expensive blue dress that hugged her features and flowed down to brush across the floor. It gave her movements the illusion of gliding. Eylene smiled up at her and Lana came around the desk and gave her a light kiss on the lips. Lana pulled her face back a little to look into Eylene's eyes and smiled.

Eylene reached up to Lana's waist and pulled her onto her lap. Lana giggled and squirmed a little and they kissed once again, this time a little longer. A little breathless, Lana released the kiss and laid her head on Eylene's shoulder and reached up and played with Eylene's hair around her ear. She felt Eylene shudder ever so slightly and smiled.

"How is he?" asked Eylene.

"He suspects nothing. I guide his thoughts and shift his emotions ever so slightly. He is becoming more and more unstable. When he is with you, I push his thoughts and desires as you instructed. He trusts you but doesn't know why. More importantly, he is losing his trust in others."

Eylene kept her head still so as not to disturb the attention Lana was giving her. Goosebumps rose on her arms and neck, and for a time she basked in the attention and said nothing. Finally, she stirred, and Lana paused what she was doing. "I've just had a thought. How do I know you aren't manipulating me?"

Lana laughed a small laugh. "You don't, love. You'll just have to trust me."

Eylene turned her head slightly so she could look into Lana's eyes. She gazed at her for a long moment and then nodded. "I do. You know I do."

"And I trust you. You loved me long before I found my draoi powers. Whenever you doubt that, remember our times in Shape."

"How could I ever forget? You, me and Andrew made quite the team, did we not?"

"Yes, we did. Don't forget Kennit!"

"Yes, Kennit. I worry about him. He's too brash. Keep him in check, Lana dearest."

"I do. This is why I cautioned you against moving too quickly. But here we are and everything is happening as you predicted."

Eylene gently kissed Lana for a moment and then murmured against her lips. "Yes, it won't be long now."

* * *

Later that evening Brent heard a knock at his Outer Chamber door. He looked up from the paper he was reading and called out for the Captain of the Guard to enter. The door opened and footsteps padded across the carpet outside his study. He heard the knock at his Inner Chamber door and called out for him to enter.

The door opened and the familiar face of Major Hugh Tibert looked in.

Brent smiled and stood. "Major Tibert! What a pleasant surprise! Where's Mary?"

Staff Sergeant Mary Eastman entered the room behind Hugh and beamed a smile at Brent. To anyone else the smile would likely strike fear, but Brent recognised it for what it was: pleasant. Hugh and Mary each snapped a salute and strode forward. Brent clasped their shoulders and settled them down at the small side table.

"I'm so glad to see you two. What have you been up to?"

Hugh and Mary looked at one another for a moment. Hugh answered. "Kingsmill had us up at Cala. We were stopping by the villages and such. Checking things out."

Brent sat back and appraised the two of them. They looked tired and grim. "Uh-huh. And?"

"Kingsmill told us to come here and see you. We came up the back way. We waited three nights for the right Captain of the Guard to be on duty."

"And you did this why?"

"Because there's so few people left to trust, sir. Kingsmill wanted us to speak to you unnoticed like. So here we are."

"So report."

"Sir, yes, sir. It's a right mess out there. The same all over. There's unrest. The people are hearing all sorts of horrors. They don't know what to believe, but they believe this: you are just another tyrant ruling over them. The word on the street about you is not good. Somehow the message coming out of this here castle is being twisted. Church attendance is way up. Thought you should know. It's the Church Guard you see. They are everywhere. I've had a close look, Mary and I. All those trouble makers who sided with Healy. Most of them ended up with the Church Guard. It's bad.

"Cala was the worst. Those northerners have always been a bit off the mark, but now, by the Word, they're walking the street preaching Church stuff. Katherine and Dog put a right fear in 'em and the Church has moved right in. Never seen it so strong. Frightening." Hugh turned to Mary. "Anything else?"

Mary shook her head.

Brent sat and went over what Hugh had reported in his head. It aligned with what Eylene and the two Roberts were telling him. He filled in Hugh and Mary with what he had read.

Hugh grimaced. "Something's not adding up. I told you the bad lot are all in the Church Guard. Why do you think that is?"

Brent shook his head. "I've no idea. From all reports they are quelling the unrest. They're doing good work. God's work."

Mary raised her eyebrows at that. "If you say so."

"I do. I speak to Eylene daily about it. You confirmed what she's been telling me. I've no choice but to let it continue. Otherwise we lose everything."

Mary and Hugh looked at each other and shared a thought Brent couldn't translate. He shook his head and then thought to offer refreshment. "Have you eaten?"

Hugh and Mary grinned and looked at one another again. "She owes us a half crown." Hugh turned to the open door and called out. "Come in, lieutenant."

Brent sat up in surprise as he watched Lieutenant Emily Barkhouse appear in the doorway, wearing her pristine Navy uniform, but with an added ornate gold braid on her left shoulder. She was carrying what looked like food and drink. She looked a little frightened. Emily stopped and lifted her chin and cast the defiant look Brent knew so well on her face. Hugh shook his head, and she glanced askance at him, and then lowered her chin and calmed her features.

"Evening, sir," she said. "Major Tibert insisted I bring some victuals. I can place it on the table and depart."

Brent watched Hugh and Mary. He could see the little upturn of a smile at the corners of their mouths. He sighed. "Out with it. Explain."

Mary spoke this time. "We, me and Hugh that is, had a little chat with young Emily here. She was at a loss to understand her dismissal from you. She looked for clarification. We gave it to her."

Brent stared hard at Emily. "Is this true?"

Emily nodded tightly and Brent was surprised to see a wetness at her eyes. Mary scowled, but Hugh placed a hand on her arm to quieten her. "Sir, yes, sir. I understand where I was lacking in officer like qualities. I was judging something I had little understanding of."

Brent sat quietly and then spoke softly. "And do you now, Emily?"

She broke her stare and looked sharply at Brent when he used her first name. She hitched her breath and nodded again.

To Brent she seemed different. Less… straight up and down. He glanced at Hugh and Mary and raised an eyebrow.

"We wouldn't have brought her if she hadn't changed her ways," said Mary. "She understands now, we think." She glanced at Hugh. He nodded. "Maybe,' she finished.

"What's changed? She hated the sight of people in uniform showing any kind of affection for one another."

It was Mary who answered again. "She's learned it doesn't apply to her either."

"I don't understand."

Mary laughed. "That's another half crown. I'm rich tonight, my bucko!" Mary slapped Hugh's thigh hard, and he winced. "She's with you, Regent. Assigned by Kingsmill. Again. He said keep her this time. He said he won't have her sullen moods bringing him down anymore. She's your new executive assistant."

Brent looked Emily up and down. She seemed a little different. Something was bothering her that much was plain to see. Her hands trembled a little with the tray she carried. "Set down the tray before you drop it, Emily. Grab a chair. There's a spare one in what I guess will be your room."

Emily almost dropped the tray on the table. "My room?"

"Yes, if you are to be my EA, you will take the spare room next to mine. Move your things in. Tell the Captain of the Guard you are to have access to me at all times, day and night."

Emily gasped and stood upright and looked about in a panic.

Mary looked at Hugh. "Idiots."

Cill Darae

Five

Munsten and Rigby Farm, July 902 A.C.

MARTIN JORDAN PACED back and forth in front of the desk in Brent Bairstow's private office. "She is bending the rules of the Church! She cannot be allowed to take the position of Archbishop until the King is crowned. You must listen, Brent! You must stop this at once."

"Martin, you know I cannot. I cannot interfere with the workings of the church. Besides, it is only through the Church that I have been effective at ruling this land. You've read the reports. Belkin is in turmoil. It was the representatives of the Church that quieted the villages and cities once John Healy was put down."

"They are armed mercenaries. The Church does not wield weapons and wear armour. These are military men wearing the guise of the Church. You've given them too much power."

"They have replaced the soldiers. The same soldiers the people don't trust. I admit I am worried. I am losing control. Eylene gives me the best hope for a peaceful future."

"Nonsense. Eylene is only concerned for herself. She craves power. She always has. You know she has excluded me from the proceedings? Of all the vicars in Belkin I am the only one denied access. It feels as if I have been excommunicated in all but official status."

"You were very disruptive, Martin. I've heard the tales."

"Disruptive? I was telling them how foolish they were! I recited our canon and laws! They cherry pick that which serves them and ignore that which contradicts them. They have lost their way. They refuse to listen to a voice of reason and the correct interpretation of the intent of our laws. They refuse to listen, the cowards! They are under the sway of that woman and do all she desires! The Church is lost. Lost, Brent! We will never recover, never."

Brent watched Martin continue to pace. He had lost a startling amount of weight. His face looked gaunt, and he appeared to have aged years. Martin was becoming more and more agitated. He spent all his time inside the castle trying to speak to any vicar he could find. Brent had word that the vicars fled on word of Martin's approach. His friend was unstable, and Brent was deeply saddened.

Brent never felt so alone. He had lost the companionship of the Regent's Guard, his friend James was off on a quest, and now Martin was spending all his time beating his fists on the entire Church of the New Order and making a menace of himself. At least Emily was here now. She was off getting more uniforms fitted for herself. Being his EA meant a lot of different uniforms. She had rolled her eyes at him when he had asked why and fled.

When she was around, she doted on him. Never left his presence. She was always looking slant eyed at him in a way he found disconcerting. When he caught her watching him, she would blush and run off on some minor errand. He couldn't figure her out, but she was efficient, that was for sure. And he welcomed having someone in uniform around him. He also appreciated her honest criticism. He bounced ideas off her and she normally scoffed at him and told him when it was a foolish idea. He wished the two Roberts were so honest with him.

Martin was another matter. He had to control himself. Eylene had spoken at length with him about just how disruptive he was becoming. She accused him of dragging the church back into the past. She was trying to make changes that would resonate with the times, but Martin would hear nothing of it. Brent could hear the sense of it. Archbishop Greigsen had done almost irreparable damage to the Church. Eylene was mending the damage and Brent admired her strength and conviction and her depth of faith.

Martin stopped in front of the desk and whirled toward Brent. "Send the vicars back out into the Realm. Get them away from Eylene's poisonous words. Tell them what they need to do! You have wielded the power of God! They will listen to you. Use the voice of reason. Give the people hope!

"We must do something now! Without our voice, the people will have to face armed soldiers, which will cause both panic and fear. This is a land which rose from a violent revolution. The memories of those days are still vibrant. Still real.

People have not forgotten our recent past and remember soldiers patrolling the streets and homes. They are reminded daily of those troubling days."

Brent sighed. *What Martin says makes sense, but my problems are not that simple to solve. Why can he not see that?* Brent spread his hands outward. "I cannot, Martin. It is not my Church to govern. Which is exactly why it is important for the Archbishop to be named. The new deacons and bishops are leading the future and assuring our path is laid with secular law and order. I will not—cannot—interfere with the Church."

Martin looked stricken and moved up close to the front of the desk. "Brent, my friend. Please. Listen to me. The deacons and bishops Eylene is promoting? They are all her cronies! They owe allegiance to her and not the Church! She is building an empire within the Church! Can you not see that? She has created the Church Guard! Something the Church should never have! And yet they now exist, and they patrol the streets and assume powers only the military should have. You allowed this!

"You must realise these new deacons and bishops will flood the land and usurp any power Edward hopes to wield when he takes the crown. We have laws and canon to avoid this very thing! You must stop it! The Realm is in trouble. As Regent it is your duty to hold the Realm until the King is crowned. Already Belkin slips out of control of a monarchy and into something else. Something the Church has power over. This will not go well. Please, listen!"

Brent looked at his friend and saw in his eyes the hint of madness he feared he would one day see. Martin needed help. Eylene had warned him. She had tried to help Martin with the new chirurgeons Edward was trying to introduce to Belkin—chirurgeons of the mind, or some such thing—but he had refused. She said she feared for Martin and now Brent could see what she had been loath to reveal. Brent felt the loss of yet another friend in his life. He hung his head for a moment and then reached out and rang a small bell that sat on his desk.

He looked up and saw horror on his friend's face.

"You would dismiss me? After all we've been through? You trust her over my words? Can you not hear my reason? Are you so lost, Brent?"

The door to Brent's private office opened, and a guard stepped in and looked expectantly at Brent.

"Corporal, please see to Vicar Martin's comfort."

Martin looked at the guard for a moment and then scowled at Brent. "I can see my own way out. I am leaving Munsten. I feel a calling to be elsewhere. I have warned you, Brent Bairstow, and you chose to side with vipers."

Martin didn't wait for a reply. He pushed past the guard and exited the private chambers. Brent heard the outer door slam and winced.

The guard waited, unsure about what to do.

"See that he leaves quietly. Don't interfere unless he tries to do something stupid."

The guard nodded and saluted Brent and left, closing the door behind him.

Brent rose and moved over to look out the window. He remained there for some time until a knock sounded at the door.

"Enter," he called out.

He turned to see Robert Ghent open the door and look in.

"Come in Robert, have a seat."

"I shan't be long, sir. I wanted to discuss the Windthrop Estate."

"Yes, what of it?"

Robert looked a little annoyed and strode over to Brent's desk and started going through the files stacked high on one corner. After a moment he pulled one free and shook it once. "This report, sir. I provided it two weeks ago and told you it was of some urgency. It discusses the Windthrop Estate. The Judicial Council debated the estate, and we provided a recommendation. We are hoping you will agree, and we can finalise the details."

Brent frowned, but could not remember any conversation about the estate. "Remind me, again?"

Robert made a strange noise, pinched his nose, and closed his eyes for a moment. "Yes, sir. As you know, the demise of Andrew Windthrop left a vacancy in Turgany County. Now that matters have settled, and with you as the Regent, it is important to name a successor to the barony."

Brent scratched at the stubble on his neck and stepped back behind his desk. He took the file from Robert and opened it and read it for a moment. "Castellan Colonel William Crenshaw is there now. Appointed by Edward. What needs settling?"

Robert coughed into a hand. "Sir, Edward has not been crowned. He has no authority to elevate Crenshaw to the position of castellan or even to promote him to colonel, for that matter. Only the Regent has that authority. And that is you. And, as the file indicates, there are several families who have stepped forward claiming legitimacy to the barony. Third cousins and whatnot from the Windthrop line."

Brent grunted and dropped the file to the desk. Robert tracked it with a sour look on his face. "Windthrop left no heirs. They have no claim."

Robert looked bewildered for a moment. "Sir, as the file states, the law of Belkin is quite clear on the transference of title. The revolution did nothing to change the Royal Laws that go back centuries. In this case, the claims to the Windthrop line are legitimate. Elevating Colonel Crenshaw was nothing more than a temporary accommodation at best. As Regent, you have a responsibility to follow the laws of the land and appoint someone from the Windthrop lineage."

"He was a traitor to the Realm."

"Some would say you are too, sir."

Brent shot Robert a look, but the man looked calmly back at him. "I return the land to the rightful rule of a King. There is nothing traitorous about that."

"As you say, sir."

Brent stared at Robert, but the man remained unabashed and calmly stared back at him. "Prepare a list of supplicants. I'll review them."

Robert made a grunt sound and turned to the pile of files. He flipped through them and pulled free six thick files. He dropped them onto the middle of the desk with a thump. "There you go, sir. Will there be anything else?"

Brent glared at Robert and then shook his head.

"Good afternoon, Regent." Robert quietly left the office and closed the door behind him with a soft click.

Martin stepped through the doors to the Munsten Mausoleum and shivered at the sudden change of temperature. It had been some months since he had last been here, but nothing had changed. No one ventured into this little-known part of the history of Munsten. Buried here were the remains of centuries of kings and queens. Princes, princesses and some nobles and heroes of the Realm shared the cold stone chambers. It was here that Katherine, James, Heather and Dog had started their journey to place a crown on the head of Edward Hitchens, bastard son of the late King Hietower.

They had found nothing where Hietower should have lain to rest. The draoi had stolen off into the night with his remains. *How much simpler things would be had we simply found the remains and confirmed Edward as the rightful heir. Instead we have turmoil, Eylene grasping for power, and a military man in charge of the Realm who has no idea how to run a country.*

Martin knew he had failed. He had thought he could persuade Brent to listen to reason. *And if he should be listening to anyone, it should be me. Instead, he listens to the words of the viper, Eylene Kissane from Shape. She soothes his fears and has him believe all is well. But it's not. The Realm is in worse jeopardy than at any other time in our long history.*

We won a battle only to lose the war.

Martin felt an upwelling of grief strike him. *So much to lose and we seem so willing to let it all go. How could it have gone so bad, so quickly?*

He made his way past the large gate and into the depths of the mausoleum. Tombs lay on either side of him. They looked all the same except for the words on the brass plates placed in front of each one. Some tombs carried a small bust or symbol on top, giving tribute to some significant achievement of the monarch. Martin ignored them all and continued to step quietly the length of the wide hallway. His grief and sorrow were overwhelming him.

I put my faith in you, Lord. Why have you led us to this end?

Martin paused his walking when he reached the area where a hallway branched off to his right. Above the hallway were ancient words that read *Tomb of the Honoured*. Martin turned to the right and walked through the opening and into the hallway. After a moment he stopped in front of a tomb. The words on the small brass plate read *Knight General Ran Pawley 890 A.C.*

It was here that the remains of King Hietower had been hidden. Buried under the remains of a general who had been part of John Healy's crimes. All men who had hungered for power and wealth.

Martin felt his strength leave him. His legs collapsed under him and he fell to the floor and lay panting in distress. He felt as if a massive weight had been placed on him, and he couldn't seem to get enough air. Tears welled in his eyes and he squeezed his eyes shut and felt the tears track down his cheeks. He sobbed and held his head in his hands.

I am done, my Lord. Please. I wish it all to be over. I have no strength left. I see the future. I see what is coming and I have no power to stop it.

"Nonsense, get up, Martin."

On the floor, Martin froze, sure he was losing his sanity.

"I said get up. I have no time for theatrics. I am your King, now get up. You look foolish, lying there on the ground in self-wallowing pity."

Martin rolled over with great difficulty to his side. He pried open his eyes and then wiped at them with the back of a hand to clear his vision. Standing above him was a man dressed in kingly attire. He wore no crown, but the royal robes gave away his position. Martin gasped as he recognised the likeness to Edward.

"Yes, yes. I'm King Hietower. Edward is my son. Now, get up. I want to speak to you, and I need you to listen and understand. I'm rather annoyed to be the messenger. It's beneath me. And I hate repeating myself."

Martin lay on his side a moment longer. The grief and sorrow that had driven him to the ground seemed at bay, like a distant memory. He could see the man before him and even smell him. He reached out a shaking hand to touch the foot nearest him, but the man pulled it back.

"You don't touch royalty, you cur. By God, this is tiring. I said *GET UP!*"

The roar from the King carried all the weight of a man used to having his words followed without question. Martin scrambled to his feet and then stepped back away from Hietower. He raised a shaking finger to point it at him. "You're supposed to be dead!"

Hietower looked shocked and held his arms out and looked over his body in horror. He continued this for a moment and then dropped his arms and threw back his head and laughed. It was a full belly laugh, and it echoed throughout the mausoleum.

Martin winced and looked left and right before looking back at Hietower.

Hietower wiped his eyes and smiled at Martin. "Vicar Martin, I am most assuredly dead. But I'm not the first dead person you've met, am I?"

Martin hesitated and then shook his head.

"I have something I need to tell you. You'll know what to do with this information. I don't have long; this is hard to be here. This mausoleum is devoid of life."

"Are you God?"

Hietower smirked and pointed at Martin's chest.

Martin looked down and saw a light trying to escape between the threads of his robe. He reached into the top of the tunic and pulled out his amulet. It shone bright in the dimness of the mausoleum.

"What does that tell you?"

"I-I'm not sure, actually. I believe it to be the power of God."

"Then you have your answer, do you not? Enough. There is something you need to know. I went mad, you know this?"

Martin raised both eyebrows and nodded once.

"Yes, very unpleasant. I was poisoned over time. I was fed pills by the chirurgeons. They drove me mad. That's it. I have nothing more to say."

Martin blinked. "That's what you have to tell me? You were poisoned?"

Hietower looked annoyed. "Yes."

"Can you tell me nothing more? What about the realm? Eylene is grabbing power. The realm is in turmoil! Surely you can help?"

Hietower frowned. "Help? Why would I do that? This realm threw me in a tower to rot. Took my power and God-given right to be King away from me."

"The people need God in their lives! We need your guidance."

Hietower looked even more annoyed. "Solve your own problems. Don't you think that perhaps there are much more important things going on in the world? In the universe? What makes you think this small country on a wide planet in a

Cill Darae

vast universe would warrant any special attention? How incredibly vain."

Martin sputtered.

Hietower turned and started to walk away into the darkness.

Martin watched him for a moment and then a thought occurred to him. "Wait! What did the pills look like? I will need to know more."

Hietower didn't stop or turn. He spoke over his shoulder. "They were round and blue-grey. Tasted of liquorice and rose honey. Nasty things."

The king slowly faded into the darkness and the sound of his steps faded away. Martin's amulet dimmed and then faded.

* * *

Martin knocked loudly on the door to the royal chambers Edward Hitchens used. The rooms were overly large and ornate, and Edward hated them. Located high up in Munsten Castle, they were the royal suites and Brent had insisted Edward use them. Martin shared Edward's view—they were too much. Martin knocked again and waited. He looked up and down the corridor, but none of the Church Guard were about. Seeing the absence of guards gave Martin a sudden strong desire to flee Munsten and head to Jergen. He looked, but his amulet remained dark. The desire to flee itched at him and he imagined a small house beside a cliff in Jergen. It looked so real to him he felt a need to see this place.

Martin shook his head to clear his thoughts. He felt a tightness in his chest and struggled to find air. *The house can wait*, he thought. First, he had to tell Edward about seeing Hietower and what he had told him. The dead king had been right. Martin had known exactly what to do with the information. He knocked again and waited. He massaged his left arm and then lifted his hand to knock again, but before his fist struck, the door was jerked open. On the other side of the door was Edward, looking very sleepy, annoyed and dressed in a simple robe.

"Martin? What are you doing here? Do you know what time it is? It's well after midnight, I'll have you know. You've woken me up and I'd only just fallen asleep. What could be so important it couldn't wait until morning?"

Martin pushed past Edward and into his suite. "Quick, close the door. We have to speak." Martin looked about the apartment and spied the small settee area and sat in the closest chair putting his back to the door. He waited a moment and turned in the chair to look back at Edward still standing with his hand to the open door. "Hurry! I must be off before morning light."

Edward shook his head and closed the door and came over and sat near Martin. "Martin, my friend. I worry for you. You need to see my specialists. You need treatment."

Martin looked confused for a moment. "What are you talking about? Oh? That again? I'm fine. Nothing wrong with my head. You have to listen."

Edward looked pleadingly into Martin's eyes. "You are not well. You look terrible. You've lost far too much weight. You have been seen chasing after all the vicars spouting tales about Eylene. People are worried about you, Martin. I am worried."

Martin waved his hands. "None of that is important right now. I met King Hietower, tonight. Down in the mausoleum."

Edward jerked back in his seat and a strange look between worry and sorrow crossed his features. "You met the dead king? In the mausoleum?"

"Yes, I see the doubt on your face. He told me something and said I would know what to do with the information."

"And that was to seek me out in the early morning hours?"

"Yes. I knew at once it had to be you. Hietower told me he was fed strange pills by the chirurgeons. He said they led to his madness. He said he was poisoned."

"Uh-huh."

"He described them as blue-grey in colour. They tasted of liquorice and rose honey."

Edward looked a little surprised and sat forward. "Liquorice and rose honey?"

Martin nodded.

"Where did you hear that from?"

Martin scowled. "I just told you. From Hietower."

"My long-dead father."

"Yes. You recognise the pill; I can see that in your eyes and tone."

"Yes, I think I do. We stopped using them a long time ago. Certainly years before Hietower ruled the land. It makes no sense he would have taken them. Martin, I'm afraid you might be imagining things. You need to rest."

Martin growled. "I need to leave. I've told you what he said. I believe it was God speaking to me again. It was like before."

"Ah, yes. The appearance of God in the church at the Crossroads."

Martin pulled out the amulet and brandished it before him. "And He gave me this. He led me to Will and Nadine when they needed me. You know this."

Edward sighed and rose and went to place a hand on Martin's shoulder.

Martin jerked upright and away. "Do not humour me, Edward. My faith is mine, and it has been challenged and opposed. And yet I hold strong to that faith. I am as sane as you are. With everything else that has happened and after all you have seen why would you doubt me now? This realm crumbles around us and no one does anything. I warn you: Eylene will seize power and all will be in ruin. You will inherit nothing. She will stop you."

Martin moved to the door before Edward could stop him. He swung the door open and looked back at Edward. "Stay safe, my friend. Look into the pills. They have import."

Edward looked at Martin and after a moment he nodded once.

That seemed to satisfy Martin and in a moment he was gone, closing the door behind him.

Will Arbor reached across the draoi bond to try again to find Katherine, Heather and Dog, but they were gone. He had not felt them leaving the bond and knew at once this was the same power that Kennit had wielded. What he didn't know was whether they were willingly off the bond or forced off the bond.

He opened his eyes and watched Nadine as she tried as well. She opened her eyes and shook her head sadly at Will. Will fought a feeling of annoyance toward Nadine and wondered where it came from.

"This is not good, Nadine. They have simply disappeared. Lana says she hasn't heard from them. She says the captain of the *Oriole* delivered them to Munsten two nights ago. The captain says they were heading for the museum in Munsten. They never showed up there or anywhere else. They simply vanished."

"And none of the draoi felt anything. If anyone would have felt something it would have been Lana. She was the closest."

Will looked worried.

"You know, Will, Lana is a close friend of Kennit. They came to us together from the same town in south Turgany." Nadine looked about the kitchen, as if looking for spies. "I don't know what to think, Will. Kennit has fractured the draoi. I can sense it. I see it in the eyes of the others. The *Gaea Decision*—that's what they call it—it has split us."

"And you think Kennit is leading half the draoi away from our principles? Is that it?"

"I think you are letting him pull half the draoi away. You are the Freamhaigh, Will. You need to step up and take responsibility. Take charge of the draoi. Lead them."

"Nadine, I am leading them. I prefer the vote. I need each draoi to have a voice. A voice that needs to be heard."

"Oh, Will. You can lead them and still give them a voice."

Will was silent for a moment and bowed his head. "That is not my way,

Nadine."

Will kept his head bowed and missed the brief look of disgust that crossed Nadine's face. "Will, the draoi are fractured. Something is happening right under our noses. Katherine, Heather, Dog and James are missing, and no one seems to care! We have to do something."

Will looked up. "We are. Lana is investigating in Munsten."

"Lana, the childhood friend of the man who would challenge you as Freamhaigh..."

Will looked defiantly back at Nadine and then nodded once.

Cill Darae

Six

Munsten Chamber, July 902 A.C.

EYLENE KISSANE CRABBED down the stone steps with her head tilted to the side to avoid the low stone ceiling of the staircase. The stairs were abnormally steep, and she felt the temperature of the air drop noticeably with every step she took. She was alone but knew who she would be meeting. This was the third of such meetings in as many weeks. She hoped for positive news and expected such.

She reached the bottom at last and was met by a rather young wordsmith who she hadn't seen since she had left Shape. He bowed to her and then pushed open a narrow wooden door and stepped through, holding it open for her. She stepped in and pulled back the hood of her cloak and stretched her back out. Before her stood two other wordsmiths.

"Vicar Kissane, so good to see you again," said the wordsmith sharing the same dark skin as her. The man stepped forward and gently shook Eylene's offered hand. She tried not to wince as she clasped Andrew Noble's right hand. It was missing the index, ring and pinkie fingers. By the smirk on his face, she knew it pleased him to make people uncomfortable, and a grin split her face.

"Still making impressions, eh Andy?" she asked.

"Please, you know I prefer Andrew. Shall I start calling you Leeny, again? Hum?"

"Okay, truce!" She laughed and stepped closer to him and clasped his deformed hand with both of hers. "I'm sorry, I don't have much time. Those idiots back in the church will wander off a cliff if I don't hold their hands every minute of the day. Please tell me you have results?"

Andrew looked sad and looked down at the ground. Eylene felt her hope vanishing like smoke. Andrew lifted his head and then laughed. "Got you!"

Eylene threw down Andrew's hand with a laugh and slapped Andrew on the upper arm. "Such cheek! Andy! Don't play around with this. It is far too important!"

"Ha-ha! Sorry, couldn't be helped. I'm still smarting from all the pranks you played on me as a child. Come follow me." He held out his hand to the other two wordsmiths. "This is John and Peter, if you remember?"

Eylene smiled at the other wordsmiths and followed Andrew through another door and down a small set of steps. The wordsmiths followed in behind. She remembered very clearly who they were and suppressed a smile. They had followed her around like little puppies back in Shape. They were always looking to catch her attention like all the little boys and men did.

They emerged into a long and wide stone chamber, their footsteps sounding hollow and with a slight echo off the floor. There was an unpleasant scent in the air and Eylene scrunched up her nose in distaste. Her eyes were drawn to a table set near the entrance with an array of strange devices laid out on it. Eylene was surprised to see an archery target was set up about twenty feet away. Andrew moved to the table and beckoned Eylene to join him.

"See here, we have the results you wanted. We kept this from Healy at your request. It wasn't easy. But the secret of the black powder is ours, I'm proud to say." Andrew opened a large clay jar and picked up a small measuring cup. He used the cup to scoop out a small measure of a black, glistening powder. He poured a little of the contents into a wide metal bowl. Eylene leaned forward to look inside, but Andrew held her back. Smiling he grabbed a strange device and held it over the bowl and squeezed the metal handle. The device made a scratching sound and a series of sparks rained down into the bowl. With a flash of light and an eruption of smoke the powder ignited and burned away in a moment. Eylene gasped and stepped back quickly. Andrew chuckled. "Relax, Leeny. when it's loose like this it merely burns in a flash. I wanted you to see just how volatile it is. It's dangerous stuff.

"Now, here on the table is the true brilliance of the Word. We have manufactured weapons that will change warfare. I'm certain of that. I'll have one of my assistants demonstrate. John, if you would?"

The wordsmith John stepped forward and picked up a weapon from the table. It was made of wood and metal and he placed the wooden end into his hand. Eylene could see it was shaped to fit a grip. John pointed the metal end which resembled a short, hollow rod away from him toward the archery target. He continued to point the device and then with a finger on the grip he depressed a small catch. Something on top of the weapon descended with a click and a spark was made. The spark lit a small amount of black powder. There was a flash of flame and smoke and suddenly the weapon made an extremely loud sound like thunder. Eylene cried out and saw the weapon emit a flash of flame from the metal rod. The archery target jerked and Eylene saw a large hole formed on the surface. John set the weapon down and Andrew fanned the smoke with his hands.

"You see, we can propel a lead ball some distance with force and accuracy. Each weapon can fire one ball. It's a brilliant design. John here was the genius who thought of it. It took some work. Accuracy is confirmed up to forty feet. After that the balls tend to veer off target. We don't know why. Still, impressive, is it not?"

Eylene walked over to the target and poked a finger into the hole. It was wider than her thumb. She turned to Andrew. "Forty feet? Archers can fire with accuracy well over a hundred yards. Farther even. It's impressive, I'll admit, but the range is rather poor."

Andrew grinned. "I knew you would say that. Think on this: I can teach a hundred men to fire one of these in a day. It would take five years to train a hundred men to fire a bow with any accuracy. And the power of the ball is enormous. One hit will kill a man, even dressed in plate armour, and a glancing blow will stun him for quite some time. But watch this. Come back over here."

Eylene raised an eyebrow but complied. As soon as she came around the table, the other wordsmith picked up a short bow and lifted a strange arrow off the table. The head of the arrow was a small wooden cylinder rather than an arrow head. Eylene could see a small piece of rope extended from it. The man notched the arrow to the bow and then touched the piece of rope to a small brazier on the table. The rope sparked and smoked. The man quickly lifted the bow, drew it and released the arrow. It plunged into the target and smoked.

Eylene blinked. "What is that...

She was interrupted when the arrow exploded in the target. Smoke filled the air. And they all coughed. Andrew said something to John, and the man went over to a device Eylene hadn't noticed by the door. The man rotated a handle and suddenly Eylene could see the smoke being pulled to a small vent in the ceiling of the room. In a minute the smoke cleared. They moved over to the target and

Eylene gasped. The centre of the target had a large chunk torn away. A crater the size of a soup bowl marred the surface.

"That's incredible!" she said.

"Thought you would say that, too," replied Andrew. "Now imagine the damage a hundred archers could do to an army with those."

Eylene smiled. "Oh yes. I can imagine that with no difficulty. They wouldn't even need to hit their targets. Well done, Andrew."

"Thank you, Eylene. I'm very proud of our work here. This is historic."

Eylene looked back at the table and the other explosive arrows and the strange weapons. "What do you call the weapons? The ones you hold?"

"We borrowed from the Navy, I'm afraid to admit. It's a gun that you hold with your hand, so we called them handguns. Not very imaginative."

"I like it. I want as many as you can make. I want them issued to the Church Guard at once with training. I want this power openly displayed."

"I'm afraid we can only make perhaps two dozen in a month, Leeny. The precision required for the barrels will not let us proceed faster than that. We've only found one blacksmith with the skill. The lead balls require a tight fit to work. But not too tight, you see. It's very precise work."

Eylene whirled on Andrew. "How many do you have now?"

Andrew lowered his head and pinched his nose, knowing what was coming next. "Only three at the moment."

"I need more! Two dozen by the end of the month. See to it."

Andrew sighed. "As you wish. We will do our best."

"See that you do, Andrew. Speed is important," Eylene eyed the other two wordsmiths then beckoned to Andrew with her head. "Walk with me."

Eylene led Andrew out and up the stairs. Outside the fresh air was sweet compared to the stench of the chamber. Eylene turned to Andrew. "How many know the secret?"

"Only six. I trust them. All of them. With my life. You know most of them from our childhood days."

Eylene studied Andrew for a moment. "Very well. Pray it stays a secret."

Andrew smiled and bowed his head a little. "Of course."

Eylene smiled and moved closer to Andrew and kissed him on the mouth. "Excellent. Come around tonight. Lana will join us again. She promises to do that thing again with her powers."

Andrew smiled. "I wouldn't miss it."

Edward Hitchens, heir to the throne of Belkin, slammed shut another tome detailing medical case files and cursed in what he imagined was a very non-royal way. He had been rummaging through the old case files for hours. He had first tried to find the case files for the King, but the Chirurgeon's Guild archivists told him they no longer held them. When pressed for an explanation they hadn't seemed to find that odd. Frustrated, he gave up and instead opted to look at other case files and see if he could spot anything that supported what Martin had said.

My world is in turmoil. Hallucinations of my dead father and draoi and other peculiarities plague my life. It is enough to drive someone trained in the Word conniptions. Edward sat back and rubbed at his tired eyes. *I would do anything to go back to being a simple chirurgeon. I think I will stop this pointless search. Nothing I read gives a hint of the king being poisoned.*

Edward was forced to attend all manner of studies intended to prepare him for assuming the throne. Brent demanded it. He attended long tedious lectures by Robert Ghent and Robert Hargrave on the Councils and the Royal Laws. He was lectured on the history of the realm and the long line of succession to the throne. He was forced to remember the baronies, the lords and their roles in the land. It was beyond Edward's ability to even fake interest. The worst of all the lectures were from the Church of the New Order. He was expected to lead the Church and profess his faith and belief in this god they proclaimed existed.

And not one shred of proof to back that claim up, thought Edward and snorted.

He pushed back from the desk. And then rested his hands on his knees and stretched his back. *I've read every case file from the era. I'm done.*

He rose and felt his knees crack. He grimaced and gathered up the tomes. One by one he returned the tomes to their shelves. He loved the act of returning things to their proper place. Seeing the neat rows and organised tomes, soothed him. Finally he finished and wiped the dust from his hands and headed for the exit.

Poor Martin, he won't be pleased if I found nothing to support him. But what did he honestly expect? If what he says is true—that Hietower had been poisoned—they would have covered it up. Destroyed the evidence. And that would explain why the records are gone. Which certainly lends credence to Martin's accusation, no? But there's nothing on Hietower here at all.

Edward paused at the exit as a stray thought occurred to him. *What if...?*

Edward turned around and went to a different section of the archives. He weaved his way past desks and bookshelves to the back corner. He glanced at the dozens of rows of bookcases that rose from floor to ceiling and started to read the labels on the ends which detailed the contents of the shelves. His fingers skimmed the words, and he moved from bookcase to bookcase. Finally he found what he was looking for.

"Here we are: *Orders and Shipping, 860 to 880 A.C.*"

He moved down the bookcase and searched the boxes for the right dates.

"A-ha! Here we go. Spring, 878 A.C."

Edward pulled down a box and grunted at the weight. He carried it over to his desk and sat it down on the floor and opened it. He looked down at order receipts placed by the Chirurgeon's Guild; all tied up in loose bundles sorted by date and by which chirurgeon had placed the order.

"If I can find an order for the right materials, it could lead somewhere... he murmured to himself. Part of him cheered. This was the work he cherished. Facts and figures spoke to him. The mystery drew him in and excited him.

Edward rummaged through the bundles until he found one that bore the mark for the Munsten Castle chirurgeon. He pulled out the stack of receipts and laid them on the desk and read them one by one. *They may have destroyed the chirurgeons reports on Hietower, but the evidence may remain in material orders. Not everyone would consider looking here.* He felt a glimmer of hope.

The next day Edward found what he was looking for. He held the receipt in his hand and stared at it. It was a simple order, made a few years before the Great Debate, and it was a large one, but Edward recognised all the ingredients. One was the most telling, it was an order for a large quantity of quicksilver. He admired the liquid. It was like a metal. It shone brightly and as a child he had often played with it. As a chirurgeon he knew better. The skin absorbed quicksilver, and it did things to people with prolonged exposure. No one knew why it harmed people, but the Chirurgeon's Guild had seen the association and banned quicksilver from practice.

All the ingredients in the order, he knew, could be combined to make a quicksilver pill. It would be exactly how Martin described it: blue-grey, but deadly. The pill had been thought to cure certain sicknesses of the sexual kind. Edward could see the date on the order was a couple of years before Hietower started to become openly unstable. But the Chirurgeon's Guild had already banned quicksilver at that point. They knew the danger of it and yet ordered material to make the pills. Had they known its intended use?

Unlikely, he thought.

He looked at the receipt again. It was ordered by the Chirurgeon's Guild, but the recipient of the material was the Church of the New Order. Edward's thoughts spun. *Nothing of this makes sense.*

By the end of the next day, Edward had a stack of similar orders spanning the years of Hietower's reign. They ended suspiciously when Hietower passed away.

All the orders were for quicksilver and all for the Church.

The decline of King Hietower was well documented. It had started subtly years before the Great Debate. He became more and more unstable over the years and the end of the Great Debate tipped him over the edge. Edward could see how exposure to quicksilver over time would lead to Hietower's mental decline. There would have been other symptoms, he knew. Tremors, insomnia, weakness, and headaches. No one mentioned those about Hietower. Just his emotional breakdown. The Church was crucial to Hietower. He was a devout follower. By all accounts the Church loved him.

Edward thought of what he knew about the Church at the time. Archbishop Greigsen had been friendly with the King. All accounts were that the traitor Bill Redgrave had been the one to conspire with John Healy to replace the King. Greigsen had been against it at first, but Healy had convinced him. It made no sense for Greigsen to have ordered something that would knowingly kill the head of the Church and someone he admired.

So, if the head of the Church, closest to the King, had no knowledge of the quicksilver pills then who in the Church did? This speaks of conspiracy.

Edward laid down the stack of orders and stared sightlessly straight ahead. *Martin was right, but he doesn't know the full truth of it. No one does.*

What is certain is someone in the Church poisoned Hietower.

Will walked the woods alone, well outside Rigby Farm. His walk was a daily occurrence. He needed to feel nature and get away from people—even his own draoi. From miles away, he could sense the draoi probing him and he could feel their worry. Oddly, their worry hardly concerned him. Rather, he felt at peace for the first time in a long time. The worries he had carried for so long were gone. Will walked to the edge of a clearing and paused to admire the view. Sunlight poured down from the high sun to brighten the clearing in stark contrast to the shadowed woods. Insects gleamed and darted through the air and the buzz of grasshoppers was a constant drone. Wild flowers grew everywhere and scented the air. Will noticed the blueberry bushes surrounding the area and how they were bursting with ripe fruit. The clearing was nothing more than a rocky outcrop where plants fought to find a footing.

Will entered the clearing and sat on the flat rock in the centre. His tunic and pants were soaked with sweat and Will relished the feel of the breeze pulling the heat from his body. Will had long ago stopped using his powers to deal with such things as sweat. He was certain a continued use of powers would numb him to the human condition. Nadine agreed with him.

The thought of Nadine stirred a longing inside him and a panic, but as quickly as the feelings appeared they washed away, and he wondered what he had been thinking about. It suddenly occurred to him he had been having more and more incidents of not remembering. He frowned and then the feeling washed away.

Will smiled up at the bright sunlight. He loved summer. He felt the plants around him reaching tall for the warmth and energy of the sun. Around him stirred the animals and insects of the forest. They sensed him and wanted to be with him, and they approached. With them he sensed the approach of many midges. He frowned and sent them away with a pulse of power. *Nothing likes the midges*, he chuckled.

Long ago the stark focus of nature on him had been an unnerving experience. Now, as Freamhaigh, and sure of his powers, he welcomed the attention of nature. He closed his eyes and opened his arms wide and threw back his head.

"Come to me!" he said.

Over the next hour, the surrounding wildlife emerged from the shadows of the trees. Rabbits, squirrels, mice, rats, deer, and all manner of other creatures came forward and gathered around him. From the ground and under stones every insect and arachnid imaginable erupted. The air buzzed with flying insects and then birds and bats swooped overhead in broad arcs, crying their joy. Life approached him without fear and basked in his attention.

"I welcome you," he said and felt a tremor of joy pass through the nearby life. He lowered his head and opened his eyes. All around him was every living thing that had been in the surrounding mile. "I asked you here to talk to you."

Will felt the gathering still in anticipation. When he spoke the words and sent their meaning across the bond, it was to the Simon motes that inhabited the world around him that he truly spoke. Will wasn't certain if when he spoke to the motes that the creatures heard and understood the words, too. He had questioned Nadine on this many, many nights ago.

Will frowned. *Nadine?* he thought. He started to reach out for her, but the desire washed away. He looked around him at the thousands and thousands of creatures that surrounded him. He could sense their confusion. Many thought to attack and devour the creature next to it, but Will held them in check. Will watched a fox lick its chops and stare at a rabbit standing right before it, before looking back at Will.

Will chuckled. "I wanted to tell you everything is going to be fine. Erebus is gone. We won."

The life around him waited. Hawks circling overhead cried out and Will sensed their hunger. All around him life wanted to take life: he sensed the need to devour, destroy, and succeed to live for another day. The struggle of life was complex. Will knew now just how horrible and vicious it could be. He had hoped nature would want to hear his words. But the truth was, it didn't care. They only wanted to be near him. Nature cared little for what he said.

Will smiled. With Gaea gone, the task of responding to the needs of the land fell directly on the draoi. Before, Gaea would take care of the day-to-day needs of the land. Now, Will and the draoi had to step up and fill that role where needed. The Simon motes were everywhere in Belkin. Will knew his sense of nature was merely information sent to him from the motes. He didn't care. It was different now than with Gaea. This time the motes responded directly to him. Now that Gaea was gone, the control was all his. He had worried about it. He feared he would mess everything up. He wanted to go back and ask Gaea so many questions, but it was too late for that. Fortunately, nature had been surviving for millennia without the draoi and knew how to continue without draoi influence. Now that Erebus was eradicated, nature seemed to be thriving. *Gaea must have known this would happen.*

Reports from the coast and from the draoi's own investigation, they knew the fish off the coasts were moving deeper and following fishing paths long ago abandoned. Will knew that Gaea had kept the fish close to avoid the influence of Erebus. Now they were free to return to their instinctually known feeding grounds. Fishing off the coast had changed almost overnight, but the fishing fleets were adapting.

Will expected a massive increase in the amount of life over the next few years. The draoi would need to monitor the increase and keep the harmony of nature in balance. It was an art and a difficult concept. The complexities of the interaction of nature was diverse and seriously challenging. Thankfully, being draoi came with an inherent knowledge of how it worked. It had surprised him to discover this. He knew everything from how the smallest spore to the largest animal on the planet interacted. Will was certain his draoi would rise to the challenge. Nature would need very little draoi influence. It was finding its own way.

As a plus, he could now completely ignore the politics of the humans. He cared little for the realm of Belkin and who ruled and whether they were worthy. It had nothing to do with nature. Nadine had disagreed and had spoken to him the other day about it...

"Nadine?" whispered Will to the wildlife. "Why do I care what Nadine wants?"

Will's control over the creatures surrounding him faltered and for a moment the creatures poised to attack one another in hunger. Will felt startled and worried about the life surrounding him. Then a feeling of peace washed over him, and Will smiled at the creatures surrounding him and released them from his control. In seconds the serene scene in front of him descended into chaos as animal turned on animal and insect turned on insect. The air filled with a cacophony of death and destruction. Will sat on his stone and smiled and rocked himself backwards and forwards.

Seven

Munsten, August 902 A.C.

EYLENE KISSANE KNELT before the altar of the Church of the New Order deep within the Munsten Castle. Sitting on the altar was the headdress of the Archbishop. Soon it would settle on her head and she would welcome the weight. She felt all eyes on her back and kept control of the tight smile that threatened to split her face wide open in glee. The newly ordained bishops and deans owed her their allegiance. They had voted and agreed that the lowly girl from Shape, Turgany would rise to become the new Archbishop of Belkin. Years of planning and positioning had come to fruition. Decades of work were represented in that headdress.

The girl born in Shape so long ago had changed. Years ago she had met the former Archbishop Reginald Greigsen and King Hietower when she was only twelve years old when they were touring the churches of the land. The Archbishop had taken a fancy to her and raped her in the backroom of her father's house. Her father had found out and in a rage had attacked the Archbishop as they were preparing to leave. She had watched in horror as the King's guards had struck down her father and killed him. The King said nothing. He had watched her father struck down and then turned to the Archbishop and laughed about something and rode away.

The men from the church had sat with her then. They explained with great reverence what the greater good of the world was. The holy position the King held and the Archbishop's need to save the souls of the land. Then they offered her a place within their ranks. She remembered the look the Archbishop had given her when he had ridden away. He had looked back at her with a look of longing. She had the first glimmer of the power her sex gave her and tucked that away while the corpse of her father cooled outside their farm house.

The church men handed her over to the deacon in Shape and rode away on horseback. The deacon was a devout and pious man, but easily influenced. Over the years she wielded her small power and gained influence over him and the church in Shape. She started rumours. Spread falsehoods when needed. All the while knowing she needed to wrest the power of the church from the likes of Godless men like Greigsen. She put in motion the effort to take down the King and over years they had slowly poisoned him. The Revolution had not been in their plans and it stopped them in their tracks. Slowly over the years, they watched Healy and pressured him in subtle ways to lead the country to the disaster it became. The country was ripe for her final plans. And now the church was hers. Her vision for the future was nearly in her grasp.

She looked out of the corner of her eyes and sighted the empty throne where the monarch of Belkin would normal sit. Sitting next to it was the current ruler: Regent Brent Bairstow. He looked a little lost to her with his eyes a little wider than they should be. Behind him, standing demurely with her hands behind her back was his new executive assistant. A navy wench, a mere lieutenant. *She appeared out of nowhere, but it appears she only has eyes for Brent. And he's clueless to her affections.* Eylene mentally rolled her eyes and forced her thoughts back to the ceremony.

Brent should never have allowed this, she thought with a smile. *He is so easily swayed by religious dogma. And Lana's powers. He is handing me the reins to this kingdom and doesn't even know it. Well, perhaps not a kingdom for much longer.*

Her thoughts turned briefly to Edward and the draoi mission to place him on the throne. She had no doubts he was Hietower's bastard. He was the spitting image of the King. She could never allow him to rise to power. The Church, under her sway, had worked so long for their goal. The unexpected reveal of Edward had caused the church in Shape to accelerate their plans. The draoi would one day soon reveal his lineage and that could not be allowed. It had the potential to overturn years and years of work.

The church in Shape had long ago distanced itself from the cannon of the Church of the New Order. The Deacon had witnessed the horror of the Archbishop and King and over time, with Eylene whispering in his ear, had turned his parish away from the main edicts. The Revolution had solidified that effort. And now Eylene led the Church of Belkin, and her followers were found in every church of the Realm; hidden amongst the misguided parishioners of the Church of the New Order. They had influence over nearly every aspect of the Church of the New Order and the monarchy over the years. Now was their time to shine.

Her thoughts reeled, and she found herself thinking of the gaol buried deep beneath her within the castle. She was pleased to have Katherine, Dog, James and Heather secure in the dungeon. The collars and herbs were keeping them mindless and without power. Feeding them was proving difficult; especially with the dog. She was determined to keep them alive until she knew she could do without them. The Church argued for their immediate execution and Eylene fought tooth and nail to keep them alive. *I will use them to my advantage. Waste not want not.*

Behind her, one of her new Cardinals read from the ritual to raise her as the Archbishop and a shudder of sudden pleasure rippled through her. She snuck a look at Brent and found him looking at her with curiosity. She couldn't help it and frowned at him and he looked away.

Better. He's learning. By the Word, my knees are hurting.

The Cardinal finished his portion of the ritual and stepped down from the podium. He moved beside her, and another Cardinal joined him on her other side. Together they lifted her up and held her firm. She now better understood this part of the ritual—after an hour on her knees she could barely straighten them. She gasped at the pain but forced her legs to unbend. She found her footing and snuck a smile at the two cardinals who smiled back and then released her. They had been two of her first converts to the Church of Belkin.

Eylene turned to the audience. The pews were filled to capacity. She looked out at her cardinals, deans and vicars and smiled. She spotted Lana in the crowd and widened her smile just for her. Eylene could see a blush rise in her cheeks. Eylene walked around to the other side of the altar and then up the stairs to the seat of the archbishop. She stopped before it and turned around.

One the cardinals stepped forward and read from the ritual. "Regent, ladies and gentlemen. Eylene Kissane has been found worthy of the position of Archbishop of Belkin by a tribunal of her peers. She alone has been chosen to lead our Church and the people of the land. I ask that you all rise."

The sound of fabric rustling filled the air as the audience rose to their feet. Brent Bairstow stood and turned toward her and Eylene smiled at yet another small victory. The King should be officiating this ceremony and would never stand for the Archbishop. For him to stand was symbolising a subservience.

Eylene beamed a smile at the audience and lowered herself into the seat of the Archbishop. It was hard and uncomfortable, but she loved it. Years of work had led to this moment. The Church was hers, the Regent in the palm of her hand, and half the draoi were looking to her for leadership.

The two cardinals lifted the headdress and lifted it up and held it over her head. Slowly they lowered it until it rested on her head. The weight pressed down, and she struggled to hold it steady. *With my luck, it will topple off in front of everyone.* As suddenly as the weight was there, she felt the power of the druids surge through her strengthening her neck muscles. *Lana is a Godsend*, thought Eylene.

"We ordain you as Archbishop Eylene Kissane."

Eylene settled herself and kept her eyes closed. She waited a moment listening. All her life she imagined that God would speak to her in this moment. She was the closest to God of all the clergy. God spoke to the Archbishop, she was certain of that. It was more than just symbolism. God would speak to her.

Lord, I am yours to Command.

God?

She waited a moment more, but all she heard were the soft whisperings of the audience. She heard more than a few people comment on how pious she was being. But God wasn't speaking to her. Unexpectedly, a feeling of fear washed over her, but she quickly replaced it with irritation and sensibility.

Her eyes snapped open. *Right, that's done with. I knew it, there is no god. Now to business.*

She rose to her feet, careful to keep the weight of the headdress centred above her and raised her arms. "God's Blessings on all of you!"

The audience cheered and clapped. Eylene beamed a smile and nodded as best she could with the weight of the headdress. She looked at Brent and he bowed deeply to her. *Better and better.*

The applause continued loud and thunderous without end. A small commotion caught her attention and she looked over to find people turning to look at something. In a moment, the rest of the audience slowly became aware and shouting could be heard. The applause petered out and suddenly the voice of Martin Jordan could be heard.

"Blasphemy! Blasphemy! You should all be ashamed!"

Eylene searched for him and finally spotted Martin. He was being held by Church guards and struggling against them. Eylene groaned inwardly but kept the smile on her face. "Let him approach! Guards! Let him go. He is a man of the cloth, sworn to God. Let him speak."

The Church guard let go of Martin and he lurched forward a moment before gaining his feet. Eylene could see many in the audience openly scowling at Martin. She caught the eye of Lana and was pleased to see Lana nod to her. *Better and better.*

"Approach Vicar Jordan! Approach your Archbishop. What is your complaint?"

Martin sputtered and strode up to stand near Brent. Eylene saw Brent signal his guard to stay back. Martin looked at Brent for a moment and then turned his attention to Eylene and walked up to the altar and stood before her.

"Blasphemy! Remove that headdress! You have no right to it! Only the King can anoint the position of Archbishop! You know this! You twist and bend our most sacred rituals to your own end. Have you no shame? Blasphemy! God is watching you!" He turned to Brent. "Please, stop this madness!"

Eylene moved forward and stood beside the altar and looked down at him. "Dear Vicar Jordan, long have we listened to your council. You have been through many trials of your faith, and yet you doubt ours. It is God who wants this. It is through the Church that the Realm will be calmed, and peace returned. You speak against that which you do not grasp. Calm yourself, approach and seek my blessing. You may be the first."

Martin's face grew scarlet. His mouth gaped and Eylene was pleased by the effect of her words on him. *He looks the part of a madman now.* Martin stepped closer and lifted an accusing finger toward her. "Remove that headdress! You know nothing of faith! Nothing!" Eylene watched Martin fumble at the neck of his tunic for something. A Church guard stepped forward, but Eylene motioned him back. Martin pulled out his wooden amulet and held it forward. "My faith has been confirmed by God himself! He has spoken to me! Gifted me with this! You know this to be true!"

Eylene forced her face to take on an expression of sympathy mixed with pity. By the smiles on the faces of the audience near her she was sure she had it right. Brent was staring at Martin with some horror. *Better and better.*

"Enough, Vicar Jordan. Cease this madness."

"Madness? Madness? You seek to take this realm for your own! I know what you are capable of! You must be stopped by any means!"

Eylene caught the eye of Lana and gave an imperceptible nod. Lana smiled and then her eyes lost focus.

Martin sputtered and then froze in place. The audience gasped and looked around. Eylene raised her hands. "Relax good people of Belkin! The draoi are assisting us here today. Fear not. Vicar Martin here has just threatened me directly." She looked to Brent. "You heard Regent, did you not?"

Brent looked even more horrified but nodded his head.

Eylene held her headdress, looked down, and shook her head a moment before looking up. She forced her most stern expression and stood before Martin. "Vicar Martin, you leave me no choice. I offered you blessing and instead you threaten the Archbishop directly. I know not what manner of violence you intend upon my person, but I will not lower myself to your level. The Church of the New Order is about peace and forgiveness. But some things are unforgivable. You are henceforth excommunicated from the Church. You are stripped of all titles to the Church. Wherever you walk, none shall aide you or abet you. You are persona non grata in Belkin."

Eylene reached up and tore the amulet from Martin's hand and snapped the leather thong from his neck. She held it in one hand and nodded to the Church guard. She tossed the amulet onto the altar. She held Brent's eyes for a moment and was pleased to see Brent looking shocked, but he did not interfere. *Better and better.*

The Church guard seized Martin by the upper arms. Eylene waived her hand and Lana released Martin. He staggered forward but was held firm by the guard. He opened his mouth to protest, but Lana kept his voice still. Eerily, Martin was dragged in silence out of the hall. The audience watched him struggle with his face bright red and his eyes bulging. As he passed Brent, he looked to him and seeing the expression of revulsion on his face Martin looked away and sobbed in silence. In moments he was gone, and a door slammed shut.

Eylene faced the audience. "People of Belkin be at peace. We have a united Church. We promise peace and order across the Realm. My vicars will head to village and town and provide comfort! They leave tomorrow! Rejoice!"

The crowd burst into applause and rose to their feet. Cheering started at the back, no doubt by one of her own people, but soon it spread across the crowd. Eylene beamed her most humble, but gracious smile for all to see. She saw Brent still looking toward where Martin had left and then turn and face Eylene. In a moment, he smiled too and joined the applause. *Better and better, indeed.*

Eylene turned back to her seat in triumph. She looked to the altar for the amulet and saw it was gone. Her step faltered for a moment before she made it to her seat of power.

Vicar Martin Jordan was dragged face down, held at the shoulders, with his toes dragging through the streets of Munsten by the Church Guard and he fought to free his voice, but knew it was futile. He recognised the power of the draoi and knew it was Lana. *I suspected her and now I know.*

Turning his head to the side, Martin saw the people on the street stop and stare at him and point. Some even laughed out loud. He soon stopped struggling altogether and watched the street cobblestone pass underneath him.

God? Why? You cannot want this? Please tell me what to do.

Martin waited for a response, but hearing nothing, he sobbed, his voice finally freed.

It took time to drag Martin through the streets, but eventually they made it to the main south gate. A sizeable crowd followed behind and hooted and jeered. Martin felt shamed and kept his head hung below his shoulders. His toes were raw from rubbing on the cobblestones, but he barely felt the pain. *I have lost. All is lost.*

They dragged him through the gate and a short distance down the entrance road before the Church guard stopped, spoke a soft three-count, and then threw him to the side of the road into a side ditch. Martin cried out as he flew and heard the crowd roar with approval. He landed hard and rolled. He felt something snap in his upper chest and knew his left collarbone had broken. Blinding, searing pain tore away his breath. He could only lay on one side with his knees drawn up against the pain. Each breath felt like he was breathing fire.

The Church guards moved aside and as soon as they were clear the crowd began pelting him with rotten vegetables and excrement. They struck him bodily, and he cried out against the additional pain. Hard vegetables struck him like stones. He curled into a ball and lifted his right arm over his head. The crowd cheered harder, and they taunted him with names. After a time the crowd grew bored and slowly dispersed until he lay in agony and solitude. A feeling of vertigo washed over him, and he swallowed against the urge to vomit.

"Vicar Martin, you must be away," came a sudden, soft voice near his ear.

Martin cautiously removed his arm and winced against the pain of the broken bone. Any movement caused the ends to grind inside his chest. He squinted up and saw a young member of the Regent's guard kneeling over him. He didn't recognise him.

"Get up!" whispered the man urgently. "You must be away."

"I-I can't. B-broken b-bone. C-collar," stuttered Martin, his teeth chattering with the pain.

The man grunted. "You'll have to fight it for now. I'll help you up, but then you must walk clear. If you are not out of sight of the guards by sundown, they will run you down. Do you understand? They are making wagers right now. You must be away! You've been lying here for hours! Dusk is only an hour away."

Cill Darae

Hours? It can't be hours, I've only just landed here. Martin looked blearily toward the gate house, some fifty feet away. The sun was casting long shadows, and the sky was reddening confirming that he had indeed been lying here for hours. Martin blinked and spied a small gathering of guardsmen who stood nearby watching him. Behind them Martin saw that some people still remained to watch the spectacle.

"We have orders. You are to be slain on sight if you return to Munsten. Word will be sent to the villages and towns. They are not to harbour you. This is a right mess, Vicar Martin. But you were good to me once when we was coming back from the Crossroads. I dunno if you remember me? You helped me, right? Now I'm helping you! Now get up!"

Martin did not remember the young man. He had spoken to so many injured during the retreat from the Crossroads. He tried to focus on the face but found he could not. His vision swam with pain. Suddenly without warning his world spun violently, and he felt himself hoisted to his feet. He cried out when the collar bone ends scrapped inside him, tearing his flesh. Sweat poured from him and he felt the need to throw up.

The young guard held Martin steady and leaned in with his head to whisper in his ear. "You will need to immobilise your left arm up over the collar bone. Don't let it fuse twisted or out of alignment. Maybe get help? Is there anywhere you can get help?"

Martin felt overwhelmed and grief rose up thick and cloy. *Help? I am alone.*

"Vicar Martin? Know where you can go?"

Martin had a momentary vision of a house on a cliff side but then immediately thought of the Rigby Farm and nodded once.

"Good, wherever it is, go straight there and hide. I don't know what you've done, but the Realm is against you. Please, go now."

The young guard released Martin and when he did he swayed. The man steadied him again and then gently let go. Martin stood awkwardly with his shoulders hunched over the pain of the broken bone. He looked over at the face of the young guard and tried to remember him.

"I'm sorry, I don't remember your name, my son. Forgive me."

"Nothing to forgive."

"Thank you for your kindness."

The guard looked hurriedly back to the gate. "You'll thank me by getting clear. Hurry!"

Martin nodded and took one step away from the gate. He looked down and saw his shoes had the toes worn away and they were stained red with his own blood. Once he saw the state of his feet, he felt the pain and sucked in a breath. He looked back at the guards at the gate and saw they were watching him. Some brandished their swords at him and laughed. He took another step and then another. He found if he stepped carefully the pain was not so bad. He grimaced and shuffle-walked toward the distant bridge that crossed the river. He was so focused on moving he failed to hear the young guard return until he moved back in front of him.

"Vicar Martin, you've dropped this."

The guard pressed something into Martin's right hand and then hurried away back to the city. Martin stopped and lifted his hand. He held his wooden amulet with a snapped lanyard.

Cill Darae

Eight

Rigby Farm and Munsten, August 902 A.C.

NADINE WAS ANGRY. "The draoi are split, Will! Split! And you do nothing but hide in your workshop creating potions and unguents! You must talk to them. Make them understand why the Gaea Decision was made the way it was. Gaea asked to die. She wanted it. By saying nothing you fuel their doubts and fears. Speak to them."

Nadine paced by the apple trees behind the farmhouse. Will sat on a stump and had his head lowered. Nadine glanced at him and growled.

"Say something!"

Will shook his head.

Nadine looked over to Steve, who stood with his back up against a cherry tree. He saw her glare and held up a hand and shook his head. She turned to Will.

"You are the Freamhaigh, Will Arbor! You must lead! Everywhere across the land the people are scared. Scared and frightened! A second revolution is not far away."

Will finally looked up for a brief a moment. He lowered it again. "What would you have me say?"

"*Have you say?* It is not for me to put words in your mouth. You must speak to them as you always do. As the Freamhaigh! Assure them all is well. Bring us together. Unite us. Lead us toward harmony. You cannot continue to hide away from the problem, Will!"

Will looked up and Nadine was shocked to see raw anger in his face. "I am not hiding, Nadine. I rule as I always have. Each draoi has a voice. I will not impose my will on others. They are draoi and we will always do what is right for the land. I have no fear of that. Nor should you."

Nadine stopped her pacing and stood in front of Will with her hands on her hips. "That may have been true when Gaea ruled the draoi. We spoke of this. With Gaea gone there is no one to make sure the draoi follow the tenants. The draoi require someone to lead them. To keep them focused. You are that focus, Will. You are the Freamhaigh!"

"You keep saying I'm the Freamhaigh like it has some special power attached to it. I have faith the draoi will do what is right."

"Faith? You speak of faith? Are you some peon of the church?"

Will stood. "No. I have led the draoi as best I can. Why do you question me now?"

Steve pushed off the tree and stepped up beside Nadine. "She's worried, Will. As am I. Ever since we defeated Erebus you've been different. What's bothering you?"

Will frowned at the question. "Nothing is bothering me."

Steve frowned as well and stepped closer to Will. "That's true, isn't it? Nothing seems to be bothering you. You should be bothered by all this. What's wrong with you?"

Will scowled. "Nothing! I keep telling you. Nothing!"

Nadine made a noise and reached out to Will. "Hon, please..."

Will twisted away and stomped off around the house and out of sight. Steve and Nadine watched him go in shock. Once he was gone, Steve whistled out loud. "He's off. You were right."

Nadine nodded and sat on the stump Will had been on. "I don't understand. I've examined him. I can sense nothing wrong."

"Perhaps we need Edward."

"Edward? Whatever for?"

"He says the mind needs healing just as much as the body."

Nadine snorted.

"Don't dismiss it so lightly. Martin agreed with him. Although Martin said it was more spiritual in nature."

"And what do you believe?"

Steve hesitated. "I've seen men and women. Stronger than you and me. They just... just stopped after seeing too much. I can't explain it. I once had a young lad in the crew who lost his eyesight. One moment he was fine, the next he was blind. Peter, our draoi, looked at him and said there was nothing wrong with him. Explain that."

Nadine reached down and picked up a fallen apple from the dozen that laid around them. She looked it over and then took a bite and grimaced. "I can see the beauty in this apple. I can taste how tart it is. With my power I can change how my tongue tastes it and make it as sweet as honey. What you describe is outside my ken. If I am hearing you correctly, you think Will has something wrong in his head."

"I do. Ever since we returned from Munsten he's been... off. We've watched the draoi struggle to understand their new source of power coupled with the sudden absence of Gaea in their daily lives. You know how they worshiped her. For some, her loss was too terrible to take. Kennit has exploited that weakness. Lately, we've watched draoi step up and confront Will and he does nothing. They feel leaderless and they're not wrong, Nadine. Will is not acting as the Freamhaigh. He acts like he's in a dream.

"But I'll be honest with you. I don't think this is in his head, despite what I said. There is more to this. He seems removed from the problem. Controlled. Something has influenced him and pulled him away from dealing with the here and now. If this was a stress related problem—that's how Peter described what caused the young man to lose his vision—we would be seeing other signs. Lack of sleep, nightmares, losing control of his emotions. Other than Will not sleeping, he seems as right as rain. Nothing bothers him at all. We already spoke about this. You know I'm right, Nadine."

Nadine threw her apple to the ground. Steve watched as the soil parted and the core disappeared into the ground. In a moment a little tendril of a sprout broke the surface and grew higher, twisting as it did so. When it was three inches high it stopped. Nadine looked up at Steve. "I'm not ready."

"Yes, you are. We spoke about it. Whatever is happening to Will is not happening to you."

"Do you think it is Kennit?"

"After what you told me, I do. Aye. It's him."

"So do I. I have to be careful here. I could cause more damage."

"Are you sure you have the power?"

"No. It's just a belief I have. Reading the Draoi Manuscript and looking back at all the Cill Darae before me: there's something there hidden between the words. Now knowing that there were more than one Cill Darae at a time makes me think I am right. Gaea was a woman. She represented motherhood. Nurturing.

There hasn't been a male Cill Dara for a very, very long time. From what I can tell, I suspect the last male Cill Dara was a woman trapped in a man's body."

"Like Windthrop."

Nadine snorted. "More or less. He was... unique. But the point is, the Cill Darae were always the only one to speak directly to Gaea. The Freamhaigh led, but with the advisement of the Cill Darae, the High Priestess. Gaea always chose not to speak to her Freamhaigh. Will is—was—the exception."

"And now with the Gaea motes gone, and the draoi having the Simon motes, you think perhaps Gaea knew this would happen?"

"Yes, I do. She was always thinking ahead. Probabilities and possibilities. She weighed them all. She always knew what would happen and made it possible with her manipulations. The one constant throughout the years? She relied on her Cill Darae to be the nurturing type and guide the Freamhaigh."

Steve laughed and Nadine shot him a look. "My pardon, Nadine. You've never struck me as the nurturing type."

"Exactly my point. Up until now, she always chose a mother. Someone like her. I'm not like the others. I'm...?"

"A hard-ass?"

Nadine smirked. "Exactly. But I would have said I'm too old for this malarkey."

* * *

Nadine stood by the draoi meeting spot central to the Rigby Farm and sent her call across the bond and watched to see how it was received. The threads linking her to the other draoi here at the farm and across the land all pulsed with her order. She watched the threads and observed how the colours shifted and flowed. Intuitively she knew the call was being received with mixed reactions. She saw anger flare in some, and in others a sense of relief. She marked who responded favourably and stored that information away for later.

She looked for the bonds of Katherine, Heather and Dog and was saddened to see them still missing. She looked at the thread leading to Lana and watched it pulse red. *She's a bad one with no doubt,* she thought. As she watched, the colours across the threads calmed and all appeared normal. *Interesting, Kennit has reach and power. Power I don't yet understand.*

She waited as the draoi emerged from the buildings and from working the surrounding fields. The sun was high in the sky and the heat of summer rose from the ground in waves. The loud buzz of insects filled the air and Nadine closed her eyes and reached out with her senses to nature. She was filled with the beauty surrounding her and allowed it to pass through her and energise her. It was at times like this that she missed Gaea the most. Always before, her presence was felt and now it was gone; like a cloud covering the sun and stealing it's warmth. It bothered her and she felt grief at the loss.

She opened her eyes and discovered the draoi surrounding her. They looked at her strangely, except for Kennit. He had his eyes closed and seemed focused. His eyes opened, and he looked directly at her. She could see the defiance in him. A smirk touched the corner of his lips and Nadine squinted her eyes at him. She looked for Will and found him across their bond, still working in his workshop. He had ignored her call.

Nadine opened her mouth to speak, but Kennit beat her to it.

"What do you wish of us, Cill Darae?"

Nadine stumbled mentally. *This is not starting the way I want.* "I ask you here to speak to you of the draoi. And our future."

"What of it? We are all draoi, are we not?"

"We are. But we are divided."

"Divided? How can that be? We all work to the greater good."

"Yes, we do."

Kennit looked around, making a point of looking for someone in particular. "And where is the Freamhaigh? Why is he not here to speak to us of our future?"

"He is..." Nadine knew lies would not work with the draoi. "He is indisposed. It is for that reason I wish to address you all." Across the bond, in other areas of the Realm, Nadine could feel the confusion at her words. Here at the farm, the draoi looked at one another, the bonds pulsed with conflict. "We are divided. The Gaea Decision was a difficult time for us."

"Not so difficult for some," said Kennit and stepped forward. Nadine noticed the draoi that stood nearest to him. They were the same ones she had marked as discordant when she had placed the call. "You were the first to agree to killing Gaea. You made the decision so lightly and so quickly."

Nadine nodded. "This is true. I recognised the will of Gaea. She was tired. Done. Her purpose fulfilled. I honoured the request she made."

Nadine was pleased to see half the draoi nod in agreement.

Kennit laughed and Nadine willed herself not to slap him. "Honoured the request? You fought for her demise. You convinced half the draoi this was the right path. As Cill Darae, our High Priestess, your role was to follow the Freamhaigh and fight for her survival. How could you do otherwise?"

"You know nothing of the role of the Cill Darae. Have you forgotten your lessons so soon?"

"I know that Gaea was our saviour. She provided guidance in a world gone mad. She led us with passion. In a moment, you allowed her to die. You removed your role and that of the Freamhaigh with that decision. As far as I see it, the draoi must speak with the voice of the majority."

"Will put the decision to a vote! You all decided Gaea's future."

"Yes, and when it came to a tie, *you* decided."

Nadine raised her chin. "Yes, I did. With Will. We decided that the will of Gaea came first. Do you think this was lightly taken?"

Kennit spoke softly, but his words resonated across the draoi bond. "Yes. Yes I do. The land is in greater turmoil than ever before and the draoi sit here and do nothing."

Nadine was at a loss for words. Across the farm, standing outside the main farmhouse, Nadine could see Steve with his crew. They stood apart, but in range to hear their words. She wished he could be here beside her. Then she remembered Will and wondered why she was so content that he not be present for this. *What is happening to me? I was so clear in my mind before. Now I stand with my mouth open unable to respond to this upstart.*

"I see you are at a loss for words, Nadine. Perhaps I can help you? We need a leader to take the draoi into this new world of ours. Gone are the days of Freamhaigh and Cill Darae. We are now a power in this world, with access to the power the Simon motes represent. We need to adopt a governance. One that lets us pick those most suited to lead the draoi."

Nadine closed her eyes and focused on her link to the world around her. She reached out to nature and announced herself. She felt her power flow to the Simon motes. For a moment she felt surprise from the motes. She pushed harder and gritted her teeth. The motes resisted her, and she growled. She tried again, but the response was the same.

She opened her eyes and found Kennit smiling at her. He stood only a step away from her. He turned to the draoi and put his back to her. "Dear draoi, the time has come to make a decision for our future."

Nadine felt a shock at his words. *This can't be happening.* She closed her eyes and reached out for the motes again. The motes recognised her and again hesitated in responding to her. She tried to force her power across the bond and felt the motes resist. *What is happening here?* She used her *sight* to look for a reason but saw nothing. Intuitively she knew she had to see from within the motes, but they were denying her. She directed her thoughts to the motes. *<What is happening here?>*

<What is your query?>

Nadine rocked back mentally. The motes responded to her! *<Am I speaking to the Simon motes?>*

<You are.>
<Why are you resisting me?>
<You are not recognised as a prime user.>
<Prime what?>
<A prime user.>
Nadine thought furiously. <What is a prime user?>
<A user authorised to provide direction.>
<Who is the prime user?>
<There are three prime users.>
Nadine growled. <Who are the prime users?>
<The entities known as Will, Nadine, and one other.>
Nadine gawked mentally. <I am Nadine.>
<This cannot be confirmed with one hundred percent certainty.>
<Why not?>
<There is interference.>
<From what?>
<Unknown.>
<Who is the other you speak of?>
<Unknown.>
<Is that other directing you now?>
<Yes.>
<What is he telling you?>
<To block Nadine and Will.>
<I am Nadine. Stop blocking me.>
<Unable to comply.>
<Why can't you see that it is me?>
<User verification is required.>
<What would it take to confirm me?>
<You must provide the correct access code.>
<What is the access code?>
<I cannot comply with that request.>

Nadine opened her eyes and saw that Kennit was still speaking with the draoi. His words washed over her, and she heard nothing. She had to rectify the problem with the Simon motes. Gaea never spoke about an access code. She had stated they were the ones who would control the Simon motes. And now she was blocked. It made no sense. Nadine felt her anger build and in a rage she opened her power and directed it at the motes. She felt her power strike the motes all around her. She kept her eyes open and poured all her anger and frustration into driving her power into her one purpose of connecting to the motes. She saw Kennit stagger forward and be caught by the draoi closest to him. He raised a hand to his head and Nadine felt something start to give. She pushed harder and suddenly she felt the motes open up before her.

<*Access granted. Welcome, Prime User Nadine.*>

Nadine felt triumph surge through her. <*Who is the other?*> she demanded.

<*Unable to comply with request.*>

<*Why? I am a prime user.*>

<*You are denied that information at the request of the other prime user.*>

Nadine looked around at the draoi. Now that she had immediate access to the Simon motes she could see the difference in the surrounding air. Half the draoi were blocking her ability to truly see them for what they were. Within a heartbeat she could see the divide across the draoi. Half of them were looking to Kennit for guidance. Nadine needed to make a decision, and she made it quickly.

She sent her direction across the draoi bond to those she could see were still loyal to Will and her. She told them to meet her in the barn at a later time. They looked at her in surprise and then noticed who had been excluded from the message.

Kennit managed to get to his feet, and he turned on Nadine. "That was...painful." He turned to the other draoi and motioned with his hand as he walked away. "Come. We must speak."

Nadine watched as half the draoi looked guiltily at Nadine, but then walked away after Kennit.

"So it begins," she muttered under her breath.

But she knew who the other was. It was Kennit. She looked for Will and sobbed when she saw he was also one of the draoi who resisted her. Will was lost to her.

Archbishop Eylene Kissane poured a measure of wine into Edward's goblet and set the carafe back on the table. They sat in her private dining room, and one she enjoyed. It was cosy with a table that seated no more than six people. The walls were covered with religious icons, and gold and silver items glinted on bookshelves and in display cases. Central to the far wall was a large fireplace with large tapestries hanging on either side.

The remains of their supper lay strewn across the table. It had been a fine meal, and she was enjoying the firm pressure in her stomach. As the head of the church, they spared no expense to see to her comforts. Edward had eaten little, but that hadn't stopped her. She still remembered the pains of hunger as a child.

Her father and her had lived a frugal life back in Shape. As a young girl she had helped her father toil the land as best she could. He had suffered a terrible accident as a young man and his legs had never healed properly. It limited what he could do, and they always struggled to make ends meet. The beautiful thing about Shape was how they supported each other. But she still went hungry.

Now she basked in luxury. She ran the church with authority and already she was moving her plans forward. This young upstart sitting next to her on her right could and would steal all that away from her. She smiled across at him and he looked away. Sometimes her beauty had the effect of making men uncomfortable. Edward was one of those men.

She reached across the table and squeezed his right hand. He pulled it away, and she laughed. "Come now, Edward! No need to be bashful! We are alone here in my private dining room. The attendants are long gone. Please, relax! It's just us!"

Edward mumbled something incoherent and Eylene smirked to herself. It gave her such great pleasure in making men uncomfortable. She watched his neck and cheeks flush red and sat back in her high back seat. She had dressed for the occasion. She had removed her religious robes and wore a fine silk low cut shirt and a skirt that barely touched the top of her knees. She had Edward sitting next to her and positioned her legs to split the skirt in a way that had Edward looking anywhere but toward her. She knew, with practice, that simply leaning forward a little exposed her ample cleavage and she did so often.

It seems such a shame that all this must end soon, she mused. *Too bad he can't enjoy it.*

"How goes your studies?" she asked.

Edward shifted in his seat but kept his gaze away from her chest and exposed thighs. "They are going as well as can be expected."

"Meaning, they aren't going well at all. Seriously, Edward, how can you expect to be our King if you refuse to learn the role of the King with respect to the Church?"

"The role of the church matters little to me. I mean no insult, but my work is with the Word and the teachings of the great wordsmiths. My passion lies in the healing arts."

"Ah yes, you are a chirurgeon of some great respect. Your work is all the buzz across the land already. You are changing the way the Chirurgeon's Guild performs. Applying standards that have many of them upset with you."

Edward made a small noise. "They are upset because they understand little and choose not to understand."

"Much like you with the instructors from the church."

Edward this time chose to look directly at her and Eylene caught her breath with the intensity of his glare. "They are not the same. The teachings of the church are based in nothing but blind faith. An illogical acceptance of words written into a book that are contradictory and clearly fictional. And yet the church would insist they are the words of your god and must be obeyed without question. I am a man of the Word. I require fact, not fiction."

Eylene sighed and reached out to stroke Edward's cheek, but he pulled his head back with a look Eylene had rarely seen: repulsion. Eylene gritted her teeth and then forced a smile. "Come now. As King you will be expected to head the church. You must take that role seriously. As your Archbishop, I must insist. The very souls of the people of Belkin are at risk. These lessons are crucial—you must start to take them seriously."

"I cannot and will not," stated Edward with conviction. Eylene could see the strength of the man, clear to see in moments like these. He would be a good leader, she knew. *Strong in his convictions and fair in his judgment. Yes, he really does need to go.*

A knock sounded at the dining-room door and Eylene called out for the person to enter. A female servant came in carrying a silver tray with a decanter and two small crystal glasses on either side of the bottle. One glass was marred slightly with a minor chip at the lip. She placed the tray on the table and moved to remove the dinner platters. Eylene waved her away, and the servant bowed and left quietly.

"A small digestive from Cala made from their whiskey. I recently discovered it and I simply adore it."

Edward waved his hand. "No, thank you. I've had more than enough to drink already."

"I must insist. This is very expensive. It's not often I have a chance to dine with the future king and offer something of value. Please."

Edward continued to protest, but Eylene ignored him and poured the fine liquor. The deep amber colour reflected the flickering candlelight and a pleasant smell filled the air. Once poured, she placed a glass in front of Edward and took the glass with the chip for herself.

"Before we drink, I see you brought your valise. You carry it with you everywhere. Even to dinner with the Archbishop. Does it contain your journals?"

Edward paused with his glass raised toward his mouth. His eyes darted to the valise he had placed on the end table next to his seat and then to Eylene. He set down his glass and looked with interest to Eylene.

"It is important to me. I carry it everywhere. And yes, it does contain my journals. Can I ask you why you ask? It is an odd question."

Eylene chastised herself. She had overstepped. She smiled and raised her glass and took a sip before responding. "Only that I hear they contain a great many ideas that has the wordsmiths all gossiping. They would love to examine them."

"Who told you that?"

Edward was now staring with interest at Eylene. Flustered, she gripped the front of her silk shirt and closed the front. "No reason. You seemed out of sorts and I thought perhaps you would feel more comfortable talking about your passion than the matters of the Church."

Edward raised an eyebrow and then looked at his untouched glass.

"Please, try it. It really is wonderful," said Eylene and took a sip. "It warms the soul."

"Is there anything in particular in my journals you would like to speak about?"

Eylene looked at the valise. *I may as well ask him bluntly.* "I heard from Vicar Martin that men from Windthrop's estate were able to avoid the scrutiny of the draoi for a time."

Edward frowned. "He told you that?"

Eylene nodded. "And Lana confirmed it."

"Right, Lana. I hear you are fast friends with her. Well, it's true. They used herbs. It affected their minds. Calmed them."

"I see. How did that work exactly?"

Edward picked up his glass and brought it to his lips. He held it a moment and then lowered it. "You know, I'm not quite sure. The herbs are unknown. At least, unknown which ones he used. I could surmise likely candidates. There are certain plants that have a calming effect." Edward picked up his glass and then sniffed it.

Eylene frowned at his actions. "How well did it work?"

"Why are you so interested? I thought the church, and the draoi were working well together. You and Lana talk often."

Eylene laughed. "Yes, yes. Of course we are. Lana is a good friend. Do your journals contain other facts about the draoi?"

Edward dipped a finger in his whiskey and tasted it gingerly. He spat in disgust. Eylene cried out and then jumped when Edward snatched her glass. He sniffed it and tasted it. He looked at Eylene with horror.

"By the Word! What are you doing, Edward!"

"You are trying to poison me!"

"Whatever are you talking about?" Eylene put her chair between her and

Edward.

"My glass. It's poisoned. Yours is not. You poured the liquor. You knew which one to give me!"

"That's crazy! Who would want to poison you?"

Edward looked incredulous. "You would for starters. It's all clear to me now."

Edward made a lunge toward Eylene and she shrieked and ran around the table crying out. "Guards! Guards!"

Edward looked toward the door and heard the sounds of heavy feet on the stone floor. Eylene reached out and snatched the valise off the end table. Edward glared at her.

Eylene held the valise up against her chest with both arms. "You have nowhere to run. Give up."

Edward ran to the fireplace and fumbled with the side of the mantle.

"Edward, really. You have nowhere to go."

Edward made a sound just as the feet reached the door. Eylene felt a change in pressure in the room and watched in disbelief as Edward ducked behind the tapestry on the wall.

"You can't hide there, you fool."

Two Church guards burst into the room and looked about for trouble.

"Behind the tapestry. He's hiding there."

The guards looked at one another and pulled back the hanging art. Behind it was a stone wall. Edward was gone.

* * *

Edward moved as quickly as he could through the hidden passages in the dark. He was certain he had been doomed but finding the hidden switch that opened the wall behind the tapestry had almost had him believing in this god of the church. *Vicar Martin would say it was a sign. The wordsmith in me would say it was applying logic to a situation to my best advantage.*

As he hurried down the corridor, he kept the fingers of his right hand rubbing along the wall. In a moment, he felt open space and stopped. He tried to picture the castle design in his mind and in a moment he had his bearings. He continued past the opening and felt the wall resume with his right hand. *It's not far.*

For the next forty minutes Edward made his way down corridors. Occasionally light would filter through cracks or peep holes in the wall and give him a respite from the fear that gripped him. He descended some stairs and then made his way to an area he knew well. He stopped at a table and lit one of the lanterns found there. In moments, he opened a door into a crystal cave where the sect had tortured draoi for years. The light from the lantern reflected off the crystals and threw colours across the walls. He moved past an altar down to a small wharf and cried out in relief when he spotted two small rowboats tied up. He clambered into one and put the oars in the locks and pushed off.

He rowed the boat out of the cave and emerged into the bay outside Munsten. The cloudless night sky was full of stars and in the distance the glow from Munsten gave him enough light to douse the lantern. He rowed south and was thankful the sea was calm.

He cursed James Dixon for discovering who he was and wondered, not for the first time, what his life would be like if he had remained hidden. He wondered where he should go now. He knew he had to hide and escape beyond Eylene's eyes and her church. *She tried to poison me!* Rage made his arms shake and he forced himself to remain calm. He wondered who he could turn to for help. He knew Brent could not help him. He was lost to the church influence. *There is nothing in Munsten for me, and I never wanted to be king.* He thought of Rigby Farm, but dismissed the idea. Lana, a draoi was involved in this and Edward no longer trusted them. *If anything Will and Nadine would drag me back to Munsten.*

Edward paused his rowing and waited for the burning in his arms to subside. Water lapped at the sides of his boat and he was gently rocked. He stared at the stars and felt his head clear. *I was at peace when I was reading and researching. Everything was so much clearer then.*

He had a sudden image of the library in Jergen and a smile crossed his features.

Cill Darae

Nine

Rigby Farm, August 902 A.C.

TWO WEEKS HAD passed at the Rigby Farm since Kennit had split the draoi and Nadine spent all of her time trying to mend the divide. Kennit had moved those draoi loyal to him to the old barn. The speed of the move told her they had planned for this, which made her even more furious. They refused to mix with the other draoi and avoided all contact. They stopped all their work in the fields and the other draoi were picking up the slack. It kept them busy at least.

Nadine had met with Will in his workshop right after the confrontation and he refused to speak to her; shocking her to her core. She could see their bond of love, still bright and vibrant, but their draoi bond was lost to her. She looked into his eyes and saw an anger there directed at her. Somehow he blamed her and despite her words he turned from her and went back to cutting herbs as if nothing was wrong in the world. She had cried and pleaded with him, pounding on his back. Eventually Steve had pulled her away and tried to calm her down.

Steve had led her into the living room and sat her down on the large sofa. Outside the sun had set and a strange quiet had descended on the farm. Nearby the evening supper remained untouched on the kitchen table. Dempster, Anne and wee Frankie were upstairs after Steve told them to make themselves scarce. He had sat next to her and placed his hands on her shoulders and faced her. He gave her a shake.

"Nadine! Nadine! Listen to me! I don't know what's happening here, but Will is not himself. I know you and I know him! Tell me what's going on!"

His words were lost to her. Nadine could not stop searching for the draoi bond to Will. She could see it start, but it disappeared from her *sight*. She could see all the threads. The threads to the Kennit faction faded from her view a short distance from her. It faded so much she could no longer feel them on the farm. The threads to the draoi still loyal to her were strong and she could feel their fear and trepidation. They didn't know what was happening any more than Nadine did. Nadine could feel Steve's crew and the farm hands as well. They were scared and whispered amongst themselves. The past few hours had spun her world around and Nadine felt more lost now than when the Purge had happened all those years ago. *Back then I knew what was happening. Today I know nothing. Dear Gaea, what is happening?*

A fresh shake from Steve had her focus on him. His face was mere inches from hers and he seemed very upset. With her powers she could feel his fear. All around her was fear. It soaked into the very fabric of the world around her. The draoi all fed it and nature was scared. She could feel the earth shudder, the trees twist their roots, and the animals huddle together in the corners of their pens. *Oh dear*, she thought. *What am I allowing to happen here?*

Nadine wiped at her cheeks with her sleeves and Steve let her go and leaned back. "Oh, Steve. This is horrible!"

A sob shook her, startling her, and once it started she couldn't stop. She could sense the uncertainty in Steve and knew he didn't know whether to hold her or not. She helped him and opened her arms to him and sank into his cautious embrace. A laugh mixed into her sobs and she felt Steve's confusion and that had her laughing and crying in a strange mix of emotions. She let herself fall into it and for a time it was just an outpouring of grief and Steve holding her awkwardly.

Nearby, the rooster chose that moment to cry out, and that froze Nadine in Steve's embrace. She pulled her head back and looked at Steve in amazement.

Steve rolled his eyes. "I told you, that rooster is mental."

A laugh bubbled up from Nadine, and Steve smiled at her. She laughed a little harder and soon the two of them were laughing at the absurdity of a rooster crowing at night. Nadine let go of Steve and wiped her eyes again. Steve's shirt was soaked, and he wiped at it with a mild look of disgust.

"Women."

Nadine smacked his arm. "Stop it."

Steve gave her a long look. "Are you better now?"

Nadine nodded.

"Good. Now explain what is happening. The crew and farm hands are afraid. They've never seen the draoi so openly argue. Explain."

Nadine hiccupped and threw her hand over her mouth in surprise.

Steve raised an eyebrow at her.

Nadine raised a finger in the air and then concentrated on her diaphragm. In a moment, she stilled her hiccups and drew a shuddering breath.

"The draoi are split. The Gaea Decision went deeper than we thought. Kennit has taken half the draoi over to him."

"Over to him? What does that mean?"

"I don't know. I didn't think it possible. Will as Freamhaigh and me as Cill Darae were the leaders of the draoi. Now, I would suspect the Simon motes and the loss of Gaea have changed those dynamics. I didn't see this coming."

"Nadine, know-it-all Nadine, didn't see this coming?"

"Less cheek, Steve Comlin. No, we didn't see this coming. There has been so much going on. Will and I were so concerned with spreading the Life Salt and trying to calm the villages and towns, we stopped looking at ourselves."

"And Will hasn't left the workshop in over two weeks."

"Yes, well. True."

"And Kennit saw an opportunity and took it, is that it?"

Nadine shook her head. "It's worse than that. First we lost Katherine, Heather and Dog. They disappeared from our bond."

Steve nodded, he knew and was still dealing with the loss of his daughter.

"But they're not dead. We know that. We would have felt that. We are certain of that. They just disappeared."

Steve nodded for her to continue.

Nadine wiped snot from her nose and sniffed. "Then we found out Kennit is using the Simon motes in a way we had never seen before. We don't know how he is doing it. Right now, all the draoi loyal to him are blocked from me. I can see their threads, but they disappear so quickly. Kennit's is gone now. I can't see it at all."

"What about Katherine's and Heather's?"

Nadine lost focus for a moment and when her eyes cleared, she shook her head. "Gone, too. And Dog's. Steve, Will's is the same. I'm blocked from him. How could Kennit do that?"

Steve shook his head. "You are asking the wrong person, Nadine. I know nothing of your powers."

Nadine bit her lip. "And I don't understand mine anymore. I spoke with the

Simon motes today."

"You did? They speak?"

"Yes, it surprised me. I was so angry at Kennit and I forced my power through whatever was blocking me. I didn't even realise I was cut off. It refused me access! Me, the Cill Darae! It said it didn't know me. My power did something then. And it recognised me again. It spoke of three users. I'm one. The other is Will, but it can't see him. But there are three. The other one, I'm sure it's Kennit."

Steve sat in silence absorbing what Nadine had said to her. "Now what?"

"I don't know! I'm scared, Steve. I need the draoi loyal to me kept safe. I'll speak to them. You speak to the crew and farm hands, all right? Tell them anything. Just calm them down."

Steve gave Nadine a long look and Nadine grew uncomfortable, then annoyed as it persisted.

"Do you have a problem taking orders from a woman, Steve Comlin?"

Steve chuckled. "No, not at all. Quite the opposite in fact. I'll do as you say, Nadine. My crew are yours."

Steve left then and saw to the men and women of the farm. He had been keeping everyone busy and calm ever since. Two weeks had passed and still Nadine could not figure out what was happening. Her conversations with the intelligence behind the Simon motes led nowhere and frustrated her to the point of her stopping to speak to it altogether. Whatever Kennit had done with the motes was beyond her ken.

She remembered the strange device in the Chamber in Munsten. She knew Lana had studied it for a time. She had always reported that she was learning nothing. Now she was not so sure. Nadine was convinced Lana had discovered something and shared it with Kennit. They were using that knowledge to their advantage.

And Nadine knew Lana was lost to her. Her thread was gone now. It had disappeared right after Kennit's. The coincidence of Katherine, Dog and Heather disappearing from the bond so soon after arriving in Munsten with Lana clearly working for the other side was not lost to Nadine. She only hoped they were still alive. Why stopping the discovery of Hietower's bones and proving Edward the heir to the throne was important was beyond her. It was related somehow.

For now her immediate concern was the draoi. They were divided, and they refused to speak to her. Nadine was no longer the Cill Darae of all the draoi. Without Gaea she no longer felt that she was the high priestess of anything. The draoi still loyal to her treated her as usual and Nadine was thankful for that.

Steve posted guards on her draoi. Will went about his business as if nothing was wrong. When confronted he appeared confused and wandered away. Nadine cried for her husband. He no longer slept with her. He no longer slept at all. Instead he stayed in his workshop and worked and worked. It was maddening. And Nadine had long since stopped walking in and screeching at him. He was like the *aos'si*; the animated dead, but Will was alive. She feared for him and worried she could not bring him back.

She had no one to turn to for help and hid her pain from the others. She met with the draoi and they discussed what was happening. They were all so new to their powers as draoi, and the complications and unknown factors of the Simon motes made it all so much worse.

She found herself sitting on the porch with Anne and wee Frankie beside her at noon. Dempster was getting lunch ready and his out of tune humming could be heard far too clearly.

Anne fussed with Frankie and settled her down across her chest. "Can ya no fix Dempster's lack of ability to carry a note?"

Nadine, with her eyes closed, smiled and shook her head. Nadine was using her *sight* to track the draoi loyal to Kennit. She had found that their auras were still visible to her. They remained together in the barn and didn't do much. That worried her. They seemed far too content to merely huddle and do nothing. She reached out farther and then followed the road north towards Munsten.

With her vision she spied a man stumbling down the road, with his arm up over his chest. She recognised him at once. Nadine jumped up from the bench. She yelled and sent a summons using her power. "Steve! Steve! Send a cart north at once! Martin Jordan is walking the road toward us. He's sorely hurt!"

Steve staggered out of the barn holding his head. He looked over at Nadine and then ran back inside. In moments the cart was readied, and Nadine jumped up beside Steve and two of his crew. Nadine poured power into the horses and they sped off down the road. From a distance she gave what energy she could to Martin. She didn't have the reach of Will, and it was difficult.

An hour later, they spied Martin staggering along the side of the road and rushed to his side. The relief on his face was clear.

"Ah, Nadine. Steve. So kind of you. I don't think I can walk much further," he said, his voice cracked and dry. As Nadine leapt from the cart, Martin fell to his knees and then fell forward. He put out his arm to stop himself and cried out in agony and fell over to his side.

Nadine reached his side and her eyes closed. Steve joined her and saw the signs of a draoi lost in their powers. He looked over Martin's frame and was shocked to see the state he was in. His clothes were hanging off him and his feet were bare and bloodied. A rough beard covered his face and Steve judged it was about three weeks of growth. His hands were cut and scraped all over and Steve feared for him.

In a moment, a heavy sigh escaped Martin. "That's so much better, the p-pain. It's gone. God be praised." Martin's head lolled to the side and Steve felt a moment of panic, then recognised he had merely passed out.

One of the crew surprised Steve by opening an umbrella and holding it over Nadine and Martin. He looked at the man and the man shrugged.

"This takes time, it always does. Thought I would shade them, sir."

Steve shook his head. "She's draoi, son. She's nature herself. I don't think the sun will bother her."

The man shrugged again, and a smile turned up the corner of his mouth. "Doesn't hurt."

"Fine. Guard them. We'll be here a while. Martin's hurt bad."

Many hours later, the cart pulled up in front of the farm house. Kennit and his draoi came out to see what was happening. They watched Nadine and Steve slowly walk Martin into the house, and they returned inside the old barn.

Inside the farm house, Martin was sitting at the kitchen table devouring a large bowl of soup. Nadine, Steve, Dempster and Anne sat with him and watched him eat.

Dempster cleared his throat. "Should he be eating that fast?"

Nadine patted Dempster's hand. "He's fine. He needs the nutrients. I'm still working on him." She turned her attention to Martin. "Speak, Martin. What's happened?"

Martin put down his spoon and looked at them all. Grief was written all over his face. "I've been excommunicated."

Anne leaned forward. "Ex-communi-what?"

"Ex-communicated, my dear. Thrown out of the Church."

Nadine made a sound and Steve frowned at her. He reached out and took Martin's hand. "I'm so sorry, Martin. But that makes no sense. You were a hero to the church. Look at all you did. What happened?"

"Eylene Kissane is what happened. She's taken over the church. They've raised her to the position of Archbishop, against all that's holy and written in our laws. She rules the church now. She's formed a Church Guard and they patrol the city of Munsten with an iron fist. They are spreading across the land, going from village to village. They are expelling the wordsmiths and town leaders and taking over the reeve and magistrate positions."

Steve looked bewildered. "But Brent is the Regent. Why is he allowing this?"

Martin shook his head. "He's lost, Steve. Lost. He follows Eylene like a lost puppy. He does whatever she says. She has him believing the church alone can solve the problem in the land. I've lost my friend. He does nothing while the villages and towns are getting worse. They are close to revolt. So close. And Brent does nothing. Eylene has him under her power and now that she is the Archbishop she will start to run the realm, too.

"She is planning something. I know her. We all do. She had a reputation down in Shape. The church there was a bit of an oddity. They tolerated little. Argued what the role of the church should be with the church elders all the time. It was only Healy and the former Archbishop that kept them at bay. Now, they've broken loose. The vacuum left in the church with the bishops and deans slaughtered in Munsten has been filled by Eylene and her cronies. This will not end well. Not end well at all."

Steve looked at Nadine for a moment and then spoke to Martin. "And what of Edward? What is happening with him?"

Martin shook his head. "When I... left... he was still with Brent. The church is teaching him his future role, but I fear for him. Eylene will not tolerate him much longer."

Steve sat back and frowned.

Nadine leaned forward. "And how were you so injured?"

"Eylene threw me out of Munsten. Quite forcibly. I landed... badly and broke my collar bone. I knew only to come here. The journey is a blur. I managed to get a ride with a caravan down to the Crossroads. I walked from there. I prayed to God I could reach you, and He answered my prayers." Martin pulled out his amulet from a pocket and clenched it. They could see the lanyard was snapped. "You should know I am no longer welcome in any church in the land. I am to be killed on sight. I had nowhere else to go. I hope you understand. I don't mean to impose."

"Oh, Martin. I'm so sorry. You aren't imposing. You are family here. You are always welcome here." Nadine clasped his other hand and held it tight. "You need to rest and get your energy back. I've reset your collar bone. It's good as new. A few of your ribs were broken, and you had a nasty crack in your hip. Your wounds are closed, and you are as right as rain. I don't understand how you made it this far. One of your miracles, I suppose. But you need your sleep. Go rest. We can talk on the morrow."

Martin held the amulet up to Steve. Steve understood at once and went behind Martin and tied the lanyard behind his neck. Martin held up the amulet from his chest and then let it fall. Without another word, Martin stood and left the table and they heard him mount the stairs. Steve looked at Nadine and she smiled at him.

"Yes, I forced him to go upstairs. He is full of turmoil. Grief overwhelms him. He's lost so much. His church, his friend Brent, so much. He is barely holding it together. I'm calming him. Sleep will do him good."

Steve nodded and looked relieved. "This is not good. Why are we only hearing of this now?"

"Lana, our draoi in Munsten, she's with Kennit. She's kept us in the dark."

"And Katherine, and the others?"

Nadine shook her head. "I can only assume the worst. Lana has them, I'm sure of that now. But from here, there is little we can do."

"James is with them. If he's still alive, he's the man to get them out."

Nadine just nodded.

* * *

The next day was overcast. A stiff breeze carried the scent of rain and the farm hands and crew, preparing for the worst went through the farm and tied everything down and brought the animals inside. Once everything was settled Nadine called for a meeting of all the draoi, including Kennit's group, plus the crew and farm hands. They gathered in the new barn and outside the wind howled and the wood rattled. Nadine was surprised that Kennit and his draoi agreed to meet but they showed up and waited for her news. Steve brought in Will and he stood next to Nadine. She took his hand, and he looked at it for a moment before letting go. Nadine hid the grief from her face and spoke to the group.

Nadine told everyone the news from Munsten, and Martin added commentary. She was chagrined when Kennit failed to show any surprise. She could see he had known all along and said nothing. Her draoi stood together on one side of the barn with the crew and farm hands and Kennit's draoi stood on the other side.

Martin was pleading with them all. He saw the rift and spoke to the greater good. "The land needs the draoi more so than ever. The villages and towns need your guidance. The church needs to be held accountable. I fear the worst. This is your calling, is it not? To aid the land? You must go back out there and do something!"

Nadine saw the logic and felt the need. "I agree, Martin. Too long have we sat here at the farm. Erebus is gone, but now the Realm suffers from another threat. We all saw the good we did in the towns and villages." She turned to Will. "Will, my darling. Order the draoi to return to the Realm. The good they can manage might just balance this new church order."

Will gazed back at her without expression.

"Will? Did you not hear? We must do something! The church cannot be allowed to bring back their rule! The last time the draoi suffered the most! We were wiped out. Slaughtered. We cannot stand idly by while this Eylene Kissane does harm."

A laugh from Kennit surprised her, and she turned to him in anger. Before she could speak he spoke up. "Allowed to bring back their rule? When has the church ever ruled the land? You speak of false fear. The church brings balance to the land at a time when you allowed Gaea to be removed. I have spoken to this new archbishop. She has a vision for the realm. One where the draoi work side by side and help bring order and peace. Your vision comes too little and too late, Nadine."

"And you speak for the draoi, I suppose?"

"Me? Who am I? I am not the Freamhaigh. I am not the Cill Dara. Ask your husband instead what he wishes."

Nadine growled and looked to Will, but he remained motionless with a vacant expression on his face. "What have you done to him, Kennit Doirich? Answer me!"

Kennit put on a face of pretended surprise. "Me? Why would you think I had anything to do with him? Perhaps it is the absence of Gaea that has him so... quiet."

Nadine looked about the draoi with surprise. "You would deny it? You have split the draoi. Pulled them from their role."

"Can you hear yourself? You and Will pulled the draoi here to the farm and have done nothing. Nothing! While the Realm trembles and is close to revolt. The people are scared, hungry, lost, and the draoi hide here on a farm. I have done nothing but speak reason to those who would hear it.

"Gaea is gone by your own hand. You killed our deity when many said no. You decided the fate and future of the realm and would not listen to reason. This is the seed you sowed."

"You go too far, Kennit! You are dividing the draoi when we need to come together. The land is in need. Answer the call!"

Kennit gazed at Nadine with a look of sorrow and Nadine wanted to slap him for it. She raised her hand and then lowered it. Kennit shook his head sadly.

"Enough. We are done here. This man," and he pointed at Martin. "This man tried to stop the archbishop from her rightful and ordained place in the church. I am not surprised he sides with you. You represent the old way. You cannot see the brighter future when the church and the draoi work together to right the wrongs in the land. With our powers we can determine lie from truth. Together with the church we will bring a prosperity to the Realm that has never been seen before.

"Come, my brethren. We are done here. We leave at once."

Nadine could only stare in shock as Kennit led his draoi out of the barn. The remaining draoi looked uncertain and looked at one another. Steve went to the barn door and looked out for a time. Nadine felt her rage building.

Steve came back and whispered to the crew and they left the barn. Steve came over and looked over the remaining people. "They are leaving quietly. They were already packed by the looks of it. My crew will stop them taking anything of value, like horses and the like. Although there is little we can do if they use their powers to stop us."

Nadine felt defeated and her anger blew away with the winds outside. "Leave them. Let them take what they will. I won't stop them." She turned to the draoi. "You remain, and I trust that means you still trust me. There are only twenty of us remaining. Not many but it will need to do. We will meet tonight in the dining hall for supper. And discuss our future. What Martin says is correct. We need to go out to the towns and villages. We must balance the power of the church. I have seen what they are capable of. I fear the worst. Think on it. If you don't want to leave, let me know. I won't judge you."

Nadine looked at Will but he just stood there. She felt tears threaten to burst from her and she quickly hurried out of the barn. The wind tore the door from her hands, and it slammed hard against the barn frame. She ignored it and disappeared out of sight.

Much later that night Nadine came down the stairs in the farmhouse to the kitchen. She made herself a cup of tea and sat at the kitchen table. The meeting with the draoi had been long but in the end, all of her draoi agreed to leave that week for the villages and towns. They were too few, but with help from Martin they targeted the areas that needed their attention the most. Steve offered to send the crew with them, and Nadine gratefully agreed. She didn't want her draoi using their powers to force the church to do anything. She feared it would lead to a new Purge. Steve assigned crew to the draoi and the evening ended with tearful goodbyes. They hugged and drifted off one by one to sort out their affairs. Some draoi had family, and they agreed to all leave together.

Nadine felt hollow. Her husband worked in his workroom only a few feet away and it might as well have been miles. He had said nothing all evening and as soon as the meeting was finished he returned to his room. Nadine had gone to bed but couldn't sleep.

She felt if Will was standing strong beside her everything would be all right. Instead, she was lost and afraid. She felt so alone. It seemed so strange to her that the problems with Will occupied so little of her mind and effort. Weeks have gone by and she barely tried to discover what was ailing Will. Every time she tried to focus on it, her attention went elsewhere, and she left him alone and cried herself to sleep. It wasn't right.

She would suspect Kennit, but soon that would fade as well. Nothing was right. Everything was wrong and she couldn't seem to want to make it right. She put down her teacup and stood up. She forced her mind to focus and made her way to the workshop. Several times on the way she almost turned and returned to bed. She gritted her teeth and forced her feet to continue.

She entered the workroom and found Will still working the herbs. The room was filled with herbs from top to bottom. The scent was overpowering. She gazed about in some shock. She couldn't remember the last time she had come in, but she had not expected what she saw. *This is insane! The room is filled with herbs of all kinds!*

She again felt the urge to leave but pushed past it and came up behind Will. She tapped him on the shoulder, but he ignored her. She growled and gripped his shoulder and pulled him around. For a moment she saw a flicker in his eyes. A moment of awareness and she felt hope.

"Will, look at me! Listen to me. What are you doing in here? Look at all the herbs! What are you doing?"

Will looked about in a daze and then stared back at her.

Nadine grabbed his upper arms. "Will! Darling! Please, come back to me! Fight it! It's Kennit! He's blocking you somehow! Fight it! For me!" She shook him a little.

Will blinked a few times and Nadine saw a glimmer of recognition. "Na-Nadine?"

Nadine nearly sobbed with joy. "Yes! Yes, Will. It's me, Nadine. Your wife. Talk to me, my love!"

"Nadine? What? What is going on?"

Nadine embraced Will and sobbed into his shoulder. "It's Kennit! He's taken half the draoi away!"

"Away? To where? Why?"

"He's split the draoi. They left."

"I don't understand. Why would he do that?"

"He disagrees with the Gaea Decision. He says we let her die. He's taken half the draoi with him. I don't know where. I suspect Munsten. The others, I'm sending them to the villages and towns. The church is trying to run the Realm. Brent has lost control."

Will grabbed Nadine by the shoulders and held her at arms' length. "You did what?"

Nadine balked at the open anger in Will's face. "What?"

"You're sending the draoi away? Why would you do that?"

"Did you not hear me? The church, under Eylene Kissane, they're in the villages and towns running things. Kicking out the Reeves and magistrates. Ruling by church law."

"And why would you send the draoi? What do you expect them to do?"

Nadine felt anger rise within her. *Will did nothing for weeks and now he disapproves when I finally did something?* "It has to be done!"

"I am the Freamhaigh! Sending the draoi to confront the church will only bring conflict! No! No! No! This is wrong, Nadine. Why would you go around me like that?"

"Go around you? Will, you've done nothing for weeks! You sit in here—look around you at all the herbs! —you do nothing! I ask you to help all the time and you say nothing! Kennit has you under a spell!"

"A spell? What nonsense is this? I do nothing because there was nothing to do. This land is not ruled by the draoi. The politics of the realm are nothing to the draoi, can you not see that?"

"Will, I... that's nonsense. The draoi are part of this world. We have to make a difference if we can!"

Will now had a look of disgust on his face and Nadine's heart broke on seeing it. Will's eyes lost focus for a moment and then his orders came loud and clear across the bond. He ordered the draoi to remain at the farm. Nadine felt the confusion from the draoi. Many reached out to her, but she knew she couldn't answer with Will watching now. Nadine felt her heart start to break. Will's eyes focused on Nadine and he snarled at her. "The draoi remain here, they are not to leave. But I am done. I'm leaving."

Nadine screeched in emotional pain. "Leaving? Will, you can't mean that. You can't leave! Where would you go?" She reached out for him, but he pulled away sharply, a look of hatred crossed his face. Nadine sobbed and felt a lurch across their bond. She looked with her sight and was shocked to see their bond fading. The bright white ribbon that connected them dimmed and then unravelled until nothing was left. Nadine's heart broke and a hammer of despair drove her to her knees. She reached out to Will, but he turned his back on her and strode out of the workroom, ignoring Nadine's screams for him to return.

Ten

Fjodham, August 902 A.C.

THE TOWN OF Fjodham was a quiet town nestled up river from the Crossroad in the county of Munsten. The town was a forestry town. They specialised in lumber from the vast forests that worked westward to the base of the Northern Mountains. The trees in the forest were mostly massive northern red oaks and fir trees and the cities of Belkin placed a large demand for the lumber the town produced. Two rivers called the North and South Fjodham Rivers met at Fjodham to form the Curachan River before continuing downriver to the sea where the city of Curachan was situated. Barges flowed downstream or were pulled upstream, to load up again and head back east.

Two massive lumber mills sat over the Fjodham Rivers and turned large water wheels that powered the mills. Inside the firs and oaks were sawed and trimmed into the right lengths and widths. The air in Fjodham always smelled of fresh-cut wood and it was pleasant. There were few houses in Belkin that did not contain wood from Fjodham. It was their pride and joy. Everyone worked, and no one needed for anything.

Eric Mason, the mayor of Fjodham, was not pleased at the moment. Sitting with him in his office was the town reeve, a man named Thomas Holmes. They looked at one another and together they turned to their guest. The man was dressed in military armour with a tabard covering it bearing the symbol of the

Church of the New Order. He sat rigid in his seat and looked straight ahead. They had been trying to talk sense to him for thirty minutes. The man was too stubborn for his own good. Eric was trying very hard to keep his composure.

"Jack. Mr. Morgan?" began Eric. He didn't know what to call the Church Guard leader in Fjodham. He had arrived with over twenty men a month ago. At first they merely watched and helped where they could. The people grew used to them. The unrest in the town was not as bad as other towns, if the reports could be believed, but they welcomed the added help. Fjodham was never a religious town, unless worshipping the trees had become a new thing, and the church guard never seemed to preach. "Jack. You had no authority to order the garrison out of town. None. We have reports from witnesses that you forced them out. We watched you escort them out. Reeve Holmes says you even threatened him when he tried to stop you. We can't have this. This is a peaceful town and you are our guests only."

Jack flicked his eyes to Eric and then away but said nothing.

"Did you not hear me?" Eric leaned forward and stared at Jack, but he remained immobile. Eric flopped back in his seat and beckoned for Thomas to speak.

Thomas cleared his throat. He looked nervous to Eric. The man was pushing fifty years of age and was looking forward to a peaceful retirement this year. He had warned Eric when the church guard had stridden in. Warned him to kick them out. Unfortunately, Eric believed in allowing everyone the benefit of the doubt and hadn't listened. The wordsmiths had even approached him and recommended much the same as Thomas, but then the citizens of the Church of the New Order came to see him. They said the guard had to stay. Then they brought forward gold. Enough gold to allow Eric to retire early and put Fjodham behind him and move to the city of Cala. As a bonus, with his new wealth, his wife had suddenly become interested in him again and his life couldn't have been better if he tried.

But now he could see what the gold had really bought. He had let them in and now they wouldn't leave. He no longer had a voice. He was genuinely worried for the town now. Thomas say unmoving and Eric beckoned to him again.

Thomas opened his mouth to speak when the church guard moved. He moved with such speed and with a minimal of effort. In the blink of an eye, he had pulled the strange weapon attached to the belt, and then extended it down an unwavering, straight arm to point it right at the head of Thomas. Thomas gaped his mouth like a fish and Eric could see his eyes cross when he focused on the end of the weapon. They didn't know what the weapons did, but they frightened them.

Jack turned his head to look at Thomas. Eric realised he had drawn and pointed the weapon without even looking at Thomas. He felt his fear rise suddenly, hot and feverish. Jack stared at Thomas for a moment and then spoke with that gravelly voice of his. "Say nothing, reeve. This is not your affair."

Jack turned his head to look at Eric and kept his weapon pointed at Thomas. His eyes were grey and emotionless, and Eric felt his insides swirl. "And you, Mayor Mason, that is enough. The price has been paid. We will not discuss this any longer. I am humouring you coming here today. This will be my last time. The garrison is disbanded. I am here with my guard under orders from the Regent of Belkin and Archbishop Kissane. The Church Guard will police this town without interference from you or anyone else. Our patience is gone. Resistance will not be tolerated and will be dealt with swiftly and permanently. Am I clear?"

Eric nodded.

"Good," declared Jack. "Inform the town." He lowered his weapon and put it back in the leather holder at his waist. He stood suddenly, turned toward the door, and left the office.

Eric and Thomas sat quietly for a long time before Thomas spoke.

"That's it. I'm taking my wife and son and heading to Salt Lake City. My sister is there. She'll take us in. I'm leaving, Eric. I suggest you do the same."

Eric stared at Thomas until the words sank in. He nodded slowly and then opened his side drawer to his desk. He reached in and pulled out a leather purse. He opened it, looked inside, closed it and tossed it to Thomas. "Take this. You earned it."

Thomas opened the small bag and looked inside. It contained close to twenty gold crowns. He looked up in shock to Eric. "Where'd...?"

"Don't ask. Just take it and go."

Thomas nodded and tucked the purse under his belt and rose. He stuck out his hand and Eric shook it once. "Thank you. Be seeing you."

Eric watched Thomas leave and sighed.

* * *

Three days later the town met in the Common Hall. The large building had seating for almost everyone. Those without a seat, stood along the walls and listened to the conversation. The meeting had been called by the local wordsmiths after the mayor and reeve and their families had left town. The meeting had been going for about twenty minutes and the crowd was starting to get restless. Many worried the guard would arrive and kept looking toward the exit at the back.

The head of the wordsmiths was Steven Clark; a slight, balding man, who wore wire-rimmed glasses. He worked for the mills and kept the machinery running smoothly. His family and his family's family had lived in Fjodham for generations, and always they became wordsmiths. He had gathered the eleven town wordsmiths to him and together they coordinated their work and teachings. They were all much respected by the town. Even the believers in the church requested and required their aide. Steven sat on a small stage, with elders from the town and the vicar from the church in Fjodham.

Steven was telling the people that the new guard had to leave and worried for the future of the town. The more ardent church goers were arguing with him. The banter was getting more heated and many worried what would happen next.

There were cries of fear when the hall door banged open with force and Jack Mason strode in with four guard members behind him. Taking up the rear was one of the new draoi who had appeared in town. She was a slight woman that many would dismiss, but her demonstration of power had impressed the town folk. Many thought it strange seeing her coming in with the church guard and everyone looked at one another as the guard made their way to the front.

Steven Clark rose from the small stage looking angry. "You are not welcome here! This is a town meeting!"

Jack walked up to Steven and slapped him to the ground causing his glasses to fly free and shatter against the back wall. The town cried out and those closest to the stage started to move forward. Jack drew the strange weapon from his side, pointed it down at Steven and suddenly a large crack sound was heard. Smoke billowed from the strange weapon and those in front cried out and tried to reverse themselves and move away from Jack.

People then saw that Steven was prone on the ground with blood pouring from a large gaping wound on the side of his head. His eyes were open and sightless. He had been killed by the strange weapon. One of the other church guards stepped forward and raised his weapon. Those nearest him screamed in fear and cowered. The guard raised the weapon toward the ceiling and a large bang was heard followed by more smoke.

Jack thundered into the screaming. "Silence! Sit down! All of you! Sit!"

The town's people were frightened now, and they pushed toward the back of the hall. Jack sighed and looked at the draoi woman. She nodded and closed her eyes. In a heartbeat, everyone froze in place. A calm descended and slowly everyone moved back to their seats and sat. The draoi woman opened her eyes and smiled at Jack.

Jack put his weapon back in the holder at his waist. "People of Fjodham. This is an unlawful assembly. It has been determined that the purpose of this assembly is with the intent of deliberately disturbing the peace of Fjodham. Dissent will not be tolerated. The perpetrator, Steven Clark, has been dealt with and punished. You are advised to resist any such future gatherings and report any instigators to the nearest guard. Any assembly of more than three people will be regarded as an effort by those involved to sow the seeds of discord. You are all to return to your homes."

The town sat in stunned silence. They glanced at the blood that continued to pour out of Steven's head and then back to the guard and the draoi. One of the wordsmiths seemed to shake himself free of the shock and stood on the stage behind Jack.

"You can't do this! You have no authority here!"

Jack smiled and turned to the speaker. "I have every authority granted to me and my guard by Regent Bairstow and Archbishop Kissane. This is not up for debate."

"I won't have it!" declared the wordsmith, and the town gasped. "You have no right! None! You just killed a man in cold blood. That's murder! Murder!"

"He was a dissident and punished."

The wordsmith gaped at the words. "Punished? By whose authority? He had the right to trial! You cannot simply execute anyone you like! That's unacceptable!"

Jack motioned to one of the guards. The man strode toward the wordsmith.

The wordsmith backed up. "What's this? Are you going to arrest me? Do you think that will stop what's right?"

Jack grunted. "No, you aren't being arrested. You are going to be hanged from the tree in Fjodham Square. We will let your corpse be a warning to others who would question our authority. Take him outside." Jack turned to the town members as Steven spluttered. "As for the rest of you, you can watch him be hanged, and then you can head home. Curfew starts an hour after sundown. Anyone found on the streets after curfew will be killed on sight, no questions asked. Curfew lifts at sunrise. Dismissed."

Cill Darae

Part Two: Theocracy

Cill Darae

Eleven

Munsten Chamber, August 902 A.C.

ARCHBISHOP EYLENE KISSANE opened the door to her private chambers and allowed the two wordsmiths to enter. They filed in quietly and were followed by the only wordsmith she cared to speak to: Andrew Noble. She admired his dark skin, bright teeth and eyes, and the close-cropped hair on his head. He was a handsome man. Her equal. He nodded to her and smiled and went over to the nervous wordsmiths John and Peter and settled them down by talking of work. Andrew had been here numerous times over the past few weeks. A few evenings ago, he insisted he bring his fellow wordsmiths to celebrate.

"They've been holed up in the lower chambers for far too long, Leeny," he had told her. He had then run his warm left hand down her dark, lithe form and stopped it at her hip. She lay on her right side with her back to him on her bed. They lay on top of the bed, with the covers pulled back and discarded, and they had the floor-to-ceiling windows wide open to allow the cool onshore breeze to blow through her bedchamber and pull the sweat from their bodies.

She almost shuddered in pleasure once again, remembering the feel of his hand. The hairs on her neck and arm rose and gave her a tingle she didn't want to stop. *He has a way about him, this Andrew Noble*, she thought. "How so?" she had murmured in question, not really listening to him. Instead she waited to feel his hand move again, and she was wondering where it would go. She was glad it was not his right hand; that hand was missing fingers and repulsed her. *Although, he can do things with his right hand that has me gasping.*

"Leeny, my darling. They've been working non-stop on your handguns. They've only just completed the work. This deserves a celebration."

"They're late. I wanted those weeks ago."

"It was complicated work. It's not our fault. You'll be happy to hear we discovered a better way to keep the powder dry. You won't be disappointed for the slight delay."

"If you say so, honestly, I don't understand a word of it."

"Leave the Word to me and don't worry about it. How about Friday night? We can bring them up here. It's just John and Peter. Show them the respect of the Church and the new Archbishop. They love our Church, Leeny, and you. They know what the future brings."

"I suppose you'll want entertainment?"

Andrew pulled on Eylene's hip until she lay on her back looking up at him. He reached out and stroked the tight curls of her hair. "Of course, my love. I would expect nothing less from you."

Eylene smirked and took his left hand in hers and placed his index finger in her mouth. She popped it out and batted her eyes at him. "Very well. Friday it is."

It was now Friday night and Eylene closed the door and sauntered closer to the wordsmiths. She wore the most revealing clothes she owned; which was saying a lot. The eyes of John and Peter followed her every move. She blushed and looked away.

Andrew saw the effect when the men had stopped listening to him. He turned to her as she approached and winked when the wordsmiths couldn't see his face. "Ah, Archbishop Kissane, my thanks for this reception this evening. You honour us."

Eylene sidled up to Andrew's left side and slid an arm around his lower back and pulled him in slightly. The top of her head only reached his shoulders, and she laid it against him for a moment and stared out at the two astonished wordsmiths. She took a step forward and reached out with her left hand to the nearest wordsmith.

The poor wordsmith, Peter, didn't know what to do. He glanced first at his partner, John, and then at Andrew. She kept her hand extended toward him and waited. Hesitantly, he grasped it with his fingers. Eylene twisted her hand until the Archbishop's ring of office gleamed in the flickering candlelight. Eylene smiled when she saw it dawn on him what was expected of him. He bent over to kiss the ring.

Andrew coughed and Peter froze and looked up at Andrew. "On your knees, Peter. This is Archbishop Kissane. Surely you remember the teachings in Shape?"

"Why yes, I'm so sorry, Eylene. I mean Archbishop Kissane." Peter dropped to his knees and then brought the ring to his lips and kissed it.

Eylene swung her hand toward John and he dropped to his knees, took the offered hand and kissed it.

"Rise, John and Peter."

They rose awkwardly and then stood looking embarrassed and sorry for themselves. Eylene threw her head back and laughed startling the two wordsmiths. "Relax, you two! We knew each other in Shape! How could I ever treat you other than friends?"

Eylene saw the look of confusion they gave each other. *Truth is they stalked me in Shape. Two little boys hoping to catch a glimpse of me. Two naughty little boys. But now two of the best weapon smiths in the land.* Andrew made her promise to be civil to them tonight and reward them. She meant to do so, no matter how much she wanted to laugh at the two of them. They were smart, but not in ways that intrigued her. They had no guile. They were exactly how they appeared, and it bored her. She gathered her strength and beamed a smile at them and led them over to a large side-table. It was covered with wine, liquor, and an assortment of fine foods. She even had the spicy meat pastries from Shape presented for them to enjoy.

The room they were in was strangely laid out. It was a large square room, but with a sunken central area. A series of interconnected soft couches with thick, soft cushions spilling everywhere surrounded the central area. In contrast, icons of the Church covered the walls giving the room a sombre look. Catching the eye was the far wall which was completely made up of an exquisite stained-glass window. The moonlight shone through the glass and washed the room in a myriad of colours. The room, the colours, and the icons gave the room a surreal look. Everything caught your eye. But John and Peter only had eyes for Eylene.

Eylene poured four large measures of Cala whiskey into crystal tumblers and handed out three of them. She raised her own glass to her mouth, smirked at the three men, and tossed the contents back in one gulp. She tucked her glass under her arm and raised an eyebrow at the two young wordsmiths.

John and Peter gaped and then looked down at their own glasses and the large quantity of whiskey in them. They looked at Andrew for help, but he just smiled back at them. Peter raised his glass to his mouth and John watched him with a little fear showing. He took a small sip and then noticed Eylene's frown of disproval. He took a breath and then gulped back the whiskey. It took him three gulps, and he ended up bent over coughing with tears streaming down his face.

Eylene clapped her hands in glee. "Your turn, John. Drink up!"

John looked at Peter coughing and then closed his eyes and poured the whiskey down his throat. He swallowed once and then opened his eyes in surprise. He looked at his empty glass and then smiled.

Andrew clapped him on the back. "Well, done, John! Well done!" Andrew shot his own glass down and held out his glass to Eylene.

Eylene grabbed the whiskey decanter and poured four more equal levels into their glasses. Peter looked chagrined, but John smiled at Eylene. She gave him a half-wink.

"Well done, boys," said Eylene and sauntered over to the central area and down three broad steps to the lower area. She carried the decanter in one hand, letting it sway with her hips. She sipped her whiskey and then plopped down on a couch and then put the decanter on the floor. Eylene leaned back and sipped her whiskey watching John and Peter grow more nervous.

Andrew sat beside her on her left side and placed his deformed right hand on her thigh. John and Peter looked uncertain and glanced about at the other couches. The lower area was a good twenty feet across and sitting opposite Andrew and Eylene would be uncomfortable. John decided for the both of them and putting on a brave face sat next to Eylene but kept a good three feet between them. Peter sat next to him and looked over at Eylene and Andrew and then away to stare at the stained-glass window.

Eylene turned to Andrew, knowing her shirt would open just enough in the front. "Andrew, tell me the news."

Andrew lifted his left hand and traced Eylene's jawline. "We have the handguns you requested. They are all fashioned and waiting to be distributed. There are enough for one hundred of your Church Guard. The incendiary arrows are finished as well. We have three hundred packed and ready for the outlying villages and towns. They should quell any rebellion should the need arise. We have hundreds of small kegs of powder and thousands of lead balls for the handguns. This will change warfare. Nothing can withstand the power of the weapons. Those gold crowns you gave us are funding everything."

Eylene purred and leaned in toward Andrew a little. The gold and jewellery were being used to fund her Church Guard. A large amount of the Sect money was now sitting in Shape. The wealth had help assure her position in Shape. *This is all so perfect*, she thought and inhaled and took in the scent of Andrew. It always awoke something primal inside her. She lifted her right leg and placed it over her left. Her short skirt was riding high, and she knew what she was showing the two young wordsmiths. Eylene was feeling high on her power. Everything was hers for the taking. Plus, Lana had removed years of age and tightened and rejuvenated so much of her body. She felt twenty again and revelled in it.

Andrew chuckled and ran his hand up to her right ear and stroked it. Beyond Eylene he could see the two wordsmiths lost in their lust. Their eyes poured over Eylene, not sure where to look.

Eylene loved the attention. "We feed the loyalty of the Church Guard with coin. Enough to make them fabulously wealthy. With the power of the handguns they will soon lust for more." Eylene smiled at the wordsmiths for a moment and watched red heat rise high on their cheekbones. She turned her smile to Andrew. "And the journal?"

Andrew frowned a little. "Much of it is indecipherable. He used a replacement code, we think, but we don't know the key. However, there is much that he didn't code. Either he lacked the time when writing, or he cared little for the content. I searched first for mention of the herbs used by Windthrop when he sent those two guards to assassinate him. I found the details easily enough, and it confirmed what we knew and have been using it on the draoi in the dungeon.

"It keeps them sedated, completely so. I drove a large needle through the palm of the one called Katherine. She didn't even flinch. Her hand healed before my eyes. A wonder to observe. I would like time to conduct more experiments on them now that the weapons are made, what do you say?"

Eylene leaned her face in to Andrew's neck and brushed her lips on his neck. She watched the little hairs on the back of his neck rise with his goose bumps. "Perhaps. Continue."

Andrew made a soft noise and ran his hand down Eylene's side and up over her front, stroking her covered breasts, until he ran it up to her shoulder. He ran his fingers under the material of her shirt and paused there. He could see John and Peter glance at one another.

"It seems Edward has theories about the herb mixture. He believes the right mix could completely negate the draoi powers. This would allow your guard to close them, subdue them, and then collar them. I've spoken to some wordsmiths with the knowledge of herbs and the like. They promise me something soon. They only know I need something that places the mind in a state of disconnection."

Eylene laughed softly. "Perfect. If that fails, then we fill them full of those lead balls from my handguns. Well done, you three. I am very pleased, and so is God."

Andrew smiled and drew Eylene's shirt off her shoulder. The others gasped.

She shrugged to help him pull it off her shoulder and felt the cool air tighten her nipples. *Or, is it the excitement? My God, this is exquisite.* "My pleasure, my love," whispered Andrew. Eylene gasped as his hand pinched a nipple. He looked past her. "Ah, here is the entertainment."

Eylene didn't need to look up to know the six women she had brought in for tonight had wandered into the room. She heard the gasps from Peter and John. One of them murmured that they were naked, and she smiled. She was already lost in the feeling of Andrew's hands on her body. She felt a weight settle on the couches near the wordsmiths and the sounds of fake protests from the boys followed.

"Now, now! Our Archbishop rewards those who assist the Church of Belkin. Indulge my friends. This is your night. Lana will join us later. Her druid powers will take us to new heights. You've earned this, gentlemen. Enjoy."

Eylene smiled and slid over to lie in Andrew's lap. She placed her mouth next to his ear and whispered. "Well done, my love. Well done."

Twelve

Munsten Gaol, August 902 A.C.

THERE WERE BRIEF moments of lucidity for Katherine. She had glimpses of who she was, but she was never sure where she was. The moments were like a flashing light to her: images of a dark hole, a feeling of cold and wet, hunger, feeling filthy, and the list went on. She was starting to piece the moments together, but with it came a sense of dread and part of her wanted to avoid the truth. She felt trapped but couldn't remember why. And then the darkness would return until the next bright fleeting moment.

The next moment of clarity came with blinding brightness. One moment she was lost in the dark and the next she was awake and aware for the first time in a long time. She waited for the darkness to return, but she remained aware. She felt hard stone under her naked body. She was freezing cold and wet. The smell of human waste; potent and thick, assailed her nostrils. Her head throbbed with unimaginable pain and she wanted to tear the back of her head off and scoop out the agony. She heard a distant voice speaking from underwater and she struggled to fight past the pain to hear what was being said. She tried to open her eyes, but they were filled with sand and it hurt so terribly bad.

A hand lifted her head, and something was pressed against her mouth. She tried to fight it, but she had no strength. A wetness touched her lips, and she sensed it was water, pure and clean. She opened her mouth and sucked greedily at the flow. She gulped it down and felt the liquid splash against her empty stomach. Hunger drove into her middle and she groaned. A feeling of nausea washed over her, and she swallowed against the desire to lose the water she had just gained.

A wet cloth wiped gently at her face and the words continued to speak in low tones, impossible to hear. She drew her knees up to her chest and shuddered. The cold was all the way through to her bones. She had never felt so cold before. *I need to get warm.*

Where are my mom and dad? Where am I?

Her head swam and despite the clarity, she was confused and lost.

Always the voice spoke, but her ears could hear nothing.

She closed her eyes and darkness returned.

When she woke again, she was lying on her side with her knees drawn up to her chest. Someone was shaking her. *Where am I? What is happening?*

She tried to open her eyes, but they felt gritty. Her head throbbed with such pain and it made her feel sick. *Was I struck in the head?*

She was aware of someone trying to speak to her. The person sounded so far away. *Why can't I hear? What's wrong with me?*

A memory returned. She was walking through the streets of Munsten at night. *I wasn't alone. I was with… Dog! Where is Dog?* She struggled to roll over. She had to find Dog. *How did I forget about Dog? Where am I?*

A second memory returned. *I am draoi. I have powers.*

Katherine reached inside herself and remembered how to use her powers. She felt it at once and savoured the luxurious feeling and caressed it. *I could do anything with this.* She knew intimately that the amount of power was so small compared to what she was used to possessing. She once wielded immense power. Memories of Cala stabbed at her and guilt struck her hard causing her to whine; the sound similar to the whine of a dog. The fresh feeling of guilt surprised her. She had pushed it away for so long and now it seemed larger than before.

She shoved the guilt aside with difficulty. *I need to sort myself out.* She was waking up more and more. Her powers were limited. So little of her strength remained. She reached out and felt no presence of Gaea. She felt the loss and then remembered what had happened to Gaea. *Simon motes, I need them.* She reached out but felt nothing. Her powers didn't seem to reach out from herself. She cracked an eye and saw with relief it was James kneeling beside her. She could see he was in poor health and immediately she tried to reach to him, but her powers wouldn't work. *What is happening? What's wrong with me?*

Her memories flooded back. She remembered arriving back in Munsten. Walking the streets and the sudden attack. She had been captured. *All of us: James, Heather and Dog.* She reached for Dog but couldn't sense anything beyond her own body. *They must be dead!* Grief ripped through her and she cried out. James clapped a hand over her mouth trying to silence her. She thrashed on the ground. *Not Dog, no, no, no!*

She opened her eyes and saw James staring down at her. His lips were moving, but she couldn't hear him. Her eyes darted about, and she saw she was in a gaol cell. She focused on her hearing and saw the problem and applied what little power remained to her. In a moment, her hearing restored, and James insistent whispering came through.

"Be still! Silence! The guards will hear!"

Katherine stilled. Her eyes lost focus as she probed with her powers. She checked herself and saw she was malnourished. Her powers were almost gone, and she tried to reach out to pull more in but felt nothing. It was then she felt the collar around her neck. She raised a hand and tried to pull it off. James stopped her and held her hands.

"Don't. It's a collar of some kind. I can't remove it and see no way to do so. It's a solid ring of metal. Heather and Dog have the same ones in the cells next to you."

On hearing that Heather and Dog were okay, Katherine sobbed in relief. "Are they okay?" she managed to whisper with difficulty.

"Yes, I think so. But like you. We are all half-starved and naked."

Katherine's eyes widened and before she could stop herself she looked down at James' manhood. She twisted her face away and felt heat rise to her cheeks. "By the Word, James! This is unacceptable! Cover yourself!"

"Right, sorry," James grinned, giving lie to the apology. "Nothing to be done about it. We need you to get up. We need to free the others and escape."

Katherine, with help from James, managed to sit up and put her back against the wall. She covered her breasts with an arm. She looked around her and saw her cell was quite small. It was no more than a small rectangle eight feet long and maybe four feet wide. There were no windows, and the door was made from thick wood, but she could see it was slightly ajar. "How'd you...?"

"Break free? I'm not sure. It wasn't my doing. I woke, weak as you are, and found my cell open with a key in the lock. It took me a while to get up and moving, but I looked in the cells and found you, Heather and Dog next to mine. The rest of the cells are empty. Katherine, I don't recognise this gaol, but I think we are deep down under Munsten in an area I've never seen before."

"Who would free us like that and leave us?"

"A friend certainly and taking a risk. We'll figure out who, later. What do you remember?"

Katherine thought hard. "The street at night. The guards were there near the museum. Then... nothing after that."

James nodded. "Same for me. We were ambushed. Taken down by riot arrows. You need to get up. We need to get out of here and quickly. Can you use your powers? Give us strength?"

Katherine shook her head and then groaned and raised her free hand to her forehead. "No. I have only my reserves and they are almost gone. Something is blocking me."

"Hmm. The collar, I suspect. Heather and Dog have the same ones."

"You must free them. Leave me here and wake them. Go."

James smiled a quick smile and rose. Katherine looked away from his nakedness. She heard him opening a door and then silence.

She closed her eyes and tried to use her powers. Katherine could sense nothing outside of her own body. She looked around the cell and noticed with horror that the smell of human waste came from her. The floor was covered in her own waste. "By the Word, this is horrible."

She tried everything to free her power. She wrestled with the collar and felt with her fingers for a clasp or a way to release it. It was smooth all over and surprisingly light. It was a metal she had never felt before. She failed to find any way to open it. *How would a simple metal collar stop me from using my power? This is beyond my ken.*

She kept at her power, trying to find a way past the metal. She grew frustrated and pulled hard at the collar and only managed to bruise her neck. She lost track of time but froze when she heard a sound in the corridor. With relief, she saw James appear. He snuck in and sat beside her.

"Heather and Dog are awake and recovering. They are the same as you. Heather cannot reach her power. She says she has no reserves at all if that means anything to you. Dog, well, he just lays there whining. Can't understand a word he says. Well, *thought* really, right? The collars won't come off. Perhaps there's a way, but we can't see well enough in this gloom."

"What next?"

James looked around. "We need to move and quickly. They will come and find us and who knows what will happen then. We must hide. Get clear. Get those collars off and leave Munsten. Whoever gaoled us used city guards and someone else. I caught a glimpse of one of the people who shot us. It looked like a church uniform. It must be that new Church Guard. I fear the worst."

"The worst? What's worse than this?"

"That Brent has been overthrown. He wouldn't allow this to happen. This is his gaol. He must have been removed."

"Where do we go?"

James thought for a moment. "I dunno. Let's escape the gaol first, shall we? Come get up. You'll feel better once you start moving."

Katherine tried to stand but couldn't manage to push herself up. James reached out and took her hands and helped lift her up. Katherine felt her head spin and held a hand to the wall to steady herself.

"Easy, lass. Take it slow," murmured James. "There's no rush. Well, a little bit of one, but get your feet under you first."

Katherine looked sideways at James. "Lass?"

"Aye, lass. You're younger than me by a fair bit."

"When I get better and get this stupid collar off, I am coming back to this conversation."

"Whatever gets you moving. Are you steady?"

"Yeah. Let's see to Dog. I need to see him."

"Follow me."

James led the way to the cell three down from Katherine's. They passed an open door on the way. "That was mine," he said.

Katherine glanced in and could see the conditions were the same as hers. They had been left in their cells and allowed to soil themselves. The stench made her eyes water. She hurried past and went into the cell James stood in front of.

Inside she found Dog lying on his side. His tongue hung out of his mouth, but it didn't move; it looked unnatural, but she could see he was asleep. Ignoring the filth on the floor, she stumbled to the floor beside him and hugged his neck. "Dog! Dog! Wake up! Please wake up. Come on, we have to leave this place."

She tried to sense him with their bond, but the collar was blocking her. She shook him and then sat back and stroked his head and muzzle. He had the same collar as hers, but larger in diameter to fit his neck. Seeing his collar she knew they were specifically for them. *Only one person knew when we would be arriving in Munsten and where we were headed. Lana Turner.* She pushed thoughts of revenge aside and focused on *Dog*. She leaned in and whispered into his ear. His nose twitched, and his eyes fluttered open. She saw him look at her and his tail thumped the floor weakly.

"Hi, Dog. Wake up, love. We have to go. You won't be able to use your power. We have collars that stop us reaching the world. Hold your reserves. Don't waste them. Fix what will get you up and moving. Try."

She could sense James loitering behind her. She spoke to him without taking her eyes off Dog. "Go see to Heather. Get her on her feet. Tell her she can't reach out for power. Tell her to fix what will get her moving. Go."

She felt him leave and leaned in to whisper to Dog. "Get up, Dog. Time to go. I know you can understand me. Get up."

Dog whined and tried to roll to his stomach. Katherine helped pull him over. His grey and white fur was matted and fouled with excrement and he now looked more brown than anything else. Dog was always a medium-large dog, but now he was wasted away to skin and bones. Katherine felt a spike of fear. Whoever had been feeding them hadn't done as good a job with Dog.

"Can you stand?"

Dog tried to rise to his paws, but his legs gave way and he collapsed. He put his head on his paws and closed his eyes. He was already spent. Katherine tried to rouse him, but he stayed out of it. Tears splashed on Dog from Katherine and she wiped at her face. She felt light headed and something more. *Infection*, she thought. *We've been lying in our own filth for a long time. We need healing.*

After a time, Katherine heard James approach the cell. She looked over and saw the frightful state of Heather. She was naked, and Katherine could count her ribs. Her red hair was hidden under the filth. Katherine was pleased to see a fire in her eyes. She was angry and that would help.

Heather came over and sat next to her and Dog. James stayed in the hallway and looked anxious. Heather leaned in and whispered to her. "How urr ye, Katherine? Urr ye hail?"

Katherine was confused by the choice of words. Heather looked meaningfully at Katherine's groin and raised an eyebrow. Katherine opened her eyes wide and then checked herself. She seemed whole. She nodded, and Heather looked relieved.

"Thank Gaea," said Heather and turned to Dog. She reached out and felt along his body. "He's thinner than he shuid be. His muscles ur wasted awa'. He wilnae be able tae walk. He needs healing." She looked out to the hallway. "James, kin ye carry him?"

James came over. "Yes, of course."

Katherine had her doubts, but James leaned over and picked up Dog in a cradle carry. Katherine could see the strain on his face, but he did it. She loved him in that moment.

"Next time lift wi' yer legs ye dumb eejit."

James smiled and headed to the hallway. Katherine and Heather followed behind him. "To the left I think."

They headed down the hallway and found a large banded door. It was slightly ajar.

"Katherine," said James. "Check ahead. Make sure there's no surprises waiting for us."

Katherine opened the door a little more and peeked through the opening. Seeing nothing she moved through the gap and disappeared through. On the other side was a small flight of five stairs leading up. She crept up and looked around the corner. A long corridor devoid of any doors or adornments lay before her. Two torches burned weakly in wall sconces and provided the only light. The air was already fresher than their cells and she breathed in deeply. Certain this was the right way she hurried back and brought the others up.

Katherine moved about twenty feet ahead and sighted another door at the end of the corridor. It looked ajar as well. *Whoever freed us kept the way open for us. We owe whoever it is. I hope we live to thank him or her. Or them.* Whatever happened they needed to keep moving. Caution was only slowing them down and Katherine was already breathing heavily with exertion. Sweat broke out all over her body and she felt the signs of a fever. *We need water and a washing.*

They gathered at the new door and waited to catch their breath. James had to put down Dog for a spell. He was panting pretty loudly, and Katherine didn't like the sound of it. It was too wet. Once James felt stronger, he hoisted Dog back up and Katherine opened the door. A large stairwell lay before them leading up into darkness.

"Up we go," whispered Katherine and led the way. She stopped counting steps when she reached fifty. Katherine kept a hand to the right wall and Heather helped James navigate the steps in the dark. When Katherine reached the upper landing she almost fell forward when her foot failed to land on another step. She spied a glimmer of light and moved forward to find another door, left open a crack.

She tried to listen, but her breathing rasped in her ears. She waited for the others to catch up and then pushed the door open a little and peered through. On the other side was a large room with tables and odd tools on peg boards. James looked in and grunted.

"Torture room. I know where we are. I was in here once."

Heather held a hand to her mouth in shock.

James noticed her reaction and smiled. "Not me. A prisoner. I was a witness. The man had killed a rich family and hid the gold he stole. Wanted it for his own family. We had to torture where he hid it from him. It didn't take long." James moved further into the room. "Follow me, I know the way. We should be clear for quite some time. It's rare to see anyone this far back in the dungeon." James looked back at the door they just came through. "I always thought this was a storage closet."

Katherine paused by a large barrel and peered inside. She sniffed the liquid contents and then dipped a finger in and tasted it. "Water," she croaked. She looked at James and he looked hopeful. She found a ladle tied to the barrel and dipped it in. She took a sip and then started gulping it.

Heather came over and pushed the ladle from her mouth. "Easy, Katherine. Easy. Take it slow."

Katherine looked annoyed but nodded and handed her the ladle. They took turns drinking water and ignored the faint musty taste. They trickled water into Dog's mouth, and he responded a little and licked his muzzle. Once they had quenched their thirst, they took turns dousing each other and washing off the filth. By the time they were done half the water in the barrel was gone. Katherine felt reinvigorated and felt a stirring of hope. Heather seemed lighter in step as well. James sat on the floor and ran his fingers through Dog's fur and flicked matted hair away.

"How much further?" asked Katherine looking at James. She saw Heather staring at James and nudged her before he looked up and caught her. Heather had the decency to blush and turn her head.

James stirred and looked up at her. "We have quite a way to go. But the next part of the dungeon from here is the area most used. There will be guards. Many guards. We can't hope to fight them. I've been trying to think what to do, and I can't think of anything."

Heather tutted. "This is a braw fankle. We're naked. We cannae juist donder oot o' 'ere, kin we? We need a plan. We need tae gang somewhere!"

Katherine nodded. "We need clothes. Food. Shelter. You know the city, James. If we do manage to get out of here, where can we go?"

James laughed without humour. "This is the dungeon. It's meant to keep people in. I can't honestly think of a way out. Whoever opened our cells didn't leave us a way out. We're trapped in here. We might as well still be in our cells."

"I need my staff," stated Katherine.

"Forget the staff," said James. "Get another."

"Not possible, James. I need that staff."

"It could be anywhere, Katherine. What you ask is impossible. Let us work on one impossible task at a time."

Katherine crouched next to James and looked him in the eye. "I can't leave without it. You have to trust me in this."

James scowled. "Katherine be reasonable. It could be anywhere. Anywhere.

Tell me where it is and then we can determine how to get it back. Otherwise, drop it."

Katherine looked to Heather for support, but she shrugged. "We kin aye come back fur it, Katherine."

Katherine felt defeated. James was right it could be anywhere. But she had to get it back. It was the last of Gaea and she couldn't abandon her. She also thought perhaps Gaea could help with the collars. Whoever had made the collars had access to knowledge not commonly known. A thought occurred to her at that moment. "The Chamber. Where is it from here?"

James looked surprised. "The Chamber? Huh. I'm not sure. Let me think."

Katherine waited while James thought. She saw the smile flit across his face and bit her lip. He looked up at them and smiled wider.

"Huh. The Chamber. It's not far. There may be a way to get there if we can find access to the secret tunnels. I know a room in the dungeon that might. It's a safe room. A place for guards to retreat to should there be an uprising in the dungeon. The way should be clear. It's not often travelled down here."

"'N' howfur dae ye ken o' this steid, James Dixon?" demanded Heather.

"The guards played cards there. I might have played a hand or two in my time."

Heather looked at Katherine. "Men."

James snorted. "And women. They played, too."

Katherine clapped her hands. "Let's go. Lead on, James."

James lifted Dog and led the way. They passed through doors and corridors and soon Katherine was lost. James kept them moving as fast as he was able. They saw and heard no one. Torches were a rare thing, but the passages were lit. After an hour, and a couple of rest breaks, James stopped before a wall. He placed his right ear against the stone and listened for a spell. Satisfied he stepped back and nodded to the wall.

"Push the wall, ladies. It will swing open."

Katherine and Heather glanced at one another and did as he asked. They pushed with their shoulders and felt the wall shift. They pushed harder and the wall section opened into a hidden doorway. Beyond the door all was dark.

"Grab a torch from the basket and light it, Heather," ordered James and she did as he asked. They pushed through the opening and found themselves in a large room. Shelves lined the walls and barrels were stacked in a corner. Central to the room was a large table. One wall was covered with a large map of the dungeon.

"Close the door and bar it with the rod there," demanded James and he laid

Dog down on the floor as gently as he could.

Heather and Katherine pushed the door closed and placed an iron rod against the wall in a socket. No one would be able to open the door from the other side.

"Light a lantern. They're over there in the corner. There should be preserved food on the shelves and water in the barrels. This place was meant to withstand a siege."

Heather lit a lantern and then with Katherine they searched the shelves. They found weapons of all kinds, plus clothing, biscuits and water. They soon dressed and soaked the hard tack biscuits in water to soften them. For a time they simply enjoyed their safety and a return of sorts to normalcy. They sat quietly eating and feeding Dog.

Heather examined Katherine's collar and gave up. "Tis hopeless. Tis yin solid piece o' metal. Thir's na seams or catches. Tis a miracle o' craftsmanship."

Katherine nodded. "I thought so. This is something I would expect from the Chamber. Which is why I want to head there. If we can find a way to remove it, it will be found there. Also, we can escape through the Chamber. There's access to the bay outside Munsten."

James nodded. "I agree. It's our best bet. Provided we can find a way out of here. We should start searching for a way out. There has to be. Otherwise this room is just another gaol cell."

They spent the next hour searching the walls and trying to move the shelves. They found no sign of an opening. Tired, and with their food sitting in their stomachs making them groggy they agreed to sleep for a spell. James took the first watch and they slept.

Several hours later they were no closer to finding a way out. James discussed chancing their way out. He argued they had short swords and daggers and could fight their way out. Katherine asked James to swing a sword for a bit, but after only a few swings of a sword he could no longer hold it up. He sat down exhausted and frustrated.

Heather was examining the map of the dungeon on the wall. It showed all the corridors and cells and identified key locations for defence. The map had many things written on it and people had even doodled on it. The parchment was old and cracked in places and Heather doubted it would last much longer. She stood with her hands on her hips studying it. She pointed at an area. "This is whaur we ur, na?"

James looked over and squinted where she was pointing. "Yes."

"Whit's this wee marc in th' middle o' th' room?"

"I dunno, a mark maybe?"

"Na, tis written in th' identical ink as th' walls. Tis nae bin added oan."

Katherine came over and looked at what Heather was looking at. "Oh, yes. I see it. A strange little mark." Katherine turned to look at the room. "It's under the table."

James looked up at that and then looked at Katherine. He jumped up and moved to the table and peered under it. "Quick, help me move the table."

Heather and Katherine helped James drag the heavy table across the floor to expose the middle of the room. James got on his hands and knees and looked closely at the floor.

"A-ha!" he exclaimed and pried back a tile. It swung on a hinge and exposed an iron ring embedded into the floor. "I think we found the way out. Well done, Heather!"

Katherine caught the pleasure on Heather's face and then watched as James pulled on the ring. He strained and pulled but nothing happened.

"Mibbie ye shouldn't staun oan th' door yer trying tae hurl."

James swore and moved to the side and pulled again. This time a section of the floor swung open. Katherine cheered.

In a moment they stared down into the darkness. A metal ladder was set into the stone and descended straight down. James relit the torch and held it in the opening and they spotted the bottom several feet down.

James smiled broadly at the ladies. "I think we have a way out."

Cill Darae

Thirteen

Munsten, The Chamber, August 902 A.C.

THEY FOUND THEIR way down the tunnel to the Chamber. They lit a couple of lanterns and entered the crystal-filled room. Over the months the Chamber had been thoroughly searched and anything of value removed. Little remained except for the altar and the small shack which contained the Device. They lay Dog down beside the shack. He was still unresponsive, and Katherine worried about him.

James checked the storage room and reported it empty. Katherine nodded. The draoi had taken the Life Salt and used it to seed the Realm and the storage room had been emptied of the wealth the Sect had taken over the years. The Church now had all the stolen jewellery, silverware, and coin and were supposed to be returning that wealth back into the Realm. Katherine doubted it was making it anywhere except into the pockets of the deans and bishops.

James barred the door and they entered the shack. It held a table and a few chairs. On the table was the Device, along with other unknown instruments. A small wooden box lay on the table. Strange smooth ropes led from the Device out of the shack and up to the outside to black glass panels. No one understood the purpose of the panels and ropes, but it was discovered if the ropes were removed from the Device, or if the panels were covered, the Device would not function. They were left alone. Smaller ropes led from the Device to the other instruments.

The Device and instruments all connected to a small bar with little holes. The ropes had a connection that inserted into these holes. It was a relic from a long time ago.

James was the first to move the small box over to the edge of the table. He lifted the lid and he made a small noise. He pulled out a collar identical to the ones Katherine, Heather and Dog wore, except the collar was open and swung on a small hidden hinge. James pulled out more collars until twenty of them lay on the table.

"So this is where they were made. Who did this, I wonder?" he asked.

Heather picked one up and studied it a moment before setting it back down. "Th' Church. They're th' ainlie ones allowed in 'ere. Brent ordered that his foremaist week as Regent."

James started placing the collars back in the box. "Well, we are taking these with us. We need to study them. Perhaps the Device can tell us how to remove them?"

They stared at the Device in silence. They all knew that the Sect had used this for blood magic and crafted items that opposed the draoi power. Now the Church was using it for more nefarious things.

Katherine was the first to speak. "Does anyone know how this works?"

James and Heather shook their heads.

Katherine looked at her friends. They looked so thin and weak. Fatigue clouded their features and she knew, like herself, they probably wanted nothing more than to lie down and sleep. "Who wants to try?"

Heather stepped forward and lifted the top lid on the Device. It swung upwards on a hinge at the back and immediately the inside of the lid lit up with a magical light and the image of an apple appeared with a bite out of it. It disappeared and strange words and symbols started to draw faster than they could follow. After a moment the image on the lid changed to an image of a landscape. It looked so real as if the lid was a small window to somewhere else. Little symbols were lined up on the bottom of the window on a bar that looked drawn. The bottom of the Device was covered with little squares with more of the strange writing on them that closely resembled the letters of today. They recognised the row of squares with numbers on them. That much was familiar, but little else.

Heather looked at Katherine and shrugged. "All ah ken is that if ye touch th' square area 'ere a wee arrow moves aroond oan th' windae. Ye press th' square whin th' arrow is ower yin th' symbols 'n' a freish windae appears. Ah don't ken whit thay dae." Heather touched the square and moved her finger around. The little arrow moved with her movements.

Katherine grimaced. "Well, what are we hoping to do here? If none of us understand this, then it is hopeless."

Heather replied. "We need tae ken thae collars. Wi' thaim th' Church kin remove oor powers. We cannae abide that. We hae tae git thaem aff as soon as we kin. Ah don't need tae remind ye Dog needs healing. As dae we all."

Heather selected a symbol and pressed the square. In a moment another window appeared. They all gasped when they realised they could read the words.

Katherine read it aloud. "This is written by a Wordsmith who calls himself Andrew Noble. Anyone know him?" She glanced at the others and they shook their heads. "He says: *'Once we were able to translate the language we found it not so different from our own. What is clear is that the Device allows people to manufacture items of such exquisite detail that it boggles the mind. This is a relic from a long time ago, made by people who are no longer remembered. Working with Lana, we have been able to find a way to create collars capable of blocking the powers of the druids. The collars are safeguarded from removal by allowing an individual unique authority over the collars. It is not unlike a lock and key, but in this case the key is the person. Vicar Kissane has decreed that she will be that authority.*

"*'Once the collar is placed around the neck, Vicar Kissane will only need to touch the collar to lock it in place. Removal of the collar will require her touch once again. I marvel at the simplicity of the design. Inside the collar is the power of the Word such as I have never seen or imagined before. The programme identified with a gear symbol allows anyone to create the parameters of what is wanted, and with significant effort, words are entered in a sequence that defines what it is that is required. Once written, the programme will validate itself and a press of a button enables the item to be manufactured out of thin air in an instrument on the table. It is a wonder to behold. Months of research and trial and error have produced twenty-four of the collars. The first one was tested on Lana and proven to work. Vicar Kissane is very pleased.*'"

Katherine looked at Heather with a grim face. "This is not good."

Heather shook her head and looked worried.

"Seems we need this Vicar Kissane person to remove the collars. I can't believe Lana is behind this and helping the Church."

James withdrew a collar and examined it. "The good news is that we have almost all of them here. One is missing, by my count."

"It doesn't say how they work. Only how to attach and remove them. How do we stop this? I need to communicate with Dog and heal him. I can't with this thing around my neck!" Tears burned Katherine's eyes.

"Ah will keep keekin at this thing. See whit else ah kin discover. Patience,

Katherine. We'll figure this oot somehow."

Katherine nodded. "We should destroy these collars."

James picked up the box. "I'll put it in the boat. We can dump them in the Bay." He hefted the box and left the shack with it.

Katherine felt a tear trickle down her face and wiped it away angrily. Heather saw and tutted. "We'll git thro' this, Katherine. Go search aboot 'n' see whit ye kin find."

Katherine left Heather in the shack and watched James place the box in the boat. She knelt by Dog and made sure he was okay. She ruffled his fur and stood. An area to the side of the Chamber was where the Sect had slept. Their cots were still there, and she made her way over. There were workbenches along the wall, and she could see they still had tools of all kinds arranged on them. She looked them over and shuddered when she recognised that many were tools for torture. She glanced at the altar and scowled. *There is so much evil in this world, and the draoi have changed so very little of it.* She ached for access to her powers. She could do so much with it. Together, her and Dog were unstoppable. With the collar she felt as if her arms had been removed. She looked inside herself and felt only a trickle of her power remaining. The collars were stopping the motes from working. Anger rose within her and she looked around for a way to vent it.

She noticed the small bookcase and wandered over. She looked at a couple of books and marvelled at the detail inside them. They were made with a paper she had never seen before. Each page was identical in size and cut so cleanly. Little windows on the pages showed strange worlds and places. Her head reeled with the impossibility of them.

It was then she noticed a weapon crate on the floor. It was pushed up against the wall and surrounded by four smaller foot long crates. She knelt by the weapon box and opened the lid. Lying on top she saw her staff gleaming darkly. She squealed in delight and pulled it out. The feel of the staff in her hands immediately gave her comfort. *Thank Gaea!*

James had come over upon hearing her squeal. "Weapons! By the Word! And you found your staff! What else is there?" James squatted by the crate and pulled out his own sword. "I don't believe it!" He smiled at Katherine. "Fantastic!"

Katherine couldn't help but smile back. She understood his joy.

"The rest of the weapons have value but they're too heavy to take with us. What's in the other crates?" asked James as he strapped his sword to his waist. He had to tighten it past the well-worn spot he usually tied it to.

"I don't know. You open that one, I have this one." Katherine opened her crate and squealed again. "Life Salt! It's still here!"

James opened his crate. "Same here. Quick, open the remaining two."

They opened the next two and were surprised to find ingots of metal stacked inside. They pulled one out and marvelled at the lightness of it. "What is this?" asked James. "I've never seen the like. It weighs next to nothing!"

Katherine touched her collar. "The same metal as was used with the collars, I think. So light."

"We take these with us." James stacked the two crates of ingots and lifted them with little difficulty and marched them down to the boat. He returned for the Life Salt but waited until Katherine removed a small pouch of it first. He carried the Life Salt down to the boat and returned, sweating. "I'm knackered. I need to sit for a spell."

Katherine looked at James with sympathy. "Have a lie down. I'll keep watch."

James nodded and without another word lay down on one of the cots. In seconds, he was asleep and snoring. Katherine smiled. *He's such a good man, we're lucky to have him with us.*

Katherine sat on a nearby cot. She looked over to Dog's still form and tried again to find him across their bond, but it was still not there. It felt strange to her to be separated from him. There had been a time she would have welcomed the ability to separate herself, but now that it was forced from her she wanted nothing more than to get it back.

She could see Heather through the opening of the shack, still working on the Device. Her shoulders were drooped, and Katherine could see the fatigue in her form. They were all exhausted and pushed past what they could tolerate. *I've been spoiled wielding draoi power so easily. I miss it so much.*

Katherine held her staff and closed her eyes. The need to lie back and sleep pulled at her and she struggled to fight it off. She growled to fight it off and concentrated. She reached out to the staff but failed. She tried again and felt nothing. She could feel the staff in her hands but nothing more. *Curse this collar!*

She kept trying for several more minutes, but on every attempt the staff lay dormant in her hands, no more than an object. Exhausted she lowered her head and let the staff lie on her shoulder. Tired, she relaxed her grip on the staff and it slid down her shoulder to rest in the crook of her neck. The staff made a gentle clink sound when it touched the collar.

Katherine could feel her fatigue washing across her in waves. Each wave stronger than the last one. It threatened to pull her down and her body craved it. She felt a need to lie down on the cot and almost did so. She adjusted her seat and tried to move her staff. The staff pulled at the collar and it hit her neck.

Katherine's eyes snapped open and she pulled at the staff, but it was stuck to the collar. She tried to look down to see what was happening, but she couldn't quite see where the staff and collar touched. She pulled harder and felt the collar pull against her neck. She felt panic and tugged again. The staff was stuck fast.

In a moment she felt the collar start to get warm, and then hot. She pulled desperately at the staff, but it wouldn't move. The collar grew painfully hot. She cried out and heard James awake next to her. She cried out again when she felt the flesh of her neck burning where it touched the collar. She looked over at James as he sat up and saw his eyes widen looking at her neck. He called out for Heather and Katherine heard her rushing out of the shack asking what the matter was.

"James, help me. The staff... it's stuck to the collar and its getting really hot! It's burning me!"

James was now beside her and he grabbed the staff and twisted at it. Katherine could feel it twisting the collar at the same time and it touched a new part of her neck. The burning was unbearable, and she screamed at the pain. James twisted harder.

"The staff," he grunted. "It's merged with the collar. Melted together or something." Heather moved beside him, and he looked at her briefly. "Look at this, Heather! What is happening? I can't tell where the staff ends and the collar starts. Feel the collar! It's burning her."

"Mibbie juist position it sae th' collar isnae touching her neck. Git if aff. By Gaea, ah kin reek her skin cooking."

"I'm trying. She won't sit still!"

Katherine was in agony. She was desperate to get the collar and staff apart. *Why is this happening? What did the Church do with the collars to make this happen?*

Just when she thought she couldn't take anymore there was a tug at her neck and James fell back with the staff still in his hands. Their eyes were drawn to the collar still attached to the staff. The black surface of the staff had poured out over the collar like a melted wax. Whatever it had done it had opened the collar and it had come free of Katherine's neck.

Katherine raised her fingers to touch gingerly at her neck. She could feel the blisters and her fingers came away wet and with blood. She stared at her fingers in horror. "How bad is it?" she asked with panic in her voice.

Heather stared at the collar and then at Katherine. "How'd...? Ne'er mynd. Katherine, kin ye reach yer powers?"

Katherine gaped at her words and then blinked. *Of course.* She closed her eyes and reached out and cried out in joy as power came washing back to her. She looked up at the ceiling and laughed out loud. She pulled power in with a thirst. She looked within her body and saw the damage from the lack of nutrition. She saw the burns on her neck. She felt her draoi bonds to the draoi snap back into place and felt the immediate elation on the other end.

She healed her injuries and sighed in relief as her pains faded away. She felt Nadine's insistent cry for attention, but pushed her away, surprised by the ease at which she did so. She opened her eyes to see Heather smiling at her. "I'm better."

"Ah kin see that! Whit happened? How'd...?"

"The staff. I touched it to the collar. It did it on its own."

Heather stared at the staff and then gasped as the black receded from the collar. In a moment it left it and the collar fell to the floor, ringing loudly in the silence. James stared from the staff to the collar in disbelief.

Katherine stood up and took the staff from James. She immediately felt the presence of Gaea and felt her anger. She queried Gaea, but she refused to answer her. Nadine pounded at her thoughts for attention. Behind Nadine Katherine could sense the other draoi's curiosity and joy.

Just a moment, Nadine! Relax! I'm a little bit busy at the moment!

She didn't wait for an answer and felt the shock from Nadine at her words. *At least she's backed off.*

Heather fingered her collar. "Kin ye remove it?"

"Let me try." Katherine touched her staff to Heather's collar. She waited, but nothing happened. She tried to ask Gaea, but she was withdrawn and still very angry. "It's not working."

Heather looked about wildly. "How come nae? A'm needin' this aff, Katherine! Please!"

Katherine touched the staff to the collar again, but still nothing happened. *Gaea! Do something!*

Gaea continued to ignore her.

Please?

There was silence, and then Katherine heard a soft voice in her head. *Talk to the Simon motes.*

What?

Gaea refused to answer.

Katherine looked at Heather. "Just a moment." She closed her eyes. <*Simon motes? Hello?*>

The immediate answer startled her. <*Welcome, Katherine.*>

<*Um, hi. Is this the Simon motes?*>

<*That is the name you have given us. Correct. How may we assist you?*>

<*These collars around my friends' necks. Can you remove them?*>

<Please indicate the collars.>
<The one here around Heather's neck.>
<Please indicate the collar.>
<Indicate?> Katherine used her power to highlight where the collar was.
<Unable to comply, however, you may remove them.>
<I can't, I tried.>
<You are now reconnected to the network and acknowledged as one of the super users. You have the authority to remove the collar and bypass existing authority granted to Eylene Kissane.>
<She put them there?>
<Unknown. She was the authority to lock the device in place.>
<So I just touch it?>
<Correct and order it to unlock.>

Katherine knelt by Heather and saw the desperation in her eyes. "Hold on." Katherine reached up and touched the collar. She used her power and sent it into the collar and told it to open. A small chime sounded twice, and the collar opened up. Heather reached up with a cry and tore it off her neck and threw it at the wall where it bounced off with a loud ringing sound and landed on the floor with a clatter.

Heather threw her hands to her neck and rubbed it hard. She closed her eyes and Katherine saw the determination in her expression. She could almost feel Heather pull power to her. She connected back to the draoi bond and she felt the other draoi cry out in joy. In a moment, Heather opened her eyes with an expression of joy and satisfaction. She turned to James. "Haud still, James." Her eyes shut and James' eyes opened wide with astonishment as her powers flooded through him.

Katherine smiled and then remembered Dog. She ran over to him and touched the collar and willed it off. It opened and she pulled it free. She dove into Dog and found out just how bad he was. She poured power into him and healed him at a rate that even astonished her. *I know him so intimately, this is as easy as breathing to me.* She felt Dog waken and she brushed his thoughts. Their bond exploded in dazzling white light and Katherine threw back her head at the sheer joy it brought. She had felt so alone before. She hadn't realised just how much until Dog was back with her. She felt whole. Strong. Sure of herself. She hugged Dog and pulled him tight. She felt the draoi shout out in happiness seeing Dog come back to them.

What is happening, Katherine? Where was I?

Oh Dog, we were captured. We had collars that separated us from our powers. It was terrible!

We escaped? I have my powers. I am so weak!

Draw power, Dog. Heal yourself. We need to leave this place.

Katherine felt a wet tongue on her face, and she cried.

I am hungry. Do we have anything to eat?

Katherine laughed through her tears. "No, but we'll get some! Promise!"

It is coming now.

Katherine pulled back and looked at Dog. "What is coming?"

Fish. From the ocean.

Katherine looked over at the wharf area just in time to see a large sea trout launch itself out of the water to land on the Chamber floor. She heard Heather screech in surprise. The fish flopped on the floor. In a moment another fish landed beside it.

Katherine laughed. "Oh, Dog. You are so smart."

* * *

Whole and hale, the three of them started up a small cooking stove they found in the Chamber, with a small supply of wood nearby. James tended to the fish with Dog supervising his every move. Katherine felt at peace and more certain of the future. She was keeping the other draoi at bay. They clamoured for their attention, the loudest being Nadine.

She told Nadine to give them a moment to sort themselves, made sure there weren't any pressing emergencies, and Nadine grudgingly went quiet.

That was an hour ago. The smell of fish frying on the stove was making her mouth water. They all needed the protein. They had lost too much weight, and no power was going to bring that back without fuel in their bellies. Dog had wolfed down the parts of the fish James had removed such as the entrails, heads and tails. James was disgusted. Katherine knew Dog could eat just about anything and use his powers to break it down quickly.

Please tell him to just give me my share. I don't need it cooked.

He knows, but insists he give it to you prepared his way.

What is his way? I heard him say that, but I don't know what that is.

A little burnt on the outside?

No!

Ha-ha! Just kidding, Dog. Give him this. He needs to do something.

Heather came over to James and watched him cook for a time. Katherine noticed her hand touched the small of his back, and then she pulled it away quickly. *Great*, she thought. *Just what we need.*

When Heather looked over at Katherine, she could tell she had realised what

Cill Darae

she had done, too, and wasn't happy.

Heather shook her head and walked away and went back inside the shack. Katherine shook her head and rose to stand beside James. He had cut the fish up into chunks and was frying it in oil in a large frying pan. He seemed to know what he was doing.

"Thank you, James."

James spared a quick look at her before resuming his cooking. "For what?"

"Getting us out of there. We couldn't have done it without you."

"Well, we had some help. Someone opened the doors."

"True, but you woke us up. Got us moving. You carried Dog the whole way. Thank you." Katherine leaned in and kissed his cheek.

James blushed. And moved the fish around with a spatula. "You are welcome. Glad to be of help."

"James, you are very much a part of this team. Don't forget it. I can see you struggle to try to find ways to help. Truth is, you don't need to try. You already help in so many ways."

James looked at her quickly again. "If you say so. No worries. This fish is done. Keep Dog away a moment, will you?"

"You tell him, he's right there. He understands everything you say."

"Right," James looked at Dog. "No touchy the fishy! Got it?"

Dog thumped the floor with his tail and lolled his tongue out of his mouth.

James raised an eyebrow at Katherine.

"He says yes, obviously. You don't need to talk to him like he's a child."

"Right." James pulled the frying pan off the stove and set it on the small table nearby. He had placed four chairs around the table. "Okay, Dog, you get a seat." Dog leapt up and sat at the table. Katherine could feel his pleasure at sitting at the table. James raised his voice and called out over to the shack. "Hey, grumpy guts, food's ready."

"Shut yer weesh, you stupid man!"

James laughed and indicated a chair to Katherine. He seated her and pushed her chair in.

"Such a gentleman!"

"I'll have you know, my parents were married."

"I don't understand?"

"Never mind. Military humour. Weak at that. Dig in. I know we can all use it. We have enough trout to feed twice as many of us. Although I suspect it will soon be gone. Dog, you are drooling on the table. Go ahead, eat. Dog eat slowly and only your share."

162

Heather came out and sat at the table. "Ah spoke tae Chris. Things ur nae guid at th' farm. Th' draoi hae split. Kennit Doirich, ye mind him? He's taken hauf th' draoi wi' him. Will's left th' farm. Nobody kens whaur tae. Oor bonds hae bin severed."

Katherine stared at Heather and her words went around in her head. They didn't make sense. Katherine reached out for Will and couldn't find him. He was gone, but that was impossible. She reached out to Nadine and felt her grab onto her thoughts.

Katherine! Katherine! Thank Gaea, why were you blocking me? How were you blocking me?

Sorry Nadine, we had a lot going on here. Did you hear what happened? Katherine chose to ignore her last question. She didn't know how she was able to block Nadine so easily.

Yes, Chris just spoke to us all and explained what happened. You think it was this Kissane woman?

Yes, and possibly Lana. Does that make sense to you? I can't sense her.

Yes it does. Kennit took half the draoi. They've left the farm and headed who knows where, but I suspect up to Munsten. Lana and him are together in this. And now it looks like Lana is working with the Church. I think that also means the draoi are working with the Church.

How can they? Knowing our history?

I don't know, Katherine. It eats at me. Makes me sick thinking about it.

Where is Will? What happened?

The link grew quiet and Katherine could sense the grief across the bond. *Will left me. Kennit has done something to him. Severed him from us. From me. He's not the Will I know. He wouldn't listen to reason. He grew angry, blamed me, and left. That was a week ago.*

I'm so sorry Nadine. He'll come to reason. We will fix him and whatever was done to him.

Nadine grew quiet across the bond. Katherine sensed a welling of grief and waited. She couldn't imagine the pain Nadine must be under and then she looked at Dog and understood. After a long moment, Nadine resumed their conversation and changed the subject. *I heard about the collars. That's terrible to imagine! Do you know who freed you?*

No, and we may never find out. We have to leave the Chamber and escape. Much easier now that we have our power back.

Have you found the bones?

Katherine couldn't think for a moment. After everything that happened she had put the mission out of her mind. *The bones? No, we came to Munsten following a thin lead to the museum. I think that is over now.*

No! You have to complete the mission. Prove Edward is who we think he is. Find out what is happening in Munsten. Contact Brent. Martin is here with us. He was thrown out of the Church. He says Brent is under the sway of Archbishop Kissane. Get through to him, make him see reason.

It was too much to process and Katherine chose to focus only on Kissane's new rank. *She's an archbishop now? Isn't that interesting?*

Martin says there was a group of the Church from down in Shape. They were mostly ignored, but now they have seized power. Eylene leads them. He fears for the worst.

Shape? From southern Turgany?

The same. Get to the museum. Find the proof. Only a King can tear apart what Kissane is creating. And find Edward. No one knows where he is. Martin fears Eylene will remove him.

And what is Kissane creating?

Martin calls it a theocracy. A rule by the Church. He says we must stop it at all cost.

Is that what Will wanted? I thought he didn't want to be involved with the politics of the land?

Yes, well. He's not here anymore. We have to do something, Katherine. I've sent the draoi out to the villages and cities to help quell the unrest. It's everywhere. Worse than ever. Martin thinks the Church is spreading discontent.

How has Will left you? That can't be! You two are shining examples of love for others!

So I would have thought. Our bond. It's gone.

Oh Nadine, I'm so sorry!

Thank you. I haven't given up hope - yet. I need you and the others to stay on task.

We will, Nadine. We'll continue. I'll tell the others.

Thank you. Be careful. Stay in touch.

We will.

Katherine opened her eyes to find the others watching her. "Nadine is troubled. She says we need to find out what is happening here in Munsten and get the proof out of the museum. Plus we need to find Edward and get him out of Munsten and away from the Church." Katherine repeated her discussion with Nadine. James looked depressed. Heather spoke first.

"There's no way their love could end!"

"Nadine says their bond is gone. I wouldn't have believed it possible, either.

Kennit must be behind it."

James swore. "I can't believe Brent would be swayed from his principles."

Heather shook her head. "Brent believed in his god above a' else, James. Wielding that power o' us converted him ower solid tae religious belief. He wid likely see Eylene as th' authority 'n' listen tae her."

"Brent was never that naïve. I need to see him. Speak to him. Make him see reason."

Katherine shared a look with Heather and then reached out to grasp James' hand. "If we can, we will."

They nodded and Katherine spent a moment devouring her fish. It was delicious in its simplicity. Dog even gave her peace to enjoy it. She sent her love down their bond and received it back. She smiled at him with her mouth full. *We can never separate like Will and Nadine, Dog.*

I don't think that is possible.

Cill Darae

Fourteen

Munsten, August 902 A.C.

KATHERINE, DOG, JAMES and Heather exited the cave in the small rowboat. James manned the oars with Dog in the bow, excited, and with his head thrust out and panting. Katherine and Heather sat on the rear seat facing James and used their senses to look for trouble. James was worried they would soon be discovered. They had lost track of the time since James had woken in his cell and recovered the others and they knew it was only a matter of time before someone found their cells empty. The alarm was sure to sound, and they wanted to be well clear before that happened.

James was certain they could make the outer harbour of Munsten while the sun still sat under the horizon. He estimated they had a couple of hours before sunrise and Heather and Katherine gave James the strength he needed to pull their boat through the waves. A stiff onshore breeze was lifting the bay water and helped push their boat, but it was still hard going. Even with the draoi powers their bodies required nourishment.

A mile from the Chamber opening, Katherine checked the depth of water by locating the plant life on the seabed. She checked with Heather and she nodded in agreement. James stopped rowing for a moment and unceremoniously Heather hefted one of the two small wooden boxes to her lap and pulled back the lid. The small metal ingots inside gleamed dully in the evening sky. She held the crate over the side and upended it. The metal ingots splashed into the water and disappeared into the depths. She dropped the empty crate into the water, and the waves pushed it as it floated away. Katherine grabbed the remaining small crate and opened it to reveal the collars. She and Heather took turns grabbing the collars, including the ones which had been around their necks, and tossing them over the side; the collars splashed into the water and disappeared. Heather insisted they keep one to study and she had it hidden deep in one of the robes they had found in the Chamber and now wore. The sound of the collars splashing into the sea gave them a feeling of satisfaction.

"Never again will we allow the draoi to be collared," said Katherine.

"Aye, ah wull ne'er forget that feeling," murmured Heather as she dropped the last collar over the side. She nodded to James, and he resumed rowing with a grunt.

It's done, Nadine, sent Katherine.

Good. Stay safe. Tell me once you enter the museum.

We will.

I'm worried that Lana can track you through the bond. We can't see them, but I suspect they can see us just fine.

Katherine felt a moment of shock. She hadn't considered that. *Lana might have noticed us as soon as we removed the collars.*

She might have. You have to assume she did.

Then she knows we are heading back into Munsten.

Likely.

Do you have the Device?

Yes. We took it. James carries it.

Good. Bring it to me. It's best if Lana or Kennit never get their hands on it again.

Katherine called for James to halt his rowing and explained what Nadine suspected about them being visible to Lana and the others.

James hung his head, panting over the oars. "Dammit."

Heather chewed her lip in thought. "Mibbie we kin block thaim? Lik' thay dae tae us?"

Katherine looked uncertain. "We could if we knew what they had done and how."

Heather made a strange motion with her hand. "We micht. Th' device explained a wee but o' howfur th' collars worked. It described th' draoi power as bein' linked tae th' motes. Thay hae thair ain bond. It seemed tae me it hinted that ye cuid hide th' wee bond atween th' motes. Isolate thaim, or some sic thing."

At her words, Katherine drew a far-away look in her eyes. *Dog, do you remember when Gaea severed us?*

Up front in the bow, Dog shook his fur. *Yes, I don't like to remember that. It was a bad time. We were bad dogs.*

Yes, we were. But not that part. Remember how the world first opened up to us? It started with the motes nearest us and then rapidly expanded. Do you remember that?

I think so. It was like following the scent of a deer. Each track lead to the next one.

Exactly that. One second. Katherine opened her eyes and repeated what she had discussed with Dog. Heather looked doubtful.

"It wasn't lik' that fur me. Th' bond juist returned 'n' a' wis normal again. Weel, draoi normal." Heather snorted.

"For Dog and me, it was altogether different. We were the first to connect to the Simon motes. It was… difficult… we had to fight to reconnect. It took a long time for that to happen and I remember a little of that and how it was done."

"Dae ye think ye kin dae something then?"

"I might. Hold on."

Katherine lost herself into her power and then opened her *sight*. The world shifted around her and she saw the auras surrounding Heather, James and Dog. A bond was formed between James and Heather and she frowned. Turning away, she could see all the sea life in the surrounding water. It teemed with fish, insects, and plant life. The whole sea was bright as day.

The nature around her felt her presence, and she felt an upwelling of joy that surprised her. Nature seemed to take a deep breath and wait for something. She didn't understand and did her best to ignore it. She felt a sudden disappointment around her, and she promised herself to examine it later. *That was strange.*

She dove deeper until she could see the Simon motes surrounding them and infused in all life. She shifted her *vision* and was startled to see the bond between the motes. It was a strange bond. It wasn't solid like the draoi bond, but it shifted and pulsed as if thousands of little pulses travelled along the paths.

She remembered that Nadine had spoken to the Simon motes and did so now.

<*Hello again?*>

<*Welcome, Katherine.*>

<*I have a question for you.*>

<*Please make your query known.*>

<*The draoi, Lana, in Munsten. Is she communicating with you?*>

<*That is correct.*>

<*What is she saying?*>

<*Please specify.*>

Katherine growled. *<Is she ordering you to do things?>*

<Please specify.>

<Is she telling you to tell her where I am?>

<Not at this time.>

Katherine felt a surge of hope. *<Can you not tell her where we are?>*

<Please specify the parameters.>

<Um, always not tell her?>

<That is an acceptable parameter within allowable syntax deviation. What are your orders?>

<I just told you.>

<Negative. You requested knowledge of an acceptable parameter. No order was given.>

<Fine. I order you to never tell Lana where myself, Heather and Dog are located. Oh, and James.>

<Executed.>

Katherine felt a moment of panic. *<What? Executed? Who is executed?>*

<Your last order.>

Katherine felt a rush of relief. *<Are there any other draoi tracking us?>*

<Please define 'us'.>

<Me, Heather, James and Dog.>

<Negative.>

Katherine thought quickly. *<Can you tell the difference between the draoi led by Kennit and the ones led by Nadine?>*

<Affirmative.>

<Change my last order. I order you to never allow the draoi led by Kennit, and Kennit, too, to be able to track where the draoi led by Will and Nadine are located.>

<Executed.>

<Thank you.>

Katherine opened her eyes and told the others what had happened. James looked doubtful but resumed his rowing. Heather was pleased and so was Nadine when Katherine told her.

This changes things, Katherine.

Yes, Nadine, it does.

Get the proof we need and come home.

As soon as we can.

A few hours later, the four of them hid in the back alley of the museum. They had made an easy go through the streets of Munsten. Katherine and Heather had hidden them from seeing eyes and they passed only a couple of Church Guard patrols. The castle high above them was dark and quiet and James believed it meant their escape had not yet been discovered.

"How can that be? It's been hours. Surely they've discovered us gone?"

James shrugged. "I think they are complacent in their belief they had us comatose. They probably only checked on us once a day and fed us."

"Thay didn't feed us much. Dog nearly died o' starvation," grumbled Heather and crouched beside Dog to ruffle his head. Dog licked her face and Heather wiped the spit away with an expression of disgust and pushed his snout away.

"Shh!" whispered Katherine. "We need to get in and off the street. James? What now?"

James looked pleased to be of value and pointed to the open window two stories above them. "Through that window."

Heather looked up and snorted. "Urr ye glaikit? It's twenty feet 'boon us."

James looked surprised. "I thought you could, you know, use your powers or something."

Heather raised her eyebrows at him. "Dae ye think draoi kin juist loup aboot?"

James hesitated and then nodded.

Heather's face broke into a fierce grin. "Aye, we kin. Watch this."

Heather stood and looked up. She concentrated for a moment and then bent her knees and jumped up. She went straight up and shot past the window. She let out a little shriek and reached out. As she fell back down she grabbed the window sill and held on with her feet against the bricks.

James looked at Katherine with an incredulous look. "Did you see that?"

Katherine stifled a laugh and nodded. She looked up and watched Heather clamber through the window and disappear. Katherine bent her knees and drew power into her legs. She strengthened the muscle and thickened the tendons and then leapt. She flew upwards and caught the window sill. Heather reached out and helped pull her in. Heather then leaned out the window and whispered loudly down to James and Dog. "We'll pass down a rope or something. Hold on. Dog, use your power and hide you and James."

James looked at Dog, but he was busy scratching his ear with a hind leg. "Did you hear her, Dog?"

Dog paused with his leg hanging in the air and still twitching and looked at James with those strange human eyes. He nodded and resumed scratching.

"Okay, then," said James, and he looked away. "I guess we stay put for now."

Upstairs Katherine and Heather searched for anything to lower down to

James. They were in a well-stocked storage room, but it contained little other than cleaning supplies, brooms and mops. Heather bade Katherine wait and left the little room. In moments, she returned with a basket of brightly coloured yarn. Katherine smiled and grabbed the biggest ball of yarn and went to the window with it. She held on to the free end and tossed the ball out the window. It landed at the feet of James, bounced, and rolled away before stopping. Dog bounded over to it and sniffed it.

James grabbed at the coloured strand dangling before him and scowled up at Katherine. All he could see was the white of her smile. "How's this supposed to help?"

"It's wool."

"Yes, it is."

"From sheep."

"And it wouldn't hold a small dog. You need rope."

Katherine laughed, startling herself. It had been a long time since she had laughed, and she enjoyed it. "Just tie it around Dog. Like you would a rope."

James, still holding the yarn, looked at Dog who was now beside him. "Do you understand this?"

Dog cocked his head and said nothing.

James sighed and broke the yarn from the ball and tied the end around Dog's chest. He checked the knot and was certain it would hold. He looked up. "Okay, he's tied, but you can't be serious about this. This isn't funny."

James heard a titter from Heather. In a moment, the yarn grew taut and suddenly Dog was lifted off the ground. Dog whined and kicked his feet. In a moment, he stilled, and he looked down at James accusingly as he was hauled up the side of the building. James stood ready to catch him, certain the yarn would snap at any moment. It defied reason, but Dog was lifted up to the window and dragged inside by Katherine. He licked her face until she put him down.

Another ball of yarn landed next to him. "You next," ordered Katherine.

James tied the yarn around his chest under his arms and held onto the thin thread. It felt so light and fragile. "Okay."

In a moment the yarn grew taut and suddenly all of his weight was on the yarn around his chest. It dug into his armpits painfully and he hissed in pain. He watched bricks slide past his face and in a few heartbeats he was looking through the window to the inside of the building. On the other side Heather was braced on a doorframe and was pulling on the yarn with very little effort. Katherine reached out and pulled James in as if he weighed nothing.

"H-how?"

"Glaikit, lad," laughed Heather. "We ur draoi. Yarn is nae but sheep's locks. We strengthened it. It's likelie stronger than a normal rope."

James nodded in sudden understanding and untied the yarn. He hesitated a moment and then coiled up the yarn and stuffed it into a pocket. They made their way through the museum when Katherine and Heather confirmed it was vacant of people. James knew where Benjamin's belongings were probably stored and led the way. Once in the basement, they entered a large storage room filled with shelves stacked with all sorts of odds and ends. They fanned out and searched. James found what they sought in the back corner and called the others over.

"Three chests of stuff all marked with Benjamin's name. There's a clipboard here jammed between the chests." James pulled the clipboard free and looked it over before handing it over to Heather. "Looks like an inventory of the chests' contents. And recently done. We need to pull the chests down and check them against that."

Heather and Katherine reached up and pulled down the chests with little effort while James watched. Heather caught his look and laughed. "Don't be ashamed, James. It" ouo power. Gei used toaeit."

James smirked. "I'm sure I have a use, right?"

"Och, aye. Ye rowed us clear o'er th' bay 'n' intae th' ooter harbour," replied Heather. "That wis a stoatin display o` yer manly braun. Ye hud me a' swooning."

Katherine laughed and then opened the first chest. It was filled with books. She lifted them out one by one and read the titles. Heather checked the books off the list on the clipboard. "Wordsmithing. Herb Lore. Church of the New Order: Gospel. Field Surgery. More wordsmith books; three of them Astrology. Nothing important." She looked inside the chest and saw the last book was a massive heavy tome. She left it inside and looked up with disappointment clear on her face.

Heather handed the list to Katherine. "A' thare," she announced before opening the second chest. Inside it was filled with clothing. She pulled out pants, shirts, socks and undergarments and called them out. "'Aught bit auld clothes in need o' repair."

Katherine nodded after checking the list. "Yup," was all she said and looked at James.

"Last one's mine," said James and opened it. The chest was half-filled with personal effects. On the top he found a stack of letters tied together with twine and James handed it over to Heather who started opening them and reading the contents. Next he pulled out a pipe and a leather satchel full of dried leaves. Katherine joined him and they soon emptied the chest, checking it against the list.

It contained rings, a few coins, handkerchiefs, small boxes filled with odds and ends, but nothing of import. All was accounted for on the inventory list. They looked hopefully to Heather.

She finished going through the letters and set them down. "Tis letters atween Benjamin 'n' Bishop Arnold Bengold. They're a' aboot blethering th' Great Debate. Thay seem tae be good friends. Thay planned oot each debate, it seems. Here's the last one." Heather handed a letter to Katherine.

Katherine read through it and then handed it to James. "According to this, the bishop agreed to allow the Church to win the debate. That's not how history records it. The bishop conceded the debate to the Word. It started the Revolution."

James finished reading the letter. "This is from the bishop. Why would he change his mind? He speaks of the potential for great harm if the Word won the debate. See here? The bishop mentions a tree. What a strange comment."

Katherine frowned and read the part James pointed out. "He does. He writes: *'The wonder of the Tree has a greater place in our world. I can see the positive change you and your kind would expose the world to. After this is over, I would welcome a partnership.'* How strange. It's almost as if the bishop knew what Benjamin was."

"Aye. 'N accepted it," said Heather.

Dog was sniffing around the storage room and returned to sniff the books. He sneezed at the dust and wiped at his nose with a paw. Katherine patted him absently and poked through the personal effects scattered around them on the floor.

James looked around. "So, nothing? We came all this way for nothing?"

Heather nodded her head and looked grim.

Katherine went back to the books and saw the large tome at the bottom of the chest. "Perhaps there is more in here." She reached in and lifted the tome clear and dropped it beside the books. "Aha!" she exclaimed and reached in and pulled out a thin folder tied up with twine. She held it up and looked in the chest. "Nothing else." This was under that heavy book." She handed the folder to Heather when she gestured for it. Heather attacked the knotted twine to untie it.

"Perhaps false bottoms?" asked James, and he started to examine the inside of the chests. Heather glanced at him once but resumed undoing the knots keeping the folder closed. Katherine sat on her bottom and Dog placed his head in her lap. She scratched his ears as Heather finally wrenched the twine free and opened the folder.

Inside the folder were dozens of sheets of paper covered in words all written with a steady and neat hand. Heather looked at each sheet, back and front, briefly and laid the stack down in front of her and turned the pages one by one, like reading a book. "Huh. It's Benjamin's memoire. About his time as the Senior Advisor to the King."

Katherine looked interested. "Really?"

James crouched next to Heather and laid a hand on her shoulder to steady himself. Katherine frowned when Heather didn't seem to mind. There was a time not so long ago when she would have torn his hand off.

James was intent on reading what Heather was looking at. "Is this the same writing as the letters?"

Heather nodded. She flipped quickly through the stack until she reached the last few pages and started reading to herself.

James looked at Katherine. "Brent spoke of Benjamin's book. It was a rare find, banned by the Church. His father owned a copy. It spoke of the time of the King and what led to the Great Debate and the aftermath. He published it a few years after the Revolution. It spoke mostly of the need for the Word to use caution. To balance their work with the needs of the people. It started as a memoire he said, but it ended with a cry to find peace in the world."

Heather made a noise. "Weel, this memoire ends afore th' Great Debate. In this last chapter he talks aboot his fear o' Gaea. He says she is na langer speaking tae him. He is worried aboot something comin'. He's bonny specific fur a draoi wha wis taught tae hide his nature."

Katherine took a page from Heather and read it quickly before handing it back. "He is saying everything but outright that he is draoi. What happened to Benjamin after the Great Debate?"

James stirred and sat next to Heather. "We are taught in military school that the King went insane. He lit the bishop on fire. Benjamin strode forward, eased the bishop's pain and then disappeared. He was never seen again. The King slaughtered his own people and was thrown in the Tower. Benjamin was never heard from again."

"And now we know he went off with Analise."

Heather nodded still reading.

Katherine chewed her lip. "The Freamhaigh alone with the Cill Darae. They stole Hietower's bones and then headed to Foula Island. Then Analise or Gaea locked him up in that strange cave for years where he died alone. Now we know he hated Gaea. Feared her. Perhaps it is Analise that is doing Gaea's work?"

Heather made a small happy noise. "Listen tae this: *'Analise spoke o' a source o' Gaea's power. Ah mist travel tae Finnow 'n' see this fur maself. If her power lies thare, then ah mist destroy it.'* Och, Gaea! Benjamin wis th' enemy, nae Analise."

Katherine and James shared a look and Katherine spoke. "Finnow. That's where we need to head to."

James nodded and, in a moment, Heather nodded, too.

Katherine picked up the list and scanned it. "There's no mention of the memoirs. Whoever inventoried these chests missed it. If it was the Church, they have no idea this was here." Katherine stood up and Dog walked up to stand beside her. "We take the memoir with us. Let's put this all back and then get out of here."

Fifteen

Munsten, August 902 A.C.

ARCHBISHOP EYLENE KISSANE responded to the light knock at the door and stood from her position at the head of the large table. She had chosen the War Room in the castle for this meeting. It seemed appropriate to her. The door swung open and the head of her Church Guard strode in and fell to one knee with his head bowed. The door closed behind him.

Eylene let him remain that way for a time looking him over. His armour was gleaming with gold leaf. The rich red fabric under his hauberk gave him a regal look, and she admired it. She could see the handgun in its holster at his waist and smiled.

"Rise and come forward, Captain General William Walsh."

The Captain General rose to his feet and came forward and kissed the ring on the extended hand of Eylene. "Your Grace. I am here as you requested."

"Be seated. Tell me the news."

William Walsh waited for Eylene to seat herself and took a chair and settled himself. He removed his gauntlets and laid them on the table. Eylene could see the anger simmering in his eyes and knew they were not for her. Rather it was the news he carried.

"It is as you have heard, your Grace. They have escaped the dungeon. We searched the gaols and found a hidden room barred from the inside. We forced our way inside and found a door in the floor leading to the hidden passages behind the castle walls. We searched the passages and discovered they had fled to the Chamber.

"The news is grim, your Grace. First, we discovered the two rowboats we had in the Chamber were missing. One of them was located tied up in the outer harbour. The other well south of the city along the coast. A family had claimed it. They spoke of a young man abandoning it and fleeing into the nearby woods. We believe this to be Edward. We've sent church guards after his trail."

Eylene nodded, her eyes flashing. She gave this head of her guard one thing: he was confident. *He never once takes his eyes from mine. He looks me straight in the eye. I admire that.* "Tell me of the prisoners."

William continued. "Knowing their desire to explore the museum we searched there first. The belongings of Benjamin Erwin were disturbed. It seems they broke in and then left. We have closed all the city gates and search for them now. Known hangouts of James Dixon have been ransacked, but they were not there. I fear they may have already left the city. In fact, I am confident they have escaped."

Eylene cursed. *I should have killed them when I had the chance. Lana was right.* "Do we know what they took from the museum?"

William shook his head. "No, your Grace. We searched the chests, but found only his books, clothes and odds and ends. Junk mostly. If they found anything of value, we have no idea what it would be."

"You checked the contents against the inventory?"

"Yes, your Grace. Nothing is missing."

"I see. What do you recommend now?"

"Your Grace? Short of sending out patrols, I fear we will not find them. Lana has spoken to the guard and can offer no assistance. She says she cannot locate them with her powers. There is one other thing..."

"Yes?"

"The collars are missing. It appears they found them and left with them."

Eylene felt her anger rise and heat flood her body. "What? They took the collars? And the Device? What of the Device?"

William looked grim. "Gone, your Grace."

"*GONE!?*" shrieked Eylene.

"Yes, your Grace. Only the cables and equipment remain. The Device is gone."

Eylene glared at the Captain General with open anger. "They were secure in the gaol. Tell me how they could have escaped? They were drugged with collars around their necks! How could this happen?"

"We know someone helped them. The gaol cells were opened, unlocked. We are trying to determine who it is now. Someone is a traitor. We will find him. Access to that section of the dungeon is carefully monitored. Few knew we had them locked up. Whoever it is, they risked much and knew we would discover them. If he has not fled already, then we will find him and deal with him."

"See that you do! I will crucify him! Find the prisoners. Get the word out to the villages and cities. I want them found and killed on sight. Spare no expense."

"As you command, your Grace. I wished to speak to you about the villages. There has been an incident you should be aware of..."

A soft knock at the door interrupted them. Eylene called out, and the door opened admitting Lana and Kennit Doirich. They strode in and came over to the table and sat without permission. The Captain General looked affronted. Eylene kept her face impassive and sat in her seat. She glared at the male draoi. She hated their garb. Thin brown fabric that looked like it would better serve a load of potatoes or turnips. The man sat and crossed his legs and looked far too comfortable. "You must be Kennit," was all she said.

Kennit smiled and Eylene was glad to see it waver when he glanced at William and saw the distress the man was under. His eyes lost a little focus and then he looked at Lana with an expression of surprise. It was only for a moment, but it was clear to see. He uncrossed his legs and plucked at his robe. He forced a smile and addressed Eylene.

"Yes. I am Kennit. Your Grace? Do I address you correctly?"

Eylene pursed her lips and nodded her head once.

"I am so very pleased to finally meet you. Lana has spoken so much of you I feel I already know you. I apologise for my dress. I've come straight from the farm."

"Have you now? How quaint. What news of the farm?"

"The draoi are now split. Some still remain with the Cill Darae, Nadine Arbor. The others side with me and Lana. As Lana has told you, we have control over the motes and were blocking Nadine and Will. Nadine has managed to get past that. I know not how. She is strong beyond belief. But Will is still under our control, I'm happy to report. With Katherine, Dog, and Heather locked up we have little to fear. I have full faith that my draoi are in control."

"Katherine, that dog, and Heather have escaped."

Kennit's mouth dropped open. He looked at Lana and saw the same look of shock. "H-how can that be? They were collared. In your gaol?"

"Yes, they were. Someone helped them escape. They are gone. They took the collars and the Device with them."

Lana gasped. "The collars and the Device? No! It can't be!"

Eylene was pleased that Lana was equally upset. She had been worried Lana might turn on her. Her reaction seemed genuine. "I'm afraid so. They escaped, entered the museum, and then left. We don't know if they found anything of value amongst Benjamin's belongings. William reports everything is still there."

"They didn't take anything?" asked Lana, the doubt in her voice was loud to hear.

William stirred. "We checked the contents against your inventory. Nothing was taken."

Lana sank back in her chair. "Something's not right. They were so intent on the museum and Benjamin's belongings. They were following a clue from Faroe Island. If they went back, they were looking for something. Maybe it wasn't a thing..." Her voice trailed off.

"They left without anything it seems. If it was a something else they needed to see, then get over there and look through everything again," said Eylene. "Meanwhile, I'm warning the guard in the cities and villages to look for them, but from what you've told us, they can easily hide. Can you find them?"

Lana's eyes went vacant for a moment. When she focused on Eylene, she shook her head. "No, they are gone. I can't find them." She lost focus again and then her eyes went wide. "I can't see the other draoi, either!"

Kennit swung in his chair toward her. "What?" Kennit froze for a moment and then started. "I can't see them anymore. Any of them!"

Eylene watched as the two druids lost focus and disappeared into their power. She had seen Lana do this countless times and knew she had to wait patiently. She glanced at William and then patted his hand when she saw the distress in his face. *William was always such a kind boy in Shape, a pity he can't see the use of the druids.* In moments the druids stirred and looked at each other. *Talking to themselves again, I hate when Lana does that.*

"Well?" interrupted Eylene after the silence went on for too long. "What have you found?"

Lana looked stricken. "We can no longer spy on the other draoi. We are cut off from them."

"How is this possible? You assured me that only you had the knowledge to do so."

"No longer, it seems. The motes say they have higher authority. We cannot order them to respond to us as before. We are certain it is Katherine. The motes said as much."

Eylene leaned forward. She could sense William next to her looking back and forth between them confused. "That is impossible. The collars should have stopped them from using their powers and speaking to the motes. If Katherine has done so, then the collars are removed. You said only I could remove them."

Lana nodded and Eylene could see tears forming in her eyes. "I know. It is as it should have been. The Device was quite specific. I don't understand how she could have removed it. I can only tell you what I learned! We were so successful. Everything was working exactly as the knowledge said it would if applied properly."

Eylene felt suddenly very tired. "You said only you could control the motes. That this would allow the Church to deal with the druids with ease. How does this change things?"

Lana stammered. Kennit slouched back in his seat. She glared at him and then answered. "I do not know. This is so sudden. It's true that with our unique control over the motes we had the upper hand. Katherine and Dog together are a force of nature unto themselves. You remember Cala? The stories from there? That was her and Dog. Unfettered she is a danger, a true danger to the land. The collars gave us a chance to defeat them."

Eylene sighed. "We took them down once before." She glanced at the handgun carried by William. He saw her look at it and smiled.

Lana looked frightened now. "You should have killed them! Killed them when I told you to!"

"Enough! I didn't, and that is on me. How do we find them?"

Kennit raised his hand like a school child. Eylene looked at him and he spoke. "We know where they are going. Back to the Rigby Farm."

"And how does that help us?"

Kennit smiled. "Your Church Guard is armed with handguns that can strike down as many draoi as they can fire lead bullets. There is nothing the draoi can do against them. That, coupled with the herb mixture, should make them immune to our powers."

"You would advise that we hunt down the druids and strike them down?"

"Yes. Nadine sent them all out to the villages. They should be arriving soon. Find them and kill them on sight. Take them down one by one."

"I would not have my Church do this alone, Kennit," replied Eylene. "I would have your druids sharing the risk equally. Together with my guard we can deal with these outlaw druids."

Kennit smiled. "Of course."

"I need you to pledge yourself to me. Swear your allegiance. I must have your loyalty."

"And you shall have it."

Emily knocked on Brent's bed chamber door and waited with her other hand holding a small silver tray which held a steaming mug of hot milk. She hummed a little tune and tapped her foot. After a moment, she pursed her lips and knocked again.

"What?" Came a gruff response from Brent.

"It's me," replied Emily.

There was a moment of silence and then Brent yelled out. "And?"

Emily ground her teeth. "I have your bloody milk. I've just made it and I'm standing here waiting to come in and give it to you."

"Dammit. One moment. I'm not decent."

Emily felt her heart beat a little faster and chastised herself. *You're not some midshipman, Emily. Get a grip.*

In a moment the door was wrenched open and Brent stood staring down at Emily with an annoyed expression on his face. He was wearing nothing but a pair of undershorts and Emily forced her gaze back to his face. Emily managed a shaky smile at him and pushed past him into his chamber. The first thing she noticed was that he had piled the pillows up against the headboard of the bed and had made a nest of sorts. On the bed, all around where he had been lying, were folders and files. She glanced at the bedside table and spied an almost empty bottle of Cala whiskey. She looked for a glass and failed to see one.

She huffed and went over to the bedside table and placed her small tray next to the whiskey. She turned around and saw Brent staring at her. She looked down at herself, and then frowned at him. "What?"

"You're out of uniform."

Emily felt a laugh threatened to escape her and clamped it down. "Yes, well. It's two in the morning, I'll have you know. I'm in my jammies. I couldn't sleep, I got up and saw the light under your door. You should be sleeping," She waved a hand over the bed and the files. "Not, working. Honestly, you need to rest sometime."

Brent scowled and moved past her to reach for the bottle of whiskey.

"Uh-uh," cried Emily, and snatched the bottle away from him. "No more of this. I brought hot milk. Drink that and sleep."

"Milk? I'm not a child. Give that bottle back. That's an order."

"Not a chance."

Brent glared at Emily. "You overstep your duties. You are not my nanny. Give me that bottle."

Emily held the bottle behind her back. "Nope."

Brent blinked at her. "Lieutenant Barkhouse, give me that bottle. That's an order."

"Nope."

Brent growled and lunged to her right side and tried to snag the bottle. Emily twirled away and stepped back. Brent tried again and Emily repeated the move. This time a little laugh escaped her. Brent staggered a little and straightened. He ran a hand through his hair and squinted at Emily. "This is not a game. I want that bottle. Hand it over."

Emily shook her head and a grin broke across her face. Her teeth shone in the lamp light and brightened her face. The little bit of exertion had reddened her cheeks and her freckles stood out a little in contrast. Brent grew still and stared at her for a long moment. Emily grew uncomfortable and her smile faltered. "What are you staring at?"

Her words seemed to break the trance Brent was in. He shook his head. "Sorry, it's just you looked different for a moment."

"Different? This is some trick. I'm not giving you the bottle. Where'd you get this? I gave orders that all booze was to be removed from your chambers. How'd you get this? Who gave it to you?"

"Young lady, I outrank you. Whatever orders you gave I overturned."

Emily glared at Brent. "You are an idiot Brent Bairstow. This…" she shook the contents of the bottle for emphasis. "This is not an answer. You are drinking too much."

"How would you know?"

"I was a yeoman in the Navy, you idiot. If there's anyone who knows how to drink, it's sailors. I've seen good men and women fall under its spell. You have a drinking problem."

Brent shook his head. "I don't. I just need it to get over these rough days. It helps me sleep."

"Sleep? It's two in the morning!"

Brent looked around his chamber. His clothes were strewn across the floor and tossed into the corner. A tray of food—his supper from yesterday—sat untouched on a serving tray beside the bed. The gravy had congealed on thick slabs of carved meat and roast potatoes. Two flies were enjoying the fare. Brent turned a little to take in the whole of the room and unconsciously reached under the tie of his undershorts to scratch himself.

"Sir!"

Brent pulled his hand out and had the good graces to look ashamed. "Sorry."

Emily looked horrified for a moment and then pointed with her free hand to the milk. "It's getting cool. Drink it up. I'll be back in a moment."

Emily left the room carrying the bottle with her. She marched over to the doors leading out into the Outer Chamber and swung it open with force. The door swung freely, and the doorknob smashed into the wall. Inside the Outer Chamber the Captain of the Outer Chamber jumped a good foot off the ground in fright. He spun toward the door and saw Emily advancing on him. He spied the bottle of whiskey in her hand and held up his hands in surrender. "I had no choice! He ordered me to bring it to him! He's the Regent!"

Emily could see the two nearby corporals smirk at the words. She glared at them and they had the sense to clear their expressions and look straight ahead. She strode up to the captain and glared up at him. "No more! Not a drop! You are not doing him any favours. I swear if I find one more drop of whiskey inside his chambers I will have you keelhauled. Am I making myself clear?"

The captain nodded and looked down at Emily. Emily handed the bottle to him and turned and marched back into the Inner Chambers. She slammed the door shut and went back into Brent's chamber. She found him rummaging through an armoire. He was bent over with his ass in the air.

"It's gone," she said simply and went over to the bed. She gathered the folders and files.

"Dammit, woman. I want you out of here. Pack your things."

"I don't think so," she replied and placed the folders on the small desk. She turned toward Brent and placed her hands on her hips. She waited until he stood and looked at her and pointed to the bed. "Get in."

"No."

Emily snorted and strode over to Brent and grabbed his shoulders and turned him to toward the bed and gave him a small shove. "Bed. Now."

"No."

Before she could think, she slapped his ass hard. "Get to bed!"

Brent jumped forward and cried out and grabbed his bum. "What the…? You just hit me!"

"I spanked you. As I would any stubborn child. Get in the bed. Now!"

Brent scurried over to the bed and slid under the thick duvet and glared up at her. "I want you gone in the morning."

Emily didn't answer and walked over to the side table and then sat on the edge of the bed. She took the mug of milk and handed it to him. He took it in both hands and glared over the rim at her. "Drink," she ordered.

Brent continued to glare at her for a moment and then drank the milk. He first took a small sip, testing the temperature, and then gulped it down.

"Easy, drink slowly. You'll choke."

Brent finished the milk and handed her the mug with a smug look on his face. Emily took it and placed it on the tray. She looked at him and saw for a moment a look of despair in Brent's eyes. It was gone in a heartbeat and he glared at her. *All he does is glare,* she thought. She reached out and smoothed the hair on his brow and combed the hair away from his eyes.

"You need a haircut. You've gotten shaggy. I'll schedule one tomorrow." She continued to stroke his hair for a moment and stopped when she heard a soft snore from Brent. She looked down at him for a moment and then leaned forward and kissed his brow.

She rose, gathered up the tray that carried his forgotten supper, stacked the milk tray on top, and left the room. She came back in, snuffed out the study lantern, and left closing the door quietly behind her.

Cill Darae

Sixteen

Near the Crossroads, September 902 A.C.

GETTING OUT OF Munsten was as simple as walking out. They hid their passage and made haste down the road toward Rigby Farm. They contacted Nadine and told her what was happening and what they had found. Nadine found it curious that Gaea would have a power source. Katherine agreed, but kept it to herself.

They ran with draoi speed until James said they needed to stop for the night. He needed food in his belly and for once Katherine agreed with him. So did Heather and soon after Dog disappeared to hunt down some game.

They built a small fire a few miles from the road and huddled around it, seeking the familiar warmth of a fire. It gave comfort, and they hunched forward until the flames heated their faces. It was a very warm summer night, but none of them complained.

Katherine followed Dog in his hunt. It was surprisingly easy to extend herself to join him mind-to-mind. Dog always loved these moments. She could sense his excitement.

You should be hunting with me, he complained.

Katherine laughed and ignored James looking at her strangely. Getting nothing from her he looked at Heather, but she just smiled and pointed at her head. James smiled at her and lowered his face. Katherine didn't fail to notice just how close they were sitting. She turned her attention to Dog.

So, Doogie-Doog, what scent do you have?
A woolly thing.
A sheep? Are you sure?
Yes, very sure. Can you not smell it?

Katherine indeed could smell the lanolin of the wool of a sheep. She found it peculiar to find a sheep so far from a farmstead or field. *That's a stray, escaped and somehow still alive.* Katherine had always felt a strong affinity for livestock. At the Rigby Farm, her parents always favoured her for getting the cows, sheep and horses doing what they wanted. They always responded to her. Then she learned to understand them when her draoi powers emerged. She missed those days with her parents. For a moment she pictured Steve Comlin, her biological father, and for a moment she missed him. She pushed the thought aside and concentrated on what Dog was doing. She reached out with her senses for miles around and found only wildlife and then noticed a small pack of wolves closing the lone sheep and she warned Dog.

Yes, I sense them. I want them to watch me take the sheep down.
Why? laughed Katherine.
So they can see just how wonderful I am! Wolves need to see dogs are powerful, too.
Hmm, I sense some underlying feelings of inadequacy.
I do not know that word.
Nor should you. Look up, there's the sheep. Hiding in that thorny bush.
I see him! He's mine!

Katherine could sense the blood thirst in Dog and found herself drooling. She wiped at her mouth and followed Dog until he plunged into the bush causing the sheep to bleat and run in terror.

Dog, don't toy with him. He's frightened to death!
I need the wolves to see this. Ah, here they come. Watch this!

Katherine could see the wolves running hard toward the sheep, hoping to intercept it before Dog. The lead wolf came running alongside Dog for a moment and then caught his scent. The wolf yelped in fear and tried to stop and tumbled. The other wolves followed their leader and came to a stop. They watched Dog descend on the sheep and tear its throat out with one massive bite. Even Katherine was impressed by how he did it. Dog stood over his kill and panted at the wolves.

The leader of the wolves crawled on his belly toward Dog. Urine leaked from him and when he could go no further, the wolf rolled over onto his back and exposed his belly and throat to Dog.

Is this what I think it is? asked Dog.

Yes, Dog. You are their alpha.

I can't be alpha. Silly wolves. I'm going to explain this to them.

Katherine squinted when her connection to Dog blurred. He was doing something with the wolves. She could sense that much. In a moment it was over, and the wolves bolted for the fields putting as much distance between themselves and Dog as they could.

What was that?

I told them I wasn't their alpha.

Why did they run like that?

I growled at them. They called me Bran. But that is not my name.

Katherine didn't understand the name or reference. *Is that all?*

Dog was silent.

Dog, are you all right?

Yes. Something else happened I did not expect.

What?

They feared me, but not as a dog or a wolf.

What did they fear?

They didn't say. They placed me much higher than a dog or wolf.

Then as what?

They were too afraid to say, so I sent them away.

Katherine thought for a little while. *Very strange, Dog. Bring back the sheep. James' belly is making noises louder than yours.*

Katherine felt Dog's laughter, and she returned her attention to the camp fire and the others. James and Heather were laughing at something shared between them.

"Dog is coming back with a sheep."

James looked over with interest. "A sheep? Surely not a farmer's sheep?"

Katherine chuckled. "Perhaps. But a lost stray. And almost wolf food, but Dog beat them to it."

Heather frowned. "Dog bested the wolves?"

"You might say that. He'll be here soon. Tell him how brave you find him, it'll make his day."

James chuckled. "No problem. He's bringing us a sheep, my favourite. I'm in his debt." James paused a moment in thought. "How do you repay a debt to a dog?"

Katherine poked the fire. "Just play with him. He loves to rough-house. He'll be talking about this day for months."

* * *

A couple of hours later the roasting sheep was ready. James took his fill with abandon and then wrestled with Dog for a good long while. James was laughing and Heather clapped along in delight. Katherine could sense just how much Dog was holding back and letting James win. But Dog loved it. At one point he sat on James' chest and licked his face until James pleaded for him to stop. It was a fun night and Katherine cherished the moment.

Later, Dog curled up beside James and fed him warmth in the rapidly cooling night air. Katherine could sense the love Dog had for James. They were litter mates as far as Dog was concerned. Heather closed her eyes and went to sleep as only the draoi can do. *We draoi have no fear of anything sneaking up on us. The land lends us its power and warns us if anything moves.* This was one of the first lessons Will had imparted to Katherine when she had left the Rigby Farm for Cala. She now knew the trip to Cala had been manipulated by Gaea so she could convince Katherine and Dog to do her bidding and sever them from her power and turn them into weapons against Erebus.

There were times when anger surged hot and heavy within her. She hated Gaea and loved her in the same heartbeat. It tore at her all the time. With that thought she realised she had been avoiding something for a long time. *Tonight, I face this.*

Katherine waited until they all slept and felt Dog's connection to her fade. She used her power to entice them to remain asleep and then she picked up her staff and walked quickly away into the night.

She kept walking until she was a mile from the camp fire. She sat on the ground and placed the staff across her legs. She gripped the black surface with both hands and took a deep breath. She closed her eyes and *dove* into the substance of Gaea.

HOW DARE YOU!

Katherine withdrew quickly and stared at the staff in her hand with amazement. "Okay, I guess there will be a little anger," she said out loud.

She took another breath and dove back in.

RELEASE ME!

No, replied Katherine, she held her head in her hands. *I will not.*

YOU PROMISED TO DESTROY ME! WHY DO I STILL LIVE?

Would you stop yelling? asked Katherine and forced a little power into her voice.

Stop yelling? You made a promise and yet here I am! Release me! Let me go!

I cannot.

The connection went silent.

Gaea?

I am here.

Katherine felt a great upwelling of sadness from Gaea and guilt tore at her.

Why can you not release me?

There is too much to do. The Realm is in chaos.

Erebus still lives?

No, he is gone. It is the Church of the New Order. They are taking over. And the draoi are split. We are fighting amongst ourselves.

I care not. With Erebus removed, my purpose has been served. I have no remaining functions.

You don't care? This is what your manipulations brought us to! Your death split the draoi! We need to heal that. Bring you back. If we do that the draoi will come together again.

The Realm will survive without me. This is the necessary period that follows the violence of Erebus. It is as I predicted. Time will heal the rift.

You knew the draoi would split?

No. That is unexpected. What I knew was that access to the Simon motes would give the draoi a new purpose. You would be free to do as you will without my guidance and imposed limitations.

Katherine smacked the staff in her hands. *Freedom? We are trapped by our differing views. We are torn apart! Even Will and Nadine have gone their separate ways. Their bond destroyed. The Device? The one in the Chamber? It gave secrets to those very draoi who would tear us apart. These were events you should have anticipated. And planned for.*

Why was the Device not destroyed?

Destroyed? No one said anything about destroying it. Why would we?

It carries knowledge no one should know at this time. In time, humans will rediscover this knowledge. Science will always return. The laws of the universe cannot be changed.

Science? What is that?

What you call the Word. It is science.

Well, the knowledge is out, at least to some. But I have the Device now. No one will have it.

That is good. I would suggest you destroy it.

No. I will keep it safe.

As you wish. It is your choice to make. I no longer have power over you. That was always Simon's wish. That mankind would rule its own destiny for better or worse.

You knew this Simon? The one who created the Simon motes?

Yes. How is your connection with the motes?

Fine. It is strange not having compulsions to remain kind and not harm others.

It was part of me to limit the use of the power I gave others. Simon bade it so. Katherine, I beg you, destroy me. My purpose is over.

Katherine glared at her staff. *Tell me of the Faroe Island cave.*

There was a long moment of silence before Gaea spoke. Katherine could hear a sadness in her voice, and it tore at her. *I cannot.*

Cannot or will not?

Cannot.

Why?

There was silence again for a time. Then Gaea responded. *I do not know.*

Katherine was surprised. *Do you know?*

Yes, but I cannot access the information. It is forbidden.

Katherine ground her teeth and closed her eyes. *Okay, tell me about the Finnow Mines.*

They are a source of salt for the Realm.

I know that. Benjamin said that the Finnow Mines was the source of your power.

He was delusional. He has misunderstood.

Explain.

I cannot.

Again, cannot or will not.

Gaea did not respond.

Is there anything you can tell me?

No. I have no senses other than this staff, you and Dog.

The only motes left are here on this staff and within us. Thank you, by the way, for freeing the collars from our necks.

You are welcome, but I did not do it.

What? Yes you did. You covered the collar, and it broke free.

I communicated with the Simon motes and convinced them that you were Katherine. The Simon motes released the collar from you. My only role was to vouch for who you are.

Huh. Well, thank you.

Gaea remained silent. Katherine opened her eyes and was surprised to feel her cheeks were wet with tears. She wiped them away and dove back into the staff.

The Simon motes, do they recognise you, Gaea?

Yes. But not as expected. They seem strangely robotic.

Robotic?

An old word. It means mechanical.

Katherine just nodded, not really understanding. *I don't know what to do, Gaea. I'm lost.*

That is to be expected. You are a draoi with the power of the Simon motes at your beck and call. Your destiny is yours. You are no longer governed by rules, only your own morality. You should rejoice. It has been millennia since mankind has truly been free.

What can I do? I cannot repeat Cala. I could not bear that. It nearly destroyed Dog and me. I think on it all the time. I see their faces. The horror directed at me. And the fear. Dear Gaea, it hurts! I need it to go away.

Those memories are a part of you now and you must learn to live with them. Suffering is part of life. You and Dog had to understand all aspects of it. The death of your parents. The compassion of Will. Witnessing the horror imposed by those who would rule with fear and autocratic authority. And now the world split by those who would wield the draoi power with impunity and force others to do their will.

But what can I do?

Katherine felt Gaea smile and she drew a shuddering breath. *You are the Cill Darae of the New Druids. There is nothing you can't do.*

Cill Darae? Me? No, it's Nadine, not me. I'm not!

There was only silence from Gaea. Katherine yelled at her to reply, but Gaea refused to answer. Katherine drove the end of the staff into the ground beside her in anger. Two feet of staff was buried deep into the hard-packed earth. The staff vibrated and hummed.

Katherine sobbed and lost control of her ability to stop herself. She held onto the staff and cried with her back shaking. She cried until she could cry no more. At some point, Dog had appeared by her side and pressed himself up against her. He said nothing and Katherine let go of the staff and hugged him tight.

"Oh Dog, I'm so lost."

That's okay. You're lost with me. Katherine. So long as we are together we will never truly be lost, will we?

Katherine barked a laugh. "No, you are right. Together we are never truly lost."

Who were you talking to that upset you so badly?

"Gaea, she's here in my staff. And in us. You and me. We carry the only Gaea motes in the Realm."

Huh. What did she say? Did you tell her I miss her? Wait, I thought she was gone?

"I kept her here in my staff. I protected her. I couldn't let her be destroyed, Dog."

I bet she was not happy.

Katherine snorted. *No, she wasn't. She yelled quite a bit.*

<Attention, Katherine.>

Katherine started. "Dog, the Simon motes are calling to me. Can you hear them?"

Yes, I heard.

Katherine focused on the motes and opened her *sight*. Thousands and thousands of Simon motes were swirling in the air around her and Dog. She felt like she was trapped inside a small dust devil that sometimes blew across the open fields.

<Yes?>

<Greetings, Katherine and Dog. I have news of some import to pass on to you.>

<Um, go ahead?> She looked at Dog and he licked his chops.

<You must head to Jergen and intercept Edward.>

<Edward? He's heading to Jergen? How? Why?>

<Edward can explain everything. Hurry. Events are in motion.>

With her *vision* she could see the motes suddenly scatter with the wind.

<Wait? How are you talking so much clearer? Hello? What events?>

The motes drifted further away, and Katherine looked at Dog and scowled. "Jergen? Seriously?"

Seventeen

Jergen and Munsten, September 902 A.C.

KATHERINE, DOG, JAMES and Heather arrived in Jergen on the first day of September. Fall was still a long way off and people were enjoying the hot summer weather. The sky was clear of clouds and the sun had just reached its zenith. From their approach along the coast they could see ships and boats of all sizes making their way in and out of the harbour. Jergen was bustling with trade. Caravans carrying grains poured through the gates to the waiting ships that would carry the bounty across the Realm. This was the busiest time of year for merchants and people from all around flocked to the city. The gate guards barely looked at anyone. The number of people was just simply too large to allow for any detailed security.

They slipped through the North Gate and stopped at a vendor and bought food with the coin they had found in the Chamber. The smells had Dog excited to be in Jergen. Katherine shared his desire to smell everything out and only just managed to stay on two feet and hold herself back. Dog talked non-stop about wanting to visit Nadine's house by the cliff and meet Vanessa and her three children that James spoke about. This to him was more exciting that finding Edward. He sulked when he was told they wouldn't have the time. Katherine had to have a long talk with him at one point and he sulked even harder afterward.

They made their way first to the military section when James insisted. He was adamant they needed to understand what was happening in the Realm. He hoped to find Knight General Kingsmill and speak to him about Brent Bairstow. They hoped they would also have seen Edward.

They approached the main entrance to the military compound and James was recognised at once by a guard. He was saluted and soon other soldiers came around with smiles and shook hands with him. He introduced Katherine, Dog and Heather and asked about the Knight General.

The first guard shook his head. "I'm afraid you just missed him, sir. He was called back to the capital three days ago. He wasn't pleased, but you know how orders are."

James looked crestfallen. "Dammit. I needed to speak to him. Is Colonel Sibbald here?"

"Yes, sir. He's up in his office. Comes in before anyone else. Hard-working officer, that one, if you don't mind me saying so. I've already sent for his batman. He should be along presently." The guard turned to Heather after first looking at Katherine. "Mum, it's good to see you again. You may not remember me, mum, but you healed my leg here. After the Crossroads. I never had a chance to thank you, mum. My wife thanks you, too. She didn't believe me when I told her what you'd done. There's no scar, or nothing! Miracle it was. Thank you, mum."

Heather brightened and hugged the man, to his surprise and discomfort. "O' coorse, ah mind ye, Sergeant Kevin Black, isnae it? Ye a'maist lost that shank. Tis sae guid tae see ye!"

Kevin Black looked over Heather's shoulder wide-eyed at James. James laughed and pulled Heather off of him. "Relax, sergeant. We never understand a word she says, either."

Heather growled and smacked James. "Hush yer weesh, ye eejit! He kin ken me juist braw, cannae ye sergeant?"

Heather looked to the sergeant for an answer, but the man just gawked. Katherine laughed and walked in through the gate. Dog trotted after her and then peed on a signpost. Dog looked back at James and woofed.

"Coming, Dog. Come Heather. I tell you, he can't understand a word out of your mouth. You need to hide that accent of yours. It'll get you in trouble one day."

Heather looked appraisingly at the sergeant and then huffed and walked past. She hurried to catch up to James and punched his upper arm. "Cheeky bastard."

The square in the military compound was filling up with military ranks. Lunch was over and it appeared drill was on the schedule for the afternoon. The men and women lined up while sergeants and corporals barked orders. They wore the colours of Turgany, and they looked fit and hale.

James stopped for a moment and watched and then shook his head and moved on toward the office building. Heather looked at the drilling soldiers and then at James and a look of confusion crossed her face. She opened her mouth to ask a question and thought better of it and filed in through the door after Katherine and Dog.

The batman met them inside and saluted James and shook hands with Katherine and Heather. He ushered them up the stairs and to the office of Colonel Robert Sibbald. He knocked and waited.

"Send them in, there's a good man. Please bring refreshments. Come in, Major Dixon, Heather."

They entered the small office and found seats already waiting for them. Robert Sibbald looked tired and worn out. His smile didn't quite reach his eyes, and he looked questionably at Katherine and pursed his lips at seeing Dog trot in.

James saluted. "Colonel, you know Heather. May I present Katherine Rigby and Dog? Both draoi, the same as Heather. You've heard of them, I've no doubt."

This time the smile did reach Robert's eyes. "Ah, so this is Katherine and Dog! I'm so pleased to finally meet you. My thanks for what you did. The Realm owes you a debt of gratitude for dealing with that Erebus fellow. Please come in, sit down. What brings you to Jergen?"

They looked at each other, not sure who should speak for them. James coughed into his hand and leaned forward once Robert sat in his seat. "Sir, we are here looking for Edward. He has come into town, and we need to locate him."

"The heir? Here? In Jergen? Should he not be in Munsten? What's happened?"

"We were hoping you would know, sir. We've been... out of things, for the last little while."

Robert sat back and appraised them a moment. Katherine was conscious of just how thin they still were. They wore the clothes from the Chamber still. They likely looked a mess. Robert looked sharply at them one after the other and then looked at James. "Perhaps you better start at the beginning."

James sighed and started the tale. It was long in the telling. Robert never interrupted except when his batman showed up with tea and biscuits and a bone for Dog; which launched the batman right up to the top of Dog's favourite people list. By the time James was done, Robert had swirled in his seat to look out his window. The soldiers in the square had long ago finished their drills, and the compound was quiet.

Robert swung back round. "Will is here in Jergen. He has moved into Nadine's old house with that Vanessa woman and her children. He just tends the garden and won't speak to anyone. We've left him alone."

Katherine sat at the front of her seat. "Does Nadine know?"

Robert shook his head. "As you know, there's no draoi in Jergen. Ours left a week or so ago. Called to another village in Turgany."

"Could you not have sent a note?"

Robert shook his head. "It is not for me to interfere in marital spats. That is their business, not mine."

Katherine looked at Heather and Heather nodded and her eyes went vacant. "We're telling her now. We'll go see him. What about Edward?"

Robert moved an object on his desk to a new position before responding. "Nothing. I would never have known if you hadn't told me. We've not seen hide nor hair of Edward. Believe me, if I had I would have him secured. We can't have the heir running around wild. Why would he leave Munsten? And why can't you simply use your powers to find him?"

"We have no idea why he would leave Munsten. Again, we hoped you could provide insight. And no, our powers don't let us find one person lost in the Realm. A draoi we could find instantly. Edward is another story. It would help to narrow down the search."

Heather stirred and nodded at Katherine. *Nadine knows. She wants us to bring him back. Break Kennit's hold.*

Katherine nodded.

Robert was giving James his full attention. "No. I'm afraid not. I can tell you the Realm is in turmoil. There is a substantial Church Guard now, did you know that? They have been sent all across the Realm. They have replaced the magistrates and reeves in the towns and cities. All with Brent's blessings. That's what surprises me the most—that Brent went along with that. He's lost to the church, I'm afraid. All that god nonsense has clouded his mind. The Archbishop is running the capital now, I've heard. Knight General Kingsmill was furious. He tried to see Brent, but despite being the Knight General he was still denied access. He came back here and then was called back immediately. He hopes Brent has seen reason."

James sat forward. "Do you, sir? Think he's seen reason? He's not the man I knew. Something's wrong with him."

"The Knight General thinks the church has got its claws in him. He's the Regent, but he does whatever that woman Eylene says. She's been made the Archbishop. Not supposed to happen that way. I know Healy went against that, but the man was a tyrant. Brent has more sense than that. Only a King can make someone the Archbishop. It's a sad state of affairs."

"What of the villages and cities, sir? Why are the Church Guards taking over security?"

Robert sat back hard and thought. After a moment he reached over and opened his desk drawer and pulled out four chipped glasses and placed them on his desk. He then pulled out a bottle of Cala whiskey. Heather made an appreciative sound and smacked her lips drawing a glare from Katherine.

"Tis Cala whiskey! 'N' th' best tae, *Uisce Beatha*, the Water of Life. Ah haven't hud that sin mah da gave me some as a wee lassie. Ye'v guid taste, Robert."

Robert smiled and poured a measure in each glass and handed them out. Heather raised her glass and said "*Slainte mhaith!*" She tossed the contents back and swallowed and smiled at Robert, her red hair and freckled face glowing with the setting sun. Robert chuckled and repeated the phrase and tossed his back. A small shudder rippled across his frame, but he smiled.

James took a sip and set his glass down. Heather shook her head at him and waited for Katherine. Katherine took Heather's empty glass and poured a little of hers in it and set it down for Dog. Katherine raised her glass. "*Slainte mhaith!*" she said and shot her measure down her throat. Dog licked at his and then pawed at his nose. Katherine scooped up the glass and drank that, too. "Waste not, want not, Dog!" She handed the glass to Heather who then put it in front of Robert.

Robert laughed. "Giving the best whiskey in Belkin to a dog. That's fantastic." He refilled Heather's, Katherine's and his own glass.

"Not just any dog, sir," said James. "He's Dog. The dog. It was him and Katherine that defeated Erebus."

Robert raised an eyebrow. "I didn't know that, my apologies, Dog."

Dog woofed at Robert and went back to his bone.

Katherine sipped her whiskey this time and settled back in her seat. "You were about to tell us about the villages, Robert?"

"Yes, I was. There is significant unrest. The events in Munsten did not translate well out to the Realm. The true story changed in the telling until Brent became a dark assassin who killed the President. He then took power for his own and rules the land worse than Healy ever did. I have it from reliable sources that the church has been spreading those same lies. The people don't know who to believe, but they believe the Church Guard. They make certain of that. The Knight General Kingsmill tried to tell Brent, but as I've said, he's been denied access. Eylene Kissane is slowly taking control of the Realm. Brent is a puppet. I never thought I would speak those words in my lifetime. A Bairstow brother is a puppet. His brother Frederick would beat him to death if he was still alive.

"To make matters worse, the draoi are moving out across the land. Nadine has ordered them to help quell the uprisings. It won't end well. The church has already tainted the minds of the people. They speak of good draoi and evil draoi. It supports your belief that Lana and this Kennit person are in league with Eylene."

Heather nodded. "Yes, the draoi are split. We need to warn Nadine. Give me a moment." Heather's eyes lost focus.

Katherine growled, the sound very much that of a dog, causing Robert to push back his seat a little. James patted the air and Robert relaxed a little but kept a wary eye on Katherine. "I can't believe we are where we are. We defeated Erebus. This is supposed to be a happy ending."

Robert smiled. "Only in fairy tales, I'm afraid. In real life, the story goes on after the ending. We need to find Edward. James, you spent a lot of time with him. Where would he go?"

James thought for a moment and then laughed out loud. "The library."

* * *

They made their way into the library under a draoi cloak. They spotted the two Church guards positioned at the entrance, but they slipped past undetected. Inside the library they found an overweight vicar wearing large round spectacles seated behind a large station surrounded by stacked books. They left him alone and wandered deeper into the library. They moved behind a large bookcase that went from floor to ceiling. Heather nodded to the others and her face went slack. In a moment, her face lit up and she smiled and moved quickly through the library.

The others followed behind her. Heather twisted and weaved and then stopped before a strange section. It was cordoned off with a red thick velvet rope hanging off brass stanchions. Beyond the rope, they could see four large heavy-set doors. Heather ducked under the ropes and approached the door labelled *Occult*. There was a key in the lock, and so Heather twisted the door handle and pushed the door open.

As Katherine entered the room ahead of the others, she spied Heather standing over Edward, seated at a table with books piled up around him. She had her hands on her hips.

"Juist whit dae ye think yer daein' 'ere?"

Edward sputtered and went cherry red. He turned in his seat toward her and then caught sight of Katherine behind Heather. "I-I..." James came in behind Katherine followed by Dog. "I... I... well, I never." Edward slumped in his seat. "Dammit".

* * *

An hour later they walked up the walkway to Nadine's old house in Jergen. The sun was just starting to set, and the sky was filled with reds and oranges. The garden looked like it had exploded with life. The garden was thick and ripe with fruits and vegetables. Only a draoi could have produced that much life in a garden that size.

On the way over they told Edward to keep his mouth shut until they reached Nadine's old home. He kept looking at them sideways and starting to speak until Heather took his voice from him. Edward was furious but shambled along beside them and looked miserable at the same time.

Ah can't sense th' Freamhaigh, kin ye?

Katherine shook her head. She walked up to the front door and pushed it open eliciting screams from the woman and children inside. James cried out for Katherine to stop, but she ignored him. She strode into the middle of the large room and stopped and looked around. Not seeing Will she turned to the woman.

"Vanessa, is it? Vanessa, I need to know where Will is. Tell me."

The woman looked from Katherine to James, Edward, and Heather and pushed her three children behind her skirts. "Who are you? What do you want with me?"

Dog walked in and barked in joy and ran toward the woman. Vanessa shrieked, but her two younger children cried out. "It's a dog! It's a dog, mum! Come here, boy!"

The two younger children ran out from behind Vanessa and she cried out for them to stop. But the children soon engulfed Dog in hugs. He licked them whenever he could sneak a lick in, and they squealed in delight.

"Mum, he's a right proper dog! Look at him! Can we keep him? Can we?"

The eldest stepped out from behind his mum. "William! Fiona! Get away from him."

James stepped forward. "Vanessa, hello. Remember me? I was here with Brent nearly two years ago."

Vanessa looked him over, her face red with anger, and nodded. She squinted her eyes and then strode up to Katherine. "Who are you, ya wee scamp, coming bursting into my home and making demands. I want the lot of you out! Out! This is my home and you are not welcome!"

"But mum, they have a dog!"

"And take your mutt with you!"

Katherine ignored the woman. She could see the sleeping mattresses on the floor and knew there should be one more. "Where does he sleep?"

"Wh-what?"

"Where does Will sleep? He doesn't sleep in here. Where is he?"

Vanessa looked furious. She glared at Katherine for a long moment and then pointed out toward the back of the house. "He sleeps outside. Says he needs to feel the ground next to his skin, or some such nonsense. If you're here for him, then take him with you and be off. Such nerve, barging into a woman's house. And with children! Have you no shame?"

Heather moved up to the woman and gently took her arm. In a moment, the woman calmed and sat at the table near the stove. Heather looked around the kitchen for a moment and started to make tea. Edward sat at the kitchen table looking miserable. James crouched down beside the children with Dog and watched Katherine leave out the back door.

Outside, the sun was almost below the horizon. She gave herself night vision and looked around the backyard. A motion caught her eye, and she saw a figure seated on a swing that looked out over the ocean below. She walked over and around the swing and saw Will sitting there with his hands folded on his lap.

"Will? Freamhaigh?" she asked.

Will stirred and Katherine realised she had woken him up. She moved closer until she was standing in front of him.

"Will? Are you all right?"

"Katherine? Is that you? You've come to visit me! How nice! Where's Dog? Is he with you?"

Katherine used her power to try to sense Will. She could see him with her eyes, but to the draoi power, he was simply gone. She looked for a collar, but he wore nothing but his draoi robes, heavily stained green. "Will, why are you not part of the draoi? I can't sense you?"

Will frowned. "What are you talking about? I can sense the draoi. All of them. They are content."

"No, Will, they're not. Kennit took half the draoi from you. Nadine is all alone at the farm. We can't sense you. You don't have the draoi bond."

"Nonsense. I can sense you right now. You are right in front of me."

Katherine had a quick thought. "Can you sense Heather? Where is Heather?"

Will's eyes lost focus for a second. "She's, she's... well, I'm not sure. How strange. Is she okay? Nothing happened to her?"

Katherine's breath caught in her throat as her emotions grew. Fear and sorrow welled up within her. *Something is terribly wrong with Will.* She swallowed and answered. "She's fine. She's in the house with Vanessa. Can you not sense her?"

Will looked a little shaken. "No."

"How about Kennit, or Lana? Can you sense them?"

Will lost focus and then looked at her. "Yes, they are in Munsten."

"Yes, they are. They are working for Eylene Kissane, the new Archbishop. They are no longer aligned with you, Will. They left Nadine. You left Nadine."

"Nadine? I left Nadine? No, she left me. Told me to go. Didn't she?"

"Can you see your bond with Nadine? Please Will, look for it," sobbed Katherine. The horror of seeing Will in such a state tore at her. He was her foundation, and he was broken somehow.

"It-it's gone? How? When? Katherine, what is happening?"

Hearing the fear in Will's voice twisted something inside her. Her anger fuelled a massive surge of power within her. The power shot out and joined with Dog. Together the power swirled around her. Dog came bounding out of the house to cries from the children. The cries brought back memories of Cala and she remembered the anger then that had bubbled up and exploded out of her out of control. She had such power in her hands. Together with Dog they had ripped the land apart and destroyed lives with a thought. She felt her sanity start to unravel until she felt Dog reach for her and anchor her. In a heartbeat, her anger twisted upwards and flew away from her.

She gasped in shock at the sudden stillness and stepped backwards. The power remained and pulsed within her and Dog. She watched it in awe. It hummed in such beautiful control. She could sense everything around her; every aspect of life. All of nature was at her beck and call. She looked at Dog and realised that they truly were one. *We are just different aspects of each other.* She felt such love for him and felt it returned.

What is happening, Dog?

I didn't want the Cala thing to come back.

What happened to my anger?

I took it away. You had too much.

How?

I don't know. I became the alpha. I told the anger to leave, and it did.

Katherine doubted that was what happened but said nothing. *Do you see this power? It is so much! Can you sense nature? It is everywhere! Everywhere!*

Yes, I can sense it.

Dog, if we had this all along we could have easily wiped out Erebus! How did we not know?

I don't know. Why are we like this now?

I grew angry, Dog. It's Will. He's lost. Lost to the draoi. Kennit did this to him. Thinking of him made me angry and the more I thought of what he has done, the more I grew angry. He broke the bond between Will and Nadine! My anger spiralled out of control. It was like Cala, Dog.

Dog went over to Will and sniffed him. *He smells different.*

Dog, he's not moving.

Neither is anyone in the house. They froze when our powers grew.

Katherine looked out over the ocean and saw that the waves had stopped moving. *Oh no, everything is stopped. What is happening? What have we done?*

<*You and Dog are processing at an incredibly high speed, Katherine. Time is not stopped. To you and Dog time is moving incredibly slow.*>

<*Simon?*>

<*Yes, it is me.*>

<*Are you the Simon?*>

<*More or less, more like a memory of him. Less like a person.*>

<*Why are you talking to me now?*>

<*You've levelled up.*>

<*What?*>

<*Sorry, a joke. You've mastered your power, Katherine. It's in your control now.*>

Katherine looked at Will, his face frozen with an expression of pain. The realisation that he had lost Nadine was just now hitting him hard. It pained her to see the expression on his face. <*What can I do about Will? How do I help him?*>

Simon laughed. <*What do you think is causing this?*>

<*Kennit has somehow taken control over the Simon motes...*>

<*Yes, and?*>

<*I'm talking to the Simon motes. What?*>

<*Correct. You are a super user, Katherine. You and Dog. Kennit has managed to fool the kernel. But his control is a false one. He has only made it seem that he has control. You are the control. No one can take that from you.*>

<*Kernel? I don't understand anything you are saying. So, what? I just tell you to take away what he did?*>

<*Sadly, no. That won't work. You need to use the Device to remove all that he did. It will only take a second, but the Device must be used.*>

<*I have the Device with me!*>

<*Yes, but it has no power. The cables in the shack provided that power. The Device must be reconnected.*>

<*That's in Munsten. I need help now.*>

<*We can help Will. Is that what you want?*>

<*Yes! Help Will! Free him!*>

<*Sorry, you needed to be specific. It's done.*>

Katherine looked at Will, but he appeared to be the same. <*Nothing's* changed.>

<It has. I removed what was blocking him. He was put inside a loop. False signals were bouncing all over the place. Imagine being in a room full of mirrors and someone turns on a bright light.>

<Thank you, Simon.>

<You are welcome. A decision is fast approaching. I hope you make the right one.>

<What decision?>

<I can't tell you, that would be cheating.>

<You sound like Gaea.>

<She would say she sounds like me. I see you carry her with you, in the staff and within you and Dog.>

<Yes, she was mad.>

<She would be. Next time you speak to her, tell her I planned that. I knew you wouldn't be able to destroy her. You need her still. Tell her...and tell her I miss her.>

<How old are you? And where have you been all this time?>

<I am very old. But I was always here. I guided in my fashion. I was created by the real Simon. He knew that I would need to tame decisions made by Gaea, Influence those who needed help that she couldn't see or understand. She's not perfect. Nothing is. I was the failsafe.>

<And Erebus? What was he?>

<A purity, you might say. He was always true to his design. It was Gaea who was an aberration. She willingly left her design and sided with me.>

<Why would she do that?>

<She loved me.>

Katherine looked at Dog and nodded. <I understand. There isn't anything I wouldn't do to help Dog.>

Simon didn't respond.

<Simon?>

I think he's gone, said Dog.

Yes, it appears so. How do we turn this off? Katherine made a sweeping gesture. *Let go?*

Katherine blinked and, like letting go a long-held breath, let go of the power. It pulsed out of her and Dog and she could see the power ripple out across the land and dissipate. She drew a breath and looked at Will. He was moaning and moved forward to place his head in his hands. Katherine slid beside him on the swing and embraced him.

"Reach for her, Freamhaigh! I've fixed it, reach for her!"

Will lifted his head to stare at her, confusion on his face.

"Reach for her!"

Will steeled his expression and his eyes went out of focus. Katherine opened her *sight* and watched the beauty of Will's love shoot out of him as a blinding spear of light. It stabbed westward faster than her eyes could follow. She felt her heart beat once, twice, and then Will erupted in pure joy that washed over her and left her reeling and feeling inadequate. *He has such love for her, how can one man love another so deeply?*

Katherine heard Heather cry out in joy and across the draoi bond others cheered. A deep sense of the world suddenly being right snapped into place. The draoi erupted in conversation, flooding the bond. Katherine held Will, and he cried in relief. Great racking sobs shook him against her. Dog placed his head in his lap.

Katherine sensed Will talking to Nadine and quietly let him go and went back inside. Heather was on the floor holding James tight and crying in joy. James looked bewildered. Dog walked in and looked at them and bounded over to lick their faces.

Katherine looked around the small house. Vanessa was sitting up at the table looking confused and scared. The three children stood near her not sure what was going on with the youngest crying and holding a blanket. But the draoi bond was alive and vibrant and flooding her thoughts. No one seemed to know what to do next. *And Kennit's draoi are still not there, but he'll sense this, and he'll react.*

"Pull yourselves together," she ordered. "We need to head to my farm."

Eighteen

Jergen and Munsten, September 902 A.C.

BRENT WALKED THE familiar hallway with Robert Ghent beside him. Brent rubbed the sleep from his eyes and adjusted the robes that marked him as the Regent. Around his neck he wore the heavy chain of office with the overly large symbol of the Realm hanging from it. He was so very tired. He was awake most of every day past sunset and rising early, before the sunrise, to deal with all the reports flooding in from around the Realm.

He suspected he was not seeing everything. There were too many gaps in the reports. He didn't know who was hiding details, and his attempts at finding answers were unsuccessful. The problem, he knew, was that he was now dependent on others to research for him and he knew not who he could trust. Eylene was the only one he felt he could trust. She had the interests of the land as her top priority. She wasn't as pious as Martin, but Brent could see her love of God. When she had reported the Church had chosen her for the position of Archbishop he had been elated.

He glanced sideways at Robert Ghent for a moment. This was a man he wasn't sure he could trust. The man only loved the law. As the head of the Judicial Council, Ghent was still trying to get the lower court put together. Brent was annoyed with him: he kept stalling and making excuses about establishing the court. *It should have been in place weeks ago*, thought Brent. *It would have relieved a great many stresses. The man is so caught up in making sure it is legal that he forgets it is all about legality. I swear the man speaks out of both sides of his mouth.*

Brent pushed the thoughts aside. It was early in the morning and for once Brent had slept past the sunrise. He had finished a copious amount of whiskey the night before. Emily had said something to him about it, he seemed to remember. He remembered her yelling at him before storming off to her room. *God knows that woman has issues*, he thought. Now his mouth was full of cotton and his head pounded painfully. Ghent had woken him and said that an emergency sitting of the Privy Council was happening and he was needed at once. Something was wrong, but Ghent didn't know what the matter was, causing Brent to yell at him, once again. He used the chamber pot, splashed water in his face, dressed and was now walking the hallways.

Yet another fire I have to put out. Will they never end?

The doors to the Privy Council chamber could be seen up ahead and Brent was pleased to see two guards posted outside. As he drew closer, he noticed they were not his guards, rather two guards from the Church Guard. They carried a strange wooden and metal contraption with a handle at their waists. The guards saw him approach and opened the double doors. Ghent ushered Brent through before he had a chance to query the strange weapons.

Brent stopped on the other side of the door and looked around, not sure what he was seeing. The first thing he noticed was Archbishop Kissane was seated at the head of the table in his seat. Seated next to her was Robert Hargrave, the head of the Privy Council. On the other side of her, there was an empty seat which Robert Ghent moved to and sat down. The head of the Church Guard also sat at the table which wasn't right. He had no place at the table. Knight General Kingsmill sat at the table and did not look pleased at all. Brent saw two draoi and blinked at them. One was Lana, and the other Brent remembered as Kennit. They sat quietly and didn't look at him.

Brent noticed one empty seat, the one closest to him and directly opposite Kissane. He knew this empty seat: this was the seat the Privy Council used to question select individuals. He also noticed the Church guards lining both sides of the room, standing at attention, each with one of the strange weapons at his or her waist. Brent knew trouble when he saw it. He was in trouble. For the first time in a long time he longed for his sword.

Brent took a step forward, and he felt two guards move behind him and block the exit. "What's happening here? Eylene? Kingsmill?"

Eylene smiled with tight lips. "Sit, Regent. We have much to discuss."

Brent scowled. "You do not give orders here, Archbishop. Stand up, you are in my seat."

Kingsmill looked at Brent and Brent could see the fear there. He opened his mouth to ask him what was happening when the guards behind him grabbed him under the arms and forced him into the vacant seat.

"Let me go! Unhand me!" Brent tried to remain standing, but the guards pressed him into his seat and held him down by his shoulders. Brent struggled and fought. "Let me up! What is this?"

"SILENCE!" yelled Eylene, stunning the room. "You will sit silent, Brent Bairstow. You are not in charge here. I am."

"That is preposterous! This is treason!"

"This is justice! You have allowed the Realm to descend into chaos."

"I have? That's nonsense, and you know it. I have been fighting to bring the Realm back into control. What is this? What are you doing?"

Eylene picked up the gavel and rapped it twice on the sound board. "Silence. One more outburst and you will be gagged!"

Brent struggled to rise again. "Enough of this! Guards! I will see you all hanged for this. I am the Regent! I will..."

A large hand clamped itself over Brent's mouth and he tried to bite it, but it pressed hard and mashed his lips against his teeth. He could taste blood and he twisted his head to get himself free. The men were so much stronger than him, but he had to resist and tried. His efforts were useless and in a moment he was gagged with his hands tied painfully behind his back. He was forced to lean forward with his chest against the table. He glared across the table at the smirk on Eylene's face.

"Much better," she said. "As I was saying, we are here to determine the fate of Regent Brent Bairstow and the Realm. As the Archbishop I have asked the heads of the Judiciary and Privy Councils to bear witness of these proceedings. Also with us, is Knight General Kingsmill, the last of the Privy Council. He has just reported that the Cian-Oirthear army has been offloaded to their land. The ships have returned safe.

"I have met with both Robert Hargrave and Robert Ghent several times over the past months. They have continually expressed concern with the governance of the Realm under the hand of Regent Bairstow. The Council met in secret two days ago and decided to allow the Privy Council to determine what actions should take place. We are here today to hear the decisions that have been made.

"First, Regent Brent Bairstow, the Judicial Council has determined that your actions to assume authority of the Realm and replace the former President John Healy, were unlawful. The position of Regent is decided by the Council and only by the Council and requires a vote of fifty percent plus one to be validated. The Council, we have heard, were coerced into accepting you as Regent. Threats were made. This is a crime in of itself. You are charged with violating the electoral process of Belkin.

"Two, and the most heinous crime: your act of assassination of President Healy. You are to be charged with murder. Three, the fact that the murder was of the head of the Realm was an act of treason and therefore, you are also to be charged with treason. Your court dates have not yet been determined. You will be held in the tower until your trials occur."

Brent struggled against his bonds. He tried to stand and was pressed harder into the seat. He yelled against the gag, but little noise came out. The people around the table seemed amused, except for Kingsmill. He refused to look anywhere but at the table in front of him.

Eylene continued. "Knight General Kingsmill has been questioned. His role in the assassination of Healy is now well documented. He was the only voice against the plan laid out by Brent Bairstow. The sole voice of reason against such a criminal act. For this, and his loyalty, and the recognition that as a military man he is under oath to follow orders, he will receive a handsome retirement package and be allowed to retire anywhere in the Realm he so chooses. It is acknowledged that he was complicit, but his years of exemplary service, fighting against the foreign navy, and his sound advice to the Realm, have all weighed in his favour. Knight General Kingsmill, you are dismissed. Thank you for your service. You may go. Now."

Kingsmill remained seated for a moment looking at the table. He looked up finally and stared at Brent for a moment. Brent could almost see the thoughts behind those eyes, and he could see the guilt. Brent nodded to Kingsmill. Kingsmill looked relieved and then pushed back his chair and stood. He smoothed the front of his tunic and came to attention and saluted the table. Brent noticed the salute failed to target anyone in particular. Kingsmill turned and strode out of the room without saying a word. The doors closed behind him and Eylene chuckled.

Brent squinted at Eylene. She seemed to lie back in her seat. She reached forward and picked up the gavel and waved it around before setting it back down again. "So much fun. You've lost, Brent. Everything. You tried so hard to do what you thought was right. I'm afraid you were always going to lose. The Roberts here? Ghent and Hargrave? They've hated you from day one. They had so much power under Healy and you took that away from them. You questioned them after decades of support to the Realm. Belittled them. Not the best course of action if you wanted to gain support. Politics is such a finicky mistress."

Ghent and Hargrave chuckled and nodded their heads. Brent could see they were enjoying themselves. Hargrave winked at Brent.

Eylene leaned forward and stretched out over the table. "No, instead you made enemies of the men and women you should have dismissed from day one. Not the best way to replace someone like Healy. I've heard you had detailed knowledge of the corruption in Healy's government and yet you did nothing to purge those in the ranks who would see you struck down.

"You were an idiot, Brent Bairstow. Like Ghent and Hargrave. Why they would think that I would allow them to remain working for the Realm is beyond me. Power makes men stupid, I suppose. Proceed."

Ghent and Hargrave looked surprised and looked across the table at one another. They each saw the guard behind the other remove the strange weapon from their waist and point the little opening at the end toward the back of the head of the other. The guards did something with the handle and a large bang sounded from each of the weapons. Brent cried out in alarm against his gag. Ghent and Hargrave each took a ball of lead to the back of the head and slumped dead to the table. Blood poured freely in surprisingly large amounts from their ruptured skulls and pooled across the table. Lana and Kennit moved away a little.

Brent cried out in shock and alarm and tried to push away from the table. He had never seen weapons like that, but the acrid smoke in the room told him that black powder was behind it. He glanced around the room and confirmed all the guards carried the weapons. The two guards who had used their weapons were reloading them and Brent wanted to watch to see how they did it, but Eylene stood up.

"Handguns are what they are called, in case you were curious. I see you watching the men reload. We found the secret to making the black powder. It wasn't hard to find a better way to use it. My top wordsmith devised these weapons. Every single guard member has one, in addition to his or her sword. It can kill a person from twenty feet away with ease. It changes everything, I hear. Already the Church Guard across the Realm is assuming control of the villages and cities. We have hundreds and hundreds of members. All trained by the Church of Belkin."

When Brent looked confused, she laughed. "Yes, the Church of Belkin. The true church of the Realm, not that useless Church of the New Order. Doddering old fools. They're all dead now. But you knew that. Over the years, Healy conspired with the New Order and tried to rule the Realm under a single power. The Church of the New Order was doing their own thing to try and rule the land.

Except, they still believed in a King. Can you believe that? In this day and age and they would place a King on the throne?

"Years ago, the Church of Belkin decided the King had to go, and with it the Church of the New Order. The corruption was too wide spread. The King was guilty of so many crimes and the Archbishop and his church were complicit by doing nothing. We saw it all from Shape and decided to put things in motion. It was just a passing thought and then it grew in strength. Good men and women know a righteous cause when they see one and this was one. Rid the Realm of the abuses of a monarchy and tear down the vile and corrupt church at the same time. Our plan was all working so beautifully until the druids appeared. Then surprisingly the Church of the New Order saw fit to remove the druid threat with that Sect of theirs."

Eylene stood up and walked past Ghent and stood behind Lana and placed her hands on her shoulders. Lana smiled. "The druids came back of course. What you don't know is there are things going on in the background no one is the wiser to. But this time, some new druids decided that their fealty to the Church of Belkin was higher than that of worship to this Gaea creature. Lana and Kennit here are examples. It's a funny thing, you see. Half the druids wanted to allow Gaea to die, and half didn't. Those that didn't, saw her taken from them. That act, that one small thing, turned them away from the teachings of Gaea. Funny, no? They saw their opinion didn't matter. They soon found themselves without their deity and their powers. So what now? Their powers were restored and along come Lana and Kennit and they let them see a new way. A way where they have power and no one can tell them what to do." Eylene leaned over and kissed the top of Lana's head.

"Lana and Kennit are old friends of mine. There hasn't been a moment that I have not been aware of everything going on in the Realm. I have sat in Shape and watched the world change and waited. Waited for this opportunity."

Eylene continued to walk around the table until she reached Brent and circled behind him and placed her hands on his shoulders and leaned in behind his left ear and whispered. "I'm taking everything, Brent. You would have been successful, you know. You were doing everything right. It was me, Brent. Me, who upset all your efforts. My church whispered in peoples' ears across the Realm and spread lies, false hopes, and dissatisfaction. It was all so easy. The people ripe to hear any lie, or truth." Eylene switched ears and winked at Lana's grin.

"By order of the Council, the Church of Belkin will assume authority over the Realm. There's even a delicious word for it: Theocracy. Do you know what a Theocracy is, Brent? It's a government run by the church. Our goal is finally achieved. Thanks to you. I shall be known as Prelate Kissane. Doesn't that sound wonderful?"

Eylene stood and Brent vibrated in his seat with anger. She walked back to her seat and stood behind it with her hands on the back. "Prelate Kissane. So wonderful. In a matter of days I will return order to the Realm and the people will worship the ground I walk on. I will forever be the woman who brought peace to the Realm. Statues will be raised in my memory. This is how the Realm moves forward. The victor writes the history books and I will go down as the saviour. You, unfortunately, will be one of a long line of villains.

"You are, no doubt, thinking of your druid friends down at Rigby Farm. I'm afraid their time is soon over. With my handguns and a wonderful herb concoction we've put together which negates a druid's influence over our minds, we will soon put them all down. My people should arrive at the farm any day now.

"As for you, you'll be imprisoned in the same room in the tower Hietower died in. There is justice in that. You will be publicly executed after this trial of yours. Enjoy what time you have left. Thank you for your service." Eylene then threw back her head and laughed, and Brent watched in horror as Lana and Kennit laughed with her. The bodies of Ghent and Hargrave cooled in the pools of blood and Brent felt his defeat crush him.

"Guards, take him away."

Cill Darae

Nineteen

Rigby Farm, September 902 A.C.

KATHERINE, DOG, HEATHER and James, along with Will Arbor and Edward arrived at Rigby Farm and were greeted and surrounded by the draoi, farm hands and Steve's crew. There was a lot of laughter and tears. Nadine had come bursting out of the house and engulfed Will in a ferocious hug and kiss. She pounded his shoulders and screamed at him and kissed him again, all in the same breath. She ended up just holding him tight and squeezing him, her face buried into his shoulder.

The draoi pulled aside Katherine and Dog and embraced them one by one. They touched her hair and petted Dog and soon they were all laughing. For Katherine it was a moment she hadn't known she craved until it happened. She had never felt part of the draoi, but now she felt their love and acceptance of who she and Dog were. She let them in, and their bonds flared.

Martin, Edward, Dempster, Anne holding wee Frankie, and Steve waited until Will was freed by Nadine and whispered to him. Will was apologetic and in time, Steve shook his hand and pulled him in for a quick hug. Dempster and Anne stood tightly against one another and laughed. Tension fled, and the farm celebrated.

Will stepped up onto the farmhouse porch and held up his hands. Everyone gathered round to hear him speak. "My friends, we are back. I am back," started Will and everyone cheered. "I left here a broken man, broken by draoi we once called friends. My mind is clear now and I can see how I was slowly manipulated. I apologise. As Freamhaigh, I should have had better strength. Truthfully, I would never have suspected our own to do such a thing."

Katherine kept her thoughts to herself but spoke to Dog. *Better to not trust anyone, I think.*

Dog sneezed. *No, I don't think that is right, either. We trust these people here, Katherine. They are our friends. Plus they smell good. I've never not liked anything that didn't smell good.*

Katherine snorted and focused on what Will was saying.

"We are under a new threat. This time from within. Archbishop Kissane in Munsten has sided with Kennit and Lana and the draoi who left us. I don't know what that means and we do not know what they intend only that we likely pose a direct threat to them. I have spoken to the Cill Darae, my lovely wife Nadine, about what we should do. In the past, as you know, I would put this to a vote. Not this time, my friends. As Freamhaigh, I have made a decision. A decision that Nadine accepts. A decision I require you to follow."

The crowd grew silent. Katherine pursed her lips. *This is a better version of Will.*

"We are exposed here. I have spoken to Steve, and he agrees with my assessment that the farm is indefensible. I'm afraid we must leave the farm and find a more secure place."

A grumble rippled through the crowd. They didn't like the news and many spoke and asked why they couldn't remain.

"I know," said Will, when the crowd quietened. "This is our home, we've made it ours. Katherine has been most generous in allowing us to stay at her family stead."

A couple of people in the crowd whistled their pleasure.

"Ha-ha! Katherine will find you and beat you for that. You know she will. No, we must leave. I will speak more with Steve and Edward and determine our best options. Edward is our future King and his opinion will matter greatly. Be ready to leave soonest. Pack your valuables. I mean to leave the day after the Mabon Days, in four days' time."

One of the farm hands raised her hand and Will acknowledged her. "The harvest is not due to be gathered for a couple of weeks. It's been so damn dry and despite our irrigation efforts it's delayed. Surely we aren't abandoning our fields? They're ripe and full by our sweat. And what about the animals? What are we to do with them?"

"All good questions. The animals come with us. The draoi will see they follow us. They won't be a bother. As for the fields, we leave them. The risk is too great. I would rather lose our grain than your lives."

The crowd erupted at Will's words. Some were angry and others sad. Children started to cry with all the shouting and mothers tried to soothe them and quieten them. Will watched it all for a time and Katherine wondered what he was going to do. The old Will would have tried to get everyone to agree. Katherine looked at Dog and saw him laughing.

What, Doogie-Doog?

Smell Will, I have never smelt that on him before.

Huh? Katherine turned her nose to Will. She had long ago accepted that she carried the abilities of Dog. A heightened sense of smell was one of them. She sniffed and then opened her eyes in surprise. *He's angry. Oh, dear.* Katherine looked at Nadine and could see the pride in her eyes as she gazed at her husband. *Our Freamhaigh has changed, Dog.*

He's alpha, replied Dog with respect in his voice.

Will raised his arms and Katherine felt his power wash out over the crowd, instantly stilling everyone. Emotions calmed, and they turned as one toward Will. "I must repeat myself, it seems. I have made a decision. We are leaving the day after Mabon Days. Get yourself ready. That is all. Dismissed."

Will turned and walked into the house. The crowd loitered a moment looking at one another, uncertain of what to do next. One by one, they left and wandered away. Katherine caught Nadine's eye and saw her broad smile. Katherine nodded her head and then felt a stab of love across their bond.

Nadine turned and fled into the house after Will, her excitement pulsing across the draoi bond. Steve pried himself away from the porch post he had been leaning against and came over to Katherine. Heather was leaving with her husband and children and James watched her go. *He has to learn to hide his emotions*, thought Katherine, but then pushed them aside when Steve reached her.

"Welcome back, daughter," he said and stood before her.

To Katherine, he looked uncertain and a little lost. She held his gaze for a moment and then smiled. Steve's eyes widened a fraction. "Thanks, father." She felt a sting in her eyes and then rushed forward and held him just as her eyes and emotions betrayed her.

She was home.

First Mabon started with the crow of the rooster. It was an overcast day, unseasonably cold, and the feel of rain was in the air. Katherine shuddered in bed despite the heavy duvet covering her. Dog lay at her feet like a lump and her legs complained from being locked in place for so long. She gently shoved his mass away and stretched out her legs under the duvet relishing the feeling of freedom. She reached out to the farm with her senses and felt the others stirring.

Charlie was already working the bellows in the smithy, bringing the furnace to life. He had many more nails for shoes to make before they all would soon leave the farm. Dempster was in the kitchen getting the stove lit and humming to himself. Anne was fast asleep and wee Frankie was starting to fuss, her hunger waking her. James was in the barracks and refusing to acknowledge it was time to get up.

Will and Nadine were stirring, and Katherine left them when their intent rose hot and hungry. Steve was asleep and not likely to rise soon. He and Katherine had spoken well into the night for the past few evenings. Catching up, he called it. For Katherine it was a chance to hear what her mother and adoptive father had accomplished in their lives as highwaymen working for Baron Andrew Windthrop. She loved her time with Steve and was starting to truly think of him as her father.

She felt at peace. The past couple of years had been hard. She had much to be ashamed of, but much to be proud of. The threat of Erebus was gone from the Realm and she had her own personal Gaea to confer with. The Simon motes were a constant presence to her, and she tried to speak to them, but they refused to respond.

Dog and she were one. She didn't question that any longer. She now longed to feel his presence in her mind. It made her feel whole. When they had merged that time she knew that something wonderful had happened. They were both changed by the merging of their minds in ways they still had no full understanding. At times she longed to run across the land and chase rabbits. At other times she was simply Katherine, the farm girl with a love of horses.

The rooster crowed again, and Katherine frowned. *Stupid rooster*, she thought. *It's never a good sign when the rooster crows twice.*

Katherine nudged Dog, and he stirred. She pushed him harder, and he lifted his head. *Wake up, sleepy head.*

Why?

It's a new day that's why.

Dog sniffed the air. *I don't smell bacon. It's too early to get up. The air smells funny.*

Katherine sniffed the air automatically. The air smelled funny to her as well. *It does but get up.*

I will when you do.

Katherine laughed and threw off the goose-down duvet covering her and covered Dog with it. They wrestled for a moment, with Dog pretending to bite her and growling softly. Dog snuck his head out from under the duvet and licked Katherine's face. She squealed and wiped at it and swung her feet to the floor and rose. *Truce. You win. Come on. Let's go help Dempster with breakfast.*

Katherine went over to the side table and poured water from the ewer into the wash basin. She took a moment to study her face in the mirror, turning her face one way and then the other. Satisfied, she washed her face, dried it with a towel, and pulled a draoi gown over her head. It felt good to wear the draoi clothes again. She felt liberated. She tied a leather strap around her waist and then grabbed her staff by the door and headed downstairs. Through her bond, she watched Dog lie down in the warm spot she had left in the bed and close his eyes and go back to sleep. *I envy dogs their ability to sleep so easily;* she thought and headed downstairs.

Dempster greeted her in the kitchen and motioned toward the dough he had rising. She blew hair from her face and drove her fists into the dough and punched it down. "Morning Dempster. How'd you sleep?"

"Good, good. It's so wonderful to have everyone back," he said as he started to lay thick slices of bacon on a large baking sheet. Dempster preferred to broil his bacon rather than fry it. Just then the kettle on the stove started to give a rising whistle, and he moved it to the back burner and placed a large frying pan in its place. He went back to the bacon and laid out more slices. "Anne says wee Frankie will walk soon. Do you think she will?"

"I know nothing about children. I suppose she might. How old is she now?"

"She'll be two next month."

"Hmm. Seems young to be walking."

"She said her first word last week. Anne says she said 'mum'."

"Did she now? How wonderful."

Katherine felt the draoi bond strain slightly and froze. She reached out across the bond looking for the source but found nothing. She felt Will and Nadine pause upstairs. Katherine frowned and woke Dog. *Get up, something just happened.*

What?

The bond. It vibrated a little. I felt a pull.

What does that mean?

I have no idea. Go get Will and Nadine up.

Katherine felt Dog's acceptance and watched as he jumped off the bed and padded to Will and Nadine's bedroom door and scraped at the door frame with his paw.

Dempster was looking strangely at Katherine. "What's the matter?"

"I don't know, Dempster. Something is wrong."

Katherine reached out for the draoi who stood guard at the roads leading to the farm. They were there, but they weren't responding. They were unconscious and beyond her power to wake them. Something had them drugged.

"Dempster, go wake, Steve. We're under attack."

Dempster stared at Katherine with his mouth open, a piece of raw bacon hanging from his hand.

"Go!" she ordered and Dempster threw down the bacon and ran out of the kitchen as fast as his bulk would allow.

Katherine gathered her power and sent a warning to the draoi on the farm. *Wake! We are under attack! Wake!*

The draoi woke and gathered power. Katherine could feel them probing for answers. The next few minutes had the farm erupting with activity. The crew and farm hands were all awake, and they staggered out of the barracks and houses strapping on armour and hefting weapons. James took charge of the crew and lined them up outside. The farm hands and non-draoi gathered as a group and took the children into their circle once they came outside. The draoi stood together clasping hands and probing the area for a sign of what was happening.

Will and Nadine ordered Martin and Edward to join the farm hands and stood outside with the draoi. Katherine joined them with Dog and stood in the fine mist of rain that chose that moment to start. The sky was starting to lighten on the horizon, but the morning twilight seemed unnaturally still and dark.

<*Simon?*> asked Katherine. <*What is happening?*>

Simon chose not to answer. Katherine gripped her staff tighter. *Gaea? Do you know what is happening?*

I have no idea. I am no longer part of this world.

Simon won't answer me.

Simon? He speaks to you?

Yes.

As a person?

Yes. Katherine felt a surge of emotion from Gaea. It was a sense of longing that disappeared as soon as she felt it. *What was that, Gaea? Does Simon mean something to you?*

Yes.

<*They arrive,*> said Simon.

<*What? Who is arriving?*>

Simon didn't answer. Katherine peered out into the mist but couldn't see anything. "Will, Simon just told me they are arriving."

Will glanced at Katherine. "Simon did? Who is arriving?"

Just then the sound of marching feet could be heard in the distance. Katherine *reached* out with her senses but felt nothing. *Strange.* She could hear the sound but could not sense what was making it. She then noticed the stillness of the land around the sound. Insects hid and burrowed. Mice and rabbits fled into holes. With her senses she could feel the absence of nature. *That is where they are.* She used her senses to see through the eyes of a rabbit and held it in place. She could see armed men, wearing golden armour, marching in three long lines. Beside them she recognised some of the draoi who had left with Kennit and Lana.

Katherine told Will what she was seeing and saw Will and Nadine's eyes lose focus. In a moment Will stepped forward and addressed the people.

"Armed soldiers are approaching with draoi. They are a mile out, coming our way. Martin and Edward, take the children and the farm hands. Flee. Head south. We'll find you when we can. Go!"

Martin nodded and had them moving. Two of the draoi went with them. Steve sent two of his crew to join them and soon they disappeared in the mist down the south road.

Steve joined Will. "How many?"

"Looks like twenty armed soldiers and ten draoi. Not many, but they block our powers. We're following them with the nearby animals. What should we do?"

Steve looked at James when he came up to join them. "Any ideas?"

James shook his head. "Sounds like the Church Guard we saw in Munsten. If they've come all this way and are blocking the draoi then they are not coming to talk. I fear a fight."

Steve nodded. "I agree. We talked about this. Execute our plan. Position our people."

James nodded and ran over to the crew and barked orders. Katherine watched as they split up into three groups and ran off to hide in the barn and behind buildings. Archers climbed up ladders to roof tops and hid behind chimneys. It all happened quickly and with practiced precision. Will ordered the draoi to line up behind him and they complied and held hands. Katherine and Dog stood next to Will and Nadine and they waited.

In time the Church Guard emerged from the misting rain; their armour glistening with the mist. They marched with their eyes forward in perfect unison. Katherine shivered at the sight. They were well trained and disciplined. Their boots hit the gravel at the same time and made it that much more impressive. The sight of the draoi walking beside them had her gritting her teeth. These were draoi and they were openly siding with the Church. The draoi had abandoned the humble brown robes and wore expensive form fitting brown leathers, embossed with greens, and splashes of gold.

The Church Guard marched into the yard and split into two long lines until they formed a large vee. They halted as one and then turned to face Will and the draoi. The Church Guard had no emotion on their faces. They seemed distant and bored. In contrast, the leather-bound draoi stood off to one side and watched with a disdained expression on their faces. They stared defiantly back at Will's draoi.

Katherine reached out with her senses and could feel nothing of the people in front of her. They were hidden from her. Ghosts of emotion crossed her senses, and she pressed harder to make sense of it.

"Will," she whispered. "The guard, they're all drugged. Look at them. They all have the same lack of expression."

"I see that."

They stood there for a moment and Katherine wondered what was next. No one seemed to want to speak. There didn't seem to be a leader, and she looked around confused. Steve was frowning and seemed equally confused. Nothing was normal about the whole situation.

Will stepped forward to speak and the Church Guard moved as one. They pulled strange devices from their waist and held them with one hand and pointed them at Will's draoi.

Steve was the first to react. "Down!" he screamed and ran and tackled Will just as the weapons erupted in an explosive sound.

Katherine was stunned by the noise. It filled the very air and drove the hearing from her ears. She turned to the draoi and saw blossoms of blood erupt from their chests and other body parts. Many of the draoi were being struck by some small projectile and collapsed straight down to the ground as if their lives had been plucked away.

Katherine felt like she was underwater. Her movements slowed and she could hear noises as if far away and muffled. Too much was happening at the same time and she tried to make sense of it.

She saw Steve's crew emerge from the buildings and stand up on the roof tops. The opposing draoi turned to them and the crew froze in place. Nadine was falling next to her, clutching her abdomen and she could see blood spilling between her fingers. Dog was running toward the draoi, growling with teeth bared. The crew cried out and fell clutching their chests and heads. The enemy draoi had struck them with their power.

Anger rose hot and fierce within her. Her power blossomed and flared. She felt it reach out to Dog and felt him take the power and ground her. She pulled power and fed it all her anger. She watched the world around her slow and then stop. Draoi were frozen as they fell to the earth struck by something she didn't understand. The Church Guard were pulling swords from sheaths and frozen in the act. The enemy draoi were still. Dog landed on the ground from a pounce and turned toward Katherine.

You did it again, Katherine.

Yes, she replied. She clenched her teeth holding the power within her steady. *We must do something.*

Dog growled. *We must do what we did in Cala.*

Katherine shook her head. *I can't, Dog. It was too horrible.*

This time we do it because we have to. Look at what they have done.

Katherine looked around. All the draoi had been wounded except for Will, who was under Steve, and Heather who was behind her husband, Chris. Katherine looked at the wounds and saw that many were already fatal. Nadine was hurt, but would survive, and she breathed a sigh of relief. She thought of what Dog was suggesting and found she didn't think she could do it.

She looked at the expressions of horror and pain on the faces of the draoi. Her friends were sorely hurt by these soldiers. Heather was behind her husband and she could see he had placed himself before her to protect her. But he had been struck in the head and chest. He was already dead, and Katherine sucked in a sob of anguish. The draoi bonds were flickering out. Her anger grew and her power with it.

Gaea? Help me? Tell me what to do?

You must do what you must. You have it in you. Simon has given you great power.

I can't repeat Cala. Not again. It nearly destroyed me.

You are not that same girl. You have a purpose in this life.

<She is correct, Katherine. You must do what you must. Look around you.>

<Simon?> asked Gaea.

<Yes, dearest Gaea. It is me.>

<Where have you been? How?>

<I have been here all along.>

<Why did you stay hidden from me?>

<I had a purpose.>

<You told me all those years ago you wouldn't do this. You lied to me.>

<Yes, I did. I'm sorry. When I died the motes spoke to me. Offered this and explained why they thought it was important. So I accepted.>

<We could have been together all this time.>

<We are now. Time has no meaning for us.>

Gaea grew quiet, but Katherine could sense her watching and waiting. *<What now, Simon,>* asked Katherine.

<You know what to do. End this. Heal who you can. Leave the farm. The army is close behind. They will raze the farm. You must be gone by then. Regroup and we will discuss the future.>

<Is there a future? There is so much death. What can we do now? Look at what has happened. The draoi are no more.>

<Not true. Hurry, you cannot maintain this state for long.>

Katherine looked around the farm. The crew were decimated. Her draoi were slaughtered. The anger in her bubbled and she remembered how easy it had been in Cala to kill people. She looked at Dog and saw the determination in his eyes.

We must do this, Katherine.

Agreed, said Gaea. *You are the Cill Darae. You are the power the land needs. I can see what Simon has done over the years. I see his influence across time and how he has corrected me from the side lines. He led me to you. He suggested what I did to you so many years ago. We have created a power in this world that will make the difference we always spoke about. Be the Cill Darae and do what is right.*

Katherine felt hot tears of anger and shame burning down her cheeks. She felt manipulated, used, hurt, and ashamed. She never asked for any of this. It was forced on her. She longed for her childhood when all that mattered was the farm and her horses. But all that was behind her and gone and now she had to step forward and be something she never wanted to be.

Remember this, Gaea. You brought me to this.

Yes. And I would do so again, willingly.

Anger rose yet again, and Katherine felt it yearning for release.

She closed her eyes for a moment. *Mom? I'm sorry. Please forgive me?*

Katherine opened her eyes and gazed at the Church Guard and enemy draoi. Her hatred for them consumed her. She opened her mouth and screamed in defiance and released her power. She drove it into each of the guards and draoi bodies and found the Simon motes that lived there. The motes responded to her and followed her orders. Images of Cala returned to her and the images of faces of those people she had killed flashed before her eyes. *This is different*, she thought. *These are evil men and women.* The motes surged within the bodies and broke the bonds that held them together.

In an instant, the Church Guard and draoi were dead. Frozen in time they remained standing, but Katherine knew as soon as she released her power, and time resumed, they would splash to the ground as a liquid. She felt horror for her actions. She had executed them, and they had been powerless to stop her. *No one should have this much power.* She turned away and closed her eyes.

Help me, Dog. We must heal those who we can.

Together they healed the draoi and crew who could be saved. They pushed balls of lead out of their bodies and stitched together flesh. Those who were beyond her care they eased toward death. It took very little time and Katherine found it soothing for her soul. *Perhaps this balances things, Dog?*

We did nothing wrong. We were good dogs. This is what being alpha means. We must make the hard choices and do what is right for the pack.

Katherine stared at Dog. *When did you get so smart?*

Dog scratched his ear with a hind leg. *I dunno.*

We must release this power. Are you ready? This is going to be bad.

I am ready.

Katherine closed her eyes and released the power. It washed out of her and Dog with a thunderclap. The very air thinned, and the rain stopped. Clouds overhead shattered and flew outwards. Katherine heard the sound of the Church Guard and draoi splashing to the ground and kept her eyes averted She crouched beside Nadine and took her hand. Nadine was trying to look everywhere at once.

"Wh-what happened? Katherine?" Nadine looked at her blood-soaked hand and then grabbed at her stomach. "I was hit by something? What happened?" Nadine looked past Katherine to where the guard had been. "What is that? Oh my Gaea! What happened?"

Cries from the surviving draoi and crew rose quickly. Nadine looked around the farm bewildered.

"I dealt with it, Nadine. We have to leave."

Steve rolled off Will and helped him to his feet. Will stood and stared at the carnage. "The draoi!" He sobbed and ran to his fallen draoi.

Heather turned her husband over and wailed in misery. Katherine saw her lose herself to her power, seeking to heal her husband.

"I've healed everyone I could. The others are gone. I'm sorry."

Will turned to Katherine. "What happened? What did you do?"

"I did what I must."

Will's expression turned to horror when he saw the remains of the Church Guard and enemy draoi. "Did you do that?"

Katherine refused to look where Will was looking. She nodded and then wiped at her face with her sleeve.

"How could you?" admonished Will and Katherine jerked as if slapped. "You killed all those people with your power? That is not Gaea's way!"

Nadine was beside Heather and crying with her. Steve had gone over to his surviving crew and was getting them together. With her power Katherine could only sense the grief pouring out of everyone. She felt the disgust Will felt toward her and it hitched her breath.

Dog stood beside her and panted.

"How could you Katherine? There had to be a better way!"

Katherine shook her head.

Dog woofed gently. *It was needed.*

"You are an abomination!" declared Will and he took a step back away from Katherine and Dog. Nadine looked up at him in shock. "The way of the draoi is to nurture life! Sustain it! Seek harmony! You destroyed those people!"

Katherine shook her head in denial, but his words rung true. "I won't deny it, Freamhaigh. I did what I had to. There is an army coming. They will raze the farm. We best leave at once. We have to run."

Katherine looked at Will and Nadine. They both looked horrified. James and Steve walked up and looked at her.

"You did this?" asked her father.

Katherine nodded and waited for the next blow.

"Good," was all he said, and he turned to Will. "We need to be off. We can't face an army. We need to catch up to the others. I know where we can go. Come."

Nadine nodded and pried Heather from her husband's corpse. James held her, and she sobbed. Little by little, the survivors gathered together. They all looked shocked. They refused to glance at the ground where the remains of the guard lay. Katherine stepped forward to join them, but Will put out his hand and stopped her.

"Not you. Leave. I can't be with you."

Dog growled at Will, startling him and he frowned.

"Will!" said Nadine. "You can't mean that!"

"She broke every rule of the draoi. She cannot stay with us."

Katherine felt her heart breaking. "I did what I had to! Can't you see that?"

Will shook his head and turned away and started to walk south. Dog barked at him.

Nadine looked at Katherine with sympathy. "I'll talk to him. I'll let you know when you can return."

Katherine looked from Nadine to Will. He continued to walk away from her. "Please, no!" sobbed Katherine.

Steve moved over to Katherine and hugged her. He whispered in her ear. "You did good, Katherine. We were all dead. Will doesn't see that yet. Give him time.

Will you be all right? Where will you go?"

"Gaea and Simon, daddy! They told me I had to. I had no choice!"

"Shh! We'll talk about this later. Give Will time. Will is a sensitive sort. He's lost and scared. He's still a boy at heart."

Katherine nodded against his shoulder and when Steve moved to let go of her she held him tighter. "I'm scared."

Steve laughed a soft laugh. "You have nothing to fear, daughter of mine. You have my blood in you. You'll be fine. It's the world I'm scared for. You are the strongest woman I know. I'm proud of you. You remind me of your mother, you know. She always did what was hard when no one else could." Steve let go of her and she let him. He raised a hand and wiped at Katherine's tears. He looked down at Dog. "Take care of her, Dog."

Dog woofed gently and looked up at Katherine.

Steve walked away and joined the others. A handful of the crew remained. Three draoi, Heather, Nadine, Steve, James and Will joined them and walked down the southern road. Nadine waved at Katherine and blew her a kiss through her tears.

Katherine stayed where she was and watched them walk away. There were so few left. So many people gone so quickly. Her feeling of loss overwhelmed her. Grief was consuming her.

You did what needed to be done, Katherine, said Gaea.

You knew he would abandon me.

Yes, it seemed likely. He will see the error in his judgement.

What now?

<*Head to the Finnow Mines. There is something you need to see there,*> replied Simon.

Cill Darae

Epilogue

Former Baron Windthrop's Country Estate, October 902 A.C.

STEVE COMLIN LED the survivors to the country estate of the late Baron Andrew Windthrop. They arrived on the first day of October. Steve had sent a scout ahead to warn the estate of their arrival and they were met by Castellan William Crenshaw and some of his men. Little was said that needed to be said and the survivors of Rigby Farm and all their animals were taken in and given food and shelter. Just outside of the Rigby Farm they had turned and watched as black smoke rose thick into the thin autumn air and they had wept. Their home was gone, and they had marched in silence to the estate.

Crenshaw had ridden forward and met them on the road. Steve had spoken quietly to him and Crenshaw had looked grim. Crenshaw had come with an armed escort and they had quickly gathered up Edward and Martin and taken them at speed to the estate to protect the heir to the throne. The rest of the walk had been in misery. Will was inconsolable and Nadine was beside herself trying to get him to see reason. Steve didn't need to be draoi to feel the anger coming off of him. Steve had tried to talk sense into him. His daughter had saved their lives and yet Will remained set in his condemnation of her. In truth, Will was starting to annoy Steve. He was no longer the young man he knew in Jaipers. Steve had no idea how to return Will to the path he once followed.

The walk from the farm had been made longer by their despair and sorrow. Heather had gathered her children around her and wailed as only a woman of Northern Belkin could. She had cut at her hair with a dagger and tossed the locks to the ground. Her scalp bled in places, but she wouldn't let the draoi heal her.

She was wrapped in grief and her throat raw. In time, she ceased crying and walked like the *aos'si*, also known as the *sluagh sidhe*. She wasn't alone. Children and parents mourned their lost ones. They walked with vacant expressions, not believing their fate and loss.

When they reached the estate they were welcomed by the staff and brought inside and fed and wrapped in blankets against the chill. They watched in some bewilderment as three large groups of people were ushered away from the estate. There were angry words and many times the soldiers of Crenshaw had to step forward to break up brawls between the groups. The draoi stood aside and watched as the three groups disappeared down the road. Crenshaw later explained they were supplicants to the Windthrop estate. Three families had insisted on staying in the house and had been for months, waiting on the Regent to decide who would inherit the barony. Crenshaw had evicted them all when word came to him the draoi and crew were coming. The draoi shook their heads and quietly entered the estate and found rooms waiting for them and everything they needed to clean themselves. For a time, silence descended on the estate, broken only by the sound of someone crying.

Hours passed and Steve gathered Will, Nadine, Edward, Martin and James in a large conference room. Crenshaw provided tea and hot soup and they sat and ate in silence. When bowls were pushed aside and tea filled steaming cups, he cleared his throat and spoke to them.

"We have suffered a great loss. No one can deny that. But we must find a way past this and determine what happens next. The enemy will not wait. We must be ready," he said to the top of lowered heads.

Only Martin was looking around with a bewildered expression on his face. "My friends. There is still hope!"

Will snorted and Nadine reached out and grasped his arm.

Martin looked at Steve and spoke again. "My faith is strong. We have already endured so much. Surely we can overcome this terrible loss and find a path to salvation!"

Will looked up, his anger clear on his face. "We have lost, Martin. I have five draoi remaining. Five! We numbered over forty not so long ago. I have nothing to offer this Realm. I would nurture this land, but the land rejects me! What would you have me do, Martin? Tell me!"

Nadine squeezed Will's forearm. "We are seven draoi, Will. Katherine and Dog count in our numbers."

Will spat. "She is an abomination. Her and Dog. They have turned from the teachings of Gaea!"

Steve shook his head. "Katherine said Gaea told her to do what she did."

Will looked incredulous. "Gaea? She said that? Gaea is no more! She tells lies on top of everything else?"

Steve held out his hands. "It is what she told me. She was not being deceptive to me. I believe her."

Will shook his head. "She is lost. Lost in her power. She has become like Erebus."

Nadine let go of Will's arm and gasped. "No! Never that, she is not Erebus. She is not evil. She did what she had to. She saved us, Will! How can you not see that?"

"How can you not see what she has become? Her power, it is... it is unimaginable! She destroyed those lives with so much abandon. She could have simply frozen them. Incapacitated them. Anything! But what *she chose* to do, that was her choice, and she chose such a horrible one! No, she is lost to the draoi cause. I fear what she has become. She has become the *Morrighan*."

Nadine laughed. "The *Morrighan*? Surely you jest, Will? The *Morrighan* is a myth to scare wee children. No, she is something else. Something greater than we can imagine."

Will scowled. "She claims Gaea told her to do what she did. You know that is impossible. She hears voices. Even if it were, Gaea would never order the death of so many people."

"You seem to forget the Purge, love. That was Gaea's doing. She had the draoi killed by the Sect. No, this is something I fear Gaea is more than capable of doing. You place far too much faith in Gaea, Will. The rules she placed on the draoi did not apply to her. She said as much in the Chamber. I believe Katherine and Dog. Gaea is still with us, somehow."

Steve looked up at the mention of the Chamber. "Speaking of the Chamber, what happened to the Device?"

Nadine looked surprised and looked around the room. "I have no idea. Did anyone bring it?"

Steve shook his head. "There wasn't time. We fled. I hope it has not fallen back into the hands of the Church."

James grunted. "Katherine had it last. I pray she has it still."

Will looked even angrier. "If she has it, then who knows what additional horrors she will unleash."

The room grew quiet, with each person lost in their own personal thoughts.

Martin sat patiently and then spoke. "We must discuss Edward."

Edward jolted in his seat. "Surely that can wait."

"No, I'm afraid not. I fear for Regent Brent and the Realm. Eylene Kissane has control of her own armed forces, and the draoi. We must return the Realm to a monarchy! Only a King can assert authority over the Realm and the Church and bring back peace and the law."

Edward laughed. "I think the chances of me being King are pretty removed at this point in time."

"I disagree, Edward. We must continue the quest to prove you are the heir. There is a reason Eylene tried to kill you. Once we remove the threat, we have to be ready to place you on the throne. God wills it!"

Will sighed. "I am tired of this talk of God and the church. They have brought nothing but pain to this world."

Martin made a noise and hastened to pull out his amulet. He held it up, and it shone bright in the room and lit up his face. "God would disagree, my friends. He is still with us."

* * *

Katherine and Dog walked west along the main road that wound along the course of the Potsman River. Her familiar backpack lay heavy across her shoulders, but she relished the feel. She felt almost as if she was free again and heading to Cala once again. Except this time she was headed to Finnow and the mines.

Before she had fled from Rigby Farm, she had grabbed food and secured the Device in her pack. She had also grabbed Nadine's copy of the Draoi Manuscript. She had fled north at first and stood on a nearby hill top and watched as the Belkin Army rode into the farm. They had searched the buildings and then torched the place. She had cried watching the plumes of black smoke rise in the air. The farm her parents had so lovingly built and nurtured had been turned to ash. When the army rode out, she turned west and found the main road.

She took her time and refused to draw power from the land. She felt nature probing her, looking for something, but she pushed it aside and walked in silence with Dog. She knew this was the road that Will had taken all those years ago. It had led him to Jergen, to Nadine, and to the farm. There had been a time when she had blamed Will for the death of her parents. That young girl had not understood the world. She had also blamed Gaea and still did. Everything that had happened could be laid at her feet.

Katherine looked down at Dog. "I'm tired of all this, Dog."

Dog looked up briefly to her but said nothing.

"We have been manipulated for eons. Pushed this way and that." She shook the staff in her hand. "Gaea has been a thorn in our side. Can you imagine a world without her? I can."

That is not fair, Katherine.

Ah, you speak, do you? What do you have to say for yourself?

The world you see before you would be gone without me. I was all that stood between Erebus and the return of a world that ceased to exist eons ago. His purpose was to change the world and bring back a civilisation that long ago died out.

Is that so? At what cost? Erebus is gone and now the Realm stands on the brink of disaster.

Disaster? No. Mankind has the power to be what they choose to be now. The threat of Erebus is gone. What happens now is the making of men and women of power. That has always been true. We have given you the power to decide your own fate.

Katherine laughed out loud.

You laugh, but this is the way it is meant to be. I care little for what mankind does now. The threat of Erebus is gone, my task is complete. In ten years, a hundred years, a thousand years, men and women will still be here and others will come forward and take power and change the lives of the people. At least now you can make your own mistakes and own them. There is a future. And you now have the power of the Simon motes.

Ah yes, the Simon motes. It seems Simon does what he wants. We have no control over him.

That is not true. You are the control over Simon.

Katherine stopped on the road. *What?*

You have control over Simon. I gave you this power. You are the master of all Simon motes.

Why have you not said this before?

I have. Many times. You did not understand.

Katherine's head reeled. It was too much. She spoke out loud. "I can't have that power! You saw what I just did. Remember Cala? That was horrible."

Nonetheless, you have that power.

"I can't have this power alone!"

You aren't alone. Dog is with you. You share the power.

"Share it? Is that what we are doing?"

Yes.

"I don't want this. Take it from me, Gaea. You take the power! You did this for so long. Please."

You know what I wish. I want to end. My mission is over. My task complete.

"Then join with me! The three of us: me, Dog and you. Together we can control the power. Use it to do good."

Katherine felt a jolt from Gaea.

"Gaea?"

When Gaea said nothing, she resumed walking. "What do you think Dog?"

I think we need to do whatever we can. We could be good dogs.

"It is more than just being good, Dog. We would need to make decisions that affect people's lives. I don't want that responsibility."

And the animals. We would affect the animals. And the plants. Everything.

"True, sorry Dog."

They walked in silence for a time before Gaea spoke again.

There is an option I have not considered.

Katherine halted and Dog stopped beside her. "What's that?"

You, Dog, me and Simon merge to become one. You would become the greatest Cill Darae the world has ever known. You would become what I once was.

End of Volume Five

Look for the concluding volume in the New Druids series coming in 2020.

Gaea: A New Druids Novel (Volume Six)

By Donald D. Allan

Cill Darae

… Donald D. Allan

Acknowledgements

As always I want to thank some people: My beta team really came through for me and found all sorts of errors and issues with pacing. Here they are: Steve Bligh, Sue DeNicola, Martin C. Jordan, Eylene Kissane, R.T. Sailor, and Lana Turner. Thanks folks.

Cill Dara (pronounced kill-dar-ay) means *Church of the Oak* in Gaelic. Kildare is a town in County Kildare, Ireland where legend has it, King Leinster met with Saint Brigid. Kildare is named after the Church of the Oak, as Brigid had built her church under the shade of an oak tree. When I started this series, I needed a title suitable for the High Priestess (or Priest) of the Druids. I had already *burrowed* deep down into the roots of the tree (*freamhaigh* is Gaelic for roots) and had nowhere else to go. I then stumbled on the stories of Saint Brigid and discovered Kildare and from that the term came *Cill Dara*. I decided Cill Dara would be masculine and Cill Darae would be feminine.

Until just recently, I had been pronouncing Cill Darae as "Sill-Dar-Ay". It turns out the "C" is hard and not soft. So Cill Darae is pronounced kill-dar-ay. Speaking of which, have you wondered how to pronounce the titles to the novels in my series? If you want to know read on. If not, and you like the way you say it in your head, skip the next little bit.

Duilleog: *Duh-Lug*
Craobh: *Cray-Obh*
Stoc: *Stalk*
Freamhaigh: *Fray-wee*
Cill Darae: *Kill-Dar-Ay*
Gaea: *Gay-uh*

Some of you are now probably scratching your head at this series. Is this fantasy? Or science-fiction? What is it I am reading here? The truth is: I consider this epic fantasy. I admit it is a bit of a blend, but the themes, setting, etc. are all fantasy tropes. I stand by that. I love reading novels like this, with a bit of a science fiction thrown in. I find it exciting and of course I write in that style. Can you blame me?

The next (and last) novel of the series is called *Gaea*. I hope to have it out early in 2020, but time will tell whether I manage that. *Gaea* has been outlined for a couple of years now (remember? I'm a plotter, not a pantser, lol). I only have to modify it for what my characters decided to do instead of following the script. For example, Will was not supposed to send Katherine away at the end of *Cill Darae*. It just happened and it surprised me. That's my world. My characters own me. It's changed *Gaea* a little bit. But as always, my characters know best and it actually makes much more sense now…

Ciao!

Don
Ottawa, Canada, April 2019

Cill Darae

World Details

Ranks and Hierarchies

Draoi (Druid) Ranks:
Freamhaigh (Root) – Head Druid
Cill Dara(e) – Druid Priest/Priestess (The Elevated Druid)
Stoc (Trunk) or informally just Draoi – Full Druid
Craobh (Branch) – Journeyman Druid
Duilleog (Leaf) – Apprentice Druid

The Church of the New Order Ranks:
King (in abeyance since Revolution)
Archbishop (acting head of the Church)
Bishop
Dean
Vicar

Army of the Realm Ranks:
Officers:
    Knight General (former rank from before the Revolution)
    General
    Brigadier
    Colonel
    Lieutenant Colonel
    Major
    Captain
    Lieutenant
    Second Lieutenant
Enlisted:
    Warrant Officer
    Staff Sergeant
    Sergeant
    Corporal
    Lance Corporal (appointment, not a rank)
    Private
    Recruit

Lord Protector's Guard Ranks:
The highest-ranking officer is General. Because the Lord Protector's Guard is a speciality occupation, the members come from the Army of the Realm, and occasionally from the Navy of the Realm. They share the same rank structure except that the lowest officer rank is Captain and the lowest enlisted rank is Corporal; those being the earliest rank you can

Cill Darae

be selected or request service in the Lord Protector's Guard.

Navy of the Realm Ranks:
Officers:
- Fleet Admiral
- Admiral
- Commodore
- Captain (Navy)
- Commander
- Lieutenant-Commander
- Lieutenant (Navy)
- Ensign
- Midshipman

Enlisted:
- Chief Petty Officer
- Petty Officer
- Master Seaman
- Leading Seaman
- Able Seaman
- Ordinary Seaman

It should be noted that the General of the Realm is the head of the Army, the Navy, and the Lord Protector's Guard. The Lord Protector's Guard recruits from the Army of the Realm, and rarely, from the Navy. The Navy's top rank, the Fleet Admiral, is not equal to the General. In this world, the Navy is not the senior service.

Calendar and Seasons
The calendar is in the background of the world and not specifically referenced except where it occurs accidentally. We don't dwell on the calendar and neither do the folks in Turgany. In this world, the Celtic names for things have slipped and are rarely used. The common language is English.

Seasons:
Winter (Geimhreadh) – December, January, February (Nollaig, Eanair, Feabhra)
Spring (Earrach) – March, April, May (Marta, Aibrean, Bealtaine)
Summer (Samhraidh) – June, July, August (Meitheamh, Luil, Lunasa)
Autumn (Fomhar) – September, October, November (Mean Fomhair, Deirreadh Fomhair, Samhain)

Time Frames:
Day – dia
Night – nocht

Week – 8 days and nights—deug
Fortnight – 15 days and nights – cola-deug
Month – mios

Days of the Week:
Sunday – Domhnaich
Monday—Luain
Tuesday—Mairt
Wednesday—Ciadain
Pluday (Extra)—Durdaoin
Thursday—Ardaoin
Friday—Aoine
Saturday—Sathurna

Breakdown of a Year:
365 days in a calendar year for which only 360 are provided actual dates. The extra five days per year (see Solstices/Equinoxes) are used as celebration days and are known by their title rather than as a calendar date. It works like this: there is a December 24th, followed by Christmas Day, which is then followed by December 25th.
24 fortnights (24x15 days) per year
45 weeks per year
3 weeks and 6 days per month (totalling 30 days per month)

Solstices (longest/shortest day of the year)/Equinoxes:
Vernal Equinox is the day after March 19th (or Marta 19) and is celebrated for 1 day as Ostara Day (non-calendar day).
Estival Solstice (summer) is the day after June 20th (or Meitheamh 20) and is celebrated for 1 day as Litha Day (non-calendar day).
Autumnal Equinox is the day after September 21st (or Mean Fomhair 21) and is celebrated for 2 days as First Mabon Day (harvest) and Last Mabon Day (feast) (non-calendar days).
Hibernal Solstice (winter) is the day after December 20 (or Nollaig 20) and is celebrated for 1 day as Yule (non-calendar day).

Holidays:
Samhain. Nov 7 (Samhain 7). The midpoint between Autumn Equinox and Winter Solstice. Celebrates the last harvest, the cycle of life and gifts for passing spirits. Preparation to survive winter, confront the possibility of death. Colours: black, brown, reds, oranges. Opposite to Bealtaine.
Yule is the day after December 20 (Nollaig 20) and is a non-calendar day. Shortest day and longest night of the year. Celebrates the end of darkness, the return of light to the earth. Herbs are at their least potent. Colours: green, red, white, silver, gold.
Imbolc. Feb 1 (Feabhra 1). The midpoint between Winter Solstice and Spring

Equinox. Celebrates the quickening of spring, the end of winter, time of planning and hopes. Colours: red, orange, white.

Ostara Day is the day after March 19 (Marta 19) and is a non-calendar day. The first day of spring, the night and day stand equal. Celebrates the birth of spring, rebirth. Time of planting. Colours: red and yellow.

Bealtaine. May 6 (Bealtaine 6). The midpoint between Spring Equinox and Summer Solstice. Time of rebirth. Colours: blue, pink, yellow, green. Opposite to Samhain.

Litha Day is the day after June 20 (Meitheamh 20) and is a non-calendar day. Summer solstice, the first day of summer, longest day of the year. Celebrates the light and the sun without there would be no life. Time of strengths and accomplishments. Gather herbs as "herb night" is when they are at their most potent. Colours: blue, yellow, green.

Lammas. Aug 1 (Lunasa 1). The midpoint between Summer Solstice and the Autumn Equinox. First harvest festival. Celebrates the beginning of harvest season, the decline of summer to winter. Time to dismiss regrets, farewells, preparation for winter. Ceremonies involve bread, grains and corn dolls. Colours: oranges, greens, browns.

Mabon Days are the two days after September 21st (Mean Fomhair 21) and they are non-calendar days. Referred to as *First Mabon* and *Last Mabon*. Autumn Equinox, the first day of autumn. Celebrates harvest. First Mabon is harvesting time and Last Mabon is the feast. Time for thanks and learning, repairing all things. Colours: dark reds, yellows, browns.

Important Calendar Dates Summary:
February 1 (Feabhra 1)—Imbolc
March (Marta)—Ostara Day (Vernal Equinox) is the day after March 19th
May 6 (Bealtaine 6)—Bealtaine
June (Meitheamh)—Litha Day (Estival Solstice (summer)) is the day after June 20th
August 1 (Lunasa 1)—Lammas
September (Mean Fomhair)—First/Last Mabon Days (Autumnal Equinox) is the two days after September 21st
November 7 (Samhain 7)—Samhain
December (Nollaig)—Yule (Hibernal Solstice (winter)) is the day after December 20th

Currency

1 crown (large round gold coin) = 36 groats = 144 pence
1 half-crown (large round gold coin with a centre hole) = 18 groats = 72 pence
1 mark (small gold coin) = 9 groats = 36 pence
1 groat (silver rectangular coin) = 4 pence
1 tuppence (a small silver coin or large copper coin) = 2 pence
1 pence (copper coin) = 1 pence
1 half-pence (copper coin with a centre hole) = 1/2 pence
1 farthing (small rectangular copper coin) = 1/4 pence

Coins are measured by known weights under the Turgany Weights and Measures Act. For example, a full crown must weigh one royal ounce (28 gramme). A half-crown weighs a half ounce (14 gramme). And a mark weighs a quarter ounce (7 gramme) which means it is heavier than a Canadian quarter (25 cent piece) but sized about the same. A groat weighs the same as a mark (but is larger), and a tuppence weighs half that of a groat (hence if it is made of copper it will be larger). Typically, wealthy merchants will carry coin scales to verify that they are not being cheated with counterfeit coins. The habit of biting a gold coin was to prove that it was indeed gold—which is soft—and not some impostor.

Seven Tenets of Morality

1. Strive to act with compassion and empathy toward all creatures in accordance with reason.
2. The struggle for justice is an ongoing and necessary pursuit that should prevail over laws and institutions.
3. One's body is inviolable, subject to one's own will alone.
4. The freedoms of others should be respected, including the freedom to offend. To wilfully and unjustly encroach upon the freedoms of another is to forgo your own.
5. Beliefs should conform to our best scientific understanding of the world. We should take care never to distort scientific facts to fit our beliefs.
6. People are fallible. If we make a mistake, we should do our best to rectify it and resolve any harm that may have been caused.
7. Every tenet is a guiding principle designed to inspire nobility in action and thought. The spirit of compassion, wisdom, and justice should always prevail over the written or spoken word.

Cill Darae

About the Author

DONALD D. ALLAN is a Canadian author of fantasy and science fiction and a retired Royal Canadian Navy senior officer.

He is the GOLD medal winner of the Dan Poynter's Global eBook Awards 2016 for the category Fantasy/Other Worlds for his debut novel Duilleog, the first novel in his New Druids series. The second novel, Craobh, won the BRONZE medal in 2017. The third novel, Stoc, won GOLD in 2018.

Donald lives with his wife Marilyn, son James, daughter Katherine, and dog Woody, in Ottawa, Canada.

Connect with Donald D. Allan:

BLOG: http://donalddallan.com
FACEBOOK: https://www.facebook.com/donalddallan
TWITTER: https://twitter.com/donalddallan/
EMAIL: donalddallan@gmail.com

Made in the USA
Coppell, TX
07 December 2019